Railroad Rising
The Black Powder Rebellion
by J. P. Wagner

I0634654

Copyright © 2015 by J. P. Wagner

2022 edition Print ISBN: 978-1-990862-02-1

Second Edition Published by MOONGATE STUDIOS, BURNABY, BC

www.revjpwagner.com

First edition Ebook ISBN: 978-0-9949865-3-5

First Edition published by HADES PUBLICATIONS, INC., CALGARY

Under the EDGE-Lite and EDGE imprints

www.edgewebsite.com

.

For Beth

Chapter 1

Yakor pulled his horse up beside his master's and spat in the mucky road that wandered through the trees ahead of them. In this vicinity, much of the heavy northern forest had been cleared for the town, of which some rough and ramshackle buildings were visible just ahead.

Nor were the two of them alone on the road. Ahead of and behind them were a number of people, mostly men, and from their dress hunters and farmers off to attend some special occasion in the local city.

"Tenerack. As you noted by the smells, you could tell we were coming up on a major town for the last couple of hours. And, Lord Carrtog, since the only large town in the vicinity is Tenerack, I tell you this one will be it. And do you also remember what I've told you about it?"

The blond young man beside Yakor frowned his annoyance with the business of learning and lessons. "It was the center of resistance during the late war, and it is still suspected of being a center of resistance against the king. And since my grandfather counted up the odds and rode behind the old king, when the king declared the necessity of the recent border adjustment, he is now in the present king's favor. Which means that if I promise my service to the wrong person, I may find myself facing one of my uncles or my many cousins across the battlefield." Carrtog waved his hand, letting his horse follow the flow of people on the road, "Don't worry yourself, Yakor, we came here mainly because I wished to see a large city. We can look around, then go somewhere safe."

Yakor snorted. "I'd still prefer it if I could convince you to go somewhere safe first. Or even better ... somewhere else instead."

Carrtog grinned. "But Yakor, we're heading off to hire on as mercenaries. That's not a safe occupation any time or place."

"You're right about that, of course. But a smart mercenary always tries to lessen the danger to himself whenever he can. Riding into Tenerack with only your faithful armsman by your side does not seem to me to be lessening the danger to you very much at all. I really don't look forward to going back to your grandfather and explaining to him that I couldn't convince you to use a bit of sense, and therefore lost one of his grandsons."

"As to that, Yakor, I'm only one of his younger grandsons, unlikely to inherit anything unless a war or a plague wipes out all the family ahead of me, an extremely unlikely event."

The bulk of the town was still hidden by trees and rising ground, but smoke was rising into the air ahead of them, and a stream of white suddenly shot up as well. A steam-whistle shrieked up ahead on the heels of that puff of steam.

It took the two a few moments to calm their horses, then Yakor grabbed the shoulder of one of the men hurrying toward the sound.

"What's happening?"

The man looked up at him. He was a broad and burly fellow dressed in the muck-brown tunic and trousers that marked him as lower-class with a short, hooded cloak over the lot, the hood almost covering his eyes.

"Far from home, aren't you, soldier? Everyone knows the king promised us a new railroad. The king himself has come to open the railway."

He spun round and went off at a near run toward the sound of the railway train.

"Well, now, Yakor," said Carrtog, looking after their informant, "That seems to be a sight worth seeing. If I'm not mistaken, when kings do this sort of thing, they tend to supply food and drink as well, even for strangers from far off."

Yakor snorted. "Of course, they may look suspiciously at traveling mercenaries, with no apparent local connection. If they don't seem welcoming, we move along without causing trouble. Agreed?"

"Oh, yes, agreed."

Yakor sent him a mildly suspicious glance, as they set their horses in motion. "I hope you don't have anything tricky on your noble mind."

"Goodness, no! I am the very model of decorous and genteel behavior!"

"When you say things like that I'm almost certain I should clout you across the head with the flat of my sword, and haul you away bodily! I might just do it, too! 'I'm sorry, ladies and gentlemen, but my master occasionally takes these fits, and the only thing I can do is take him someplace quiet until the fit passes.'"

"I promise you, Yakor, I will behave myself." He pointed ahead to where the station stood forth, a brand-new building, no longer hidden by trees and other buildings. It was decorated with royal pennants, while in front of it sat a small train. "Ah, there it is! Much more fancy than the bit of a train that runs through my grandfather's holding of Tsingallik, down south, isn't it?"

"Yes, it is. But you must consider that this is more or less a bribe from the king to make the local people think well of him. For that reason, it has to look like a royal train."

Carrtog grinned. "As so often happens, Yakor, I believe you are correct. That must be one of the reasons why I put up with your surly nature."

Yakor cast his eyes heavenward. "All the Gods keep me! I bend all my efforts to keeping you safe, and as comfortable as out-of-work mercenaries can make themselves, and the only appreciation I get sounds more like a complaint."

"And I try to assure you that I have no intention of causing you trouble and I'm rewarded with suspicion and threats. We seem to be a pair of badly-matched scoundrels, don't we?"

Yakor smiled slightly. "It's probably too late for either of us to go back and choose a different companion."

"I suppose so. I expect we'll just have to bear with each other as well as possible."

As they spoke and urged their horses toward the station, the crowd assembled on all sides of them. Most of the onlookers gazed intently at the royal party standing on the platform that had been attached to the railway car just behind the fuel-carrying tender.

Carrtog suddenly lifted his left hand and looked at the ring on his third finger. "My ring's prickling, Yakor! Danger's on the way!"

"Nothing more specific than that?"

Carrtog shook his head. "It's not infallible, Yakor, but any time it signals me this hard, I know something's coming up." He continued to regard the ring: an ordinary looking pale yellow circlet which had been carved from a beef-bone and polished while certain incantations were recited over it.

"We should ride quietly away."

Carrtog shook his head. "Given the circumstances, I think we should at least warn the king's Guard. I mean, the king's here, and my ring signals trouble in an area known for disaffection toward the king, so isn't it the greatest likelihood that the trouble involves the king?"

"Now, why would I have expected anything different? You do realize, don't you, that the king's Guard will likely take a wild-looking pair like us to be part of the danger?"

"I've got to at least try. You could hang back here and wait for me."

"I'll come up behind you, at a little distance, so I can rush in and drag you away if I have to."

Carrtog rode on without hesitating, and soon could see the whole scene. It was only a modest train, five cars, including a coal-car to fuel the engine.

The king had not ridden up on the train itself, Possibly, Carrtog thought, for fear of starting jokes about the railway being for the purpose of transporting kings, swine, and other livestock. The king and his retinue had arrived on horseback, in proper gentlemanly fashion. There were a few ladies with them, royalty and royal servants from the look of their clothing. Carrtog was surprised to see the princess, recognizable by the tiara on her head. Even she and her ladies-in-waiting appeared to have come on horseback, though Carrtog noted a wagon in the background, in case any of the royal bottoms required a rest from the rigors of the ride.

There were soldiers as well, all horsemen, all dressed in decorated metal back and breast with a powder-blue coat over the steel, as well as a gold-colored sash. These were the king's Gentlemen. Their numbers seemed a bit low to Carrtog. Of course that made sense, if the king was coming here to make friends with the people by presenting them with a train and railway; best not show too obvious distrust for the locals by bringing along overwhelming force. He'd only seen King Bornival from a distance, but some things he'd heard about the man made this sound like a thing he would do.

He could spot the king on the platform amongst his men by his dress, which was similar to that of his Gentlemen but a touch more elaborate with little bits of extra decoration here and there. Carrtog also noted the captain of the troop; not only did he have a golden sash around his waist, but he wore a diagonal sash of bright red.

The crowd gathering around them seemed mostly to be made up of rough-looking men wearing short, hooded cloaks, and carrying large sacks. Were these part of the danger, he wondered. They all still look like farmers or hunters, or even tradesmen, taking a bit of time off for the occasion.

Carrtog pushed his horse forward through the crowd. The prickling of his ring grew in intensity, was this crowd about to turn into a riot? What did they have in those sacks besides their lunches?

He pulled up in front of the line of guards and said to one of them, "I must speak to your leader. Immediately!"

The fellow looked at him suspiciously, and without taking his eyes off Carrtog, he called "Captain Gwailants! Man wants to speak to you, sir!"

Shortly, the captain came over on foot, there being no room for horses on the platform. He was a hard-looking man, his face browned by the weather, and his short beard and mustache had all gone pepper and salt. His sword was unsheathed in his hand.

"Come up here and talk, and I hope for your sake that you have something important to say."

The guardsmen grudgingly let him through the line, and the first thing he did was to display his ring to the captain. "My ring tells me that there's danger here, sir."

The captain sneered and displayed his own ring. "It does, does it? Would it surprise you at all to know that I know that very well? Our king, however, has decided to ignore the danger in favor of making his political point."

"Oh." Carrtog felt deflated.

"Your news is not as vital as you thought, eh? Perhaps you should turn and leave us before—"

There was a shout somewhere in the crowd and what looked like a smoking ball of cloth came whirling through the air to land on the platform.

Carrtog felt a touch of confusion. Recognizing a battle-magic spell, he waved his ringed hand in front of him as if waving away the smoke. The confusion cleared from his mind. That first ball was followed by three others, thrown from other points in the crowd.

He spun to face outward, drawing his sword and shouting "Tsingallik for King Bornival!"

With any luck, that yell might convince the King's Gentlemen all around him that he was on their side. On the other hand, members of the King's Gentlemen seldom took risks with the king's life; it was too likely that one or another of them would stick a sword into his side just to be sure.

Several among the guard swept hands before them — it was no surprise that a large number of them knew battle-magic, some likely knew much more than he did. Men among the crowd flung back their hoods, revealing caps of metal or leather, though a good number wore only a cloth bonnet like his own. There seemed to be only a couple who wore metal breastplates — the rest had a jacket of leather. The weapons they pulled from their sacks were mostly short swords and stout cudgels, but several had wheel-lock pistols.

The pistols were only accurate at close range and took some time to reload. Carrtog knew how to use a pistol; in fact, a pistol would have had more than one use for him at this moment given his training in battle-magic. His grandfather had offered him one before he and Yakor started off on their journey, but he had turned it down. The things were very expensive, particularly in a hinterland place like Tsingallik, and though he hoped at some time to earn the money to buy one of his own, he hadn't wanted to ride away carrying one that his grandfather might well need worse than he.

The pistol-men in the crowd opened fire, the King's Gentlemen replying. The powder-smoke began to gather, obscuring visibility, though not to the extent of hiding either of the two sides. Several men in the crowd went down. Carrtog noted at least two pushing their way back out of the crowd, just trying to get away.

An attacker stuck a pistol into his face, but Carrtog managed a frantic chop just before the fellow pulled the trigger. The pistol fired off to the side, and the man staggered aside clutching his bloody wrist.

Carrtog thrust at him, but his sword glanced off the man's leather jacket as he went sidewards. The thought went through Carrtog's mind that he should grab the dropped pistol, but good sense told him he didn't have time. Indeed, there was a man jumping forward, extending his sword in a thrust. Even as he reacted, Carrtog noted that something had taken off most of the man's left ear, leaving the blood streaming down his left side. He parried, and did his own thrust, then pulled his sword free, jumping back to avoid further attacks.

He called out once more, "Tsingallik for King Bornival!!" Then stepped forward, thrusting again.

He noticed that the attackers did not seem to be trying to kill the king or his party, but working to force them backward into the train car where the ladies and the rest of the retinue had already taken shelter. If the attackers were trying to force them inside, it seemed to him that the best thing to do would be to try to force their way out.

But with Captain Gwailants shouting "Rally round the king! Rally round the king!" It seemed that they would be playing into the enemy's scheme.

The King's Gentlemen tried to close in around the king, and one glimpse that Carrtog was able to get of Bornival showed the man standing tall and grim, his bloodied sword in one hand, and blood soaking his left sleeve. Obviously, someone had gotten closer to him than his guard would prefer.

Carrtog could hear Yakor's wisdom telling him not to get trapped in a train-car with the enemy's target. But with the next surge of rebels he had little choice. He fell into formation with the king's Gentlemen. Then they were all inside fighting to prevent the numbers of foe inside with them from growing. Strangely, several of the rebels were pushing backward out the door, while trying to prevent any of the royal party from leaving.

Shouts went up from outside the car, shouts that Carrtog couldn't make out, but he suspected a signal of some sort.

The train jerked into motion. There was a great groaning as the fastenings tore from the outside platform. Then the train was dragging the outside platform with it, leaving bits scattered along the way as they gained speed.

Chapter 2

They're trying to take the king hostage!

Even as that thought went through Carrtog's head, wooden poles sprang up from the floor, each pole shooting out branches to join with the next as they formed a cage around the king and his party. Several rebels jumped back and pressed against the car's walls just in time to avoid being imprisoned with them.

By the Gods, this is powerful magic, Carrtog thought.

More was to come though, as the walls and the floor began to fall away revealing a smaller cage attached at the front by means of a long framework of seemingly flimsy wood, wood that Carrtog had a feeling was heavily reinforced by more magic. The roof spun sidewise, forming itself into a long pair of wings which shot out magical extensions from their ends.

Now there was magic!

The winged contrivance began to lift away from the bed of the train, listing badly to the left. Some of the attackers had fallen away with the disappearance of the walls and floor but others clung desperately to the cage.

One of the operating crew turned and shouted, "Jump off! Jump off you fools or we're all going down."

A rebel near the front turned and growled, "You jump! I volunteered to risk my life fighting, not to splatter myself all over the landscape!"

Another rebel lost his grip and fell with a scream, his pistol skittering across the cage floor. Carrtog grabbed it just before it fell through one of the openings and thrust it into his sash. The glider lurched upward, but the sideways list remained. The crew didn't do any more shouting, but saved their breath to manhandle the controls. For a moment it seemed they might succeed, then the nose tilted sharply towards the sky and the craft stalled. Carrtog's stomach climbed into his throat as the glider slipped sidewards in the air and dove towards the ground.

Shrill yells went up, both from people in the cage and those hanging on the outside.

The crew fought the machine all the way down, but Carrtog knew by the prickle of his ring that they hadn't the height they needed. They were almost straightened out when the lower left wing clipped the trunk of a medium tree, smashing the appendage irretrievably despite its magical strengthening. The glider turned leftward around the pivot of the tree-trunk, then hit the ground still moving, only the right wing scraping across the patchy snow cover and bits of underbrush prevented a tumbling roll.

The men on the outside shook loose with the first and succeeding impacts and the people inside the cage were thrown against the walls.

Carrtog slammed headfirst into one of the bars and lost consciousness...

HE CAME BACK TO HIMSELF with pain in both his head and his left ankle. He was lying on something soft, which revealed itself to be the princess' lady-in-waiting...

He pushed himself off almost frantically, then laughed to himself. She was unconscious and couldn't begin accusing him of taking liberties, though his mind insisted on recalling her warm softness — Stop that, Carrtog!

He investigated his ankle and found it not broken as he had feared, only sprained. Using bits of the smashed cage and a couple of strips of his shirt, he immobilized the joint. He then took the pistol from his sash and considered it. There was a spell, a powder-charged spell, that could cut down on the pain. But it would have to wait, discharging a pistol in these circumstances could cause panic unless everyone knew what he was doing.

He put the pistol back in his sash and began checking the rest of the cage's occupants where they lay tangled beneath the broken and collapsed wood.

The results were not encouraging. There had been twenty-two of them in the cage; of those, eight were dead, either from wounds received in battle or from injuries sustained in the crash itself. Three more had suffered crushed chests, which were beyond Carrtog's ability to heal or patch. Others had suffered various fractures rendering them incapable of helping out to any degree. Only four could lend a hand if necessary having suffered cuts or scrapes and bruising.

The princess' maid was dead, a broken neck, while the princess' lady-in-waiting had regained consciousness and was seeing to the princess, who apparently had broken her right forearm and was barely aware of the world around her.

The king was still unconscious but didn't seem in any great danger from his wounds. One of the the King's Gentlemen had already done what could be done for his royal charge's hurts.

Carrtog noticed that Captain Gwailants was dead; his face ruined by a pistol ball. Carrtog turned to speak to the nearest of the Gentlemen who seemed to be recovering somewhat from the shock. "Who's the senior man left to you?"

The man gave a glance at Gwailants, then shook his head. "Don't rightly know, sir."

Carrtog gave a mental shudder; he'd been going at doing things just because they needed doing, and now it seemed that this fellow was assuming that he, Carrtog, was a voice of authority.

Well, the worst thing he could do was to stop doing things and wait for someone else to take charge. Though the people who had tried to kidnap the king had been a bit hit or miss regarding some parts of their plan (having the train start moving before the attackers could dismount, for instance) one couldn't count on similar faults in the rest of their plan. They would probably have people out looking for the glider.

The survivors of the king's party had to be ready for that.

"Do you, any of you, know healing magic, or at least a pain-killing spell?"

There was silence for a bit, then one man, after looking around at his fellows, answered. "Most of us know how to do bandages and set broken bones, sir. I know how to cast the pain-killing spell with a pistol. The others, if I'm not mistaken, know only bits of combat magic besides."

Carrtog nodded. "I see. What's your name and rank?" If he were going to assume command, even temporarily, best try to do it right. He could almost see Yakor shaking his head at him with that 'you always get yourself into these things' look.

The fellow straightened, his training taking over. "Trained Private Roisilan Harrad, sir."

"Right, Private Harrad. You get some reliable people to see to all the bandaging and bone-setting you can manage. Then take one person and see what you can find for weapons on those other fellows. I'd be surprised if they don't get some people out here looking for us when the glider doesn't turn up where it's supposed to. We left my companion behind at the railway station, and I expect him to come looking for us as well, though he might try to find some trustworthy people to bring along. If we bet on the rebels getting here first, though, we can avoid nasty surprises. Any questions?"

"No, sir."

"Get to it, then."

As the man went off to carry out his orders, Carrtog inspected his command — such as it was. Several of the worst-hurt had already died and there were several others who would almost certainly do the same without application of more powerful healing magic than anyone present had available.

For the sake of the morale among the sadly battered royal party, it was likely best to keep the obviously dying and the seriously hurt separate from the rest.

Carrtog knelt by one of the wounded men who was barely conscious and gasping with the pain of broken ribs among other hurts. "Would you allow me to use the pain-killing spell on you?"

He could, and might well if he thought it best, use the spell without the man's consent, but it was a proven fact that the spell worked better on willing patients.

The man gasped out agreement.

"Then hold still while I work," Carrtog said.

He spoke the incantation, then aimed the pistol down just next to the man's battered chest. He squeezed the trigger. The wheel spun shooting a stream of sparks into the priming pan. The pistol fired, and the man settled back, breathing a little easier.

Carrtog leaned forward and extinguished the sparks the discharge had left on the man's vest. He wished he could do more, but the spell could only be applied once in eight hours or so and the man's wounds beget more pain than the spell could remove. The best the man could hope for was this amelioration.

A woman's voice broke into his thoughts. "You killed him?"

Carrtog turned to see the princess' lady-in-waiting looking at him having just finished bandaging the princess. "No, Lady, just a pain-killing spell. The nearer the discharge is to the patient, in particular to the part giving pain, the more effective the spell is."

"Do you intend to use this spell on the princess?"

He never claimed to read minds and even his ability to read expressions and tones of voice were limited, but it seemed to him that she was challenging him with the full expectation that his spell was nothing but fakery.

"This sort of spell works best if the patient gives her willing consent. If you will ask her, and she agrees, I willl do it. In the meantime, I will deal with the others who are presently suffering."

"Hmph." She snorted. "If it truly does them any good. Go ahead, then."

Carrtog gave her a quick bow. He had not convinced her, not by any means, but though the fact annoyed him, he was not going to allow her disbelief to affect him.

He went from one wounded man to the next, asking permission to do his spell and carrying it out. When he was done, he looked at the king. He was still unconscious but, from the look of him, he might be coming around any time. Bornival was taller than most of his soldiers and looked to be as hardy as the toughest of them, still he was fortunate that his wounds were not all that bad.

Carrtog checked his supply of powder. He was glad that, though he had turned down the pistol his grandfather had offered, he had accepted the bag of spell-grade gunpowder. It would quickly prove the most useful of his possessions if he were to treat a king.

He glanced back to the princess and the lady-in-waiting. The princess seemed to be having trouble following the lady's questions, though she was much more aware than before. Carrtog, who had suffered a broken bone from time to time, suspected that her pain was making it difficult to concentrate. It was likely time to intervene.

"Does the princess wish me to do the pain-killing spell on her, Lady?"

The lady raised her chin. "She has given her consent."

"What of yourself? I am not extremely proficient at the spell, but I can probably ease the pain for up to three people at once."

She looked at him, startled. "I hadn't thought—" She let her voice trail away.

He shrugged. "Your choice, Lady. I will force nothing on you."

She touched a hand to her forehead, then said, "Then I suppose you may try."

He made his preparations carefully. This time, instead of using ordinary powder, he reached into an inside pocket and pulled out a small pouch of spell-grade powder. Much of its special nature came from the incantations spoken over it at various stages of mixing, caking, and grinding, which increased its ability to carry out spells.

It was possible that by rejecting the possibility of the spell's effectiveness the lady could prevent it from having its full outcome. Unless her doubt was extreme however, the most she was likely to achieve was a weakening of the spell.

Whether she would allow the spell to have any credit was another matter. From her attitude, he suspected she would claim the amelioration of her pain was due only to her having grown used to the discomfort. Of course, if she decided to be fair about it and took into account the effectiveness of the spell on those soldiers who were conscious, she might just admit that he'd done her some good.

"Now, Lady, if you will please lie down, and remain still. Try not to flinch when I fire the pistol. In order to make the spell more sure, I have to aim close to you, but you will notice that there is no ball in the pistol. On the other hand, sparks of only partially burned powder will land on you, and I will extinguish them as quickly thereafter as I am able."

She looked at him a little doubtfully, then clenched her teeth. He could almost hear her thinking that she had planned to show this self-declared magician a thing or two, and she would not pull back now.

He pointed the pistol at the ground beside her and squeezed the trigger. Though the spell worked best if the pistol was fired as close as possible to the affected body part, the sensation of firing even a blank round near the head might affect the patient's ability to accept that the spell had done its good. He had therefore picked a spot about an arm's length from her head. The pistol fired, and the lady winced despite his warning. Carrtog dropped to a knee and quickly brushed the sparks from her hair before they could do more than singe.

The lady gingerly put a hand to her forehead, then said, "It does feel better. Of course, I may have grown a little inured to the pain."

Carrtog bobbed his head without speaking. There was little to be gained by arguing with royalty — or the servants of royalty. If the king accepted the spell, she might change her mind, but he wasn't going to worry over it.

In the meantime, here came Private Harrad and the four Gentlemen who, though injured, were still capable of working. From the path they had left through the patchy snow, they had gone straight to where the section holding the crew of the glider lay canted against an evergreen, then made their meandering way back, pausing here and there to pick something up, or to search a body.

They were hauling a litter made of two long poles thrust through the sleeves of two coats, the whole strengthened by a couple of belts. On the litter were piled several more coats with the metal glint of weapons here and there underneath. "We thought it best to bring along more coats, sir. It's likely we'll be out overnight, and the cold's going to be hard on us, particularly the wounded."

"Good thinking, Private Harrad. Anything else?"

"We brought along whatever scraps of food we could find, sir, though truth to tell, it wasn't much. We picked up all the weaponry there was, but if those buggers catch up to us our problem is going to be finding hands to wield them."

"Yes, I've been thinking of that. Have any of you had experience with the Grove of Battle?"

The others looked at each other, then Private Harrad looked back at Carrtog. "No, sir. That is, we've heard of it, but none of us have done it, nor seen it done."

"I see. Well, it would have been useful if you could have helped me with it, but I should be able to do a reasonable job of it by myself. Don't fret yourselves over it, just be ready to do what you can."

He was still hoping that Yakor would bring a rescue party before the rebels found them, but experience in warfare and life in general had taught him to prepare for the worst.

He began to make preparations for a spell to increase his hearing. He considered calling his available soldiers together and putting the spell on all of them at once, but people experiencing it for the first time often had difficulty with it. If they were out here more than overnight, he would begin training them in using it for brief times. Probably get a survey of what battle-magic they did know, maybe even teach them more.

This spell didn't require a full shot of powder, burning a small pinch should suffice. While firing the powder in a pistol was more effective in terms of powering spells, some spells were not much weakened by simply tossing a pinch of powder into an open flame.

He called his men to him. He could see that they were all wondering what he had in mind.

"The next thing I intend to do is to increase my hearing temporarily. This will make it more difficult for anyone to sneak up on us. Have any of you had experience with such a spell?"

It turned out that Private Harrad and one other had previous experience under the spell and were willing to undergo it again.

"Don't any of you agree just because you think you should. We're likely to be using it for serious this time, and that's not the best time to be having your first experience with it."

He recalled back in the late war, the old and battered commander of his grandfather's troops had expressed the same notion, though there'd been times when it didn't work out that way. He'd had to deal with the fact or die, and he'd managed to survive without even becoming appreciably magic-shy.

He carried out the spell and watched the changing expressions on the two soldiers' faces. Satisfying himself that they did not seem to be overly surprised by the increase in their hearing, he nodded, then said, "I will now cast a ward around all of us, to warn us if any enemies come on us in the night."

He poured a small circle of powder on the ground in front of him, then spoke the words of the incantation, not quietly as most times before, but in a loud voice.

Then he touched off the powder. It flashed in a blue-yellow flame, then died down to a pale yellow gleam expanding out of the camp on all sides.

"It will go out about fifty yards," he told them, "and it will let us know if an enemy crosses it."

He had no idea how the spell differentiated between friend and enemy but he was not going to mention that: doubt did not mix well with magic.

"You may be interested to know that the effect of the expanding ward kills all fleas and lice and the like, so you will find yourself itching less for a time."

He saw grins on their faces and answered them with a smile. By now, evening was well on its way so he ordered Private Harrad to schedule watches for the night.

He watched as that was done, then oversaw the distribution of what food was available, stretching it with liberal quantities of water derived from melted-down snow.

Following that, Carrtog made the rounds of the camp and discovered that several more of the gravely-hurt had died. He felt those deaths in the pit of his stomach despite the fact that he knew full well that he could not have prevented them. Still, he had taken command of the situation and they had died under his charge.

On the other hand, one of the men Carrtog had considered most likely to die had seemed to rally just about the time he'd established the ward.

That brought to mind the rumor he'd heard about the occasional curative properties of the ward. Some day he would look up a real magician, not just someone who knew various magics involved with war and battles, to pose his questions. For instance, how did it work? And why only one or two occurrences at any time? He shook his head, pulling himself back to the present.

He sat down and forced himself to relax. He looked over at the king who had been drifting in and out of consciousness. What kind of reputation could he gain as the man having taken charge of the party where the king died? Even despite the fact that the king's death would not be attributable to any action he had taken. It was a worrisome thought.

Then suddenly he was waking up with Private Harrad's hand at his shoulder, "Pardon, sir, but His Majesty is awake and asking for you."

Carrtog shook his head to rid himself of the fuzz, and said, "Ah, how is His Majesty doing?"

"About as well as could be expected, sir. That is, one has to step carefully around him."

Yes, what was supposed to be a simple ceremonial function has ended with uprising and battle with his command cut to pieces and now stranded in unfriendly highlands. He's likely been brooding.

Those were not safe thoughts to express aloud, so he got up and followed Private Harrad to the king , who sat on a couple of coats, his back propped against a sack apparently stuffed with another coat or two. His outstretched legs were covered by a pair of coats in lieu of blankets. He held his sheathed sword in his left hand, and with his right twiddled at the gold knot on the cord which, in battle, would be wrapped around his right wrist. The expression he turned on Carrtog was fierce.

"Your Majesty?" Carrtog said respectfully.

"Humph! So you're the young soldier from nowhere who has taken command of my Gentlemen?"

"With respect, Highness, I did ask first who was the most senior of those left on their feet. None of them seemed willing to put themselves forward, so I gave what directions I thought were proper. I'm quite willing to turn the command back to you, Highness."

"Are you indeed? And what payment were you expecting? A wandering man, armed, and skilled at the use of those arms, but with no marks to show you belong to anyone's army, or under hire to anyone. That would make you a mercenary, and no mercenary does anything except in expectation of payment."

"I did not expect a reward, Highness. Let me introduce myself. I am Carrtog, third son of Gwahalad, son of Dlestan of Tsingallik. And I do seek to hire on as a fighting man though I know not where."

The king straightened a little and a quick flicker of pain twisted his face. "Dlestan of Tsingallik? He served my father well in the late war. Though I believe he took our part because our numbers were more favorable." He snorted, briefly, "But then any leader would prefer the side with the better numbers," he looked up at Carrtog. "You were calling 'Tsingallik for the king' if my mind recalls properly. That suggests I can put my trust in you, and yet, the people of Tenerack cheered me when first I arrived before things turned ugly." He narrowed his eyes, "How far then do I trust you?"

Then the king shook his head. "Hmph, listen to me. This bash on the head has turned my thinking foolish; it seems hardly likely that you would have been fighting on my side merely to give yourself the opportunity to do me ill. No, I think you had better go forward as you've begun. When we reach safety, we'll see to what reward you merit. Though positions among my Gentlemen are filled months, perhaps years, in advance. Unless you are carrying a recommendation from your grandfather particularly asking for such a position..."

It occurred to Carrtog that he ought to have asked for better letters than he had. "No, Highness, all I have is a letter of introduction from my grandfather's Master of Arms."

The king grimaced. "Intent on making your way without playing on your grandfather's reputation, then? So be it. It may make finding a place for you a little more difficult. But that all depends on our surviving this debacle. What do you think of the attempt to take me hostage? A near thing, was it?"

"Yes and no, Highness. It was too complex for the way they handled it. Certainly they did well at subverting the building crews, but they had no opportunity to practice the actual kidnapping. That meant that when the train started to move, apparently a little sooner than was expected, no one was ready to improvise.

"Furthermore, they hit the spell turning the railway car into a glider too suddenly, leaving the men who had not been able to get off with no choice except to hang on to the glider, which in turn was fatal to the glider's attempt to fly."

"A flight we were lucky to survive. You have thought all that out, have you? I don't think I dare let you get away, young man, whatever political battles I have to fight in my court."

"Father?"

The two of them looked up to see the princess approach. Carrtog scanned her face for indication that she might need another pain-killing spell to bolster her against the ache of her splinted arm.

"You need to rest, Father." There was determination on her face as well as concern but it seemed she was handling the pain well enough on her own.

The king smiled. "She's right, Carrtog of Tsingallik, if one assumes that we're going to survive this thing. You will also need your rest, particularly if we assume that the rebels will find us before our own people. You have done well today. Continue to serve me well, and I shall do well by you."

"I did only my duty, Highness."

Carrtog bowed first to the king and then to the princess, and went back to his place, the spot from which he could oversee his small force. They were not likely to face an attack while it was dark, not in this kind of country, rough and hilly, with patches of evergreens, and the snow that hung about in shady patches reminding one that winter was not far in the past. He recognized, though, the breadth of difference between 'not likely' and 'impossible.'

Twelve hours was the maximum time for the ward-spell to maintain its full power, after which it would begin to weaken. He would then be required to make the decision as to whether or not to replace it.

They all lay down to get what rest they could, save for those who had the first watch.

It seemed only shortly thereafter that a sound as of several hundred faint brass bells sounded in his head. Enemies had crossed the line of the ward-spell.

Chapter 3

"Take positions!" he shouted, "They've just passed the wards!"

With very little wasted motion the surviving soldiers, who resembled beggars wrapped in extra garments against the cold, took up positions around the king.

Having so few soldiers, Carrtog had them all take up covered positions around the camp. Now, having a direction from which the enemy were coming, he quickly shifted two of the men into other positions he had previously noted on the side of the camp from which the enemy were approaching, then took his own position among them.

"Have any of you had experience with the Grove of Battle?" Carrtog asked of the men around him.

As he'd come to expect from this lot one spoke up diffidently, "Here, Sir," while the rest wore expressions of varying degrees of blankness and confusion.

"I'm going to set up a Grove of Battle around us. Among its main features is the ability to conceal us and reveal the enemy. Be ready to take advantage of that, but don't expect too much of it."

He took up a previously charged pistol and pointed it at the sky, calling out the incantation. The pistol held no ball, only powder and a loose clump of wood-slivers and similar debris.

He squeezed the trigger and the wheel shot sparks into the priming. The charge went off, flinging a mass of flame and sparks into the sky.

As the sparks began to settle, a grove of evergreens sprang up around them. He heard the muttering of his troops; this was visibly powerful magic.

He hoped they did not depend too much on it; it might be that someone among their attackers might know a stronger spell, one that would show them a safe path through the Grove, or worse, one that would whiff the Grove out of existence. The best they could hope for was the momentary advantage while their attackers worked out their own best tactics.

There was movement out in the Grove beyond his line of defenders, Carrtog raised another specially-charged pistol; this one had a smaller charge of powder behind five balls. "Fire when you see a decent target!"

Speaking an incantation, he himself fired.

The pistol bucked ferociously and four of the moving figures out in the Grove went down. Hah! The Accuracy Spell was more effective than he'd hoped. It guaranteed at least three out of five hits, and four meant luck was on his side today. Might it also mean that the Grove would be particularly effective as well, today?

He let go his pistol and drew his sword, then took his dagger in his left hand. From the look of things, unless the Grove was very effective, the enemy would soon overwhelm his tiny group of fighters; surrender, however, was not an option.

He wished he'd had more power to put into the Grove. His previous experience said that the attackers were in for a tough time working their way through the Grove as he had cast it. They might force their way through the tangle, and still like as not come back out on the far side of the Grove, within a yard or two of where they'd gone in.

He even knew of a man who'd gotten lost in one of his Groves, only to find his way back out when the power upholding the Grove failed. That was not a happy memory. The man was half-mad when they found him, and though he did recover somewhat, he was never fit for much after that. Certainly, he had been an enemy, determined to kill Carrtog and all his fellows, but this punishment had seemed extreme; death, he thought, would have been preferable.

Keep your mind on this battle, Carrtog.

One of the enemy who had made their way through came right at him, thrusting his sword at Carrtog as he came.

Carrtog parried it and put his dagger into the man's gut. A moment later another stumbled out of the Grove, eyes wide and staring.

Carrtog feinted a thrust toward the man's eyes with his sword, and when the other's sword came up to parry, he brought his dagger up at the rebel's side.

The enemy managed to get his own dagger in the way. Carrtog thrust his sword at the fellow's throat. The rings of the man's gorget parted with the force of the thrust.

As the fellow went down, Carrtog had time to note that the gorget had been patched, but poorly.

Carrtog kept his eyes on the Grove while he reloaded a pistol. He noted that several of the other soldiers were following his example, and he also noted that at least one of them had a fresh wound, though it didn't seem serious. As he worked, he recalled the staring eyes of the enemy who'd managed to come through. Obviously, they'd seen strange things in there. The Grove was clearly having an effect.

For a long while there was no more action. He wondered if someone on the other side was working on a spell that could be used for finding their way through a Grove of Battle.

Unlikely, but not impossible. Upon coming on a Grove the sensible thing to do would be for the attacking force to pause long enough for the leader to poll his men to see if anyone had such a spell; on the other hand, the sensible choice was not always the first one that came to mind.

There was a flicker of movement out there in the brush, "Here they come again!"

A moment later a storm of pistol-fire broke out somewhere beyond the Grove. What on earth were they shooting at? They wouldn't be able to see the defenders from there.

He swung his pistol up to aim at the flicker of movement and suddenly the man appeared, running toward them.

Before he could squeeze the trigger, one of his men fired and the attacker went down.

Behind that one, men began coming through the Grove in twos and threes, This is it, Carrtog thought, They'll overrun us this time, for sure.

He fired his pistol, then took up his sword and dagger. There followed several hurried minutes of ringing, clashing blade-work, ending with one man mortally wounded in front of him, another badly hurt, and a third approaching him with great caution.

More men came pouring through the Grove; they must have found someone with a spell after all. Even as that thought went through his mind, he realized that these new arrivals were attacking the men in front of Carrtog's position. The distance was near enough that he could hear people shouting "For King Bornival!" This sort of thing was vital on battlefields like this, where friend and foe might be intermingled, and uniforms might be non-existent. And yes, there was a figure, recognizable by his movements. "Yakor!"

Carrtog's remaining attacker approached with a careful series of feints, never committing himself wholly.

Carrtog himself fenced cautiously in return. Even though help had arrived, it was no time to get careless; it would be stupidity to let himself get killed or wounded just as the rescuers had come.

And one of the arriving rescuers was coming up behind the rebel. Carrtog crowded the man a bit and his opponent, hearing the sound of someone behind him, panicked.

Frantically, he knocked Carrtog's sword out of line and jumped to the right rear, trying to turn while he did so. Carrtog thrust once, violently, right through an attempted parry by the man's dagger.

A moment later, he was standing over the fallen body, leaning on his sword. The man coming up lowered his sword slightly, but remained watchful; after all, Carrtog was not wearing the uniform of the king's Gentlemen.

"You are?" he demanded.

"I am Carrtog, third grandson of Dlestan Lord of Tsingallik, and I fight for King Bornival."

The man was still wary, "You do, eh? Can someone vouch for you?"

The fellow was obviously an ordinary townsman with some amount of military training. Carrtog wasn't surprised the man was leery about taking anybody's word for much of anything, he'd likely witnessed a bunch of rough-looking types hijacking a train and kidnapping the king.

"Hold up, Druthan, put up your sword! That fellow's my master, and a good supporter of the king!"

Carrtog glanced over at Yakor who was coming up behind the other fellow.

It was just like his companion to have gotten a band together to come out after them and to have learned most of the important names on the ride.

"Good to see you, Yakor, I wasn't sure how long we'd be able to hold out."

"Nonsense, sir! The moment I smelled your magic on that Grove, I knew we were in plenty of time. From what I could see by the tracks and the casualties out there, less than a dozen out of something over a score managed to get through. Only problem would've been if one of that lot had a spell to get them through the Grove, and if they'd had it, they'd've used it already."

"You smelled my magic on the Grove? Gods above, Yakor, you're always saying things like that, but you never explain them!"

Yakor shrugged and grinned, "If I tried to explain it, you wouldn't understand the explanation."

"And you always say that, too!"

Yakor only grinned the wider, "Because it's true. Anyway, what kind of situation do we have here, sir?"

Druthan was looking from one of them to the other and finally he slipped his sword back in its scabbard.

Carrtog gestured around to the battlefield where men were taking care of each other's wounds and stripping the enemy dead of any useable weapons. "Those bits and pieces of shaped wood that you see scattered around are the remnants of a glider partially formed by magic. I don't know what you know of gliders, but the Chief smith on grandda's steading was interested in flight and used whatever spare time he could find to test them, and he was willing to talk. From what I recall, gliders have a limited range of flight. Those people you just rescued us from arrived within a day of the glider's crash, which means that their base is nearby, so we had best get ourselves back to town as quickly as possible." As they spoke, he led Yakor a little way apart from the townspeople. "Who's in charge of the group from the town?"

Yakor grimaced. "Near as I can make out, there's a fair crowd of people who'd have helped the rebels, but are just a little bit annoyed that the rebels didn't see fit to ask them. What we've got is several of the leading people in the town out to rescue the king and every once in a while one or another of them will express their claim to be in charge."

Carrtog nodded. "We've got a lot of men battered up badly in the crash. Any means we use to get them out of here is likely to make their condition worse, but can you imagine the sort of treatment they'll get if we leave them here for the rebels to find?"

Yakor's expression went grim, "You're right, that's the worst of a bundle of bad choices. How did you come to be in charge of the king's Gentlemen?"

"I was willing to stand as advisor to a senior man, but with their captain dead none of them were willing to take on this mess, for which I can hardly blame them. That left me to give the orders and try to keep us alive until you showed up with the rescue party."

Yakor's eyebrows went up, "Expecting a lot, weren't you?"

Carrtog grinned, "As you'd said, you wouldn't want to go back and tell my grandfather that you'd lost me and didn't try looking for me."

"Huh! Perhaps facing your grandfather doesn't sound so terrible after all."

Carrtog glanced around to be sure he and Yakor were still alone.

"Don't be so grouchy, I'm about to introduce you to the king as the man who saved his royal hindquarters."

"All right. But I'll tell you right here and now that I'd just as soon not have the king take too close notice of me. A lot of things can come of it, most of them bad."

Carrtog grinned, "If I don't introduce you, he'll think I'm trying to hog all the credit. That would put a limit to my ability to rise in his service. He'd even refuse to let his daughter marry me."

Yakor gave him a sharp look, "I hope you're joking! kings don't marry their daughters to nobodies, even if those nobodies have saved their royal hide." Then he chuckled ruefully, "But trust you to make a go of it anyways. Fine then, let's go talk to the king."

The king was sitting up, watching them approach, his face carefully expressionless.

"Highness, this is my companion, Yakor, who urged the townspeople to put together this party to come to our rescue."

King Bornival nodded, "Well done, Yakor. As you see, your noble master has managed to keep us alive until you arrived. What sort of reward do you think I should give him?"

"Me, Highness? I hardly think it's my place to say, Highness."

The king frowned, "I'd say it's your place to answer if your Sovereign asks a question."

"Ah..., Yes, Highness. In that case I'd say to give him a small bag of silver and your thanks."

"A small bag of silver? Is that how you value the life of your king, then?"

Yakor did not hesitate for a moment, "No, Highness, never that! Only that if you reward him too well he'll be insufferable on the trail."

Bornival stared for a moment, then roared with laughter, "I see. That would hardly do, would it? On the other hand, I can offer no reward at all until we get back to town, and then only providing no one has plundered my baggage."

THE RESCUE PARTY HAD brought along several spare horses and Carrtog noted with satisfaction that Yakor had brought along his own horse as well. They had horses enough for those who were fit to ride, but the few horses they did have didn't solve the problem of transporting the wounded.

In the end, they decided on sleds and began to gather pieces of wood of varying lengths to put together several makeshift sleds with which to transport the wounded soldiers. Carrtog cautioned the party against attempting to take anything from the Grove of

Battle. His warnings amounted to vague suggestions of possible ill luck. Most of those present were fortunately willing to take his word for it; after all, his magic had created the Grove.

For himself, Carrtog knew little more than that, that the taking of wood from a Battle Grove was reputed to bring ill luck, particularly if the one who had taken the wood was also the one who had produced the Grove. He wasn't absolutely certain if the bad luck would follow if the one who produced the Grove merely stood by while others of his company did the taking, but he preferred not to risk the chance.

As he watched and thought, he wondered if there were some means of cleansing the wood from a Battle Grove to make it usable for other tasks: another matter to be brought up with someone more knowledgeable than he about battle magic.

While the men set to work on the sleds, the leaders of the rescuing party — there were at least two — assured themselves that the king was still alive. Then moments later, a tug-of-war of commands broke out between the two commanders, one short and squat, one tall and lean.

The short one began the argument by shouting, "Divlan, get yourself back to town and tell them that His Majesty is alive and well!"

The tall one shouted, "Divlan! Hold on there! Neddivar, you've got a faster horse. You go back and tell the town that His Majesty is alive, but wounded, and much of his party dead!"

The shorter one glowered at the other, then burst out, "Look here, Penllucos, I'm the mayor! I'm in charge!"

Penllucos snorted. "And I'm the commander of the town militia, Mayor Ffulgos." The title and name came out as an insult. "In a military situation, I'm in charge."

The mayor subsided, but the militia commander's victory only seemed to whet his appetite. Penllucos, apparently seeing Carrtog as the person in charge of the king's forces, urged his horse over to stand in front of him. The mayor pushed his own horse to follow so as to force his own inclusion.

"You don't appear to be one of the king's Gentlemen; how is it you've taken charge of them?"

"I'm Carrtog, third son of Gwahalad, son of Dlestan of Tsingallik." Carrtog waved the bone ring on his left hand. "My ring warned me of trouble, but when I came to warn the king, the riot broke out before I could do more than speak a few words. Being there in the midst of things, I did what I could in the king's defense. After the glider crashed, it turned out that Captain Gwailants had already died, and I had already started giving orders. The remaining Gentlemen were just as well pleased for me to continue doing so, and when His Majesty recovered consciousness, he decided to let matters stand as they were."

He made no mention of the fact that, being a son of a lord, he sounded like a lord; in some sense, the soldiers had deferred to him naturally.

"Probably for the best, then," declared Penllucos, and Mayor Ffulgos muttered what sounded like an agreement shortly after.

They moved off to argue over the contents of the message that would be sent to the town with the courier and Carrtog left them to their discussion, thinking the mayor might have cause to win this one; the townsfolk were, after all, his people.

He wondered then just how loyal the respective commanders were to the king. The militia commander would certainly have been vetted by the king, most likely even the previous king, and would very likely be dependably loyal with reliable military ability. Among the other ranks, though, it would be almost certain that a number of less dependable men would have slipped in.

As for the mayor, he was also very likely loyal, but many of the men under him might well just be looking for the most effective time to turn their coats.

Their enemy had not had far to come to find them after the crash; it made him wonder if the town was as safe as they were all wishing. Carrtog set the thought aside. They would need to get to the town before they could worry over it.

The building of the sleds took a bit of time, but when they were finally complete, they began loading up their people.

That meant loading their dead as well; they had neither the tools nor the manpower to dig proper graves in the frozen ground, and no one was willing to leave them for creatures of the wild to scavenge.

As Carrtog supervised the loading, he found himself occasionally watching the princess' lady-in-waiting, who was staying close enough to her mistress to offer help when needed, but appeared to be doing her best not to hover annoyingly. The two of them appeared to enjoy a close rapport, despite the pains of their wounds and the stress of the situation in which they found themselves. (That same pain and stress was probably behind a lot of her initial negative attitude. It might be nice to try to change her mind.) Carrtog shook his head. No, despite all the jokes with Yakor, a lady-in-waiting to the princess was only slightly less beyond the reach of a landless third son than the princess herself.

Chapter 4

The railway had been built to generally follow the main road to Tenerack, with differences, such as the fact that the railway could not turn as sharply as the road, nor could it climb so steep a grade. The rebels' glider had not, fortunately, gone far off the railway line before crashing, so that the rescue party from the city had been able to see the smoke of the campfires from the road. On the other hand, the rebels had also been able to see those fires when they came looking for their glider.

Another result of the railway being built along the road was that, once the king's party had gotten on the road, they were able to make fair time getting to Tenerack. That was in spite of the burden of the homemade sleighs and their passengers.

As a result of the courier having gone back to town ahead of the main party, there was a small crowd out to greet them when they arrived.

Carrtog, having willingly let the militia commander take command, rode back beside Yakor among the rest.

"What d'you think, Yakor? Are the townspeople right to seem as nervous as a bunch of cats at a hounds' parley?"

Yakor shrugged. "Don't ask me; you're the one who's been hobnobbing with royalty. If you don't know what he's likely to do, how would I? I will say they're probably safe for the moment; there aren't enough left of the king's troops for him to dare trying any out-right destruction. I would suggest they keep a careful watch a month or so down the road. If they spot a royal army coming this way, they should start evacuating. Or fortifying, whichever they decide is best."

"Sounds right. If anyone is fool enough to press him on his intentions, he'll likely say whatever he has to say to get out of town safely. He can't ignore outright rebellion and attacks against his person, and particularly not in a part of his realm that was just recently added by conquest. It's going to be a long while before the city of Tenerack gets any more royal favors, and the next royal army it sees will supply itself from the locality while it hunts down rebels."

Yakor frowned. "Best you don't talk to the townspeople. If you point out all those facts to them, they might decide they're best off to slaughter the lot of us and then deal with the king's successor."

Carrtog shrugged. "Most of them aren't stupid; they'll be able to think of things like that for themselves. If we're lucky, though, they'll try to mollify the king rather than deal with his heir when he comes up with blood in his eye. Perhaps the two of us should quietly drift off into the night to be safe."

"Says the youngster who jumped into the middle of an uprising shouting Tsingallik for the king."

"What should I shout jumping in among the king's Gentlemen, and me, dressed as a wandering mercenary, not known as the most-trustworthy of people? But you're right Yakor, here now just as in that moment, I don't think I'd find myself easy to live with if I abandoned the king when he needed me."

Yakor grinned broadly. "Strange, nearly the exact words I'd expected to hear from you."

Carrtog smiled in return. "Well, the king has promised me a reward, and our purses aren't quite so heavy I can turn that down on the grounds that I was just doing my duty."

THE CHIEF MEN OF TENERACK found quarters for the king's party in some of the local inns, while the wounded were placed under the care of healers, mostly old women — sometimes men — with a knowledge of healing herbs and bone-setting.

Carrtog and Yakor took advantage of the opportunity to get themselves cleaned up and paid a few copper coins to have their clothing washed by a local laundress. Yakor was a little concerned. As they were walking back to their lodgings, he asked, "You don't think it's a bit of a risk leaving our clothing with the laundress? If we have to run during the night, we'll be leaving it behind."

"But if we go about looking all confident that we won't have to leave in a hurry, any prospective enemies will find themselves wondering what we know that they don't."

"Or perhaps take us for a pair of overconfident idiots."

Carrtog grinned briefly. "Well, yes, in the best of plans there is some risk."

"'In the best of plans?' If this is your best plan, Gods preserve us from your worst!"

"Maintain your self-confidence, Yakor. None of my plans has killed us yet."

"Yet! I fail to find that reassuring."

As they came in the door, one of the king's Gentlermen approached them, one whose wounds still allowed him to get around."Sirs, the king is at table, and he asks you to join him."

"Certainly," Carrtog responded. "Lead the way."

The king was at table in the city's highest-quality inn, though all the dishes were painted pottery, nothing of gold or silver. The rag wrapped around the king's temples had been replaced by a clean white cloth, and he looked up as Carrtog and Yakor came in.

He snapped his fingers, and one of his Gentlemen, who was serving as temporary butler for lack of any other available servants, bawled out, "Two more place settings, quickly!"

Two place settings were produced and the two of them were directed to seats of prominence, Carrtog next to the king, and Yakor next to him.

When this was done, the king spoke to Carrtog. "A good evening to you gentlemen. I appreciate the risks you have taken for me, but unfortunately the risks are not yet done."

"Yes, Highness, I can appreciate that fact," Carrtog answered. Yakor stayed quiet, but cast a glance at his master.

The king carried on. "With uprising going on in the neighborhood, we dare not stay here long; indeed, my intention is to depart tomorrow for Comgwiddiog. There is a small garrison there who will be happy to see us safely to the capital. I would be grateful if you would accompany us; counting all who are fit to travel with us, we are too few. It will be a risky business travelling through this country, even adding the two of you."

He gave Carrtog a long look, and Yakor a look only a little briefer.

"Of course, Your Majesty, we will be ready to march as soon as you need us."

"Good, good! And we have not forgotten the service you have already been to us. There will be a suitable reward for the both of you when we reach the capital. Now let us eat, gentlemen. Afterward, we will call all our people together to discuss matters. It will save a lot of tedious repetition."

It will also save us from repeating several painful and embarrassing admissions, Carrtog thought, but did not say.

The rest of the conversation revolved around the benefits the royal railway would bring to the area, and how he, Bornival, would not allow a band of rebellious ingrates to thwart him.

"Meaning no disrespect, Your Majesty," Carrtog said, "but certain aspects of this particular attack speak to a higher degree of planning, indeed, to sabotage in the Royal Iron-works. The attack was poorly carried-out, for certain, but it is striking that they even attempted such a complex attack."

The king scowled. "It sounds as though you admire this pack of rebels and bandits."

Carrtog smiled. "It does us no good to falsely denigrate an enemy. Best realize that they may well be as brave and intelligent as ourselves, and be ready to fight them, whatever they try."

The king continued to frown, but he waved his hand in dismissal. Carrtog got the impression that he felt it better not to say anything that would cut back on his already tiny force.

Yakor waited until he felt they were far enough out of earshot of anyone, royal or local, before he muttered, "We won't be taking the wounded with us."

"No," Carrtog replied. "I believe the rationale is to get the king out of danger, at all costs."

"I might feel better about that if he'd admitted it, but he talked all around the matter. It sounded as though he had a guilty conscience about it, but he didn't want to confess to it."

Carrtog glanced around. "The whole thing is a bit of a mess. To be sure, he wanted to gain favor among the local people, but he'd have been better to send some royal relative to declare the railway open. What he's done is to stir up a rebellion that's going to be hellish difficult to put down."

EARLY IN THE MORNING, one of the King's Gentlemen knocked on their door. "Are you awake? The king summons us to meet in the stables at sunrise."

"We're awake," Yakor answered, though they had just barely been wakened by the knocking. "We'll be down in a moment."

It was still dark, but the stables were all a-bustle. Several horses were already saddled and bridled, and King Bornival was holding himself upright, looking almost noble despite his wounds. He was standing on his own but near enough to one of the posts of the horse-stall that he could lean on it if necessary.

Private Harrad approached the two. "We've been getting dark looks from many of the populace, sirs, so His Majesty has decided to leave early."

Carrtog nodded. "I see. And has he given any order as to where amidst the party he wants us to ride?"

"His Majesty feels you would be best used riding forward to scout the way to Comgwiddiog since you wear no uniform. If you spot any large bodies of armed men along the way, you and your man are to return immediately."

Carrtog nodded in agreement. His ring had been intermittently signaling him during the night and evening, so he already had some notion that trouble was on the way.

"His majesty further orders that we should all walk, leading our horses, until we are out of the town at least."

Carrtog nodded. "Leading the horses seems the best course to take to try to avoid the greater numbers of the enemy considering how few we are. If we're leading them, we can try to keep them from making too much noise."

"Good, then," Private Harrad said. "I will take my report to the king."

When Private Harrad had gotten sufficiently far away, Yakor muttered "Not a word about the poor wounded buggers we're leaving for the rebels to slaughter."

"You were perhaps expecting a speech expressing his royal gratitude that their deaths allow him a better chance to escape unnoticed?"

"Some small reference to their sacrifice would have been nice."

Carrtog smiled bitterly. "That might have required something close to an admission of the poorly-thought-out and even-less-well-executed nature of the plan. He might even find himself blaming himself for the whole fiasco. A king can't allow that, can he?"

THE STREETS OF TENERACK were quiet as they led their horses through. Carrtog's nerves were on edge, expecting at any moment to hear a challenge from the darkness.

Yakor spoke quietly. "You worry so hard, lad, one can near enough hear you."

He looked over at Yakor, walking quietly and easily beside him. He composed his mind then, and concentrated on moving quietly. They kept to uncobbled side-streets and alleys as much as possible, to avoid the distinctive sound of horse-shoes on stone. No one had thought, until much too late, of getting rags to wrap the horses' feet against the sound.

They were near the city's edge when Yakor spoke again. He pointed with his chin towards their left, where the houses had become sparse. "That gowk skulking at the base of that branched willow down there; he isn't as well hidden as he thinks."

"Will you take him or should I?"

"I'd do it myself, but I think you need the practice."

"I do, do I?" Carrtog responded.

"You do. Remember, you won't always have me handy to take care of nuisances like this."

Carrtog twisted his face in a grimace. "You think I love all these fellows!"

"Not that you love them or any such nonsense, but you have a hard time putting things out of your mind, such as their widows and orphaned children. Think instead about what could happen to us, to you and me and the king and the princess' lady-in-waiting."

"All right, all right, no need to beat me over the head with it." Carrtog stepped into the saddle and urged his horse on along a path that led somewhere behind the fellow in the willows, all the way looking down as if he were following a track, though by no means was there light enough to find footprints from horseback.

The man, still trying to remain hidden, looked around to see if there were anyone else in sight.

Carrtog turned his horse's head leftward toward the skulker, urging his mount into a run. The man realized his predicament and jumped up to flee. Carrtog's horse overtook him, though, and Carrtog, kicking his feet free from the stirrups, dropped on him from behind, one hand raised to plunge home his dagger. A moment later, it was done.

Carrtog's horse had pulled up a little further on and began to graze allowing Yakor to catch up the reins and lead him back. The smell of blood made him shy slightly, but the familiar touch and smell of his usual rider had a calming effect, and soon the two were on their way again.

THE EVERGREENS WERE silent about them, most wildlife having become scarce along the path cleared for the track of the railroad, though occasionally a deer bounded into and out of sight, or an eagle soared high overhead. Beyond that, there was little sign of life.

On the afternoon of the second day, they began to scent smoke.

"If we're lucky," Yakor said, "That's just the cook-fires of Comgwiddiog."

"And I suppose I'm expected to ask, 'what if we're not lucky?'"

"You're not expected to ask, you're supposed to list several less fortunate possibilities."

"Possibilities such as the rebels having taken the town and burned it to the ground with less than the usual amount of burning, and are getting ready to use it against us?"

"Very well thought out. So, now, what are our best notions? Should we go right back and inform the king, or have you a better idea?"

Yakor was looking at Carrtog as though urging him to make up his mind quickly, "One usually has more time to make up his mind than is safe; on the other hand one might just barely have time to pull one's tail from the fire."

Carrtog, his mind made up, nodded sharply. "Let's find a little body of water, preferably a stream."

"Didn't we just cross a stream a little bit back?"

"You're right, of course." Carrtog was already turning his horse back.

Moments later, they came to a small dark stream. "This will do very well. Yakor, get out a silver coin, near pure silver as possible, and cut off a few shavings. Save them on a chip of wood."

Without questions, Yakor began to obey, while Carrtog dug a small ceramic bowl out of his saddlebags. A bowl of silver would have been preferable, but carrying such a large piece of silver in one's saddlebag through these wilds was dangerous to the point of stupidity. A ceramic bowl, well-washed, along with incantations, would have to do.

He washed it thoroughly, reciting the proper incantations, then filled it with water. He drew a pistol ball from his pouch, and dipped it into the bowl, repeating further incantations to make the magical connection, then dried it so as not to dampen the powder.

He then took some of the silver chips Yakor had produced, and using the flat of his sword as an anvil, pressed them into the soft lead of the pistol ball

He glanced at Yakor as he began priming and loading, "This is known as 'The Ball Over the Wood.' I'll want you to watch carefully what shows in the bowl, if anything."

He aimed the pistol forward and at an angle that would take the ball high in the air and near to as far forward as guesswork would allow. He spoke an incantation, which, among other things, was intended to dampen the sound of the shot.

Despite that, the discharge was uncomfortably loud. Carrtog grimaced. He hoped this got some result, for he had no wish to repeat this. He couldn't hope to go unheard by enemies for long, nor could he count on being mistaken for a hunter.

He wished he had more experience with this particular spell. He suspected that Yakor could read his nervousness, and was quietly grateful to the man for not showing it in his expression.

He glanced at the bowl; at first the water's surface showed only a passing woodscape, mostly evergreens and low underbrush. Suddenly there was a flicker of movement, and Carrtog spoke a sharp word.

The view held still, expanded a little, and, for the space of about ten heartbeats, they were able to scrutinize it closely.

"Headed this way," commented Carrtog. "What d'you think?"

Yakor nodded in agreement. "Here before midday, I'd guess."

"Right. Let's clean up here and head back to the king."

'Cleaning up' consisted of emptying the bowl, sloshing some clear water around in it, then drying and stowing it in the saddlebag. There was little point in trying to wipe out their tracks in the patchy snow.

Carrtog glanced around. "It's possible that someone who knows their magic could figure out what went on here, but I don't know anything I could do about that. Let's go."

They hurried back down the track towards where they had left the king's party. Shortly they saw the others, who, as soon as they saw the pair coming back, had begun to get themselves into a sort of defensive formation, displaying more confusion than skill.

"What now?" demanded the king.

"Comgwiddiog has fallen, and there's a party of armed men headed this way. They'll be on us by noon."

The king snorted. "I expect those traitors in Tenerack found some way to pass the word on as to which way we were travelling."

Carrtog, who knew half a dozen ways to pass a message through the distance between the two towns, forbore to comment.

The king continued to glare. "Do you have any suggestions for us, other than that we cravenly surrender ourselves?"

It occurred to Carrtog that King Bornival did not know much history. Tsingallik having betrayed their cause during the previous war, the best any of his descendants could expect from people loyal to the pre-war situation was execution out of hand.

"No, your Majesty, I prefer flight and evasion. I am not a complete Master of Battle Magic, but if you follow my instructions, I believe I can get us safely away."

The king gave him a suspicious look. "If I follow your instructions?"

"I shall endeavor to ask nothing that would offend your Majesty's honor."

The king nodded grimly, but Carrtog could see that his agreement was only grudging. "So. What next, then?"

"The first thing we do is to get off this trail, so as not to run headlong into the rebels. I will prepare a spell of confusion and illusion. If they come in sight of us, I need only speak one word and we will be off at a run, leaving them only fleeting glimpses of a herd of deer in flight."

"And they will mistake the gait of running horses for running deer?" scoffed the king.

"Part of the spell, Highness," Carrtog replied. "Besides which, the spell will keep them from seeing more than glances of us."

"Had you not considered that firing a pistol-shot will attract their attention, make them aware that something is up?"

"True, a pistol-shot is preferable for the powering of a spell such as this, Highness, but I can get equal results by the open burning of good-quality powder a little bigger than the size of my thumbnail. Now, Highness, I ask you to excuse me while I make my preparations. I would suggest that you follow Yakor off the trail, and I will catch up to you as soon as may be."

The king frowned, hesitating. Please, Your Majesty, don't make any snide hints about my betraying you. I may not be able to maintain my courtesy if you do.

But the king only nodded curtly and turned away.

It didn't take long for Carrtog to gather a few twigs and make a tiny fire, then he carefully spoke the words of the several necessary incantations and tossed a pinch of powder into the flame.

It flashed, putting most of the fire out and scattering the smallest sticks.

He carefully stamped out the rest of the fire, kicking loose snow over the remnants, then got up on his horse and rode after the rest of the royal party.

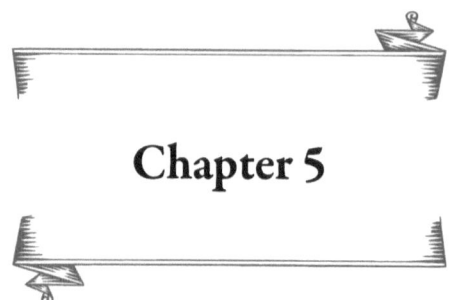

Chapter 5

He followed the trail through the brush and under the low-hanging evergreen boughs until he found himself coming up behind the rear-guard.

"It's only me, Lord Carrtog," he said warningly. Pistol half-raised, the man turned around in his saddle to satisfy himself that Carrtog was indeed who he said he was. The man nodded and turned back to face front.

Carrtog rode on up the column, shortly coming to the lady-in-waiting and the princess, who was riding well despite her broken arm. Her mouth, though, was grim and tight against the pain.

"Highness, would you like me to cast another pain-killing spell on your arm?"

She looked at him, forcing a smile. "I thought you didn't want to fire any shots so near to our pursuit?"

"True, but there are spells I can do without a pistol-shot."

She shook her head. "No, I think it would be better to wait until we stop to rest the horses, then you can do spells for all those who still bear wounds."

He nodded, seeing the good sense in her suggestion. "Yes, you're right. I'll see you when we rest."

He was turning away when the lady-in-waiting called, "Lord Carrtog?"

"Yes?"

"I believe I must make apologies. I see so many people intent on doing service to Their Highnesses, often to the point of pretending to abilities beyond what they possess. In your case, not only do you possess the abilities you claim, but I must confess that I had ignored the fact that you had treated the men for pain, even the ones who later died."

Carrtog inclined his head, surprised at her apology. "Uneasiness around magic is not an uncommon thing my lady, I take no offense."

"Given the circumstances in which we find ourselves, and will for the next many days, I find no need for you to call me merely by my title. I am called Adengler."

Perhaps he could convince himself that princess' ladies-in-waiting were not so far out of reach.

WHEN CARRTOG CONTINUED up the column, King Bornival was wearing what seemed to be his usual displeased expression, but he didn't hail Carrtog and insist on talking to him. For his part, Carrtog was just as pleased not to have to remain unfailingly polite in the face of the king's snide allusions.

"Do you have any suggestions for us, other than that we cravenly surrender ourselves?" That one had left a particularly foul taste in his mouth.

He rode beside Yakor for a bit. "Anything happening that I should be aware of?"

Yakor shrugged. "We can't hurry very much in this underbrush and loose snow, not unless we want to risk laming a horse or two. Anything to report from behind?"

"Her name is Lady Adengler."

Yakor turned to look at him, frowning. "That's what's got you smiling like a fool, is it? Watch yourself, boy, you're moving into dangerous territory."

Carrtog, who hadn't thought that his facial expression was revealing so much, protested, "Come now, Yakor, it's not as if I plan to begin courting her out here in the wilderness!"

"You just see to it that your mind is on getting us home safely, and not on the charms of the Lady Adengler. If we run into an ambush while you're trying to make up a poem to her in your head, I'll be seriously annoyed with you."

Carrtog wanted to protest, but he had to admit that Yakor had a point. He'd found thoughts of Lady Adengler haunting his mind before he'd known her name; now that she'd introduced herself to him — thereby suggesting that she found him worth talking to at least — he was going to have to force himself to be doubly wary of letting his mind wander. Oh, Carrtog, my lad, how easy it is to give yourself such commands, yet how hard it is to carry them out!

WHEN THEY PAUSED A little later, Carrtog, mindful of the warning from Yakor, was careful not to approach Lady Adengler first, but rather went to the king. "Does your head pain you, Your Majesty? I can produce a charm to decrease the discomfort, if you wish."

The king scowled. "I need none of your piddling charms! Just leave me be!"

Carrtog bowed. "As you wish, Your Majesty. I will see to the others, then."

He still did not go immediately to Lady Adengler, but made the rounds of the wounded troops who had been hale enough to ride along with the party. That brought to his mind the men who had been left in Tenerack, and even the fact that he had put himself under the king's orders did not assuage his guilt particularly.

Most of the soldiers were willing to accept his pain-killing spell, though two of them took their cue from the king and refused him brusquely.

He didn't bother wasting any time attempting to convince those, but went on to the princess and Lady Adengler, who were both grateful to accept whatever he could do for them.

He didn't speak to Lady Adengler, not more than to make his offer and to accept her thanks, though he did try hard not to seem to be rejecting her offer of friendship.

That done, he went to rejoin Yakor. Yakor muttered quietly, "I suppose it would be treason to suggest you use a spell to put His Royal Grouchiness in a better frame of mind?"

"I'd say we should be careful not to be seeming to talk secrets in his sight; he might well take it as evidence we were plotting against him."

Yakor's face went grim. "Gods above, the pupil teaching the teacher! But you're right; we're walking a very fine line."

AFTER A SHORT REST, they were riding again. They had been traveling for about an hour when Carrtog heard the sound of an owl hooting twice. That was the agreed-on signal from the rearguard that the rebels were closing in on them.

"Close up!" Carrtog shouted. A moment later he called out "Now go!"

He shouted the last words of the incantation; suddenly they were galloping through a fine mist. *Carrtog, you fool, you didn't warn them what to expect! We'll be lucky if we don't lose someone through confusion!*

On the other hand, the mist was the sign that the spell was working, and that the pursuers, if they saw anything, saw only brief glimpses of deer bounding away through the brush ahead of them, brush that suddenly seemed thicker and more impenetrable.

IN THIS SORT OF TERRAIN, it wasn't safe to run the horses for very long; laming one of the beasts could be little short of disastrous. They ran for about as long as Carrtog dared, then he called another halt.

The king was still not pleased. "They'll be following our tracks, of course, once your magic fades. That means they may be a little delayed, but they'll catch us."

"They won't find it quite that easy Your Majesty. All we could see of the magic was a fine mist. They'll see patches of fog and some quick glimpses of animals. While the spell lasts, they won't be able to see tracks at all, not even their own. As well as that, they'll keep hearing sounds, including what seems to be far-off shouts of men, coming from various directions. When the magic fades, they'll have been drawn so far off the trail that they'll be a long while finding it again."

The king was not mollified. "What you can hide with magic, cannot another find with magic?"

"Quite possibly, Your Majesty. On the other hand, I have set a charm to warn me if magic finds us, at which point I will take further countermeasures. We haven't yet seen any sign of combat magic from our pursuers, but I'm sure that a party of their size would include at least one competent magician."

The king continued to scowl, but Carrtog had a feeling that his dissatisfaction was mainly due to the fact that Carrtog had an answer for each of his concerns.

"May I be excused, Your Majesty? I should see how the others are holding up." *Actually, the others are likely holding up very well; I just* have a fear that if I stay here much longer, my courtesy will end up worn to a shred.

"Go, then," the king replied, ungraciously.

Carrtog bowed and left the king, going straight to Yakor who had taken it upon himself to check on the others. "How are we doing, Yakor?"

Yakor shrugged. "Surprisingly well, but then we've just barely begun, and we have no idea at all how wide-spread the rebellion may be."

Carrtog nodded. "When we stop for the evening, I'm going to try some spells to see what I can find out. I don't dare try it now, this kind of magic is likely to wear me down completely, and I'll need a long sleep afterward."

Yakor nodded in his turn. "Let's be on our way, then."

THEY HADN'T GONE VERY far when they came out of the brush into a clearing. A second glance showed the clearing to be man-made, for it ran almost straight from northeast to southwest, and the trees and bushes that had been cut down were piled in piles here and there along the sides.

In the center was a slightly raised embankment, on top of which could be seen the ends of the cross-ties, and on top of that the long gleaming line of the rails.

Yakor led them up the embankment and down the other side. When it was clear that he was leading them toward the forest on the other side, the king called out, "Would we not be better following the railway track? It's all clear land."

Carrtog answered. "Yes, Majesty, but unfortunately the rebels are aware of that as well. I expect they'll have parties waiting here and there along the railway line to catch us should we do just that."

The king did not respond, but Carrtog could see he was not pleased. Was he displeased because he would have preferred to follow the railway, or just because he was annoyed with himself for not thinking of the reasons why it was not a good idea?

Having made their way into the brush on the other side of the railway, they continued to move, tending south-westward as much as possible. Late in the afternoon, as they worked their way painfully through the underbrush, they heard the sound of the train coming from the northwest, and looking back saw the trail of smoke from the smokestack.

The king spoke up. "I suppose you have a reason why we should not go back and stop the train?"

"Yes, Your Majesty, I do. It's coming from the north, and most likely has two or more companies of rebels riding on it hoping we do just that."

"You think it's packed with rebels under arms, but you won't even go close enough to see if that's true or not?"

"Correct, Your Majesty, because if we are close enough to see them, we're also close enough for them to see us. Best we don't take the risk."

The king sat up straight. "My train hijacked by rebels and we skulk here in the woods and do nothing about it!"

"Our numbers are too few and those we have are not fit to fight, Your Majesty."

The king continued to scowl. "I tell you, when I have put down this rebellion, I will personally see to the punishment of whoever dared to drive my train for their cause!"

There didn't seem to be any appropriate response to this so Carrtog remained silent and they continued on their way.

WHEN THEY STOPPED FOR the evening, Carrtog first made sure that all the wounded were as comfortable as possible, though again the king — and the two other Gentlemen — refused his ministrations.

That done, he informed the king, "Your Majesty, I am about to attempt a very complex series of spells, attempting both to discover whether or not anyone is searching for us with magic, and as much as possible, how much of the surrounding territory has gone over to the rebels. As I say, the spells are complicated, and when I am done, I will be able to do nothing but sleep for some time. Therefore, if you wish to ask me any questions, or if you have a request of me, please speak now."

The king sneered and waved a dismissive hand. "No, go do your muttering and chanting and all. I believe I shall get along well enough."

IN THE MORNING, CARRTOG found himself with a vicious headache. He wasn't surprised; his teacher had warned him about such effects, especially for sets of spells like this. The truth was, while he had learned the set of spells, he had never used it for something so complicated. And now he could not properly remember what the magic had told him.

He remembered his teacher telling him, however, "Don't expect to be functioning properly the next day until you get rid of your headache."

He sat with his legs folded under him, staring at a knot in a tree-trunk across the way, concentrating on a mental process akin to untying several complex knots in his head. When he was done, the headache had practically faded away. Then, after he finished a series of muscle-stretches, he was feeling close to decent.

The king was still sleeping, a stroke of good luck, Carrtog thought, since though he himself was feeling better, he still did not feel up to maintaining politeness in the face of the king's usual attitudes. He spoke to Yakor.

"The news isn't as bad as it might be," he said, "The next ten miles or so are pretty firmly in rebel hands, and the next twenty miles after that are mostly controlled by the rebels, with some patches either still on our side or trying to stay neutral."

"What about people looking for us?"

Carrtog nodded. "There are indeed, several of them, or perhaps several lots. There is one small and fairly powerful group that's looking for us with our safety in mind, which isn't really surprising. If it wasn't for our present position, I'd let that lot find us, but— Oh, the king is waking up. I'd better go talk to him."

The king, of course, was not in a mood to talk to anyone, and even after his share of the sparse breakfast, his mood did not seem to have improved. He looked over at Carrtog. "Well, Lord Carrtog, stop hovering over there and come tell me the latest bad news!"

"Well, Your Majesty, the news is not completely bad. The next ten miles or so are pretty much under the rebel control, and the following twenty miles are mostly under rebel control but with several patches trying to show favor to neither side."

The king gave a sour look. "And which side they decide to support will likely depend on which side first gets a significant body of troops into their area."

"I wouldn't disagree with that, Your Majesty," Carrtog responded, "but there is also slightly better news. Though the rebels have several people, singly and in groups, looking for us with magic, there is also one very powerful group on our side searching out there."

"Then the answer is simple; let that group find us!"

"Unfortunately, Your Majesty, the matter is not quite so simple. The rebels are closer to us than our friends are. If we stand still, they are likely to arrive before any help. And I think the risk of trying to slip between two or more bands of enemies to find our friends is too high."

The king scowled. "So with this good news and bad news, what are we left with?"

"I'm afraid, Your Majesty, we are left with the necessity of maintaining our pace to attempt to join with the favorable forces before our enemies catch our heels."

"I see. Then I suppose we had better get to it."

As Carrtog went back to his horse, the Lady Adengler approached him. "I do hope that when we have gotten out of here, we will find it possible to talk together."

He smiled at her. "If I do nothing else, I will make sure of that, Lady Adengler. At present, most of my mind is taken up with getting us all out of here safely."

"Especially the king."

He shook his head. "Especially all of us. I ask you to please not make me decide who I would leave behind if the necessity arose, which it won't, Gods willing."

She smiled., "Gods willing indeed!"

Carrtog had taken to having Yakor ride ahead of them to keep his eyes open for anyone or anything that might appear in their path. About an hour after they started out that afternoon, he came back with a smile on his face.

"We're about to cross the road into a village."

"Why're you smiling? In this neighborhood, they've probably sided with the rebels."

"I think it'd be wise to have someone go into the village and try to buy some food. We're a little short, I shouldn't have to tell you."

"Who should we send? They've probably got posters up portraying His Majesty. And the remnants of the Gentlemen's uniforms are too distinctive. The ladies look too upper-class, and that leaves you and me."

"Actually, that leaves me. You're the one with the bit of combat magic; the party can more afford to have me taken or killed than it can you."

"I don't like it."

Yakor's grin broadened. "That's what I like about you; you don't like sending people into danger, but you will if there's no alternative!"

Yakor spent some minutes brushing his horse, not so much as to remove all traces of travel but enough to remove most signs of having pushed many miles through thick brush.

"You have enough money?" Carrtog asked.

"Probably not," Yakor answered. "On the other hand, best not to have too much. Somebody might get suspicious if I buy every loaf of bread in town."

Carrtog nodded. "We'd best find you a selection of small coins. Wait until the rest of the party arrives, and we'll make a collection."

By this time the rest of the party were coming up, and the king, in his usual manner, simply demanded, "Well, Lord Carrtog?"

"Yakor is going to cross the road into town, Your Majesty, to buy what food he can manage."

"Why don't we all go in, demand their support in my name?"

"Not a good idea, Your Majesty. This town is firmly in rebel territory and the chances are good that they have posters up describing yourself. Best only one of us takes the risk of going in while the rest of us circle around the town."

"I see."

To Carrtog it seemed more as if the king saw that he had just made a fool of himself again, and didn't like it. When no useful comments were made, Carrtog went to roundup a small handful of coins that he passed on to Yakor.

"Off you go, then, and we'll meet you on the far side of town."

Yakor waved a hand and moved away down the trail.

Carrtog looked around at the rest. "Come now, if you please, Your Majesty and the rest of you, follow me."

THEY MOVED OFF INTO the brush bordering the road. Carrtog kept a careful watch all around; some of the local brush and trees had been cleared away for fields, and as unlikely as it was for people to be out in the fields this late in the year, anyone would be suspicious seeing a band of horsemen riding across those fields rather than openly down the road.

In addition, the nearness of the town meant the likelihood of hunters out in the surrounding woods. If they came upon such a hunter, there would be no choice but to kill him, much though Carrtog would prefer not. Though the hunter might make strong protestations of loyalty to the king, the reward that was undoubtedly offered for the capture of the king would be difficult for an ordinary villager to reject.

A further difficulty was the likelihood of their pursuers coming on their trail sooner than he had counted for. Surely the tracks the royal party had left on the road back there told a clear tale; one of their group had gone into the town and the rest had circled around. The best bet for the pursuers would be to surround the village, nearly as possible, and hope at least to take Yakor. Then hurry down the road in hopes of coming on the rest of the party. What could he do aside from praying that the pursuers didn't come up too fast? There wasn't very much he could do while riding, save devote whatever free part of his mind that existed to coming up with useful spells and making preparations for those spells during their rest periods.

As for hunters from the village, from either luck or good management, they met none.

At their first rest stop, he made preparations for the Grove of Battle, with a vague notion of using it in case the pursuers suddenly came on them.

He noticed the king glancing at him as he worked, but was just as happy that the king did not decide to ask him what he was doing. Shortly, they started out again, and a little later again, they were crossing the road once more.

Carrtog threw up his hand. "We'll stop here and wait for Yakor."

The king approached him. "And if, instead of your friend, we find a troop of rebels roaring down on us?"

"I've made preparations for that case, Your Majesty."

The king paused a moment, then said, "I see."

Carrtog suddenly realized that the king had expected him to explain just what his plan was so that King Bornival could suggest modifications, or perhaps even a whole different plan. It was too late now, and the king was already seriously annoyed at him. Of course, a good deal of the king's annoyance was the king's own fault, but even telling him that would only make the situation worse.

As he sat waiting, Carrtog tried to consider just what preparations he might make. Any preparations he did make should fit a number of circumstances; there were several cases, for instances, in which he could make good use of the Battle Grove, such as the case the king had suggested — Yakor coming back with a whole troop of rebels on his heels.

His mind was growing decidedly weary and thinking was becoming a chore.

He suddenly realized that he ought to have had Yakor see about the availability of a horse or two while he was dealing for food. They'd had tremendously good luck so far with none of their mounts suddenly coming up lame. They couldn't count on that luck carrying on, though; they were going to have to buy some more horses, or perhaps even steal some horses if this chase south didn't end soon.

He felt his mouth twist into a grimace. He doubted if they had enough money to buy both horses and food for the rest of their journey; they could attempt to trade their present mounts, but people would be suspicious of anyone trying to trade a horse of the obvious quality of the king's mount for any horse that could be found in a highland village.

And that assumed that no description was given of the horse the king was riding. No, stealing was the only alternative. That would mean he'd have to prepare a spell to hide their traces from the place of the theft, otherwise they'd have the victims of their theft chasing them as well as the rebel troops.

A black spot in the sky caught his eye. At first he thought it was some kind of soaring bird, but he noticed that its wings never moved. "A glider, Gods help us! Quickly everyone move under the trees!"

Most of the party began to move, though not as quickly as he would have liked. The king and two of his Gentlemen sat staring at him as if he'd gone mad. He looked at them and pointed up into the sky. "Your Majesty, it's a glider! The people who're most likely to have gliders looking for us are the rebels. We've got to get under the cover of the trees, and far enough that they can't catch sight of us."

He moved in deeper under the trees himself, conscious of the fact that he might have given them away with his gestures if the person or people in the glider had some kind of long distance vision equipment.

The king and the others were making their way under the trees with a bit more speed, now, apparently seeing the seriousness of the situation.

The glider, however, continued on well overhead, not pausing or circling or showing any other sign it had seen them.

After a few moments in their new place, Carrtog said, "I'll have to go back to the road to wait for Yakor. The rest of you please stay here and wait for us. Stay under the trees, please. That glider may come back in this direction."

"You're leaving us here for any bunch of rebels to find?"

"Your Majesty, I don't believe any rebels will fall on us in the next few minutes. If I should happen to be wrong, I've already put out a ward in a one-mile circle around us, which will let me know if anyone approaches us with ill intent. In that case, I'll rush back to take care of the situation."

He turned, not waiting for the king's leave to go. That would surely offend the king, but he'd already demonstrated to them all that they needed him if they were to get home safe, and he didn't want to spend any more time arguing.

Furthermore, he didn't want the king to ask him why that spell of his hadn't warned him of the glider's approach. The answer was that he hadn't thought to cast the spell he'd just mentioned, but he would do so immediately after he reached his post by the road.

Very shortly, he reached his post, a little spot enclosed on three sides by a bunch of willows. He cast his ward spell, burning a pinch of powder by setting the powder on a chip of wood and striking sparks on it with a steel dagger blade and a flint, rather than risk alarming the nearby town by firing a shot through the pistol. Then he settled down to wait.

Chapter 6

Shortly thereafter, Yakor came trotting up the road, a sizable sack hanging from his saddlebow. Carrtog stepped carefully out from his place, slowly enough to give Yakor plenty of time to recognize him. He grinned at his man. "Stand and deliver!"

Yakor returned the grin. "I'm sorry, my dignity will not allow me to be robbed by a bandit in such a grubby state as yourself. I suppose the rest are hiding nearby?"

"Ah, yes indeed, the others. You saw the glider go by overhead?"

"Yes I did. I thought you'd be likely hiding them further under the trees."

"Exactly so. And speaking of which, we should join them." He mounted up and headed back into the trees, very much enjoying the feeling of not having to explain or argue over every word.

When they rode back into sight of the others, Carrtog saw the king scowling blackly at him. Uh-oh! he thought, I forgot my own warning about seeming to conspire privately with Yakor. I suspect we're in for trouble.

"Yakor!" The king ordered, "Come over here."

Carrtog made to come along.

"Not you, Lord Carrtog! I'll let you know when I wish to speak to you next!"

Carrtog got down and began to brush his horse. He was careful not to look in the direction of the king and Yakor, but he certainly hoped the king was not browbeating Yakor or making accusations.

He wondered how many of the Gentlemen would accept an order to arrest the pair of them, and whether the threat of the Grove of Battle would hold them back. Well, it would certainly keep them off long enough for him to make his escape.

If it came to that, though, he would no longer be welcome in the kingdom of Cragmor; from what he'd seen of Bornival's reactions, even his grandfather might suffer.

He stopped that train of thought altogether. No sense borrowing trouble, not until he saw what the king intended.

A voice broke into his thoughts. "You're looking particularly bleak just now, Lord Carrtog."

He looked up to see Lady Adengler standing next to him.

"I'd suggest you not get too near me, Lady Adengler. I'm not in good odor with His Majesty just now."

"Actually, I serve the princess, and the king particularly dotes on the princess, especially since her mother died. I would have to commit some egregious act for him to punish me against her will. Don't worry, I won't press my advantage too far. I may, however, persuade the princess to speak a word on your behalf."

Carrtog felt a frown come over his face at that. "Thank you, Lady, but I don't wish to trouble you."

"Trouble me, Lord Carrtog?" Her face took on a grim look. "I'd say you need someone to trouble themselves on your account." She turned and strode away.

Carrtog took a half-step after her, then held himself. The king would certainly notice him chasing after Lady Adengler and notice even more if he began shouting after her. He went back to his horse. A few moments later he was interrupted again, this time by Yakor, his face bearing a sour expression.

"You look as though you'd swallowed a toad."

"I've had to swallow worse than that. He's put me in charge of the party. Did you actually turn your back on him without asking his leave to go?"

Carrtog sighed. "I'm afraid so. He was starting to get into a bother about the way I had arranged things and I was starting to worry about my ability to hold my temper through another Royal Fulmination. And of course I knew I'd done the wrong thing before I'd gone more than a few steps, but it was already too late."

"Gods and all their minions, boy! You're going to kill us both someday! I can understand the temptation, but you're going to have to learn to hold on to your temper with iron gloves!" He paused. "Well, as it stands, he will no longer speak to you nor be spoken to by you. He's retained enough sense to allow me to consult with you and for me to give orders for such spells as are necessary. That's just the kind of mish-mosh of a command structure as to make the whole party little more than a moving disaster looking for a place to happen. I'm hoping, Lord Carrtog, to leave you in charge of such magic and spells as you think appropriate, without the necessity of the two of us consulting together as the enemy thunder down on us. Is that feasible?"

"I'll manage. One thing I've been thinking is that we're going to have to come up with some fresh mounts before long. I'd be surprised if you hadn't come to that conclusion already."

Yakor grinned. "This time the student wasn't ahead of the teacher. Yes, but I don't think we should hang around this locality for too much longer."

"Agreed."

Yakor turned and called out orders, and very shortly the party was mounted and riding on in a generally southward direction.

✕

THE HOUSE WAS DARKENED, the farmer and his family likely in bed for the night. There was sufficient light from the stars, though, for Yakor and Carrtog to survey the five horses in the corral. Carrtog had already dismissed two of them as too old for the kind of journey they would have to make.

The other three were somewhat slender, but hardy-looking. He pointed. "Those three, you think?"

Yakor nodded.

"Those three. You're sure we're invisible? I can see you just fine."

"Strange, isn't it? But we'd be a danger to everybody running around out here and bumping into each other at every step. I assure you, it wasn't easy to tailor the spell so that we could see each other while nobody else could."

Actually it had required two different spells — both of them exhausting to cast; one to make them invisible and one to allow each of them to see through the spell, but if he went on to tell Yakor all that, the older man would know how nervous he was.

They led their own invisible horses over to the corral entrance and threw down the bars, then went inside. The horses stamped and whinnied; they could hear and smell strange men and horses but not see them.

As a result, it proved impossible to drive the three chosen horses out the gate, and they had to settle for dropping a halter around the necks of two of them and leading them out. The one Yakor chose went along, though unwillingly. The one Carrtog chose, however, stood stiff-legged and refused to move, until Yakor came up behind it and slapped it on the backside with his gloved hand.

At about this time, Carrtog heard the door of the farmhouse slam open and a dog rushed forth, barking. The dog halted part way across the yard, unwilling to go any further but barking itself ragged. Like the horses, it could smell and hear strange animals but not see them.

A moment later a man's voice bellowed across the yard. "Who's there? Show yourself, or I'll fire!"

Carrtog recognized that as an idle threat. The man couldn't see them, and wasn't likely to take the chance of injuring one of his own horses by firing blind.

Shortly they were back in the brush where they had begun; the stolen horses following more obediently the farther they got from their home corral. Carrtog muttered another incantation and suddenly the tracks they had left through the trees on route to the farm were glowing in the dimness.

They followed the sets of tracks for some time until they came to the point where the rest of the party was camped. The sun was just beginning to lighten the eastern sky.

"I expect we'd best wake up the rest and have them start moving," Yakor said.

"Yes, you better be getting at it; the king isn't likely to have changed his mind and decided he wants to hear it from me."

Yakor glanced at Carrtog. "Don't allow His Majesty's snit to spoil your day. He'll probably feel much nicer toward us when he's gotten back to his comfortable castle."

Carrtog grinned. "If his castle is comfortable, then it's different from any castle I've known. Cold, drafty piles of stone all of them, built for defense and not for comfort."

"Ah, but the most uncomfortable castle is preferable to sleeping out in the wilds with nasty men hoping to stick a sword in you."

With that, Yakor went off to wake the party.

ON THE AFTERNOON OF that same day, Carrtog felt the ring on his finger giving him notice of danger coming near. He called out a warning to Yakor, who passed it on to the rest of the party. Worse yet, Carrtog felt the presence of magic searching for their trail.

The pursuers hadn't had any notable magic with them, but now they did; those two facts pointed toward a dangerous conclusion. Most likely the magician had communicated with the pursuers from a distance and, discovering their need, had used his magic to join them. That was the kind of magic that was beyond Carrtog's ability.

Well, he wasn't about to give up until he'd tried everything he could. Rather than worry the whole party, he reported quietly to Yakor. "The fellows behind us have got a magician with them, one who's more powerful than I am. I'm not ready to quit just yet, but we may have trouble the last bit of the way. Let's just pick up the pace."

"'Pick up the pace?' Do I have to remind you that these horses we're riding are no longer as fresh as they were?"

"I know that; we'll just have to do the best we can. I'll leave a couple of snares in our trail to slow them down."

The others noted the increased speed, and when they paused that afternoon to rest the horses, the king inquired, "Why the sudden rush, Lord Yakor?"

"Your Majesty, Lord Carrtog has detected a very capable magician on our track. While he still hopes to delay the pursuit, we must move as quickly as possible."

"I see." The king paused. *Trying to work out a way this is my fault, too,* Carrtog thought. He had also noted the king's promotion of Yakor to 'Lord', and wondered what Yakor thought of the matter.

But the king merely nodded, albeit with his near-habitual scowl, and dismissed Yakor.

While they rested, Carrtog considered what sorts and kinds of spells would be best to use to slow the pursuers. The first notion that came to him was a snare, of sorts. When a number of people passed a certain old moss-covered rock along their way, the spell would be released. Nothing terribly complex, just an intense smell of skunk, which would cause them to scatter a bit.

The magician with the pursuers would probably be able to dispel the stench, but it would delay them a bit, especially if they grew wary of further traps.

The terrain through which they fled had changed from wooded slopes to lightly-wooded slopes and Yakor led them to the rough road.

"I thought we were avoiding roads," complained the king.

"Not any more, Your Majesty. We're coming to the place where both they and we know pretty much exactly where we're headed. That being so, they can send a part of their force to move down the road fast and cut us off. We're best off to head for the road ourselves, and make as good a time as we can."

There was a sudden howling of hunting wolves behind them. Carrtog called out a phrase, and the howling ceased. "I was wondering when that fellow back there would join in on the magical harassing." He grinned.

One of the traps Carrtog had laid was a sudden series of lightning flashes, and he had felt the trap spring, and suddenly felt his opponent totally quash it. He did not let this disappoint him, for he knew he was dealing with a competent foe.

He didn't hold out too much hope for his next trap, a brilliant flash of light that ordinarily would have blinded men and horses, for he assumed that his opponent would simply quash it as easily as Carrtog had cast it. He was surprised, therefore, when he felt the extreme consternation among the pursuers.

His best guess was that the magician back there had overstretched himself in dealing with the lightning, and so was not able to detect or deal with the bright light quickly. Carrtog knew he daren't depend on that in future, though.

The next three days were a series of long-distance skirmishes between the two magicians, much of it illusions which were easily dispelled if the magician on the receiving end was fresh and rested.

On Carrtog's part, this meant trying to set up a spell-proof circle around the camp at night, which still required him to break his sleep at least once in a night. Being fully aware of his own limitations, Carrtog did not dare respond in kind too often; he had to reserve as much of his power as possible for the final confrontation which looked more and more likely as they went on.

Toward the end of the second day, Yakor approached him. "How are you holding up? You're looking a little worn."

Carrtog summoned a grin, but only briefly. "I'm glad to hear I look so well. I feel as worn as a ten-year-old saddle blanket."

"My own magical abilities aren't worth a spit in the wind, but is there anything I can do to help?"

Carrtog shook his head. "Nothing that I can think of, but thanks for the offer — uh-oh, here comes something else!"

He snorted as a humming mass approached them. "Swarming bees at this time of year! He must be running short on ideas!" On the other hand, he considered as he prepared to dispel the swarm, it's that much more strength taken out of me, when I can bare afford to waste any.

LATE NEXT DAY, WITH their horses still gamely pressing forward on the brief rests and snatches of food they were allowed, the party crested a rise and saw below them a military force just in the process of camping for the evening.

Cut off!

Discouragement swept over Carrtog's weary mind. So near, and yet so awfully far!

Then he heard Yakor cheering and looked again. There were two smaller baronial pennons, but in the center of the camp was a vice-regal pennon, signifying that the force was at least part of a force being led on the king's behalf.

Even as he began to think that they might be safe, he heard shouting and looked back to see the pursuers breaking cover. Now it would all depend on their already weary horses.

"Ride!" Carrtog shouted, completely forgetting that the king had removed him from command.

No one, not even King Bornival, bothered to quibble, but set spurs to their horses.

Yakor kept to the rear, and Carrtog stayed just behind him.

It was probably due to two things, the weariness of the horses and the poor footing, but suddenly the princess' horse went down, and came up limping, with the princess sitting up on the ground clutching her splinted arm and shaking her head. Carrtog pulled his own horse beside her and jumped down. There was no thinking of his horse bearing double, not with what the animal had been through recently.

He pulled the princess to her feet and swung her up into the saddle. "Hold on!" He slapped his gloved hand on the horse's rump and saw the king turning his own horse to come back for his daughter.

Yakor was beside him. "Jump up!"

"Nonsense! No use both of us being lost! Get out of here!" He put every last ounce of command into his voice.

Yakor paused a moment, then kicked his horse after the pair. Carrtog turned to the approaching enemy and fired his pistol, speaking the spell that brought the Grove of Battle into existence.

A wave of forest-scent came over him as the trees and underbrush flashed into being. He heard men shouting and horses screaming on the far side of the Grove, and his hands went to work reloading his pistol, preparing the Spell of Accuracy.

He didn't allow himself either disappointment or regret when the first bolt of lightning hit the Grove before he had finished recharging his pistol. One bolt after another struck the Grove, and by the third bolt, gaps were showing in the trees.

He didn't dare turn back to see if anyone was coming to his rescue, all he could do was to make the best stand possible. Three more bolts and the Grove was gone. The rebels still hesitated before rushing across the empty ground where the Grove had been; most likely one or two had rushed forward and been caught up in the dangers of the spell.

The enemy magician seemed to be reeling in his saddle; Carrtog suspected the man had used himself up bringing down the Grove of Battle. But then the magician was shouting, and his men moved forward. Carrtog raised his pistol and, near as possible aiming at the magician, squeezed the trigger.

The magician slumped down on his horse's neck then slid to the ground. Two other rebels also fell, which Carrtog considered great success at that range.

But the enemy magician pushed himself up on one hand and pointed a finger, and suddenly the air in front of Carrtog solidified and struck him like a massive sandbag. He collapsed to the ground.

Chapter 7

He woke in a strange bed in a room, which he shortly recognized as a solid building, not the camp tent he had somehow expected. A man in the king's livery was looking down on him. "You're awake, then? Good! His Majesty will want to talk to you."

He went to the door and spoke to someone outside, then came back to offer Carrtog some water.

Carrtog discovered two things: First, that he was weak as the proverbial kitten, and second, that he was dreadfully thirsty.

"It's good to see you awake, Lord Carrtog. You've spent several days unconscious and about two weeks mostly asleep, only waking up for a moment or two now and then to take some water or some broth. From the look and feel of you now though, I think you'll be with us more often from now on."

Carrtog closed his eyes for a moment, or so he thought, but when he opened them again, King Bornival was there.

The king was very much changed from the weeks of their flight from the north. The dirt of the trail had been washed away, his hair and beard freshly trimmed, and he was wearing a clean, properly tailored suit.

In addition to that, the expression on his face was more friendly and accepting than Carrtog had ever seen it.

"I am in your debt, Lord Carrtog. You saved my daughter's life, at great risk to yourself. There is no way I can properly repay you for that, though I shall do my poor best to reward you suitably."

"Your Majesty, I did only what I saw to be my duty, and not for any hope of reward."

"Of course you didn't! All the more reason for me to do what I can to see that you are repaid to some degree."

"Thank you, Your Majesty."

"No, it is I that thank you! But I see that you are still tired; I will leave you alone, now, though I believe your man will wish to talk to you for a moment or two. Never fear, though, I will be back from time to time."

The king bowed and left, and a moment later Yakor entered. He looked back toward the door and then faced Carrtog again. "Congratulations, Lord Carrtog."

"Don't you start fawning around me, Yakor! You know me better than that!"

Yakor grinned.

Carrtog shifted up in bed. "But tell me Yakor, what news from the North?"

Yakor glanced at the door again. "There seems to be little to tell. The leader or leaders — we have no name or names for them as yet — of the rising are continually retreating before General Maelgwyn, fighting only a skirmish here and there to keep him advancing. No great victories, no great defeats. Although the rebellion itself is being styled the Black Powder Rebellion after the black powder magic that acted against the king in Tenerack."

Then his expression turned serious. He leaned forward and spoke so quietly that Carrtog could barely hear him. "It's been determined that the fault for the fiasco in Tenerack that cost the lives of so many of the King's Gentlemen and members of the king's household lies with the late Captain Gwailants. You understand?"

"Yes." And indeed he did understand: not only the fact of the one decision, but no matter how much the king favored him now, it was entirely possible that something might happen to overturn that favor in a moment.

WHEN HE NEXT WOKE, it was to the sound of nervously shuffling feet and feminine giggles. The first face he saw was that of Lady Adengler, and right beside her was Princess Ellevar .

The princess spoke first. "My Da is an old dear, but something of a fussbudget. He felt it necessary to order me to come in and think you personally for saving my life, as though that were some nasty chore that I might shirk. You may be sure, Lord Carrtog, that I am not here under duress. I'm here willingly, very willingly, to thank you for my life."

Carrtog felt himself redden. "Highness," he protested, "I did no more than my duty!"

"And near died for it! Lord Carrtog, I will hear no more foolish talk! I am in your debt, and it is a debt I doubt I can ever repay. Now, I'm told that you are recovering well. Is there anything I can do to help you, even if it's only to make you a little more comfortable?"

"I can think of nothing at present, Highness."

"So, then. If you ever do think of anything I might do, be sure to inform me." Her face went stern. "If I ever find that you had any small complaint that I could have dealt with and you did not let me know, I will be very angry with you!"

"It won't do any good, Your Highness," Lady Adengler broke in. "He's a warrior, you know, and they're not allowed even to say 'ouch' if it hurts." There was laughter in her eyes as she spoke.

Carrtog smiled and said "Ouch! Sorry, I must not be a very good warrior."

"If you can joke about it like that, you must be getting better. Actually, I didn't come just to be company for Her Highness; I wanted to add my own thanks to you for bringing us safely home."

"I didn't do it all by myself. Yakor had a good deal to do with it, and even the King's Gentlemen did their part."

"Next thing you'll be telling us that it was all luck, and you just happened to make a few good decisions. Nonsense! You were still the one making the decisions. Because you made those decisions, we are now safe at home. And because you are still not completely healed, we had best leave you to your rest. We will be seeing you from time to time, though; you can rely on that."

DAYS WENT BY. CARRTOG forced himself to get out of bed and walk, first around the room — discovering himself to be dreadfully weak — then up and down the hallway in front of his room. He began to do other exercises as well to the point where Yakor began to chide him.

"Don't wear yourself down by trying to build yourself up, Lord Carrtog. You took quite a battering, you know, and you can't expect to jump out of bed and be totally recovered in a couple of days."

Carrtog grinned, a little tiredly. "But the longer I lie around in bed, the longer it'll be before I can be back in shape. I expect the king will be wanting me to follow him when he goes to put down the rebellion."

Yakor looked around to see that no one was near enough to overhear him, then said, quietly, "I don't think the king is going to want you near him to be a reminder of certain instances where he showed himself in a less than admirable light. I think you'll find that he has some sort of good reason for you not to go along with him, whenever he leads the punitive expedition."

"It's that bad?"

"'That bad?' Boy, do you remember nothing of the journey back out of the North?"

Carrtog grimaced. When Yakor called him 'boy,' that usually meant he had been being more than normally foolish.

However physically tired he might be, he could still recognize facts when his man hit him over the head with them. He forced a smile. "You're right, of course. Well, I suppose I'll have to deal with whatever comes."

THE GREAT HALL OF THE High kingdom of Cragmor was a massive high-domed structure built of gray marble hauled from far-distant quarries at great expense by the great-great-great-grandfather of King Bornival. Tales were told of how magicians had cut and transported the stones in the space of one night. In the tales, a mist had come down on the site, and in the morning, the hall had stood fully built.

Certain spots outside of the walls of the Great Hall had been found to be pits containing the bones of men tossed in and covered over with no sign of proper burial. Some said these were the bones of people sacrificed to give strength to the building spells. Others pointed out a more likely alternative, that the bones were those of many slaves who had died during the building of it.

The inside walls were decorated with hangings and tapestries depicting scenes from history and legend, sometimes mixing the two. Carrtog remembered similar wall-hangings from his Grandfather's hall and realized the intent of such things. No one really thought that the hero Boldavor had actually appeared at the birth of Cedwin, son of Dolvar, but in the case of that Tsingallik tapestry, if Boldavor had been around at the time of the birth of Carrtog's far-off ancestor, he would have been aware of the special nature of the babe, just because he himself was special.

At least, that had seemed the best explanation.

The Great Hall was packed with colors today, all the lords present wearing their family tartans, along with cloaks in the main colors of the banners of their lands. The fashion now was shirts with slashed sleeves, and some lords went so far as to have the inserts in the sleeves done in the main colors that made up their tartans. In some cases, of course, the main colors of the tartans were not suited for such use, and in those cases the lords used whatever colors suited their fancy, trying not to use any colors that matched, or seemed to match, the tartan of another lord. Lords had been known to start quarrels, even occasionally leading to bloodshed and years-long feuds, over some lords 'misappropriation' of certain sleeve-colors.

During the reigns of certain kings, such quarrels, or the continuance of long-standing ones, were frowned on by the monarch, but the fractious nature of the nobility was often not amenable to even royal legislation.

Carrtog had managed to find a weaver who was capable of and willing to produce a measure of cloth in his family tartan, and a tailor had turned the cloth into several kilts for him. The craftsmen, knowing Carrtog stood high in the king's regard, quite willingly did their work on the promise of future payment. Carrtog privately hoped that nothing would happen to remove the king's favor before he could find the money to pay them, though he was also very careful not to mention that concern to anyone, with the exception of Yakor, who could be trusted not to speak out of turn.

Carrtog stood just inside the main door to the Hall, and before him, the lords of the kingdom — save those who were on campaign with Maelgwn Longarm or who had not managed to get to the capital in time — were gathered in two roughly equal groups on each side of the path between the door and the king's High Seat. The king's steward, in giving Carrtog his instructions, had dropped some hints as to the impossibility of convincing the status-proud lords to allow themselves to be mustered into anything approximating neat ranks.

By this time, the name of the leader of the Black Powder Rebellion had become known. He was a man by the name of Rhadfel Llorsan, a third cousin of one of the previous lords of a part of the conquered north. Carrtog glanced around the room and found himself wondering which lords present may have sympathy or quiet understandings with Rhadfel Llorsan. He was sure there must be some.

Finally, the door behind the king's High Seat opened, and two trumpeters stepped in, put their horns to their lips and blew a fanfare. The steward, still out of sight beyond the doorway, announced in a loud voice, "Gentlemen, the King!"

The lords pulled themselves into erect postures, intended to indicate their respect for the king, who immediately strode into the room, stepping to a place before the High Seat, where he turned to face the lords and seated himself.

The king spoke, "Lord Carrtog, step forth."

Carrtog, following the directions the steward had given him, stepped forward, coming down the gap between the two groups of lords, and placed himself just a little in advance of the front row.

After a short pause, King Bornival began to speak once more. "You will all know much about the events of this spring, how we took ourselves to the town of Tenerack for the opening of the railway line which we had built for the benefit of the people of the region. The ungrateful folk of that town and its environs chose that time to rise up in rebellion, and made an attempt to lay hands on our person.

"Lord Carrtog did not hesitate to put himself in danger on our behalf, fighting valiantly by the side of our Gentlemen. By the help of the Gods the plot of the rebels failed, though very few of our Gentlemen survived. We being incapacitated, Lord Carrtog took charge of the few that remained and organized a defense to stand off the rebels who came out to see what had become of their associates.

"In the following days, Lord Carrtog led us in our escape from the midst of the rebels, bringing us at last into the sight of our own troops marching northward. In that last moment, within sight of safety, Lord Carrtog did put our beloved daughter on his own horse, and set himself between her and danger, at the risk of his own life."

The king paused for a moment, then went on. "For all these reasons, it gives us great pleasure to declare Lord Carrtog Lord of the Territory known as Nandycargllwyd, The Brook of the Gray Stones."

The king raised a hand. "Steward., the colors!"

The steward came forward and beckoned to a young page carrying a folded cloak in the colors of Nandycargllwyd. The steward took the cloak, shook it out of its folds, and set it on Carrtog's shoulders. Carrtog reached up and fastened it at the neck. The Steward withdrew, followed by the page.

The king spoke once more. "Lords, I bid you all welcome among yourselves Lord Carrtog of Nandycargllwyd!"

The lords broke into a resounding racket of clapping, stamping, and shouting of "Bornival forever!"

When the noise died down a little, the king called out, "Lords, make yourselves known to the new Lord of Nandycargllwyd!"

The lords came up, one by one, in order of precedence, to clasp hands with Carrtog. There were several occasions where lords, though allowing themselves with poor grace to be ordered into the not-quite-ranks before the king, took up the quarrel again, declaring that they would not allow themselves to be put behind this or that man. Most of them eventually allowed the steward to convince them that they would be better off to allow the question of precedence to be settled for certain at another time, rather than disturbing the festivity surrounding the rewarding of the man who had saved the life of the king's daughter. In one case, unfortunately, two lords allowed themselves to become so worthy that they would not be mollified and left the hall rather than either one give up what he considered to be his rightful due.

The king watched this conflict with a grim face, and Carrtog thought, neither of those two had best require anything of the king for a long while.

Yakor had told him beforehand, "Don't expect great sincerity from all who give you their hand today. There'll be some who had hoped to get the Brook of the Gray Stone for themselves, and some who are just jealous of your place as a new friend of the king, and a few who just don't like to see anyone getting ahead."

Carrtog had grinned back at him. "And nothing like that went on back at Tsingallik? No one thought that my grandsire's youngest son wasn't given unwarranted favor? Don't worry, Yakor, I won't forget to watch my back."

He watched all the faces of the men who shook his hand, but there were simply too many to remember. Most merely shook his hand and muttered some words of congratulation, some more seriously than others.

His own grandfather, a tall and well-built old man smiled as he grasped Carrtog's hand strongly. "So you went out with only a sword to find your fortune, and indeed you did. Well-done, boy! Tsingallik for true!"

Carrtog smiled in return. "Tsingallik for true," he responded. "My father is well?"

"Yes, and your brothers as well. We thought it best that we not take too many away from Tsingallik, with the border in turmoil."

"Of course. You'll take my good wishes to them when you return."

"Most certainly." His grandfather stepped away and let the line continue.

Carrtog suddenly found himself facing an older man whom the steward named as "Melwys of Cwm Gwyrdd," A name he recognized.

"You're the father of Lady Adengler!"

Strongly-built, with scars on his hands and wrists to show that he had been a fighting man, he was of some age but it was clear he was still someone to be reckoned with.

He smiled at Carrtog's outburst. "Lord Carrtog, I'm pleased to meet you at last. I've been hearing fine things about you, the kind of things that concern a man when he hears them from his daughter."

Carrtog felt himself redden. "I'm sure she can't have built me up that much, Lord Melwys!"

The gray eyes twinkled. "Oh, no! The most worrying thing she said was that you scarcely needed someone to speak up for you."

Carrtog felt a flicker of near panic. What was that supposed to mean? It was scarce the time to dwell on his terror, with the lords lined up behind Melwys becoming more restive every moment, but Carrtog's mind could only come up with the polite request, "My Lord, may I have your permission to speak to your daughter?"

He hardly thought it was possible for his face to become any redder, but when Melwys laughed out loud, he thought the glow must be visible across the room.

"Don't you think that request a bit tardy, Lord Carrtog, coming as it does after you have spent so many days in each others' pockets in the journey down from Tenerack?"

The older lord continued to grin as he said, "When you've gained my years of experience, you will undoubtedly discover the futility of giving a daughter a command you know she won't obey. I will only say that I trust you will not make her unhappy."

The steward moved restively, almost certainly on the point of breaking up a conversation that had gone on much too long, but Carrtog held firm just a moment longer, long enough to say, "Of course not, Sir," before Melwys allowed the steward to pass him along and introduce the next lord in line.

IN THE DINNER THAT followed, Carrtog, being the guest of honor, sat at the king's right hand and could practically feel the waves of jealousy from the Lord of Silver Mountain to his own right. That lord was usually seated at the king's right and apparently begrudged his replacement, however temporary, and treated Carrtog to a series of frosty glares and sneers.

Carrtog worked at ignoring him and managed to enjoy the main course: a well-seasoned roast pig.

The next course, however, a pastry delight on which the cook had expended his considerable talent, was interrupted by the entrance of a man in a dusty cavalry uniform, accompanied by two of the King's Gentlemen. They hurried to the king's side where the dusty messenger murmured into the king's ear.

As the man spoke, Carrtog watched Bornival straighten and his face turn grim. When the man had finished delivering his message, the king stood and called for the attention of the company.

"Lords, your attention if you please! Serious news has just been brought to us! General Maelgwn has brought the rebels to battle in the North, at a place called Fallen Hills. The result has been a severe reverse to our arms. General Maelgwn himself has fallen, and the remnants of our force that could escape are fleeing southward. Tomorrow morning we will hold counsel to decide what will be our response."

He paused and looked down at Carrtog. "My apologies, Lord Carrtog, for interrupting your celebration for such unhappy news. Let the feast continue."

He seated himself, and the feast continued, but the festive air was somewhat strained.

Carrtog himself could not pull his mind away from the woods of the North, and the scattered, beaten soldiers fleeing southward, harried at every step by rebels like a pack of wolves.

Chapter 8

The day after the ceremony and subsequent celebration, Carrtog returned from his walk to find two well-dressed gentlemen waiting for him. One was older, slender, with graying hair and a receding hairline. He wore a snug-fitting suit of black with silver trimming.

The other was more toward middle-age, somewhat heavier, with red-gold hair and a colorful outfit in a mix of reds, blues, and greens.

The older one spoke. "Good day, Lord Carrtog. We are among the King's Magicians, and he has asked us to wait on you. My name is Enemantwin, and my companion is Gwaitorr. I am well-trained in the usual gunpowder magic though my passion and skill lie in magic involving plants. My companion is also well-versed in gunpowder magic, but specializes in the magic of mechanics. His Majesty desires us to give you further training in magic."

"I'm happy to hear that. Especially in the later days of our flight from the North, I was very much aware of my limitations."

"I'm pleased to hear that," Enemantwin said. "You'd be surprised to know how many young men come for magical training who already know everything."

"I see. And when can I expect the lessons to begin?"

CARRTOG HAD NOT FORGOTTEN how the rebels had managed to suborn the workshop that had produced the carriages for the train that had been supplied for the opening of the station in Tenerack. Suborned it so well in fact, that the rebels had successfully mounted a complex spell, using a blend of magic and mechanics, to form a glider with which they had attempted to seize the king.

With those thoughts in mind, he approached his two tutors with the question even before his lessons began.

"Gentlemen, you will recall how the rebels set the magical-mechanical trap in the railway carriage bound for Tenerack? Are you aware if any efforts have been made to uncover any other such plots down here where we least expect them?"

Enemantwin pursed his lips. "Some days after His Majesty returned, his magicians undertook a severe magical investigation of that particular plant. I do not have at my fingertips the results of that investigation, but I do recall that the results were astounding. I understand that several people lost their positions, and I believe that only the vast extent of the rebels' secret involvement in the workshop prevent there from being more than a few executions. No one wished to have it publicly known how severe the problem had been."

"With that as a warning, were there any other investigations made of other workshops, other groups or organizations that might be important to the kingdom?"

"There certainly were! Though very little was found that was so complex as the plot against the king."

Gwaitorr spoke up. "What of the firearms workshops?" He turned toward Carrtog, "They discovered that several capable magicians had gotten employment at several workshops that provided firearms for His Majesty's forces. They did not sabotage every weapon, but they did manage to put out a significant number of weapons that seemed to function perfectly, but only awaited a magician to speak an incantation and problems would suddenly happen. Small parts, such as triggers or springs, would break leaving the weapons useless. They had not yet had sufficient quantity of weapons produced to be a severe problem to the Army, but I suppose in a battle, even a small quantity in the wrong place could result in a victory turned into a defeat."

Had that contributed to the defeat at Fallen Hills? Surely it must have played its role, Carrtog thought. "Do I dare to hope that the King's Magicians have continued to work at hunting out other such nests of subversion in the king's lands?"

Enemantwin's face turned grave. "Lord Carrtog, such activities as that are only brought to the public attention when the King's Advisors think it useful. However, occasionally a prosecution and sentencing will be announced, one supposes to ensure that the public is aware that such investigations are going on. However, how extensive those investigations might be is hard to say."

"Well, better than nothing. I don't suppose the official investigators would appreciate any unsolicited extra assistance?"

Enemantwin's face paled. "Lord, don't even think such things too often! The men in charge of such magical counter-espionage have no sense of humor at all! The ability to read thoughts reliably has never been proven, though those same investigators have various abilities that are not commonly known. While a person of your stature would never be prosecuted for merely thinking such things, any evidence at all that you were trying to help them would lead to further inquiries, and very likely something would be uncovered with which to charge you."

Carrtog considered the man's reaction, seeing its similarities to Yakor's warnings, and Enemantwin, taking his silence to mean the subject was closed, began his lesson.

$$\times$$

"CONTEMPLATE THE LEAF of the linden tree!" He fumed to Yakor. "What is that supposed to tell me, I ask you? That it shares its shape with many a spear-blade, in particular many of the antiquated ones, that it is veined like any other leaf, and green when new? And aside from that, what?"

"I'm sure I cannot say," the older man replied. "But you might consider that the man claims to be knowledgeable in plant-magic. Might this not be in the nature of a warrior familiarizing himself with a dagger before performing weapon-drills with it?"

Carrtog calmed himself, if only because he could hear the not-yet spoken term 'boy' in Yakor's tone. "You're probably right, of course. I wish that magicians were not always so mysterious; that they'd give you some hint as to what you were looking for."

"And how much better will you retain the knowledge if you have to find it out for yourself with few or no hints at all?"

Carrtog forced out a smile. "You're right again, of course. And you demonstrate once more that if I come looking for sympathy, I should not come looking to you."

ENEMANTWIN WAS NOT particularly impressed with the results of Carrtog's contemplation of the linden leaf. "'The shape of a spear-blade?' The sort of thing one can expect from a man whose first training is as a warrior. Not good enough, young man."

Carrtog had the feeling that 'young man' from Enemantwin carried the same weight as 'boy' from Yakor. There seemed to be even less scope for response to Enemantwin than to Yakor, since Carrtog could only confess that he knew less about contemplation than any point of contention he might have with Yakor.

Enemantwin continued, "So let us both consider the linden leaf."

When they were done an hour later, Carrtog was not sure what he had learned, and his mind was awhirl with a lot of new terminology, much of which seemed to refer to little outside of itself.

The last thing the elder magician said to him was, "Magic is, to a great deal, tied to the mind. It is said that if a person is well-enough trained, he can use a gesture," he mimed a pistol-shot at the wall with his thumb and forefinger, "and achieve the same result for which another will require the actual combustion of powder. This is still only theoretical, and to my knowledge, no one has accomplished it, but it is a goal toward which we all work."

By this time, Carrtog was sure that he was going to need every little bit of help gunpowder could give him, though he wasn't willing to say so out loud.

CARRTOG WAS DEEP IN another lesson, from Gwaitorr this time, when the king strode in. "I hope, Lord Gwaitorr, that you won't mind if I interrupt your lesson to speak to your student a moment."

"Certainly not, Your Majesty."

The king gestured to Carrtog, and they stepped aside, Carrtog's mind awhirl with thoughts of pulleys and gear-ratios. Gwaitorr had been less understanding than Enemantwin. "Think of the advantage of bringing a force of fresh cavalry to a battlefield, rather then bringing them up worn with forced marching? The difference might well be made up with mechanics.'"

Carrtog glanced down at his ring and wished that it would consider the sudden appearances of the king to be a sort of danger. There was a sort of danger in every instance in which the king interfered in his life. The latest discovery of such having come from the reaction of the lords at the granting of his title. Any move by the king to reward Carrtog further would invoke more jealousy among the other nobles. And as Yakor had pointed out, it may not take much to upset the king's mood and find him at fault.

The king was smiling though, which seemed to indicate no immediate danger. Of course, that did not mean that any decision of the king would not mean danger in the future.

"One very important duty for a noble, Lord Carrtog, is to marry and produce an heir. To that end, I propose to arrange a marriage between yourself and the Lady Adengler."

"With the Lady Adengler, Highness?" he protested. "I have had little chance to speak with her father, yet, let alone to speak more than a few everyday words with the Lady herself."

The king waved a hand at the objection. "As to that, her father is overjoyed at having his daughter serving as lady-in-waiting to my daughter. If I suggest to him that his daughter be given to a new lord, one who has my favor, he will be ecstatic. As for your second objection, you don't suppose, do you, that I have missed your glances at her, and her glances at you? Besides which, our little party suffered extremely close quarters on our way down from the North; you will recall that the situation almost forced us all into near-familiar terms."

Carrtog felt his cheeks redden. "Thank you, Your Majesty." What he really wished he could say was some very polite and inoffensive form of, "Your Majesty, please stop interfering in my life." Of course, such a polite and inoffensive statement did not exist; one thing worse than having a king too interested in giving you a hand was a king offended at your refusal of his aid.

The king seemed thoroughly delighted at Carrtog's discomfiture. "Now back to your lessons, Lord Carrtog. I expect you to be of increasingly better service as time goes on."

"Yes, Your Majesty."

CARRTOG CONSIDERED himself fortunate that he was of sufficient age that his tutors did not dare to use a wooden rod to accentuate their lessons as they might for a young boy. On the other hand, they were capable of using sarcasm and biting humor to the extent that Carrtog would almost have preferred the hickory.

As the lessons progressed, he did manage to ask some of the questions he had thought of on the trip from the North. He chose Gwaitorr, hoping that the younger man would be more approachable.

"Sir, on our first night up north, I put a warding spell around the camp, and in the wake of it, I found that several of the wounded were in better condition. My tutors had mentioned this as an occasional and sporadic effect of the warding spell, but had no explanation as to how it worked, and even less explanation of why it did not work on some, while it might work on the man next to him. Do you know if anyone has made a study of this matter, and what conclusions they might have come to?"

Gwaitorr's eyes widened a bit. "Ah, the young student desires to push his learning beyond that of his teachers? No, young man, I have not studied that particular magical quirk, nor do I know of anyone who has. You could ask my colleague, but I suspect his answer would be an even more brief and pointed suggestion that you concentrate on the studies we are giving you and not on complex theoretical problems."

Chapter 9

Yakor approached him one afternoon. "Lord, I'd like to talk to you privately. Could you meet me this evening at the inn known as The Overflowing Keg?"

If Yakor had a reason for meeting him outside the palace, it was undoubtedly a good reason, so he agreed.

That evening he made his way to the inn and looked it over briefly before entering. It was neither of the finest quality, nor so dilapidated as to suggest the possibility of personal danger from its regular patrons.

It was dimly-lit inside in the fashion of inns everywhere and contained the usual scents of wood-smoke, burning tallow, stale food, and people unused to bathing. After a moment, his eyes grew accustomed to the light, such as it was, and he saw Yakor waving at him from a table across the room where he sat with five other men.

He recognized one of them as Roisilan Harrad, though he was not in uniform. The other four were the other soldiers who had traveled down from the North with them.

Curiosity made him move quickly across the room where Yakor swung out a stool for him. "Roisilan asked to talk to you privately, so I arranged for us to meet here."

There was a pause while a harassed-looking barmaid took their order for another bottle of wine for the table and a cup for Carrtog. Carrtog then turned to Harrad and asked, "What can I do for you?"

"Well, Lord, we're not sure of that, but we're hoping you could perhaps give us some advice. Just this morning, you see, we were informed that the king no longer needed our services. No reason was given, but that was the condition of our hire, that His Majesty could dispense with our services at any time, with no reason needing to be given."

Of course, Carrtog thought, His Majesty will not say that he is dispensing with their services for fear that they might spread tales about His Majesty's behavior on the trip down from the North.

Roisilan went on. "We've been paid up to and including today, though they need not have paid us for today. No commands were given, but it was suggested to us that we'd best not stay around the city beyond the week's end. Now we have a problem; if a person is dismissed from the king's service without a reason being given, how likely is it for that person to find any other lord to take their services? So we thought that you had led us well on the trip from the North, and we hoped you might be able to give us some advice." He paused then, waiting expectantly for Carrtog's response.

Carrtog, for his part, thought furiously before speaking. If he did anything for the five and the word got back to the king, he himself would be in serious trouble. In fact, there was a risk that the king might find out about this meeting despite their attempts at concealment. This might even be a ploy by the king, an attempt to catch Carrtog working against his purposes.

But no, that was not the way Bornival worked; he simply decided that someone was, or was not intending to do something against him, then he acted to remove the problem.

This is not the way to think! He told himself. What can I do, not 'what are the reasons for not acting.'

"I'd take you into my own services, but I doubt that would be a help to either of us. Give me a moment to consider."

He thought deeply for another moment, then looked up. "How about if I give you a letter of introduction to my grandfather? My personal good word will almost certainly outweigh the king's lack of recommendation."

He stopped himself on the brink of warning them against boasting -- that would be an insult to their intelligence.

"Can you stay here for another day or so? I'll send Yakor down with a letter from me to my grandfather."

Roisilan nodded. "For certain, Lord. As I said, His Majesty in his generosity paid us up to today. We will wait at least another day."

As they were returning to Carrtog's room, he said to Yakor, "I'm going to have to word my letter to Grandfather carefully. I believe I was correct, that he will take my assurances as to the quality of the men I send him, but I'd best make sure."

"I agree. And by the way, I think you did very well back there; you could have sent them off with a spoken message, but a letter will be much more effective."

"Thank you."

He sent Yakor off the next day with the letter, as well as a small pouch of silver. "To help with travel expenses."

THE NEXT DAY ENEMANTWIN sent him off to the Royal Gardens with instructions to find a particular herb with only the wizard's verbal description — given some weeks before — to go on.

Enemantwin's directions as to how to find the herb were extremely vague, though he did assure Carrtog that, "It is there, at least it was last night, and the Royal Gardener does not work that fast."

Carrtog was trying to find the first landmark Enemantwin had given him when he heard the sound of women's voices. He could not make out the words since they were some way to his left with several small stands of trees and other plants, large and small, between him and them. He did, though, recognize the two voices; one was the Princess Ellevar , and the other was Lady Adengler.

Setting aside the instructions of his tutor, he followed the path toward the sound of the voices, telling himself that it was only polite to let them know he was in the Garden in case they were talking of private matters.

The sound of the voices was coming from his right front, but even if he were willing to trample on the flowers to come to them directly, there were bushes, even small trees between him and them, so he found the next cross-path and looked down it. No one. He continued on the path he was going and realized that the trees and plants in the garden muffled the sound, so he needn't have worried about accidentally eavesdropping. On the other hand, they seemed to be moving, and moving generally in his direction, so best he should carry on as he had intended.

He looked down the next cross-path, but it curved to his left a little way down, and the voices seemed to be coming from around that curve. He walked down the path.

He came to the curve, and now he could see them; Princess Ellevar and the Lady Adengler strolling casually toward him.

The princess looked up and saw him first, and he saw the smile on her face as she spoke to Lady Adengler. Lady Adengler looked up, smiling, and called out "Hello, Lord Carrtog."

The two were similarly dressed with a ruff around the neck, a ruched neckline, and a fitted bodice above a full skirt. Their arms covered by puffed sleeves ending in long lace cuffs. Much of this was covered by cloaks in royal blue, fastened by knotted frogs at the neck, though the cloaks opened sufficiently in the front to reveal that the skirts were plaid, the royal tartan for the princess, and the family tartan for the lady-in-waiting.

Carrtog could see subtle differences in quality of the cloth, and it seemed that the princess' seamstresses had had slightly better material to work with. On the other hand, Lady Adengler's clothing was only slightly inferior, probably because, on the one hand, she was expected to present a decent showing on her mistress' behalf, but on the other hand, she must not put the princess in the shade.

"Hello, Your Highness, Lady Adengler. I heard you speaking and thought I ought to make my presence known, so as not to be thought a rude eavesdropper."

The princess spoke up, smiling, "I would never think that of you, Lord Carrtog. Are you enjoying the Royal Gardens?"

He returned the smile. "Not as such, no, though I will admit they are quite remarkable. Actually, I am here as part of my training; Master Enemantwin has sent me to find, based on his rough description of the plant and its location, something called goat's foot. One of its most common usages is in the treatment of inflammation, though I believe it has other more magical uses as well."

"Very interesting. And how are your studies coming?"

"I am continually learning how little I know. I had commented several times on the way down from the North how limited my knowledge of combat magic was, and your father has introduced me to two gentlemen whose purpose is to increase my ability whether I wish it or not."

"Come, now, Lord Carrtog, I'm sure you appreciate the teaching more than you let on!"

He smiled broadly. "Yes, I suppose so. When I go to join the Army in the North, I will be more ready to be of use to them."

"You expect to join the Army, then?" Lady Adengler spoke up.

"That depends on where His Majesty thinks I can best be of service. All my training would suggest that I could be best used in combat. As I said, though, that is all in the king's hands."

"What do you know of the war in the North?" asked Lady Adengler. "We are told very little, since we are ladies, and young ladies at that. We have to make do with bits and pieces that we overhear from our elders."

"I've heard the general had trouble feeding his troops."

He looked at the princess. "That's true, but the general was using the railroad line that your father built up into that territory and building extensions on it to continually move his magazines forward toward the advancing troops. Unfortunately, the further north he took the lines, the more difficult it was to protect them from destruction by the rebels."

"How interesting!" The princess turned toward Adengler, bringing her back into the conversation. "That means that the North will have all those ready-built railroads when this trouble is settled!"

"My understanding is that the general had been tearing up any lines that will not be of use to him as he moved. Of course, the roadbeds are left; too much trouble to tear them up as well, so in a sense, you're right. All they'll have to do is lay lines on the beds again, and they have a whole net of railroads."

Adengler spoke up, then. "It's good to think that something useful can come of all the present trouble."

Carrtog found the lady's point of view very thoughtful, looking as it did beyond the end of the war to positive consequences that might come of it. He had, during the trip from the North, gained a favorable impression of the way Adengler's mind worked. "Very true," he told her. "A person might even say that it's unfortunate that it needs a war to be fought and won to achieve the good results that follow."

She smiled at him. "Beware, Carrtog! Don't you realize that, as a young warrior, you're required to be enamored with the glory of war?"

Carrtog put on a smile, but he could feel that it was a very thin one. "Unfortunately, my most recent experience with war held very little in the way of glory, only a good deal of being hunted like animals. Don't worry, I will still go to war when and as necessary and fight to the best of my ability. On the other hand, however, I don't think I'll ever be in love with war, as some are."

Something else also occurred to him. His purpose in the garden was not to chat with the ladies, however enjoyable it might be.

"Much as I would like to stray here talking with you ladies, my teacher is going to wonder if I am too much delayed. If I may have your leave, Highness?"

"Of course, Lord Carrtog! I would not wish to be the cause of your receiving a scold from your tutor!" Princess Ellevar 's smile suggested that she thought no one would actually scold him, though he himself had less confidence in the matter.

When he returned with the cutting, Master Enemantwin looked at him with raised brows, though he said nothing immediately.

Purposely misunderstanding his tutor's expression, Carrtog asked, "Is it not enough?"

"Enough? Oh, I suppose it is. It took you long enough to track it down, though. Had the Royal Gardener moved it, then?"

"Oh, that. I chanced on the princess and Lady Adengler walking in the garden. Courtesy required me to stop and talk for a moment."

The brows rose again, and a slight sardonic smile touched Enemantwin's lips. "Of course. Young men and young women are all too easily distracted from what is important. Now, as to the plant itself..."

The lesson continued.

Chapter 10

The steam engine was comparatively small, about the height of a man, much of which was taken up by the boiler and the burner. They had begun work at the steam engine shortly after Carrtog had begun his lessons, though much of the work, the production of the boiler, the pistons and the like, had been done by smiths. Gwaitorr and Carrtog had overseen the various stages of the production, so that Carrtog had a fair notion of the very fastidious work that went into producing a piston, for instance.

Servants had already laid and kindled the fire in the boiler some time ago, and by this time the steam was jetting straight out of the exhaust valve. Gwaitorr looked at Carrtog. "As the student, to you goes the honor of starting the engine for the first time, whose building you have overseen."

Carrtog grasped the handle that would close the valve and send the steam to the pistons, but first checked the steam rising from the exhaust valve. Yes, it seemed to be strong enough. He wondered about the possibility of producing some sort of device to measure the power of the steam, and then thought idly that this was unlikely to be the first start of this machine -- he suspected the smiths would have started it up just to be sure it ran before they let the lords try it. The lords would be embarrassed by a failure, especially if it had been at all public, and the smiths would suffer for it.

He pulled the switch, then grasped the throttle that would allow more steam to come out of the boiler to increase the power of the engine. He opened the throttle three notches, as Gwaitorr had suggested. The rod protruding from the end of the piston moved downward, pushing the crankshaft which turned the large pulley a half-turn; at the end of the stroke, a valve closed off the flow of the steam to that end of the piston, while another valve opened to allow the steam to escape from the side of the piston. Another pair of valves, mounted to work in conjunction with the first two, shifted the flow of steam to the bottom half of the piston, drawing the crankshaft to complete the circle, at which time the valves reversed their flow again.

All this happened, several times, in the time it took to explain it once. The wheel spun faster and faster. Carrtog opened the throttle two more notches, watching the machine carefully, but everything seemed to be running well.

He looked at his tutor, who returned the glance with a bare smile. "Congratulations, Lord Carrtog, it works. Turn the throttle up two more notches, and let us watch it for a while. With machines, and in particular steam engines, one can't tell until they've run for a while at reasonable speed, whether or not they are really functional. Hold your oil-can handy and keep all the moving parts lubricated, being careful not to use too much oil; that is not as dangerous as using too little, but it still has its problems."

Carrtog nodded and hefted the long-spouted oilcan. He'd heard that some aristocratic mechanics felt plying the oil-can was work for servants, but Gwaitorr was not of that persuasion, and Carrtog himself thought it much better not to trust something so vital to servants. If the machinery failed catastrophically, one might die as a result, and it would be little comfort to know that one's heirs could blame the servant, who would likely also be dead.

They watched the engine run a little longer. Finally Gwaitorr signaled to Carrtog, and they both moved away from the machine.

"We can talk here without having to shout," the magician said. "We'll want to let it run for some time, just to make sure that nothing goes wrong when it warms up a bit. With the sort of heat the boiler puts out, all the metal parts will expand. We'll have to watch for things like that, or for the boiler getting hot enough to burst. I'd prefer not to be having to remind you every time something needs to be oiled, but on the other hand, I'm not willing to take the risk that you'll finally notice the necessity before something goes wrong in a fashion involving death or dismemberment. Or both."

"Understood." Carrtog also understood that if Gwaitorr felt it necessary to tell him to apply the oilcan, it would result in a very low grade, perhaps even a failure.

"I'd also like you to give some thought to what sort of machine you might consider powering with this engine, and how you would set up the belts and pulleys, and gears, if necessary. I won't want the answer today, just give it some thought, while still paying attention to the oilcan." The older magician smiled drily. "I'll expect some preliminary notions in our next session."

"Understood." He stepped forward, lifting the oilcan. Nothing showed signs of immediate need of lubrication, but neither Gwaitorr nor Carrtog saw any sense in waiting until the last moment.

THE SMOKE CLEARED, and the long wooden rod lay before them. It had been pine wood, a yellowish-white color, but now it was a dull purple-gray, a disgusting shade, as far as Carrtog was concerned, but—

"What does it feel like?" Enemantwin demanded.

Carrtog touched it. "It's still a bit warm."

"No surprise. The spell used up a fair amount of powder. What else?"

Carrtog had long ago gotten used to Enemantwin's style, brusque, very seldom admitting satisfaction with anything a student might do or say. He continued, showing no sign of his own annoyance.

"It feels a bit like iron." He picked it up and attempted to bend it. It was sufficiently thick that, even in its previous form, it had little give to it. Now it had even less, if that were possible. "It seems more rigid than wood."

He drew his dagger and tapped the rod with the blade. The sound it made was like tapping iron, but subtly different. "It sounds nearly like metal, but not quite, I would venture to suggest that the spell was a success."

Enemantwin gave him a sour look. For an instant Carrtog thought he might be considering a denial of the spell's success — he had a tendency to be upset if a student seemed to trespass on what he felt to be the teacher's prerogative — but he only said, "Fairly successful, I believe."

He lit a touch of gunpowder, speaking a brief incantation. "Yes, it appears to be a success. The readjustment of the material of the rod is very close to optimum."

And no matter how near to perfect I come, you would not admit to anything better than 'close to optimum.'

"Now, what are the uses of this material?"

That was a test of Carrtog's memory. Enemantwin knew quite well what it could be used for and had mentioned those uses several times during the teaching of the spell.

"It can be used for nearly anything where a similar piece of iron would be used."

"'Nearly anything?'"

Quietly annoyed at himself for careless wording, Carrtog spoke up quickly. "Nearly anything," he reiterated. "It is more brittle than iron, however, and does not lend itself to working in a smithy. One must take care, as well, for any knots in the original piece of wood will show up as faults in the resulting length of converted wood where it may break more easily. Even without knots, it cannot be bored out for firearms, since any fair charge of powder is likely to burst the barrel."

Enemantwin frowned, but nodded, grudgingly. "Somewhat better, Lord Carrtog. This field of study, however, requires a fair degree of precision in both execution of the spells and terminology regarding the results. Some fields of magic are more forgiving of laxity, but not this branch."

"Yes, sir," Carrtog spoke in agreement, but was quietly thinking how the field of mechanics required a good deal of precision, perhaps more than the modification of plant life, or the modification of plant products.

The tutor glanced at the pendulum clock in the corner. "I believe this day's lesson is done. Please see to the clearing up of the equipment. Our next lesson will involve the modification of willow-bark tea for more efficacious relief of pain. Please read the appropriate texts in the Royal Library."

"Yes, Sir."

The tutor did not expect his student to actually clear up the equipment with his own hands; after all, he was a lord. And though Carrtog himself was not averse to doing the work, he knew it would make the servants unhappy, as if he did not trust them to do the work they were expected to do. Instead, he rang for the servants, and when they appeared, he simply said, "See to this stuff, and clean up the room."

"Ah — is it safe, Lord? No magic left in it?"

He carefully kept his expression neutral. The servants knew little or nothing of magic, and what they did know, or thought they knew, was scary. "It's completely safe. You can be sure that if there were any danger in it, I would have warned you of what safeguards to take. The magic that was done took place in a moment, and left no residue, save for the scent of burned gunpowder, and you can be sure that can do you no harm."

As the servants went to work, Carrtog glanced at the clock himself. With any luck, the princess and Lady Adengler might well be out for their usual walk in the Royal Gardens.

He watched while the servants stowed the equipment, then cleaned the tables and, for good measure, swept the floors. When they were done, they snuffed the candles. At this time of day there was not enough light coming in the room's eastern windows to do anything that required the use of the eyes.

He dismissed the servants and started out immediately for the Royal Gardens. At first, no one seemed to be there, but the Royal Gardens were extensive, and it would take a bit more time to be sure they were unoccupied.

He strolled up and down the paths, amusing himself by noting various plants and herbs he was now familiar with and listing in his mind their uses.

He saw nobody familiar at all, though he did see a few couples, young lords and ladies, always accompanied by some older lady for the sake of appearances.

However, as he came around a corner planted with a certain foreign tree that, if not carefully watched, would reseed itself anywhere its seeds might drift to, or anywhere it might put up suckers, he stopped suddenly. "Yakor! What, have you suddenly taken up an interest in herbalism?"

Yakor gave a crooked little smile. "No, I've just heard some news I think you should be aware of, and I was led to understand that occasionally you found the company in the Royal Gardens to be enjoyable."

Carrtog was pleased to note that he did not redden so fiercely any longer at Yakor's digs regarding Lady Adengler. He grinned. "Company? What company? Your own? Yakor, I think you suffer from an inflated sense of your own worth. Of course, that is easily understood; after all you are in the service of the justly famed Lord Carrtog, the hero who has caught the attention of the king himself."

Yakor frowned. "Be careful of jests like that, boy! If the wrong person were to overhear it, they might twist your words around to make a snare you'd be hard pressed to escape from."

Carrtog, alerted by the sudden use of the word 'boy,' gave Yakor a searching glance.

"What is it?"

Yakor shook his head. "Not here. Let's go out to the Keg."

Carrtog maintained his patience, knowing that it would do no good to ask for even the slightest of hints when Yakor was in this sort of mood. Even arrival at the doors of the Overflowing Keg was not sufficient; Yakor was quiet until they had found themselves a table that was not within easy eavesdropping range of anyone else, with a pitcher of ale and two mugs on the table to keep anyone from coming near even to fill their cups.

"Now, then, what is the problem that requires such cautiously private discussion?"

"This sounds so much like a romantic ballad from years and years ago. I can't say how much truth there is in the story, but it seems that one of the young men of the King's Gentlemen who had suffered a broken leg, among other injuries, was left with a family that included a young daughter. After the king left, when the rebels were hunting down the wounded survivors, this daughter, at risk of her life, spirited this soldier away to go into hiding with an elderly uncle and aunt. Other versions of the story say that it was a grandfather and grandmother, but whatever the relation, the young man was saved, and he and the girl later on made their way down south to take refuge with some distant relation of his."

"You're concerned there may be specific mention of the king rushing off and abandoning them?"

"Precisely, though nothing as yet it seems. Luckily, the soldier is not named, nor is his family. That means two things, first that the king cannot hunt him down and kill him and his family, and second, that the king can merely say that this is all unsubstantiated rumor and need not be believed. On the other hand if news does get out about what happened in the North... What if people come to you to ask if it's true that the king abandoned wounded men in Tenerack?"

"But should the king have stayed with his wounded men to let the rebels take him as well?"

Yakor nodded sharply. "You can see that, I can see that, perhaps most of the population of Cragmor can see that. But if the story is passed, concentrating on the king's urgent desire to escape, I doubt His Majesty is going to pay much attention to your justifying what is described as a cowardly act. I'm afraid he'll be more likely to expect you to add the tale about his putting me in your place in a fit of pique because he thought you weren't being sufficiently polite to him."

That would be grave indeed. Carrtog felt his brow furrow as he considered the possible implications. As challenging as it was to have the king meddling in his life, Carrtog much preferred that to the black moods the king had suffered on the run south. And if the king were to take an active dislike to his newest noble, that noble might not have time to flee.

Yakor sipped his ale. "You've done well so far, enjoying the king's favor and looking like just the man who would never admit to knowing anything unfavorable about His Majesty. But you know very well how the king can change his mind over the slightest bit of evidence; even trying to calm his mind over the situation might just have the opposite effect."

"Do you have any suggestions as to what I should do?"

Yakor scowled. "Nothing terribly useful, save to suggest that you never engage in passing rumors, and especially not rumors about the king. I'd suggest you even be cautious about passing favorable stories of the king. It's just possible that whoever tells tales to him might be good enough to let him know that you don't gossip yourself."

"On the other hand, I may do all of that and still discover that not only does His Majesty no longer consider me a favorite, but that he has suddenly brought charges of sedition against me. What sort of plan do you suggest we make to deal with a change of the king's mind?"

At this point Yakor frowned. "That's just the problem; could you invision the king's reaction to something like quietly accumulating a bit of money just in case of emergencies?"

Carrtog nodded. "Sure evidence that I'm planning to kick over the soup-pot and run."

"Unfortunately, yes. On the other hand, it'd be pure foolishness not to start putting by a little bit here and there, always trying not to make it obvious that you're doing so."

Carrtog gave a crooked little smile. "Make some careful little plans while seeming not to be making plans? That should be easy for a man of my great skills."

Yakor returned the smile. "Just be sure your great skills don't end us up with our heads on pikes over the front gate."

Chapter 11

The king had sent a servant to summon Carrtog to his presence. Given his talk with Yakor just the evening before last, Carrtog had a little concern that the king was about to change his mind in some way.

The king, however, was smiling when he saw Carrtog, "Ah, Lord Carrtog. Good day to you!"

Carrtog bowed properly. "A good day to you, also, Your Majesty."

The king's expression was the one Carrtog remembered whenever Bornival had proposed another reward. Carrtog tried not to feel trepidatious about that either.

"Lord Carrtog, I am about to go out at the head of the Army to deal with this so called Black Powder Rebellion. I realize I may be rushing you a bit, but I would very much like to see you wed before I leave."

That was a surprise. "Highness, I have not yet spoken of marriage to her father!"

The king waved a hand. "Lord Melwys has agreed to allow you to speak to her. I am quite sure he will have no objections to your wedding her, a matter of a standing up before witnesses and swearing to the promises."

Carrtog was left with nothing to say, save perhaps a complete rejection of the idea, which would almost certainly ruin his status with the king and most likely toss him out of the palace, and thus out of any chance of even speaking with the Lady Adengler.

Another thought occurred to him; it might not be good for Lady Adengler's status if he were to object to strongly.

"Your Majesty, I will agree with your suggestion, with one proviso, that her father be asked and his consent granted beforehand."

Of course, the wedding ceremony would require her father to be present regardless to give his consent to the match before witnesses. So it wasn't much of a proviso, Carrtog knew, but at least it gave him a small illusion of control.

YAKOR FROWNED WHEN Carrtog told him the news. "You know what he's doing, don't you? He's trying to make sure you don't go along with his army to deal with the rebels. Once you're married, he'll say something on the lines of 'Of course I can't ask a newly married man to leave his wife and march away to war.'"

Carrtog opened his mouth to protest, then was quiet. He remembered how the king had been on the flight from the North; he didn't think King Bornival would expect a minor lord to suddenly take on leadership decisions and make the king look bad. Most likely he didn't want that minor lord to be around to remind him how poorly he had shown up on that same flight from the North.

"Yes, I see what you mean. And if I disobey him, I'm sure he'd find ways to demonstrate his displeasure."

"Ah, perhaps you're starting to get a little wisdom in that hard head of yours. Just be careful you don't get yourself in trouble when some of those lords who're jealous of your sudden elevation start making hints about your arranging not to have to go to war for fear of your hide."

Carrtog clenched his teeth for a moment, then relaxed. "I'll deal with that when it happens."

THE GREAT HALL OF KING Bornival was ablaze with color. There were not so many lords present as had attended the ceremony by which Carrtog had been officially granted his new lands and title, though to make up for that, almost all lords were accompanied by their wives and older children. All the wives and daughters were dressed as well as the pocketbooks of their husbands (or fathers) would allow. The occasion being a marriage, all the women were wearing at least some small item of green, though of course none of them wore gowns of green, that being reserved for the bride herself.

Carrtog, in an outfit that was so fancy as to render him extremely uncomfortable, stood beside Yakor.

Yakor leaned a little toward Carrtog and muttered, "We might still be able to make a run for it."

Carrtog glanced over and realized that the man was speaking only partly in jest. "Too late. We'd have His Majesty and most of his Gentlemen, along with the bride's father and a fair bunch of his retainers on our tail before we managed to get to the city gates."

Yakor managed a twisted little smile. "In all that magic you've learned, was there not something about turning invisible?"

"There was— Too late! Our retreat's cut off!"

Behind them, Lady Adengler had entered the hall on her father's arm. One quick glance was enough to drive out all thoughts, however much in jest, of fleeing the marriage.

The bride's gown was green, green for the beginning of new growth, green for the fertility of spring, and set off by a short-sleeved tan jacket and a necklace of polished amber beads. A pair of black shoes showed under her dress as she walked. Afterward, though he could remember clearly every item of Adengler's attire, he could remember nothing of Melwys' garb. Save, for some reason, that his sword was no fancy ornamental thing such as many lords wore at gatherings such as this, but an ordinary, well-worn fighting weapon, which a man might wear when there was a possible prospect of fighting. Carrtog wondered whether this might be some kind of warning that he, Carrtog, should treat Melwys' daughter well. Not that he had any intention of doing anything else.

When they came even with Carrtog and Yakor, Melwys paused, then took one step diagonally forward, with Adengler turning with him, so that they faced Carrtog.

Melwys then took his daughter's right hand from where it lay on his left arm and held it out to Carrtog, who took that right hand in his own left. As the tradition had been explained to Carrtog, the groom was required to keep his right hand free to use his sword. Apparently, in earlier times, a man might find himself only one of several claimants for a woman's hand and might have to demonstrate that he was capable of fighting for her and thus, if need be, of defending her.

The old lord spoke the traditional words, "Lord Carrtog of Nandycargllwyd, in the sight of the Gods, the King, and this assembled company, I offer you the hand of this my daughter Adengler, to be your wife forever. Will you take her and keep her, with none to come between you, in good or ill, for so long as you live?"

"I will."

He then turned to Adengler. "Adengler of Cwm Gwyrdd, will you take this man, Carrtog of Nandycargllwyd, to be your husband forever? Will you hold to him in all times, with none to come between you, in good or ill, so long as you shall live?"

"I will."

The old lord drew his sword, setting it point-first on the floor, then took the joined hands of the couple, placing them atop the pommel, and said, "Before the Gods, the king and this assembled company, I declare you joined in wedlock, and woe to whoever seeks to pull you asunder."

There was a small pause, and the assembled company began to clap, stamp, and shout, mostly things on the line of "Nandycargllwyd forever!"

THE KING HAD INSISTED on having the Wedding-feast held in one of the larger feasting-halls in the palace. The father of the bride, as was normal, underwrote the cost of the feast and much of the entertainment, though the king had provided for a significant part of that entertainment.

The feast included several courses with several kegs of wine.

During the feast, several jugglers, tumblers, and minstrels performed to the great delight of the assembled guests. Once the feast was done, a small orchestra took its place on a platform and began to play.

As was traditional, the bride and the groom took to the floor to begin the dancing, and fairly shortly, in pairs and groups of pairs, most of the rest of the gathering took to their feet.

Though the tradition called for the bride and groom, whenever they were dancing, to dance mostly together, they did occasionally dance with others, and sometimes did not dance at all. Of course, not all dances, not even a majority of dances, were danced as couples; there were many circle dances and line dances as well.

Wine was being served throughout, so that by the end of the evening most of the company were feeling quite mellow. Carrtog discovered, at the end of the evening, he couldn't recall more than a few distinct faces of people he had danced with; the rest were a blur. There were several customs concerning the ending of the wedding day. Since the king had provided a suite for the married couple to spend their wedding night, Carrtog and Adengler followed the custom that had a great deal of the assembled company, mostly the younger set, escorting the couple to their wedding suite following the end of the dance, with a good deal of singing and ribaldry.

Part of the custom involved hanging around in the hallway outside the suite until late in the night, in extreme cases, waking the newly-weds in the morning with more ribald singing.

On this evening, some of the crowd attempted to gather inside the suite, but Carrtog was not about to allow such an interruption. In a struggle, which was somehow half-serious, Carrtog ejected the last of them, locked the door, and turned to Adengler. "So, that's done."

"Yes, that's done."

"I'm told that last bit, there, was the last remnant of the situation where a man might well find himself fighting to kidnap his bride from amongst her family. I hope you don't feel too much as though you've been kidnapped."

Adengler, a baffled look on her face, stood watching while Carrtog prowled around the suite. Finally, he called out to her, "Heart of mine, come through here a moment!"

Still bewildered, she walked through the suite until she found him in a small antechamber with a servants' door in one wall.

"What is it, Carrtog?"

"Did you really wish to have that noisy lot greet the dawn outside our door?"

"Not really, but how could we avoid it? The king has seen fit to give us the use of this suite, and we can hardly hide our presence."

"Not if we stay here. But that is one advantage of having a man around who can chat with other lords' servants and hear what the people say in the hearing of those servants."

He rapped on the door and heard an answering rap from outside. He opened the door to reveal Yakor's grinning face.

"All preparations made?" Carrtog asked.

"Carriage ready and waiting outside, baggage packed and stored, servants already loaded in carriages, ready to make their way to the railroad station, fares paid for everyone, carriages ordered to wait at Harragush station to take us to Nandycargllwyd itself, and the staff at Nandycargllwyd warned to be ready to welcome their new lord and lady."

Carrtog, hearing an exclamation of surprise from Adengler, turned to look at her, questioningly.

"Will the king not be offended if we don't make use of the suite he has given us use of?"

"Perhaps so," Carrtog answered, "but I've left a polite letter begging his leave to spend a bit of time on the lands he has so graciously granted me and stating my willingness to return whenever he wishes. Even if he commands me to return immediately, given the time it takes to get a messenger out Nandycargllwyd, we should still have time to spend a day or so on the estate."

She still looked a little doubtful. "You remember how upset he can get over the slightest things."

Carrtog frowned slightly. "I'm hoping all the business of preparing his attack on the rebels will keep him too busy to worry about a mere annoyance of a minor lord running off to his estates for a bit. He's already insisted that, as a very recently married man, I should not have to go off to war immediately. I suspect there's many a young bride in a cottage in a small farm would wish the king were so understanding to her own man."

Adengler's expression showed she had not thought the matter through to that conclusion. "I suppose that young bride would feel the same even knowing that you saved the life of the king's daughter."

"I imagine that's still the word that goes round. I doubt if many consider the real truth."

"The real truth? The real truth is that I doubt you've given thought to what I'll wear for this trip. I'd certainly not prefer to travel in this wedding-gown, fancy as it is."

Yakor laughed. "You wrong us, lady! I consulted a young maid-servant, who thought the notion of your husband stealing you away on your wedding night to be most romantic, but insisted that the bride would prefer something comfortable to travel in. In that closet, you will find a dress more suitable for traveling, along with cases containing various things to make your trip more comfortable. I will step outside and call in two ladies who will make your dressing easier."

Yakor stepped back out into the hallway and called two names, and momentarily two young ladies came in, each carrying a case that Carrtog thought could easily carry enough for two. All that for one lady to dress for a night's travel?

But he said nothing. By now he had at least heard various tales about what ladies needed for any sort of occasion. But the princess and her lady-in-waiting had made do with just the clothing on their backs on the flight from Tenerack, and he'd heard few complaints. He could imagine the resulting comments were he to bring that up. But in that case there was no choice, so why complain? Now, however, we have time and facilities to bring practically whatever we want, so let us take advantage of the fact.

The two young servant-girls looked at him and, giggling, disappeared into the changing-room.

Yakor came over to stand beside Carrtog. "From what I know of women and clothes, they'll be a while. We'd best find ourselves a place to sit down and wait. I'd suggest another drop of wine, but it's already late, and I'm led to understand that the jakes on the train are not much to brag about."

"No, you're right about that. So all the plans went right, did they?"

"Yes, pretty much so. I still think you may be taking a bit of a risk, almost spitting in the king's face like this. As your wise young wife mentioned, His Majesty's mind is very changeable, if he takes it into his head that he's been insulted."

"No, as I explained to her, I wrote him a very polite and careful letter, earnestly begging his pardon for my leaving so suddenly, giving my careful list of reasons, none of which has to do with avoiding a lot of marriage-morning revelers, and seriously offering to come back to the capital if he really wishes it. I sincerely hope that I can sound sufficiently humble and obedient that he will forgive me willingly."

"Says the joking young man, maintaining his humor even as the Headsman sharpens his axe."

Carrtog shrugged. "As I've already said, I've written the best letter I know how to write. Besides, this way he'll see he won't have to find other ways to keep me from going with the Army. Nor will I be in Cragmor to cause concern over rumors."

Even as he spoke, he realized that he would need to be careful to say nothing aloud as to what he meant by that statement. Too many people talked in the hearing of servants as if the servants were deaf, then wondered why gossip got them into trouble. There was little likelihood of the young servants hearing what was said in the main room; still 'little likelihood' was far from 'no likelihood at all,' and he was not about to take that chance.

Given his expectations, Carrtog was surprised when the door of the changing-room opened and Adengler stepped out, wearing a rather simple gold dress, trimmed with black. The dress showed her figure well, but was not so close-fitting as to become uncomfortable during a long trip.

One of the two serving-girls was carrying both suitcases, the other slipped out the servant's door; the two still wore expressions that said this was still a delightful secret adventure. Adengler smiled. "Shall we go?"

Carrtog sprang to his feet. "Of course."

He looked toward the door where the one girl had left. "Where is she going?"

"She's taking a message from me to the princess, explaining where we're going and why. I'm her friend, inasmuch as a princess can have a friend who isn't merely looking to curry favor. If the worst happens, she can speak to the king on our behalf. He might heed her words where he might not heed another's."

Yakor peered out the rear entrance to the chamber, looked left and right, then turned and signaled them to follow. They made their way out into the courtyard. It was late night, cool and dark, with no light save for that cast by a pair of oil lanterns held by a pair of menservants.

A pair of coaches stood on the road, the coachmen waiting by the opened coach doors. The man at the lead coach called out quietly, "My Lord? My Lady?" Carrtog took Adengler's hand and led her in that direction. He handed her up into the coach, then climbed in after her. The coachman closed the door, quietly but firmly, then they felt the coach rock as he climbed to his place on the box. Carrtog called out "The Railway Station!"

A moment later the coachman's whip snapped in the night, and they were off on their bouncing, jolting way to the Railway Station.

Carrtog glanced at Adengler and said, "Well, Adengler, this may not be the sort of wedding night you'd imagined, but I think the result will be better than spending the next little while at Court, with everyone watching us to see if we're getting along well. If that kind of situation didn't lead us to spending a lot of time in argument, I don't know what would."

She gave him a thoughtful look. "You may well be right. I think it would be better if you called me by something other than my full name. I love my parents, and they chose for me a nice romantic name, but it's too much of a mouthful to use all the time. Even they took to shortening it to 'Addy' except when I was in trouble."

"My family generally called me by my full name. The least objectionable nickname any of my peers ever came up with was 'Thirdling', since I was my father's third son, and therefore could expect no inheritance."

Adengler grinned. "If I ever call you 'Thirdling,' you'll know I'm trying to get your goat."

Carrtog returned the grin. "I'll have to try to think of something to call you in revenge."

"Don't bother. Being a magician and used to dealing with all kinds of incantations, I'd be afraid you were about to turn me into a toad or something."

"Sorry, one of my tutors specializes in mechanics, the other in plant magic. The worst I could likely do is turn you into a weed."

Chapter 12

When they finally stopped at the Railway Station, Carrtog noticed that his new bride wakened with a start, looking round for a moment before remembering where she was. He recalled the rough ride they had undergone and felt a tinge of guilt that he had near enough forced her to this sudden long journey at the end of what could only be considered a trying day.

"Addy, my dearest, I apologize! I hadn't thought how tired you must already be! Would you prefer to go back to that bed that is so near, rather than go rushing all over the kingdom on a noisy, smelly train?"

She paused, then pulled herself up straight. "Nonsense! I knew at the start I was being invited along on a long trip, and I'd think myself a poor sort indeed if I suddenly changed my mind now. Besides, I've never yet ridden on a train, and it should be some sort of an adventure."

The train yard was lit by a number of oil lanterns on poles, which provided a faint orange glow. The engine was very much in shadow, and though the light was poor, Carrtog could recognize the sights and sounds of a working engine. In fact, many of the lessons Gwaitorr had taught him had involved visits to this same train-yard so he could see and even on occasion be in the cab with the engineer. To have the man himself explain the use of the various controls, and how a person could tell from the sound the engine was making whether it was time to pull out the throttle, or to apply the brakes, or take other actions.

In fact, he had a slight sneaking hope that he might be able to convince the engineer to let him ride in the cab for a little part of this trip.

He realized that a great part of achieving that would be convincing Adengler to let him do so without argument. He smiled, a little guiltily, understanding that that, too, would be another burden he put on her. Perhaps he should put the notion aside altogether. He would have to see how matters proceeded as they traveled.

Despite the lateness of the hour the maids were all still quite cheery and romantic, though the men, of varying ages, were less happy about the whole affair. Yakor took a pouch of silver and divided it among them all, which encouraged them at least to the point of grim smiles.

The men took charge of getting the luggage to the appropriate cars, after which the train crews saw to getting things stored. The crews inquired as to which bags might have items that would be required on the journey. Yakor had given the servants careful instructions regarding this very matter so that packing had been done with this in mind and therefore there was very little confusion.

In the normal run of things, should they all be traveling separately, Carrtog and Adengler would be traveling in one coach toward the front of the train and all the rest would be further back. However, it was understood that Lord Carrtog and his wife might at some time have need of their servants, so in this case they were established in the rear section of this coach with a discreet dark green curtain dividing the two portions.

The train started off slowly in its first jerking motion, but soon settled down to a fast and relatively smooth ride. Even at its smoothest, though, there was a constant clicking of the steel wheels as they hit the joints between the iron rails.

The seats were upholstered and reasonably comfortable, but Carrtog was a little keyed up to actually fall asleep immediately. Adengler, on the other hand, dropped off very shortly.

With nothing but starlight to view the scenery through the small glass windows, only the occasional copse of trees or rounded shoulder of a hill and sometimes a small farmstead could be seen.

Dawn began to break, but Carrtog still continued to drowse much of the time.

When the sun had completely risen, a man came through with a large metal pot from which he poured cups of a dandelion-root tisane sweetened, if desired, with honey. This was provided as a service to the travelers, and both Carrtog and Adengler took advantage of it. Carrtog gave Adengler a quick description of what he had learned of the benefits of the drink, at which she smiled and said, "I'm afraid, my dearest, that marriage to you may be a very educational experience."

He felt himself blush. "I'm sorry, I just sometimes find myself wanting to pass on some of what I've learned."

She reached over and put a hand on his knee. "No, no, that's not what I meant! I really like to learn things. Well, most things. I don't think I want to try to learn any magic, but even that might change."

A little later that morning, the train stopped at a small station for more fuel and water. The passengers were allowed to step outside and stretch their legs a little, though they were warned that the train would start moving shortly so they should be ready to reboard as soon as the whistle sounded again. There was nowhere really to go, only a few buildings on a hillside, all the surrounding landscape still green with the grass and foliage of the summer. The buildings housed the crews who handled the water and the fuel for the engine. Most of the travelers did get out and walk around. Few had slept well during the night and most had been drowsing during the morning.

A man and wife team had set up a small booth from which they sold wine and skewers of cooked meat. "The railroad company would be wise to offer some similar service on the train itself," Carrtog commented.

"But the swaying motion of the train would make it difficult to serve food, let alone to eat it," replied Adengler.

"That wouldn't be an insurmountable problem," Carrtog responded. "And it would definitely make long railroad journeys more tolerable."

"I haven't found this trip to be intolerable!" Addy protested. "Long, but not intolerable. And I'm seeing a part of the kingdom I'd never seen before."

Carrtog grinned. "So am I. And in the best of company, as well."

"My lord Carrtog, you are an inveterate flatterer!"

"Me? Lady Adengler, I only tell the truth!"

Her eyes shone with laughter. "Indeed? I shall have to watch myself in your company, I can tell. I—"

She was interrupted by a blast from the train's steam whistle, and the train-crew began to call out, "Lords, ladies, and all, please come aboard! The train must be under way!"

The passengers boarded, first the lords — there were two in the 'lord' class other than Carrtog and Addy — and then the lower class. This latter included the servants traveling with them.

Carrtog noted from the sound of the engine that the crew had started gathering steam somewhat before the boarding call so that shortly after they had boarded the train began its first jerky movement. It wasn't long before the train had reached its normal traveling speed, and once more they were making their way through the hills and forests.

By this time, they had become somewhat used to the scent of burning coal and hot oil that permeated the air within the coach. They had been traveling for about two hours when one of the train crew came in to announce, "Lords, Ladies, one-half hour to the stop at the station in Harragush Village."

Carrtog realized that he had been too involved in conversation to even think of asking to see the steam engine. He felt a bit embarrassed to have even considered it.

"This is a beautiful countryside, Carrtog. Is it part of your land?"

He shook his head. "My understanding is that Harragush Village is a village with a free charter. There is a history behind that which I don't quite understand. The village performed some particular service to one of the early holders of the title."

The Station at Harragush Village was of larger size than many other stations whose main function was to provide coal and water for the draft engines. Indeed, the quarters provided for the Station Crew — at least Carrtog suspected that was the purpose of the several buildings on the same style as the Station — were much larger than similar buildings at other fuel and water stops along the way.

Harragush Village itself was a bustling little town, almost too large to rate the designation of 'village.' It was no surprise to Carrtog that a village with a free charter would attract numbers of people for that reason alone, merchants, shopkeepers, smiths, and various artisans.

Two carriages were waiting at the Station for Carrtog and his party, along with twelve armed guards. A number of villagers were also gathered there, looking on.

The Chief Coachman, a strongly-built man with a short black beard, introduced himself and his companion. "Lord Carrtog? I am Manwydan, Chief Coachman of Nandycargllwyd, and with me is my assistant Sawyl." Sawyl was younger a little slighter, but still strongly-built, with reddish hair and a slight beard.

Manwydan glanced at the villagers and said, "We'd best be loaded and away, Lord. This lot won't likely cause any trouble, but best not to let them get started."

"Why should there be any trouble, Manwydan?"

"There shouldn't, Lord. But some eleven years ago, a lord name of Pentarric was given the land, and he made an attempt to revoke the free charter. This upset the villagers badly, and they blocked off the roads to the town. Pentarric was killed in a skirmish, and having no heirs, the land revoked to the throne. The king of that time sent a message to assure the villagers that their charter remained. When the people heard that a new lord had been appointed, one who had the favor of the new king, rumors began to spread that you would use the king's favor to try to revoke their charter once more."

Carrtog looked at the Coachman. "Other than that, what are the relationships between my land and the village?"

Manwydan frowned. "Hard to say for certain, Lord. They're willing to buy and sell from us, but some are right touchy about what they consider their 'free rights.'"

Carrtog turned to Addy, "You stay here, heart of mine. I'm quite certain I can manage this without trouble, but just in case, you should keep back. Yakor, come with me."

"You aren't about to do something foolish, are you, boy?"

"I hope not. In fact, I hope to ease a number of minds."

He began to walk toward the villagers. His sword had been clumsy to wear in a coach or a train, so he had taken it off and left it with the baggage. He hoped that would show that he had no ill intentions in mind.

He looked them over. Most of them were men who seemed of no trade, who perhaps worked as laborers for whoever would hire them, though several looked like tradesmen or shopkeepers.

"Good morning," he said. "I would imagine you have heard of me, probably all sorts of things, no more than a few of them having the least connection to the truth. However, I wish to assure you that I have no intention, now or in the future, of making any attempt to change the relationship between your village and my land. You have been free up to now, and you shall remain free from now on, so far as I am concerned."

He stopped and continued to look them over. Finally, one of the more prosperous-looking tradesmen stepped out of the group and spoke. "You wouldn't be trying to smooth our ruffled feathers for the moment, so you can come back later with more soldiers and take us by surprise?"

Carrtog drew himself up. "I have no idea what sort of lords you have dealt with before, but I have spoken, and I will stand by my word."

The tradesman nodded. "And I give you my own word that, so long as you deal with us fairly, we will deal with you fairly."

"A good morning to you all, then, and I shall be driving out to my home."

The tradesman bowed, then walked away, with first one, then two of the more prosperous-looking ones following. The rest began to look around at each other and a few of the more ruffianly sort muttered together, a few of them looking down at the roadway for stones, then, deciding that nothing was about to happen here, they too wandered away.

Yakor muttered loud enough for Carrtog to hear, "Well, you were successful, this time boy. More good luck than anything else, I think. What if one of those toughs had decided 'Gods blast it all!' and flung a stone, and neither you nor I with more than a belt-knife to hand? It could well have turned out that way, you know."

"But it didn't."

"Huh!" The older man snorted. "At the very least, you ought to have called those troopers to stand behind us, those troopers someone had the forethought to send and watch us for just such an occasion."

"And that would have made those people certain that I was about to bully them. Let's continue to and see this new home of ours."

THE DRIVE WAS A LONGISH one, a drive which wound in and out among hills, some wooded and some not. Carrtog marked the occasional neatly-kept farmstead, and some neat herds of small, long-horned, shaggy cattle.

"If these are my lands, as I assume, my bailiff seems to be taking his task seriously. Everything seems well-looked-after."

"It does, doesn't it?" asked Yakor. "Of course, all these are along the road in, and would be the first you see as you come in. Might there not be others, not quite so easily found, that might not be in such good condition?"

Carrtog looked at him. "That could indeed be so, but until that proves to be the case, I will believe the man to be doing his job, and doing it well. If it does prove that he has put a high shine on this one strip of lands to the detriment of others of my people, well, I will not let that go, either." Yakor nodded, the expression on his face being that of a teacher who finds his student giving a series of proper answers.

The House of Nandycargllwyd was large and well-built. Gunpowder, steam-power, and magic had made castles useless, but even still the large house was mostly built of stone, with only some parts made of wood. It went without saying that it was largely protected by magic, likely of various sorts.

He would have to look into just what spells were protecting it and decide whether or not they needed refreshing.

Of course, whatever magicians were on staff would likely have their opinions as to the necessity of any changes to the spells at

all; depending on their attitudes, he might well have to approach
the matter with caution. It would not do to have a fairly powerful
magician annoyed at you, particularly one who knew the defenses of
your home backward and forward.

"Carrtog, my dear." Addy's voice broke into his thoughts. "What
are you thinking of so deeply?"

He lifted his head sharply, then gave a description of his general
thoughts. When he finished describing his concerns regarding how
the staff magicians might react to the thought of a new lord with
some pretensions of magical ability, she laughed out loud.

"My dear, you do choose the queerest things to worry about!
Suppose the chief magician is a fellow who learned his magic long
ago and is well aware that he has not been able to keep up? Might he
not be just as happy to leave the burden in someone else's hands?"

"That's possible, I suppose, but all my knowledge of magicians
says that they're a jealous lot, unwilling to admit that anyone knows
as much as they, let alone more. But you're right, I should wait until
I meet the man, or men, before I make any sort of decision."

The coach started up the long road that swept up into a
half-circle in front of the manor house. From there the coachmen
could drive the unloaded coaches around to the coach house.

Someone had clearly been watching from the windows, for when
they were still quite some way from the doors, the doors opened and
a crowd of people poured forth. It was no unorganized mob, though,
for first about twelve troopers wearing the uniform of the house
came out and took up spaced positions along the drive, centered on
one whose uniform marked him as the commander. Following them
were people wearing the clothing appropriate to major servants, such
as the bailiff, the steward, and the magister magorum, and so on,
ending with the servants who would be responsible for carrying their
luggage and showing them to their rooms.

"Well," Carrtog said, "they're ready for us at the house at least."

The others were looking out the windows, and Adengler's face took on a look of trepidation.

"Don't worry, dear. Remember that you're the mistress of the house, but also that a servant who always has to fear your anger over the slightest of things will not likely be a happy one, nor one capable of giving good service."

She glanced over at him, but the expression of concern did not lessen appreciably. "Thank you, dearest, but a woman learns very early that at some time she will have to take charge of a household, with servants who have often been serving for longer than she has been alive, and it can be dreadfully easy to get a bad start and be known as someone who constantly has to change her orders because she's made a mistake as to how easy or difficult something is to do. And if she deals with such problems poorly, she can get a reputation as one who is impossible to satisfy."

He continued to smile, saying, "The worst thing to do is to fret yourself over things that are unlikely to happen. Your mother must have trained you for this, surely? Then all you need to do is to act confident, but be willing to take advice if it seems right. And in the very last instance, you are the mistress, and your husband will support what you order. So come, put on a confident smile, for surely a lady-in-waiting to the princess has learned to deal with servants."

When Carrtog got down from the coach and turned to hand Addy down, she was wearing a smile that seemed confident enough. Carrtog returned the salute given by the household troops and with Addy on his arm, moved forward to the first of the servants.

The bailiff stepped forward. "Welcome to your home, Lord Carrtog. I am your bailiff, Lugan, and at my right is your steward, Bragan."

The captain of the household troops strode over smartly, halting in front of Carrtog and saluting sharply.

Carrtog returned the salute, and the captain said, "Captain Gwaim'nash, commander of your household troops, Lord Carrtog."

"Thank you, Captain. What is the strength of our troops, and how are they equipped?"

"They presently number fifty-four, Lord. A contingent of one hundred ten went to the North under General Malgwyn, and to date thirty-three are reported as surviving and are presently still in the North, being re-equipped for further service. Royal decree permits us to have up to seventy-five under arms on our territory, but the royal command to send a contingent to the North plus some accidental deaths and deaths due to disease have left us considerably under strength.

"Our men are armed with a brace of wheel-lock pistols each, plus a sword, and are all trained to fight as cavalry or, at need, as foot. Three of every ten are also trained in combat magic. Unfortunately, our most skilled combat magician was required to march north, and it has not yet been determined whether he has survived."

"Thank you, Captain; we will discuss this situation later on. For now, my wife and I need to find our quarters and freshen up after a very long ride."

"Of course, Lord." Captain Gwaim'nash stepped back, and the steward snapped his fingers at some servants, who rushed forward to take charge of leading them to their quarters and having their luggage carried in and placed in its appropriate rooms.

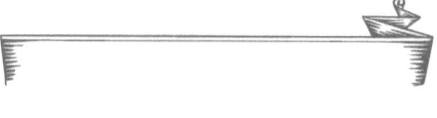

Chapter 13

S omewhat later, Carrtog and Addy were enjoying a glass of wine together in a small drawing room. They had changed out of their traveling clothes and were beginning to relax from the trip. Addy wore a gold dress with a reddish-brown jacket fastened by two black frogs. Carrtog wore his family plaid topped by a white shirt with lace at the collar and cuffs, with a loose black jacket, also fastened by three black frogs.

"Well, Addy, my dearest, how are you finding it in your new home?"

She chuckled. "It seems I was wrong. The servants all seem to be trying their hardest not to act as if they were superior to a new bride. They almost apologize for knowing more about the workings of this house than I do."

Carrtog pursed his lips. "Consider what they must know of us; you have been a lady-in-waiting to the king's daughter, and I am a jumped-up younger son promoted for saving that same king's daughter. In their view, we must both feel that all our servants should treat us as two steps lower than Gods; you because of your nearness to royalty, me because I'm still a little unsure of my actual status. Every one of them is at least a little afraid that either of us may take the least offense as a reason to cast any or all of them out of their positions, without a reference, and you know what that means for them?"

"It almost certainly means that they will never find another household job, leaving them to take whatever jobs can be found, if any."

"Well," Carrtog said, "all we can do is demonstrate, as time goes on, that we are more fair than they expect, leading," he continued, smiling "to the time when we will eventually have to demonstrate that we will not put up with unsatisfactory service. But they shall learn to live with us, and we shall learn to live with them, I hope."

THE BEDCHAMBER WAS lit by several beeswax candles, expensive, but without the odor of tallow, or of oil lamps. Addy was dressed in a plain white nightgown, tied at the waist with a narrow sash.

"I apologize," Carrtog said, "for the much delayed wedding night."

"No, no, no, my dear, no apologies are necessary. All in all I think this is best, to start our lives together in the house that will be ours together."

He smiled and took her into his arms. "And thank you for that thought, my dearest." He kissed her.

LUGAN HAD JUST FINISHED explaining the state of the land's finances and was leaning back in quiet pride. "As you can see, Lord, the land is in good condition. We have maintained the expenses for upkeep of tenants' properties at a reasonable level, so that the income is still favorable."

"That report is indeed encouraging, Lugan, seeing as we have some resources at our disposal I should like to start construction on a machine-shed of medium size. It should contain a smithy and have enough space to build a steam engine, perhaps two. I also wish to experiment with gliders, but for these I foresee using only some sort of large tent which can be erected and taken down as necessary. Of course, I do not expect to do all these things at once, but to take them on as funds permit. The machine-shed is the first priority. Would you look into this as soon as possible, and let me know how matters stand?"

The bailiff frowned. "I will see how matters stand. It would be best if we could make this machine-shed large enough to deal with production and repair of various landholders' tools and equipment, and thus defray some of the costs. As for the gliders, I'm not familiar enough with them to be aware of any possibilities of using them to make money."

"I hadn't expected these endeavors to necessarily make money, though any means of partially defraying expenses would be all to the good. The main purposes are experimentation."

Lugan's frown deepened. "Lord, your lands provide quite a reasonable sum annually, but to toss away any significant part of that sum on mere toys and the like is hardly the best use of those funds."

Carrtog frowned himself. "So long as I do not overspend the limits of the funds available, I fail to see the problem. And the sort of thing I plan to build could hardly be called 'toys.' Furthermore, referring to your lord's deepest interests in that manner is not the kind of behavior I expect from my subordinates."

Lugan flushed. "My apologies, your Lordship. Of course, as you have seen in the records, your estate, while not perhaps wealthy, can still afford to undertake some new building. And while it would be preferable to produce something that could in some way defray at least some part of the cost, it is, after all, your land to do with as you will."

"Fine, then. Be assured that I have no intention of overspending the limits of my income. Also, if there is any way of making my projects help pay for themselves, I will not be averse to that. Indeed, if you yourself can come up with a means of using the projects to help fund themselves, please bring that to my attention. So long as it does not interfere unduly with the aim of the project, I will give it serious consideration."

He couldn't tell by the man's expression whether or not Lugan believed that promise, but only time would tell.

"One further thing, Lord, when had you wished to start the building on this project?"

"I would actually like to begin work as soon as possible. I was thinking it might be possible to hire some workmen from the village." I was also thinking that the king might demand my return to the capital at any moment, so I'd like to get started before that happens. But you don't need to know that.

The bailiff shook his head doubtfully. "The tradition is to hire your own tenants as much as possible for building on your own lands. Not that you cannot hire whomever you please, but it will make your tenants unhappy, and thus unwilling to do their best for you."

Carrtog considered this; he knew there were steadings on which the lord and his family thought it beneath them to deal with any menial labor. This was not the case on Tsingallik estate, and particularly not for third sons. He remembered very well the days when he had overseen work parties, the various things that could affect the willingness of the people to do the work and thus the actual outcome of the work itself.

On the other hand— "Are the rents so onerous that the people are seriously dependent on other income?"

Lugan drew himself up. "The rents here are no higher than anywhere else of comparable size, and indeed, lower than some. It is only that the custom is to offer work first to the tenants, and only then to people other than tenants. Going against that custom, however, will cause discontent."

Carrtog nodded. "I understand. I would like to have work done on the main work-shed as soon as possible, though. I understand that having a full work-crew involved at that may not be immediately feasible, only see to it that one is in place. If there are not enough men for the task available immediately from among the tenants then please hire additional workers from the village. I will also wish to employ certain young men, capable young men, with good heads on their shoulders, to assist me in my work."

Lugan looked doubtful. "You'll not likely find young men on any of the farms capable of dealing with magic, Lord."

"You might find yourself surprised, there, Lugan. However, my plan does not require young men to become magicians, but more to assist me in my work in mechanics. For that, though, I think we'd best be looking among the villagers."

"You think so, Lord?"

"I do. Unless, that is, my smith has an apprentice he is willing to part with. Much of my assistant's duties will involve work more akin to the smithy, and even then, not quite completely similar."

The bailiff took on a thoughtful look. "Lord, a man on one of your farms typically has several sons, so as to have one to take on the farm when he passes on. However, he cannot divide the farm among several sons, which means finding places for his other sons, typically apprenticing them to tradesmen. I think I might be able to find a young man suitable for your purposes."

Carrtog raised his brows. "I will need a capable young man, Lugan, not someone who is too much trouble to place anywhere."

"Not at all, Lord! The young man I have in mind is quite capable."

Carrtog still wondered. His bailiff had gone from general disapproval of his lord's plans to seeming enthusiasm for him to

employ one particular young man, which seemed a little suspicious.
Well, if this young man was totally unsuited, Carrtog need not take
him on.

"Bring the young man to me when you can, then, and I will see
how he suits."

ON THEIR THIRD DAY at Carrtog's new estate, a message came
from the capital. A messenger was sent to find Carrtog where he was
out looking over his acres. The bailiff insisted on accompanying him,
and the man had a slight expression of disapproval on his face, as
though he were almost insulted that his lord did not take his word
for the state of things among his tenants.

Carrtog, for his part, felt that simply taking the bailiff's word as
truth was the first step in letting things slide to a point where he had
no idea what was happening at all. If the man were annoyed at this ...
well better he be annoyed than that Carrtog get a rude shock when
he get set to undertake an expense only to find that he could not
afford it.

The messenger, a young farmer's son riding a plough-horse
without a saddle, came up to them at as near a canter as his mount
could manage. He slid down off the horse and bowed, saying in a
very thick local accent, "My Lord, there's a Royal Courier waiting on
you at the House. They told me to take a horse so as to find you the
quicker."

The bailiff undertook to respond. "Well done, Nwalan. You have
brought us the message. Go tell them that his Lordship will be in
very soon, then be about your tasks."

Lugan turned to Carrtog. "Will you come in immediately, Lord,
or finish your inspection first?"

Carrtog was on the verge of telling the man that he ought to have
let his lord answer for himself, then he realized that Lugan had really

said no more than that he, Carrtog, would come in soon, but not how soon or late, so he might as well let it go.

"I believe that if the king has seen fit to send a courier to find me, I'd best not dilatory in hearing what the king has to say. Let's go in now; we can always finish this inspection another time." If the king does not demand I load myself up and present myself before him as soon as possible.

He was not about to demonstrate too great a fear of the king that he come in at a gallop to hear the king's message, nor would he come at such a slow pace as the courier might report to the king as insulting, but rather at a pace that might be called at least brisk.

When they arrived, though, they found there had been a mistake. When Carrtog approached the courier, he asked, "You have a message for me?"

The courier, a stocky man, presently covered with the dust and sweat of a long ride, looked surprised. "No, Lord, there has been some mistake. My message is from the Princess Ellevar , to the Lady Adengler."

There was immediate shock among the servants who had first met the man and assumed that the message was from the king to the Lord Carrtog. He could almost see the sudden fear among them, the near certainty that some, if not all of them, would be dismissed immediately.

The highest ranked among them immediately knelt before Carrtog. "I'm sorry, sir, the fault is mine. Please don't be blaming the rest. I ought not to have made the assumptions I did!"

"Get up, man," Carrtog said. "Let's not make the matter worse by continuing delays. Send someone immediately to find the Lady Adengler to let her know."

The man got up and sent one of the maids, one who seemed the least flustered by the situation. While they waited, Carrtog asked, "Has no one offered this man a cup of water, at the very least?"

The courier spoke up then. "It is not allowed for me to take any refreshment until such time as my message has been delivered, Lord."

So everyone stood around feeling foolish until Addy appeared. Addy looked around, seeming bewildered, then the Courier turned toward her. "Lady Adengler?"

"Yes?" she said, doubtfully.

He held out a rolled message for her. "A message for you from the Princess Ellevar ."

She took it, looking at it first as though she were sure there must be some mistake, but she read the address, which appeared to be correct, then she reached into the purse at her waist, took out a coin, and handed it to the man.

He looked at it, and said, "Lady, are you sure you mean to give this much?"

She had turned her attention to the message, but when he spoke, she looked back at him. "Of course. It means at least that much to me, and you have had a long journey. I hope you can be allowed to at least have a meal and a bed under our roof and another meal in the morning before you leave."

"My extreme thanks, most gracious Lady."

The servants, rushing to make up for the previous error, immediately led the man away. Adengler looked up at Carrtog. "If you don't mind, I'd prefer to read this in private, first."

He shrugged. "It's your letter. You need never read it to me at all, if you don't wish."

She smiled, and went into another room.

Carrtog dismissed the bailiff. "You might as well go, Lugan; I doubt I will wish to continue my inspection today. Another day perhaps."

CARRTOG TOOK A SEAT in a somewhat overstuffed armchair looking out over the front lawn while he waited for Addy to finish reading the letter and to decide what part of it, if any, she should make known to her husband.

He remembered as a boy making secret forays into his older sister's letters from her friends and being disgusted to find it mostly about clothes and the prospects (and results) of balls they had been allowed to attend, and the charms of certain as-yet unmarried men. Though, there had also been the occasional statement which seemed to be replies to his sister's complaints about "that pest, Carrtog."

He grimaced at that memory; looking back, he could see that he had indeed been a pest. He hoped he had improved since then; well, he must have. After all, Addy had agreed to marry him.

And suddenly, Addy was entering the room again, carrying the letter, and wearing an expression of at least mild concern.

"Does the princess say anything of import?"

"She does. Listen to this:" She took up the letter, found a place, and began to read. "'Da was somewhat fierce about your rushing off to leave the palace and go to Nandycargllwyd. Fortunately he talked to me about it, since he didn't want to hurt me by punishing the both of you too badly. I was able to point out to him that Lord Carrtog had begged his pardon in advance, and made a great point out of agreeing to come back immediately if Da wished it, so he calmed down somewhat. He probably will send for Lord Carrtog in a while, but he's no longer so fierce about the whole matter.'"

She looked up at Carrtog. "If you'd be willing to take some advice from me on the topic, I'd suggest we start back to the capital sometime before the king sends for you. To come before he calls you might well ameliorate whatever anger he has built up by that time."

Carrtog nodded. "Thank you. And you should never fear to offer me advice. I have no notion that I know or can think of everything, and I'm sure that anything you tell me will likely have some good sense behind it."

She smiled, a little doubtfully. "I suspect you have too much faith in me. For my part, I'm quite sure that I'm as capable as anyone of giving poor advice."

He grinned at her. "Nonsense! You had enough sense to marry me, didn't you?"

She laughed at that. "Are you sure that shows good sense, or utter foolishness? After all, you're steering very close to offending the king."

THE NEXT MORNING, BRAGAN the Steward informed Carrtog that the bailiff had brought a young man to see him.

Ah, yes, the young man he recommended.

"Tell them I will be right out."

When he came out, he found the bailiff waiting with a young man obviously of a farming family. The man was slender, but muscular, with a face that revealed intelligence.

There was also a trace of concern in his expression, which Carrtog understood as well. For the son of a farm-holder, being brought to the attention of the Lord of the Estate could mean many things, not all of them favorable.

The young man bowed deeply, and Lugan said, "Lord Carrtog, this is Gryff, son of Llych, of Cwmddon Farm. I believe he might be a suitable candidate to serve as your assistant."

Carrtog looked at the young man, then at the bailiff. "I assume you have reasons to suggest him as my assistant, other than that he has the sense to show up before me fairly clean and well-dressed?"

Being clean and well-dressed is not easy for a boy on a farm-hold.

"I do, Lord. I understand that, as a small boy, young Gryff tried to gather enough material to build a small water-wheel in the creek that runs by their holding. At the age of twelve, he put both his parents into a fret when he ran away to look at the new railway train. I understand he earned something of a hiding for that one."

Carrtog noticed that Gryff reddened at that and thought it a bit unfair of the bailiff to have brought that up. On the other hand, perhaps Lugan was trying to indicate that the young man's parents took their duties as parents seriously.

Lugan continued, "Furthermore, he has, within the last two years, asked his father to see about the possibility of apprenticing him to the Railroad. Llych has indeed made some inquiries in that regard, though nothing has come of it so far. When you stated the need of an assistant, he came to my mind. What is your feeling in the matter? Or had you preferred someone of noble birth?"

In fact, noble birth was not one of the chief characteristics Carrtog had in mind, particularly given the attitudes of the young nobles he had met at court who were mostly given to pursuit of women and pursuit of fame and glory in the upcoming war. This latter was more of a factor since the rebels had proven themselves more than just a group of ragged peasants annoyed at being ruled by King Bornival.

"No, I think the main characteristics I need are an interest in mechanics and a willingness to learn. What do you say, Gryff? You seem to be interested in mechanics, right enough, but are you willing to learn? By that I mean not just standing at the controls and making the machine function, whatever it might be, but learning how such things work, from the very basic principles on up, and even learning how to build them so that you can build better ones. What do you say to that?"

A smile lit the boy's face, making him indeed look little more than a boy. "I say yes, Lord!" Then his face went still again, and he said quietly, in the manner of one who has seen his hopes dashed more than once, "That is, if you are truly serious, my Lord."

"Oh, I am serious indeed, Gryff. The only thing that could change my mind is if you prove to be unwilling to work, or unwilling to learn, and from the look of you I don't think either one is likely to be true. Now, I suggest that you go tell your parents this news and come back here. I think that, rather than have you come in from the farm each day, you should live here in the house. Will that be well with you?"

"Whatever you say, Lord."

Of course it will be well with him, Carrtog; you're the lord and he is the third son of a farm-holder.

"Good. I will instruct the steward to arrange quarters for you here and we will begin your training immediately."

"Training, Lord?"

"Yes, of course. At the very least you must be taught to read, write, and cipher. It might be possible to learn mechanics without that knowledge, but it will be very difficult."

"Yes, Lord." Gryff sounded doubtful.

"Come, now, Gryff; these things are not impossible to learn, and once they are learned, many good things flow from the knowledge."

Chapter 14

The first arrangements for Gryff's accommodations and the beginning of his education were actually simple matters to arrange: Carrtog called his Steward and said, "I've taken on an assistant, a young man named Gryff, son of Llych, of Cwmddon Farm. Rather than having him come all the way from his farm every day, I would like to see him given some sort of quarters nearby. Would you please arrange for that, and for his meals, and some sort of decent clothing, along the lines of stable-hands garb. I would also like to have him taught reading, writing, and ciphering, as soon as possible. Could you see to that?"

Bragan spent a moment considering this, then said, "The lodgings and the clothing, as well as the food, are easily enough done. If he will report to me as soon as possible, I will have his measurements taken, and garments should be ready within at most a day. As for the teaching, I can have one of my assistants begin that as soon as possible. Will that be suitable?"

Carrtog, who had expected some hesitation, even objection, to having a farmer brought into the household, could only say, "Very much so. Thank you."

Bragan only bowed. "I am at your service, Lord."

At lunch with Addy, Carrtog commented on how everything was progressing satisfactorily. "And how do you find things yourself, Addy?"

"Well, having received reports from all the chief house-servants, and having inspected the living-quarters, the kitchens, the store-rooms, the pantries, and all such, I find myself with nothing to do save sewing. And all save the least capable of my maidservants can sew better than I."

FOR THE FIRST FEW DAYS, Gryff concentrated mostly on learning to read, write, and figure. At other times, Carrtog taught lessons on mechanics, though the lessons were hampered at first by Gryff's inability to read or write. Gryff did not lack for intelligence, though, and proceeded quite well.

Work had begun on his work-shed, and though it was going to be some time before he could actually put it to use, he got out a set of plans for a steam engine and, with Gryff and Yakor along, visited the smith to see what the man might say.

"The smith at Tsingallik has taken to steam engines heartily, and the last I heard he was trying to build gliders and launch them using a steam engine. Not all smiths are so forward-thinking, and some are downright unwilling to change. We will have to see what sort our smith is." Carrtog explained to Gryff as they went.

The smith of Nandycargllwyd, a stocky and well-muscled man named Fforchan, with a shock of graying hair, had apparently heard of his Lord's interests, and had already taken a dislike of them. He watched, in a barely polite manner, while Carrtog unfolded his plans and explained what he wished.

Barely taking time to think, he said, "I can't take the time from my real work for this sort of thing, Lord. I don't believe it can have any real usefulness."

"You think not? With steam railways already covering half the kingdom?" He was careful not to lose his temper; that would be worse than useless.

The smith shrugged. "With all the fiddling work to be done to put those boilers together so they don't burst when any amount of steam is put through them, not to mention putting those piston-things together so they hold in enough steam to actually make things work? Too much trouble for all the good it does, Lord."

Carrtog could, of course, remove the smith from his position, but that would be wasteful, and not really any sort of punishment; Fforchan could take his anvil and his tools and move to anywhere else — a good smith could always make his way, and there was no denying that Fforchan was a capable smith.

Carrtog began to fold up his plans. "Well, I will just have to go elsewhere, then."

The smith watched, expressionless, as the lord took his plans and left.

CARRTOG SENT FOR HIS bailiff. Gryff spoke up, a bit nervously. "Your pardon, Lord, but do you intend to dismiss the smith?"

"I doubt it very much. From all I've heard, Fforchan is a very capable smith, and replacing him would be difficult. No, I think I will set the bailiff for searching for a smith specifically for my workshop. I will want a reasonably capable man, and one who is willing to produce the sorts of things I wish. Fforchan will maintain his position as smith for the estate and its farm-holds."

Gryff nodded. "I understand; thank you, Lord."

The bailiff was a while coming, so Gryff eventually asked, "Lord, while we wait, may I review the reading selection my tutor has set for me?"

Carrtog, pleased to see the younger man's eagerness, said, "Certainly. And if you need help, don't hesitate to ask."

"Yes, Lord."

Actually, he didn't ask for any help, though Carrtog was not sure whether he didn't need any help, or was just unwilling to ask help of his lord.

For his own part, Carrtog brought out a book on the subject of mechanical principals, which Gwaitorr had recommended to him.

When the bailiff finally made his appearance, the two packed up their books.

Carrtog spoke first. "Fforchan refuses to lend his hand to any smith-work involving steam engines and the like."

Lughan looked serious. "Do you intend to dismiss him, Lord?"

"Not hardly. He is a competent smith, and would be difficult to replace. No, I simply wish to hire a second smith, one who has no objection to building new-fangled machinery."

"I see. Am I to understand that you wish me to engage in hiring this new smith, Lord?"

"Yes."

"I see. I will begin to make inquiries immediately."

"Very good."

A WEEK AND A HALF LATER, before the bailiff's inquiries could have any success, another Royal Courier arrived. This time there was no doubt that his message was for Carrtog, and it read, "Lord Carrtog, your Sovereign requires your presence at his place in the city of Waliauchel. Please make your way here with appropriate haste."

It was signed by the king's hand and stamped with his seal.

"What do you think he means by "appropriate haste?" Carrtog wondered aloud.

"I believe he means you've been out lollygagging around your estate long enough, and it's time to come back and put yourself under his careful eye," Yakor said.

Carrtog nodded, smiling. "That's pretty much the way I read it. If he wanted us to rush, he'd have said 'immediately,' so I'd say we have some time to wind things up here before we go."

Addy had long been familiar with the king's attitudes, and it had required only a few words of explanation of Carrtog's specific situation for her to understand how matters stood.

She pursed her lips and frowned. "I'd seen things happen to other people, but nothing ever happened to anyone I knew well. Until now. And of course, nothing is happening now, either, nor will it likely happen unless some other event happens first. If you understand what I'm saying."

Yakor nodded his head briefly. "Yes, Lady, I believe we understand you very well. The king is not demanding our immediate presence, but we should not spend too much time on preparations. We should have our people begin packing as soon as feasible."

Carrtog had one of the servants fetch Gryff and when the young man arrived he seemed worried.

"You are worried, Gryff?"

"Ah—" the young man hesitated, then went on, swiftly. "The rumor among the servants is that you are summoned to return to Waliauchel, Lord. Does this mean I must return home?"

Carrtog's eyebrows went up. "Not unless you wish to. I will be continuing my work and studies when I return to the capital, and I will still need an assistant. Did you not wish to accompany me?"

"With all my heart, Lord. I had just thought that in the capital, you would be able to find an assistant who already knew reading, writing, and figuring, and would hardly need me."

"Gryff, barring some totally unforeseen circumstance, you need not concern yourself about being replaced. You will be my assistant for so long as you live, as far as I am concerned. You've shown the ability to learn quickly, which is the most important qualification for one in your position. I would greatly appreciate your willingness to come with me and continue to be my assistant. Besides, if I were to replace you with someone else, that person and I would have to begin all over again to get used to each other." He smiled. "You understand?"

"Yes, Lord." Gryff smiled, still a little diffidently.

BY THE TIME THEY WERE preparing to load the coach to go to the Railway Station, the bailiff had still not found a smith for Carrtog. He was apologetic about the matter, but Carrtog told him, "Don't bother yourself further about it. When I come to Waliauchel, I will seek a smith there."

THE RETURN TRIP WAS done in a less cheerful spirit; despite their parsing of the king's message as a nonthreatening one, they all knew quite well that there was a strong possibility that they could have been mistaken, or even that the king's temper might have changed for the worse since he sent the document.

They passed through the village of Harragush without incident this time. Carrtog, his mind moving through his concerns as to just what might be waiting for him back at the capital, only had a slight awareness that things were different, but did not comment on it.

It was Yakor who said, "They seem to have gotten past their fear for their charter."

Carrtog looked up at him sharply. "What do you mean?"

"The people of the village. They don't seem to care about us this time."

Carrtog glanced up and around at the village, and how the people were paying little attention at all to his party. "I see. Well, that's an improvement, isn't it?"

Yakor gave a brief smile. "So what was keeping your mind so busy, then?"

Carrtog had to laugh at himself, then. "I'd been wondering if I was right to be so easy about the king's summons."

"Huh!" The older man snorted. "You've already made your decision that the summons doesn't mean anything serious, and even if you're wrong, there's nothing you can do about it until you get to Waliauchel, so be easy and enjoy the trip."

ON THE TRAIN RIDE BACK, Carrtog did arrange to ride in the locomotive for a short way. The engineer, when approached as the man in charge and asked for a favor, proved willing to allow Carrtog, Gryff, and Addy to ride in the locomotive between two watering stops, and was quite willing to explain the controls and how they worked.

When they got back to their car, Carrtog turned to his three companions, "Now I hope we all enjoyed the experience as well as learned something from this."

Gryff said, quietly, "Yes, Lord."

Addy said, "I enjoyed it very much, though, he seemed to object to my asking questions."

Carrtog frowned. "There are some people who object to women doing anything save for what women have always done."

"At the very, very least, I can learn for my own satisfaction." Addy smiled, her face glowing with a newfound excitement.

Carrtog returned the smile, feeling suddenly that her beauty grew by the day the more of them he spent with her.

WHEN THEY PULLED INTO the station at Waliauchel, there was a small guard of twelve soldiers there to greet them. Carrtog's very first thought was that they were all under arrest, but the commander of the troop saluted and said, "Lord Carrtog, the king has commanded us to meet you and Lady Adengler, and to escort you to your quarters."

Carrtog returned the salute. "Thank you, captain."

His first thought was, at least if they're detaining us, they're detaining us in comfort.

Immediately after that he had to laugh at himself. No, the king was simply indicating that you're still in favor. No mention of detention has been made, so relax.

THINGS RETURNED TO something approaching what had previously been normal. That is, Enemantwin and Gwaitorr called on him to set up a new schedule of lessons.

Carrtog, having no desire to upset either or both of them, did not attempt to have Gryff included. So Carrtog continued to give lessons to the boy in private. He also undertook the purchase of a building for his own workshop and began furnishing it with tools and equipment. This he did a bit at a time, since the proper tools and equipment were at least moderately expensive, and Nandycargllwyd, while not impoverished, was not wealthy either.

Furthermore, he had to engage a smith. Gwaitorr favored that, since otherwise, for any of their smith-work, they had to hire a local smith at piece-work rates. If Carrtog was sufficiently well-off to engage a smith of his own, that would be one advantage.

"I would suggest, though," he said, "that you engage a smith on the understanding that he be allowed to take on piece-work for others, since we will not likely have sufficient work to keep him busy all the time. That way, he will not feel the necessity to charge you so steeply for his services."

"Thank you. I had not thought of such things."

The magician bowed. "Pleased to be of service, Lord."

YAKOR WENT BACK TO his casual intelligence gathering activities in the wine-shops and alehouses of the capital. 'Casual' meant that he was not digging for specific information, but that he kept his eyes and ears open for anything he thought might be important — or merely interesting — to Carrtog.

In fact, the first interesting — and important — piece of information came from Addy herself.

On the morning of the third day after they had returned from Nandycargllwyd, at the breakfast table, she announced, "Carrtog my dearest, I'm expecting!"

He looked at her waist. "Are you sure?"

She chuckled. "I'm not showing yet, but yes, I'm fairly sure. Do I understand from the look on your face that you're happy?"

"Happy? Oh, yes, I'm that, for certain. Do you feel all right?"

"Feel all right? Oh, my dearest, I'm expecting a baby, I'm not ill!"

"Is there anything I can do?"

That got another laugh. "You've already done your part, and quite well, too. I take care of the next part of the procedure, and in some months, you get to help with the raising of the child. Are you capable of that?"

He smiled. "Never having had a child to raise, I've never tried, so I don't know what sort of father I'll make. The best I can say, I suppose, is that I'll try. Will that do?"

"I will hold you to that, then."

THE NEWS ABOUT THE baby, though important to Carrtog and Adengler, was only of minor importance given what else was taking place in and around the capital. The fields were white with the tents of the army assembling to march North under the personal command of King Bornival intent on the reconquest of the North for Cragmor.

Food was becoming harder to come by, with the army not only requiring a huge amount to see to its daily needs, but also requiring massive amounts, either to be loaded into wagons to accompany the army, or else to be sent by rail along the proposed route to set up huge supply-magazines at certain towns on the way.

One thing that was not in short supply was prophecies regarding the coming war. These prophecies were, with very few exceptions, all positive, though some seemed to suggest that the king need only show his face at the head of his army and the Rebels would surrender en masse. To his credit, the king gave scant credence to such prophecies, but put rather more trust in prophecies that predicted a severe struggle before any success. Some few, of course, were totally negative, declaring that the king and all his great army would be lost in the mists of the north, never to return. Of those who predicted failure, a few did so in public only to be taken and hanged for spreading sedition.

Yakor's comment on one such was, "Could the man not predict what his fate would be? Or did he think that the king would reward him for foretelling disaster?"

Other such prophets were more cautious, tacking up their anonymous disastrous predictions on walls and disappearing into the crowds.

The king who was preparing his army to march seemed a different person from the one who had rushed and scrambled southward from Tenerack. This king seemed almost calm and poised, ready to listen to his advisors, but still able to make a firm decision for himself when the time came.

Yakor, in private talks with Carrtog, said, "I don't believe this is the real king. If real trouble comes, I'm afraid we'll see the same king come forth, the one who scampered away from Tenerack, leaving behind some loyal soldiers whose only fault was to be so badly wounded as to slow his flight. I'm afraid that we will only survive because he's afraid we might hint at his actual behavior, and so he will insist on leaving us back here in the city. It will also be certain that he'll have people around to listen to every word we might say, just in case we say the wrong things. So you make sure you guard your tongue, and you might also speak a warning to Lady Adengler, though I think she can be depended on to be careful."

"Yakor, my trusted advisor, remember that she has served as lady-in-waiting to the Princess Ellevar for a good many years; I think if I were to have the nerve to warn her about the king's changeable moods, she would fetch me a clout around the ears. And I'd deserve it."

Yakor smiled a twisted little smile of embarrassment. "My apologies to you and the Lady Adengler. I'm afraid I'm a little too cautious about this situation we find ourselves in. And perhaps I sometimes fail to realize that you are no longer the rash and careless boy that rode out from Tsingallik a year and more ago."

Chapter 15

On the second day preceding the king's departure with his army, he summoned Carrtog for a meeting. He started off immediately with the reason for the meeting. "Lord Carrtog, I am leaving you here in the capital with a specific task, to ensure the safety of my daughter, Ellevar. Yes, she has a particular force of guards who are responsible for her well-being. You, however, will serve as a sort of second line of defense. You will not be under the command of the captain of the guards, nor will you command them, but I would wish that both of you would be willing to consult one with the other if you think of anything that the other might need to know. You may wonder why I have insisted you have more training in magic; this is the reason. The guards may well be able to fight any attacks by normal means, with ordinary weapons. You, I hope, may be able to defend if magic should be used. Indeed, you may use your magic even against nonmagical foes, at your discretion."

The king paused, and smiled. "If the Gods favor us, you will not be called upon to do anything, only stay here and be alert until I return. However, it is much better to be ready and not be needed than not to be ready in a sudden desperate time of need. Do you have any questions?"

"No, I think not, Your Majesty."

CARRTOG WAS STILL FUMING when he talked to Yakor. "I knew he'd try to use the advancement of my magic lessons as a reason to leave me behind. Now he adds in this duty for me, to make it almost seem another part of his reward to me!"

"And so it is. But remember that he's going to make you a more competent magician, something that has to be counted as good."

"But you will remember how some of the lords at my investment were less than half-willing to have me among their numbers. Some of those will be happy to tell anyone who'll listen that I took advantage of the king's favor to stay out of danger instead of marching North."

Yakor gave him a ferocious frown. "Now there is the boy afraid that his reputation will suffer because he's the one left behind to look after the herds while his elders go out on a cattle raid! For sure and certain, that boy will not likely face any danger staying back home, but he doesn't consider that there will be more than one cattle raid to come in the future, when he will indeed be old enough, and most likely face danger enough and to spare!

"Enjoy your time at home with your new wife, and think that, barring some great misfortune, you will be alive to see your first child born." The older man waved a hand toward the unseen tents beyond the walls. "There is more than a few out there who have left a pregnant wife behind, and will never come home to see that new child. So put on a smile, or I'll have to thump that solid skull of ours a time or two again."

Carrtog looked at Yakor's face and realized two things; first, that the man was right, he was fortunate, and second, that the man was indeed capable of thumping his skull, though he hadn't done it in a few years.

He pushed a smile onto his face and said, "You're right, I'm too fortunate to be complaining, and for another thing, I don't think I'd like to have to explain to Addy why I suddenly come to dinner with several extra lumps on my head."

KING BORNIVAL RODE off at the head of his army to reconquer the North. To be more precise, the king rode off at the head of a large section of his army, while another part of his Army was sent off by railroad to assemble further up along the track.

"Several highly competent mathematicians have spent a good deal of time," Gwaitorr said, "working out the schedules of how far up the railway they will set up the first assembly point, and where and when the trains will meet the marching Army to load further troops to take up to that advance point. They were also required to work out the amounts of food required to be loaded with each train-load of troops, plus the amount of fuel needed to power the trains on their various journeys. There were also the things that could only be guessed at, such as the number of cars, or even worse, locomotives which might break down and require repair, or perhaps replacement. But all this enables the king to advance a larger number of supplied troops for a greater distance than they could march on foot. I hope this serves to demonstrate the usefulness of modern mechanical methods for warfare, Lord Carrtog."

Carrtog nodded. "It does indeed. And it also seems to indicate that generals will need to be more accomplished mathematicians, whereas they previously used to employ inspired guesswork to work out march routes and situation of supply-magazines."

The magician gave him a sharp glance. "Very true; in fact, probably more true than you realize."

When the king had taken his Army off northward, he left the city and its environs seemingly deserted. All the tents that had surrounded the city had been struck, packed up, and sent off, leaving that patch around the city with the grass flattened and, in some places, worn away to bare earth.

The rest of the city began to fall back into the habitual patterns of behavior and Carrtog turned his mind back to his growing engineering passion.

Carrtog had asked Yakor to try to find him a smith, one who would be willing to work on steam engines and other 'new-fangled' notions, and it wasn't long before his man-at-arms delivered.

The smith proved to be a short and stocky man by the name of Fflanaval who had no problem with novel smith-work and, in fact, was somewhat intrigued with some of the notions Carrtog suggested to him.

Rather than build or rent another building for a work-shed, Carrtog made arrangements to use the same premises that Gwaitorr and Enemantwin used for his lessons and their work-shed. With the decision to use the same work-shed came the inevitable need to fit Gryff into the equation. Gwaitorr was not entirely pleased with the thought of a farmer's son being taught mechanics, but the king would be less than pleased if Gwaitorr ceased training Carrtog and since Carrtog was determined that he himself would pass on his lessons to Gryff regardless, the tutor capitulated. Gryff wasn't much interested in learning magic, but since there were some elements of mechanics — as Gwaitorr taught them — which involved spellcraft, he learned at least that much magic. Carrtog found that having to teach Gryff the lessons up to the point where they were at least near to even footing was useful in that it reinforced his own knowledge.

And so, with the aid of Fflanaval, it wasn't long before they'd built a small steam engine. On the day when they successfully fired it up, they sat around with a cup of wine in modest celebration.

"The next thing to do," Carrtog said, "is to attach it to something, such as a wagon, or the like."

"That can be done, Lord?" asked Gryff, there was a glint of eagerness in his eyes that Carrtog made passing note of.

"I believe it can be done, though just how it can be done will likely take some testing and trying. Though, first I would like to find a way to launch a glider using a steam engine, other than by train of course; I have little desire to repeat that particular experience."

Gryff stared at him wide-eyed. Perhaps he had forgotten that Carrtog had been present at that disastrous attempt at kidnapping the king.

Gwaitorr snorted, "I'm surprised you would even want to build gliders at all after an experience such as that."

"Truth be told, the flight itself was quite invigorating. I would not be averse to trying it again, though, perhaps with more success and less risk of certain death. The smiths of Tsingallik have already begun experimenting with gliders, launching them by a drawn winch connected to a steam engine, but it seems the engines do not produce enough force to create the necessary speed on the winch. It is my thought to create a steam engine of higher pressure that might perform the task."

Gwaitorr frowned. "With that comes greater risk to the engineer."

"Just so. There must be a way to fold or seam the pieces to improve strength by design, but I have not yet come upon the answer." As he said it he knew that it was not quite true, it had already occurred to him that the answer perhaps lay in the spell Enemantwin had taught him about turning wood into near-iron. If he could alter the spell, perhaps by adding additional effects, then maybe the results could be stronger, but less brittle, than iron; metal made, so to speak, to taste.

All these endeavors kept Carrtog busy, busy enough not to worry excessively about the rumors that had been growing about the king's flight from Tenerack. The worst of those describing how the king had chosen to abandon his wounded men to be slaughtered in their beds by the rebels.

As Yakor had predicted, most people of good sense did answer those tales by asking whether the king ought to have stayed to be slaughtered with those wounded men, or even worse, to be taken prisoner and held to ransom.

But a more insidious tale began to make the rounds, in the form of another pair of questions: Had not the king himself decided to take only what amounted to a token force of his Gentlemen up to Tenerack, so as to demonstrate his peaceful intentions? How was it then the fault of Captain Gwailants? And since the man could no longer speak for himself, was that not just a convenient place for the blame to lie?

Carrtog seldom went out among the people who would say such things, and Yakor, known as Carrtog's man, did not involve himself in such conversations, so they hoped that whatever reaction the king made would not touch them, though Carrtog kept a stock of money at hand in case sudden flight was necessary.

REPORTS OF THE PROGRESS of the King's Army were not continuous at first, but they did come down from time to time. There was a report, with moderate rejoicing, when the whole Army had reached the point where the first magazine beyond the Northern Border had been set up, a town by the name of Kilgarhai.

Some skirmishing was reported when the Army moved north from there, but the Rebels did not seem to be at all determined to fight a real battle just yet. People who recalled the fate of General Malgwyn suggested that the rebel leadership might well follow the previously successful strategy, to lead the King's Army far north, stretch their supply-lines, and at the end attempt an ambush of some sort.

The officer in charge of the garrison of the capital began to send trainloads of supplies up to the supply depot at Kilgarhai. The continual train traffic between the garrison and the supply-depots meant that news from the North began flowing readily. Part of the news came in the form of official news reports, stating that the Army was pushing the rebels steadily northward, still with only occasional skirmishes, but no serious battles. While other reports spoke of attempts by small irregular forces of rebels to cut the railway lines, both south of Kilgarhai and to the north, though General Hartovan and the garrison at Kilgarhai prevented all but minor damage.

"Actually," Yakor told Carrtog, Gryff, and Addy, "Things aren't quite so sunny as the official reports say. The rebels are retreating, that is certain, but the King's Army is taking more casualties in these skirmishes than the rebels. That is shown by the near constant requests for reinforcements. Also, General Hartovan isn't completely successful in keeping the rebels away from the tracks. Talk to the train-crews, and look at the constant requests for new rails and railroad ties."

He raised a finger. "Don't talk to anyone about that. Lord Carrtog, Lady Adengler, I know you won't be saying anything in the wrong places, but Gryff, take this as a warning. It may make you feel good to know something that none of your companions know, but if the wrong person hears it, or someone you tell merely repeats it in the hearing of that wrong person, it could end in all of us being arrested for sedition. You understand?"

Gryff, a serious, almost frightened, look on his face, nodded.

Chapter 16

PROCLAMATION!
Let it be known to the citizens of Cragmor, and in particular to the citizens of the capital. Whereinas it has come to the attention of His Majesty the King that seditious statements have been made and passed by word of mouth among the citizens and that such statements may well be prejudicial to the well-being of the kingdom.

It is therefore commanded that utterance of such statements shall be considered an offense against the Crown, and shall be punishable by a term of imprisonment, or death by hanging, according to the decision of the court.

CARRTOG STOOD BESIDE Yakor reading the broadsheet posted on the outside wall of the inn. Somewhere off in the distance, they could hear the ringing of the town crier's bell, along with his shout. Although his words could not be distinguished, they were essentially the same words as were written on the proclamation.

Yakor spat on the ground. "Well, there'll be some damn fools get their necks stretched. Most people will just be really careful who they open their mouths to. Other than that, not much will change."

"We hope." Carrtog responded. "If His Majesty starts worrying too much about the kinds of things I might say regarding the trip south from Tenerack, he might decide to do something about me beforehand. I wouldn't be the first hero to fall from glory."

Yakor spat again. "That's true, of course."

"SO THAT'S IT, MY LOVE," Carrtog told Addy. "There's a possibility that the king will blame all or some of these stories on me. If that happens, he may not have me hanged, given that I did save the princess, but on the other hand, what would be better show that he was utterly serious about stamping out sedition than to hang the man he'd previously declared a hero, and one of his favorites? If that happens, I've made plans to flee the country, much though I dislike the notion. The first part, at least, would be rough and uncomfortable, much like our jaunt down from Tenerack. I'm considering leaving you behind and possibly sending for you later. The princess might not be able to help me if the king were to take it into his head to do away with me, but she'd probably be able to shield you."

Addy stood up straight, and her expression turned grim. "Is this the situation my mother warned me about, a man getting me pregnant and then going off and leaving me and the child alone?"

"No!" Carrtog protested, "It's nothing like that at all! I'm just trying to think of what's best for you!" He was wondering if this were one of those strange moods pregnant women sometimes got; surely she couldn't think this was all part of some convoluted plot to desert her? After all, he'd married her before he'd got her pregnant.

"Of course, I'm not trying to run off on you! I'm just thinking of your welfare! If we have to flee the country with you in your condition, it'll be terribly hard on you. I wouldn't want to put you through that."

"So you say!" she declared, her face stiff with anger. Suddenly her wrathful expression dissolved, and she began to laugh. "Oh Carrtog, my love, I'm sorry, I just couldn't resist the opportunity to tease you! But my dearest dear, surely you don't think I'd agree to let you go off without me — without us." She put a hand on her swollen middle. "If you tried, you'd find me coming after you, running as hard as I could waddle. And you wouldn't put me to that nasty trouble, would you?"

Carrtog took a deep breath, then allowed himself to laugh a bit, too. "All right," he said, "but I think I'm going to have to insist that you stop that sort of teasing. I was beginning to worry about you having your father coming after me for desertion."

She was still grinning. "Oh, but if I made that sort of promise, what could I do for amusement? Well, I suppose I could promise not to overdo it, or do it too often. Would that do?"

He wrapped his arms around her. "No," he said. "I certainly wouldn't want to make life too difficult for you. Yes, I suppose I can put up with it from time to time. Now if our first child is a girl and she grows up capable of copying her mother, her poor father will certainly be in dire straits!"

PRINCESS ELLEVAR HAD invited Carrtog and Adengler to join her for dinner. It had been a small and intimate affair, just the three of them along with one lady-in-waiting, and when it was done, the princess asked Carrtog and Adengler to stay for a glass of wine.

The wine was poured, the first few sips drunk, and some casual conversation undertaken, then the princess took a deep breath and spoke.

"You will most certainly have seen and heard the proclamation regarding seditious talk?"

"Yes, indeed." Carrtog wondered where this was leading.

The princess nodded. "My Da— my father has his faults, among them a too-serious fear for his reputation, which leads him to take strong measures to protect that reputation. He often fails to

understand that those same strong measures can do the opposite to
what he wishes."

She paused. "You may think he has deluded himself as to what
happened on the flight from Tenerack. He knows altogether too well
what happened, but knows that the truth will harm his reputation,
so he insists that the truth is otherwise than what it really is. He
also knows that you two, and Yakor, know what really happened as
well. In his letters to me he wonders if you might have confirmed
the present rumors, even if you weren't the original author of those
stories."

She paused again. "I have written to him, assuring him that you
had nothing to do with these tales, and I hope he will believe me. My
greatest concern, though, is that he will begin to feel that I am merely
protecting you because you saved my life. Ironic, isn't it, that the very
reason why you have the position you've gained is the same reason
that might convince him that I'm misleading him in order to protect
you from his anger?"

"I suppose it does no good at all to assure you that I have no
interest at all in gossiping?"

"None whatsoever. The one you have to assure is my father, and
even mentioning it reminds him that you were indeed there and
could, if you wished, do serious harm to his reputation. For him,
that means that you probably would do so, out of jealousy or mere
annoyance, which could well lead him to take action, hoping to
prevent you from doing so.

"When next I write to him I will tell him I have had a talk
with you, with both of you, Addy, about the danger of rumors. I can
hope he will read that as me warning you seriously against spreading
rumors." She held up a finger, smiling, "Not that I really feel you
need to be warned, but if he hears me say so, and if his spies in the
household tell him that we had dinner, followed by a private talk,

without the presence of servants, it may well ease his mind on the subject."

Carrtog smiled, "Thank you, Highness."

"Carrtog, you saved my life. The least I can do is try very hard to protect you from my father's ill-founded suspicions. And now, Addy, how are you doing?"

For the next short time, which seemed an eternity to Carrtog, he sat there uneasily while Princess Ellevar and Addy discussed the symptoms of his wife's pregnancy. The only redeeming fact of the conversation, so far as he could understand, was that everything seemed to be going well with her.

When they had covered everything they knew for a fact and all the (sometimes contradictory) notions the midwives proclaimed, the princess turned to Carrtog and smiled. "I'm sorry," she said, "I'm sure you didn't want to know all that, Carrtog, but it was important to Addy, and thus to me as a friend of hers. I hope you weren't too disturbed by it."

"Not at all, Highness," lied Carrtog, valiantly. "If it's important to my wife, it must be important to me."

Shortly thereafter, they took their leave of the princess and went back to their quarters. On their way, Carrtog heard Addy snicker. "Share the humor, please, my dear Lady."

She snickered again. "'If it's important to my wife, it must be important to me.' How nicely you lie to the princess, Lord Carrtog."

He found himself capable of chuckling. "I should have told the truth and had two ladies angry with me? In particular, one lady who separates me by one short annoyed note to her father from serious trouble? No, you need not look around with that worried look; I was sure no-one was within hearing before I said that."

YAKOR WAS VERY INTERESTED to hear of the night's conversation (less the discussion of the pregnancy).

"Her Highness is perhaps a little overconfident of her ability to sway her father if he should begin to suspect the previously so heroic Lord Carrtog of spreading sedition."

Adengler frowned. "She makes no promises, save that she'll try her best. And truly, Yakor, the princess can sway the king, sometimes beyond what one might expect."

Yakor sat still for a moment looking at her, and Carrtog hoped he wasn't about to tell her that 'loyalty to a friend was fine, but it wouldn't help much when the noose went around her husband's neck.'

When he spoke, though, it was only to say, "Well. We'll all hope it turns out for the good, but in the meantime, we'll all keep our eyes open."

THE NEXT DAY YAKOR came in with news. "The railway line has been cut at several places south of Kilgarhai. They say the irregular rebel forces are running free up there, while General Hartovan flails around wildly, accomplishing little or nothing."

"What of the main Army?" Carrtog asked.

"So far as anyone can discover, the king is still marching northward, skirmishing at every river-crossing, but still pushing on. Most recently, the commander of the capital garrison has stopped sending up troops in anything less than regimental size, and when they go, they carry weapons and ammunition. Does that suggest anything to you?"

"That those same irregular forces of rebels that are playing hob with General Hartovan's railway line are doing much the same with His Majesty's even longer supply-lines."

Yakor grinned fiercely. "He's been paying attention to more things than building steam engines and other sorts of strange mechanisms!" He glanced around to make sure that no one was near enough to hear, before continuing. "Yes, indeed. And we can only hope that His Majesty is paying attention as well and paying heed to his officers' advice. If he's not careful, he might end up in the same situation as Malgwyn did. And if that happens, I doubt Cragmor would be able to get another army together. And that would be the end of the expanded kingdom."

"Likely worse than that," Carrtog said. "Some of our larger lords might just think it was time they promoted themselves, and we'd be seeing a civil war until some one of them ended up on top. One might even see whoever's the head of the rebels up there coming down to take over a few parts of Cragmor. And that would be a fine irony, wouldn't it?"

Yakor spat on the ground. "A fine irony indeed."

DAYS WENT BY.

Suddenly the city was abuzz with a new report. The king, it was said, was withdrawing his army southward, without having fought any major battle. The explanation given was that it would be difficult to feed the Royal Army so far in the north, especially with the northern winter coming on.

"They say that the Army's going to be foraging as it comes, partly to build up the supplies at whatever place they decide to winter, and partly to punish the rebels by leaving them hungry this winter." Yakor paused. "I'd say it's the kind of plan the king would come up with, or at least give his wholehearted blessing to. Those people not only endangered him at Tenerack, they led him way up there, hoping to spring some kind of trap on him. So let them starve!"

Carrtog nodded. Rumour said that the king had given orders to have any captured railway engineers executed out of hand. Apparently he was making good on his threat made on the trip south from Tenerack.

After a moment, he spoke aloud. "I wonder if he'll winter in the north, or come all the way down to the capital."

Yakor shrugged. "Myself, I'd wager on him coming all the way down. I have a feeling the events of Tenerack left him ill-disposed toward the notion of winter in the North."

Chapter 17

A week later, a messenger came from the princess asking Carrtog and Adengler to join her for dinner once more. There were only the three of them and the meal was a simple one. Conversation over dinner was light, mostly involving the work that Carrtog and Gryff were engaged in. The princess was greatly interested in the small gliders they were planning during the times when they were, as Carrtog put it, "resting from working on steam engines."

"It's only a small thing," the princess said. "When you do get it flying, what will you use it for?"

"I'm hoping," Carrtog said, "that we can control it by magic and use it for sending messages, and perhaps even small packages, over considerable distances."

"And how close are you to success at present?"

"We have a number of drawings on paper right now. We're fairly confident that any one of them could fly; we'll try one of them as soon as we've got a way to launch them into the air. My hope is that our work with the steam engines will provide our answer to that problem."

"That's fascinating. Only — I almost feel I should be apologizing to you, because my father's magicians seem to have made your small glider out of date before it's built. My father's magicians have been working at a process of magically sending messages over great distances."

Carrtog smiled. "No apology is needed, Highness. My glider will not only carry written messages, but small packages, depending on the size of the glider. Indeed, it is even possible that I will never get the glider to be more than a nice idea on several pieces of paper. It would be better for the kingdom if long distance messaging would be set into motion long before that."

The princess smiled, "Set into motion indeed. They have had sufficient success that they have just yesterday evening sent a message to the garrison commander here to inform him that the king intends to winter here in Waliauchel. We are to make ready for his arrival."

"Are we to spread the word ourselves, Your Highness?" asked Carrtog.

"No, I think that would not be for the best if you were to spread abroad word that I gave you in private, particularly in light of the difficulty we have had of rumors running round the capital. The garrison commander will make the announcement when he sees fit. In the meantime, you may tell the immediate members of your household, insomuch as you can trust them not to spread the word further. I believe, for instance, that your man Yakor can be counted on to keep his own council."

"Agreed, Your Highness. Nothing will be said until the garrison commander makes his announcement."

"Thank you, Carrtog. Now," The princess wore a grim expression, "Perhaps we should retire to the drawing room, there is other more concerning news."

When they moved to the drawing room and settled with their wine, she spoke seriously, almost angrily. "It would seem that someone is determined to cause trouble in the kingdom. The town-tales continue to be more and more provoking, to the point that my father is not going to be able to ignore them, even though that would really be the best thing. What I fear, Carrtog, is that he will blame you for this latest, even though it is hard to see what you might gain from it. The tale speculates that there were five surviving Gentlemen from the original men my father took to Tenerack with him and that they were discharged quietly and without cause only to disappear shortly after. The rumor claims that these men must have known something about the flight from Tenerack, something that reflected badly on my father to the point that he desired them not only removed, but dealt with after their dismissal. The first fact, that there were five of the King's Gentlemen who survived the flight from Tenerack, is true, as is the second fact, that they were discharged without cause. I will even admit, here, to you, that if they had told their stories, they might well have cast the king's behavior in a bad light. Neither my father nor I know where those men have gone, and I suppose, for their own safety — if they are indeed innocent — it is best if that remains as such. My concern is that this information has come to light now."

She looked at the two of them. "It is just the kind of thing that the rebels, were they aware of it, might pass around to ruin the morale of the nation's army."

"You're right," Carrtog agreed. "I wonder if Rhadfel Llorsan up there is shrewd enough to have looked at matters down here and come up with just this notion. For my part, I feel somewhat uneasy."

He stopped there, abruptly, and the princess looked at him suddenly, her expression softening. "Yes, I know. He's my father, and I love him, but I know his faults. And indeed, some of his actions coming down from Tenerack do not reflect highly on him. And he will know, just as well as we all know, that you are aware of those actions, and even though confirming those same things would be counter to your own interests, he might fear that you would not be able to deny them sufficiently firmly. But Carrtog, I do remember that it was you who flung me onto the back of your horse and sent us rushing off to safety, staying behind to hamper the pursuit. I believe that, even if my father does decide to punish you, I can remind him of that sufficiently strongly to make him ameliorate whatever punishment he has settled on."

Carrtog bowed, a seated bow, toward the princess. "Thank you, Your Highness. We can hope, however, that matters will not come to that point."

"SO," YAKOR SAID, "HIS Majesty prefers to spend the winter in the comfort of his capital?"

"So it would seem. Personally, I wonder if part of his plan is to come back and step down hard on all the rumors."

Yakor looked up at him sharply. "You think so?"

Carrtog shrugged. "I make no claim to be able to know what is in the king's mind. It just seems, knowing the little I do about him, that this might not be the furthest thing from his mind."

Yakor thought a while, then said, "Yes, it seems to me that he might well have some sort of notion that his presence alone might make the rumor-mongers beware."

A WEEK LATER THERE was a sudden clear chime in the drawing room where Carrtog and Addy sat reading. They looked over to the side-table where a small crystal circlet sat, giving off a soft flashing green light, then Carrtog looked at Addy. "Aha!" He said. "Apparently it works."

"Apparently so," she answered as he got up and went over to touch it.

He had not said anything to the princess about it, because they were still testing it, but he had built, under Enemantwin's instruction, a small device to be used for communicating over moderate distances.

"What does he have to say?" Addy asked.

Carrtog did not answer, but instead spoke toward the circlet. "Yakor?"

"Lord Carrtog?"

"What is it?"

"A courier has just passed through the gates. It seems the king will be arriving in three days time. I suggest you determine how you plan to meet him."

THE KING CAME IN THROUGH the main gate of Waliauchel at the head of four regiments of his army, more than sufficient to keep him safe on the journey from Kilgarhai to the capital.

The citizens turned out in force to welcome the king back from the field. Lord Carrtog and Lady Adengler came out in their coach, seated among those of the nobility who decided to make their presence known. Some nobles, though they were in the capital at the time, felt safe enough in their status that they did not bother. These were the ones who were sufficiently powerful that they were quite sure that any move of the king against them would set the others of their class up in arms against him, on the ground that they might be next.

Carrtog, with his allocation of seventy-five men under arms, was definitely not in that class. There was, however, one reason why he perhaps ought not to have come; if King Bornival had heard the latest round of town-tales, the sight of Carrtog might just enrage him. Carrtog had taken the precaution of sending Yakor into hiding, with sufficient preparations to be able get his lord free, either by paying fines or bribes or other means.

The king's entrance, however, passed off uneventfully, the king not even seeming to notice Carrtog. When the monarch had gone by, Carrtog turned to Addy and said, "Some might consider themselves snubbed by this; I hope you don't mind if I feel relieved."

"I agree," she said, smiling. "But remember, there is still a good deal of time yet for him to decide he's offended. In fact, he may not yet have heard the latest story."

"Unfortunately, you're right. Well, the other coaches are beginning to move; we'd best be getting out of here ourselves."

TWO WEEKS AFTER THE king had marched in through the front gate of the city, he sent a message summoning Carrtog to meet him. "Well," he said to Addy, "At least he just asked me to come, he didn't send a group of guards to make sure I did. I'd say that was a good sign."

"If you're not back by tonight, I'll call Yakor."

He kissed her lightly. "Try not to fret too much while I'm gone, dearest."

THE KING SEEMED TO be in a good mood when he met Carrtog.

"Good afternoon to you, Lord Carrtog. My daughter is a very profuse correspondent, and from her writings, I understand that affairs here in Waliauchel have been mostly quiet during my absence."

"Yes, Your Majesty, that seems true." If one sets aside what almost seems like a campaign of sedition carried out by alehouse and wine-shop rumor.

The king frowned. "I am less than happy about what seems to be a concentrated campaign of vicious rumors aimed at myself."

Uh-oh! Here it comes!

"Be assured," the king continued, "I shall bend all efforts towards tracking down the authors of these stories and having them punished severely."

Carrtog sat silent, wondering why the king was telling him all this.

"That aside, I have another task for you, Lord Carrtog. First of all, how far have your magical studies advanced?"

"Quite well, Your Majesty." He smiled. "I have discovered, however, that no matter how far I advance, there seems much more to learn."

"But your abilities are better than when you started?"

"Yes, Your Majesty, I can definitely say that."

"Good. In that case, I will set you in charge of the munitions depot at Kilgarhai."

"Your Majesty has great faith in my ability."

The monarch dismissed that with a wave of his hand. "You have already demonstrated your ability during the journey from Tenerack, and you have spent several months studying to be better. Take a week or so to decide what you will wish to take along with you and what preparations you wish to make, and I shall talk to you again to decide when you shall leave."

"Thank you, Your Majesty."

"YOU UNDERSTAND WHAT His Majesty is doing, of course?" inquired Yakor.

"I believe so. His thoughts might follow along the line of: 'General Hartovan was unable to keep the railroad to Kilgarhai open. We're not sure if Lord Carrtog was responsible for the latest round of town-tales, but we worry about what he might say if someone asks him about the truth of those stories. So if we put Lord Carrtog in charge of Kilgarhai, we can expect that he will have as little success as General Hartovan, and then we can retire him in disgrace, and be rid of him.'"

Yakor smiled grimly. "And if the stories continue, we can accuse the embittered Lord Carrtog of spreading such tales to revenge himself on the king who gave him an impossible task to do."

Carrtog nodded. "My best course of action, then, is to succeed where General Hartovan could not. One of the first things I ought to do is to read as many reports as I can gather from General Hartovan regarding his methods. And if I am able, I'd like to find some lower officers to give me some notion as to what the situation was like out amongst the people."

FFILIVAR WAS A VERY minor lord, having just come into his inheritance. He was a year or two short of Carrtog's age, short, stocky, and with a muscular build. He had a large round face, with large features to go with it, though his nose was short and upturned. His hair, including the beard that was beginning to dominate the lower part of his face, was a dark red.

"You ask how matters went among the citizens of Kilgarhai and the region, Lord Carrtog? They went badly, that's how they went. The people up there hate the king, and they hate the king's soldiers. There wasn't much outright hostile action, save now and again when too much wine was involved, but any time they did what we required of them, it was done grudgingly, and often as not, poorly done. All too often, anything the general ordered done had to be redone later by soldiers, which was not the best use of soldiers.

"We knew, Lord Carrtog, that they surreptitiously aided the irregular bands of rebels, though we could seldom prove it; they were usually too careful for that. There was even a case or two of irregulars living in the town itself, but seldom were they that brazen.

"The merchants were quite willing to sell to us, and though the prices were higher, the goods were mostly of good quality. That was the limit of their cooperation with us, Lord Carrtog."

He paused to take a sip of the wine Carrtog had provided for him. "You needn't address me by title all the time, Ffilivar; I know that the tables of precedence have me somewhere above you, but that is only because my title is the result of one particular action. Other than that, we are near enough the same age. So what of the irregular actions? What sort of things did those irregulars do, and how were they supplied?"

"They were supplied by the town, and by the local farmstead-holders, though of course there was seldom any proof. After we burned the first two or three farmsteads, they stopped coming in numbers to any one farmstead, but would send one or two to collect whatever any selected farmstead could afford. They never came in numbers to the town, nor were the people who came ever obviously fighters. They didn't take any great amounts of anything, either, but a time or three we found stocks of the sorts of things a fighting band might need, concealed in the woods on the edge of town. Several times we were able to take the men who came to collect the provisions, but mostly they had some method of telling that we were watching."

"Did anyone try magic to watch the supply-sites?"

"It was tried. Somehow, they seemed able to detect the magic, and they never approached those positions. On the other hand, several times they attempted to hide the supply-sites by magic, but our own military magicians were able to detect them by the presence of the magic itself." He looked at Carrtog. "You being something of a magician yourself, you probably understand that one better than I, but it seemed strange to me that a spell intended to hide something gave away the presence of the thing it was hiding."

Carrtog smiled. "That is one of the constant contests going on between opposing magicians, to hide the presence of a spell versus to reveal the existence of that spell. Of course, you wouldn't have known of the times when their magical hiding of the sites was successful."

Ffilivar's eyes widened as he realized what Carrtog was telling him.

"Of course!" an expression of chagrin came over his face. "I wonder how many we missed?"

Carrtog smiled. "Let me assure you, General Hartovan's magicians were undoubtedly aware of the fact that the rebels had accomplished magicians and were doing their very best to track down all traces of hidden spells, just as the rebels were working at disguising their spells of concealment. For certain, they missed some, but they found some as well."

Ffilivar's expression took on a little more ease. "Too much complexity for a soldier used only to handling sword and pistol. May you have better luck with the matter, Lord Carrtog."

"Inasmuch as it is a matter of luck, I thank you, Ffilivar. I hope to arrange things so that luck is no longer so large a part of the affair."

"WELL, MY DEAREST LOVE, I so dislike the thought of going all the way up there and leaving you behind." Carrtog embraced Addy, who was by now very much of an armful.

"Then why do you?"

Carrtog pulled back and looked at her. "I've been ordered to go, and I can hardly refuse—" he began.

"No!" she interrupted. "I know you have no choice, but why do you leave me behind? It is not as if you were marching off to be at the front of battle, but you are marching off to command the garrison of what is probably a town of some size. For certain there must be some place up there where you can rent us a house for the duration of our stay. For all of that, you might well build us a small house for the time, and then sell it when we leave."

He held still a moment, looking at her. "Addy, my love, this is not a nice friendly little town, this is a place where the people either dislike us, or downright hate us."

"On the other hand, Carrtog, my love, while you are not marching away to battle, you will, if I know you at all, be leading your troops out on occasion, and quite possibly to battle, and deaths happen in a skirmish of two-score just as likely as in battles of two hundred thousand." She patted her abdomen. "And this child of mine will be born this winter. It would be sad if he were to be born and never have the chance to see his father."

"And it would be sad indeed for his mother to be killed by some overzealous northern scoundrel simply because she happened to be married to the commander of the royalist enemies."

Now she stiffened and pushed herself back from him. "So you say, and so I say, and I will tell you, my most dear husband and father of our child, that if you somehow keep me locked away so that I cannot come with you, I will escape and follow you. I make this suggestion to you, that you take me and our child along with us, to save the three of us all this added fuss and bother."

Carrtog put his palms softly on her shoulders and said, "Addy, my dear, I am sure you are telling me no less than the truth, so be easy. I will take you along, and I will set Yakor to watch over you, and I pity that supposed northern scoundrel who dares to give serious thought to harming either you or our child. Will that make your mind easier?"

She smiled in return and replied, "Yes, indeed. It will until the next time you think of another such ridiculous notion."

"PERHAPS IN TIME YOU will come to see the futility of arguing with Lady Adengler," Yakor commented.

Carrtog grinned ruefully. "Perhaps I will. After all, I've stopped knocking my head against trees, haven't I?"

"Have you, then? I hadn't noticed."

AT LAST, CARRTOG AND his party were ready to leave. Since the party included only a few troops, Carrtog decided to take the train as far as the border. He took his leave of the king in the palace.

The king was dressed in some of his more colorful clothing, his royal kilt, of course, with matching stockings, a red vest, trimmed with black, and a dark blue cloak, trimmed with ermine. The king raised his right hand.

"Go forth in my name, Lord Carrtog, and may the Gods go with you. May they grant you success in all your ventures, and may you return victorious."

"Thank you, Your Majesty, and may the Gods grant our requests, and may they show favor to you all your days."

"Go, then, Lord Carrtog."

Carrtog and the small party with him bowed, then turned and went out the palace gates.

Chapter 18

Winter was setting in, which made the trip to the frontier a tedious journey. The carriages were provided with small stoves in an attempt to render the cold a little more tolerable. Even so, those who understood the nature of steam locomotion envied the crew who had their station next to the great boiler. The passengers dressed in layers of the warmest clothing they had and huddled in groups as near to the stoves as they could manage.

Carrtog could tell that Addy was suffering badly, but she gave no sign of it, undoubtedly keeping in mind how determined she had been to accompany him on this journey. He cast a small spell to increase the warmth of her clothing. He didn't want to do anything too obvious, since even he could not keep all the passengers in this car warm all the way without wearing himself down and leaving him unable to do any magic at all should the necessity arise. It was entirely possible that the rebels might make an attempt on him and his people even before they reached the border, if only to embarrass him at the very beginning of his campaign.

If the rebels had any success at all, he might find that difficult to overcome.

In the event, Carrtog's party reached the little border town of Gwarasai with no attacks, not even any attempt at blocking or tearing up the tracks. Carrtog had decided to march from there to Kilgarhai, on the grounds that the train was a very large target and might be attacked simply by removing or cutting one rail on the track.

However, when they arrived at Gwarasai, they found there a small party of horsemen from Kilgarhai, under the command of a long lean man who introduced himself as Boroddai.

"We're patrolling the track between here and Kilgarhai, Lord Carrtog," he said. "The general has a small troop come out three times a day, and rest for a bit here, then ride back. It means a lot of men out riding, but it makes it nigh impossible for the Northies to come out and make a hole in the track unseen."

"Good work, Captain Boroddai. Of course, I have not yet arrived at Kilgarhai, let alone taken up the command. Tell me, this train that has just arrived and is preparing to continue on to Kilgarhai, is it likely to arrive safely?"

"Well, Lord Carrtog, that depends. The party that preceded us along the way, it has already started back an hour or so ago. If the train manages to keep its schedule, it should catch up that party about halfway along. Somewhat past that point, the train should meet the next party coming down. If the general and his aides have planned matters carefully enough, the Northies won't've had time to do anything to the track."

"Captain, I have no right to command you, not even to ask a favor, but would you object if I rode back with you, just to see how things go? If you would prefer not to be burdened with me, I will understand, nor will I make an issue of it when I take over the command."

"Are you equipped to ride in the cold weather, Lord? If so, I see no reason why you should not accompany us. I ask only that you should refrain from giving orders to me or my men and that you should not argue if I suggest something to you. For my part, I assure you that I will make no suggestions save for matters of your own safety."

"I agree. As I have already mentioned, I know that I have no right to command you until such time as I take over the command from General Hartovan."

"Then welcome to our noble band, Lord Carrtog. We will be leaving an hour or so after the train."

"Thank you, Captain. I will go arrange for my wife to continue on the train and will join you shortly."

"Your wife, Lord Carrtog? Does she understand anything about the kind of circumstances she will be living in here?"

"I believe she has some idea. She was a lady-in-waiting to the Princess Ellevar when the rising opened in Tenerack."

Captain Boroddai's eyebrows rose. "Indeed? Well, I hope that neither of you will regret coming back to the North, Lord Carrtog."

"So do I, Captain Boroddai, so do I."

Addy was annoyed that Carrtog would not ride the whole way to Kilgarhai with them, but she restrained her annoyance, in particular after Carrtog presented her with a smooth rounded stone. "I've put a small charm on this; it will retain its heat for several hours, and if you hold it in your hands, it will help keep the cold away for some time, I hope until you reach Kilgarhai itself."

"Beware the kind of magic you give me, my most dear, for I may start to prefer this magical warmth to the magical warmth that comes from your embrace, and then you may find yourself out in the cold."

She was smiling when she said it, though; a smile that held its own particular warmth.

"My dear, if it should come to that, I might give up all the magic I have been taught for that one little bit of magic of which you speak. And though 'little bit' is not the appropriate description, still I fear that this magic would not serve me well when it comes to armed combat. So I beg you not to force me to make that decision so suddenly."

Her smile broadened. "My dearest love, please use every least scrap of magic you've been taught, if it will make it more likely that I see you safe and sound in Kilgarhai."

She embraced him then, and he felt a determination to do whatever he need do in order to feel that embrace at least one more time.

"For that," he said, "I will most certainly do everything in my power to be sure to see you in Kilgarhai." With some reluctance, he let her go, took two steps back, smiled at her, and forced himself to turn and go.

AS THE SUN BEGAN TO set, the temperature fell, and Carrtog felt glad that he had taken the time to repeat the spell he had given Addy and put it on a shot, once for himself and once for Yakor. He had put that enspelled shot into a separate pocket; it would do him little good if he were to shoot it into some enemy in the heat of combat tonight, he told himself with a smile.

He'd also made the offer to Captain Boroddai to do the same for him and his men. The captain had thought over the offer, then said, "I think not, thank you, Lord Carrtog. Not unless you can teach that spell to every captain in your command. You see, my men, Gods bless every one of them, would brag to their friends when they get home. The story would pass to the rest of the garrison by tomorrow evening, which would cause dissension among those whose commanders could not provide the same advantage."

"Of course. I ought not to interfere with General Hartovan's garrison, at least not until it becomes mine. Would you prefer, then, that neither I nor my man should have that advantage?"

"Neither you nor your man are under my command, nor anywhere in General Hartovan's line of command, and I think I can depend on the two of you not to boast to my men, which is the only way they would ever find out. Otherwise, why should either of you suffer needlessly?"

"Thank you, Captain."

"It's nothing, Lord Carrtog."

THE ROYAL FORCES HAD produced a pathway paralleling the railway line in order that the garrison at Kilgarhai could send out patrols to check on the condition of the line. Most recently, each patrol had been issued a magical communicator so that they could call either back to Kilgarhai or forward to Gwarasai, whichever was closer, when they found a break in the line.

It was not unusual for the rebels to attempt to ambush a patrol, so it was almost certain that the patrol-commander would be wearing a danger-sensing ring, or some other device.

There were spells that could mask the presence of danger and therefore conflict with such a device's effectiveness, but if the danger-sensing device had been recently refreshed it might well sense the presence of that covering magic. Much depended on the comparative strengths of the caster of the masking spell and the one who produced — or most recently renewed — the ring. Carrtog had renewed his trouble-sensing ring as a part of the most recent lesson Gwaitorr had taught on the subject. A good deal depended first on if there were an ambush at all, and second, if there were an ambush, how strong the man concealing it might be. Or alternatively, how recently Captain Boroddai's own ring had been renewed.

They continued even after dark, for even a few men working quickly could damage a rail with a little light and perhaps some magical assistance.

"From what I've been told, Lord Carrtog, the general's magicians have been working very hard on the detection of damaged rails. I gather they've had some success in discovering the damage, but saying how far along the line the damage has been done is apparently another matter. That means they can say that the Northies have been out doing their nasty work, but we still have to ride the whole length of the road to find out where."

Carrtog nodded. "Interesting. Perhaps I shall have to see how they're approaching it. It's an intriguing problem, or rather, an intriguing set of problems."

The captain glanced at him. "Interesting for you, perhaps, Lord Carrtog, but I know only the sort of magic that can help me stay alive in a fight."

Carrtog smiled. "For many, that's all that's needed. But the king thought I might do well for some extra training, so who was I to object? And I've already found some of it useful."

On they went, stopping from time to time to rest the horses but covering the ground fairly rapidly. Carrtog discussed the situation thoroughly with Captain Boroddai, though the man was very loyal to his general and avoided any topic that showed the general in a less than favorable light. Early in the morning they came into Kilgarhai, guided by magical lights, which allowed them to see the trail but did not ruin their night-vision if there should happen to be an ambush.

As they drew up to the guard-post at the garrison barracks, Captain Boroddai said, "Well, it seems the Northies have decided to welcome you to the North by not attempting to ambush our patrol, Lord Carrtog."

"Do they ambush patrols all that often, then?"

The captain grinned. "No, I will admit that they do not often ambush patrols. Just sufficiently often to keep us on our toes. Their main purpose is to sabotage the railway line, so ambushing troopers is only an occasional nuisance. Their attacks are more likely to be against the parties sent out to repair the breaks."

The captain rode with Yakor and Carrtog to ensure they made their way safely to their quarters. Carrtog was not certain whether it was mere politeness on the captain's part, or whether he possibly hoped to gain some favor with his new commander. On balance, from what he knew of the captain, he thought it more likely to be politeness.

Addy was sound asleep when he arrived, and he endeavored to undress and get into bed without waking her. Despite his care, he heard her give an incomprehensible sleepy mutter before she dropped back into sleep again.

Later on, but still early in the morning, he was awakened by a sharp poke in the ribs. He opened his eyes to see Addy leaning over him, her small fist pulled back to poke him again, if necessary.

"What is it, my dear?"

"You ought to have wakened me when you came in, rather than letting me lie here worrying until morning!"

"But you were sound asleep! How could you possibly be worrying about me?"

She poked him again, then changed her mode of attack, tickling him in the ribs. "No excuses, you mean, nasty little lord, making me wait all night long to be sure no sneaky rebel shot you from a distance while you were on your jaunt along the railroad line to make sure it was still there."

He finally managed to grab hold of her wrists to protect his sensitive ribs, then he kissed her firmly. "There!" he said, "Does that not feel like I'm here, safe and sound?"

She chuckled. "Well, perhaps so. But possibly you should try again just to be sure."

All in all, it took some little while before they were willing to rise and face the new day.

GENERAL HARTOVAN WAS a short, fussy man, with the beginnings of a considerable paunch. He was near bald, with a ruff of gray hair around his head, and a red face which became more red as he grew more excited. He had a tendency to finger the hilt of his sword, so no one could be certain that he was not ready, at any moment, to draw the weapon and make use of it.

He was quite aware that he was being removed from his command for failure to carry out his duties; maintaining the railway line in order to bring up supplies for the King's Army in the North. He was also, apparently, of the opinion that no one could do much better than he had, and some of his officers, trying to curry favor with Carrtog, had reported that the general considered him a jumped-up little nobody, riding high on the king's favor, who was about to be handed his head by a bunch of ragged northern bush-dwellers.

He returned Carrtog's salute sharply and properly, and rather than make any great effort to explain the situation, merely said, "The command is yours, General Carrtog."

"Thank you, General Hartovan."

"If you will permit me, General Carrtog, I will leave on the next train."

"Certainly, General Hartovan."

The general saluted once more, turned, and strode away. Yakor muttered, just loud enough for Carrtog to hear, "It might have been nice for him to explain what sorts of efforts he made to carry out the task given him."

Carrtog shrugged slightly, saying, "Since I am expected to do better than he did, what does it matter?"

Yakor smiled slightly, "There is that all right. Though it depends very much whose expectations we're considering."

Carrtog nodded. "Well, I suppose the first thing I ought to do is speak to my officers, and see what they think."

THE OFFICERS WERE A mixed crew, some showing little enthusiasm for the task they had been set, some looking to Carrtog with curiosity, as if wondering whether he might be the man who might come up with a method to make their task a little more feasible. Captain Boroddai had taken a position in the front of the group, and it seemed he was one of the ones who hoped he would lead them to success.

Carrtog wondered if Boroddai had spoken to any of the other captains, and if so, had he influenced them at all?

The ones further to the rear of the group seemed to have lost hope of doing their job successfully. He wondered whether he ought to try to win them over, or just dismiss them and ask for replacements.

Well, it was definitely time to say something to them.

"Gentlemen, as you already know, I am General Lord Carrtog of Nandycargllwyd, and I have been sent to replace General Hartovan and to attempt to keep the rail lines open."

There was a little movement in the rear group of officers, and his impression was that he had said approximately what they had expected, that they were afraid that he had no new ideas in mind and thus was unlikely to do better than their previous commander.

"I have already talked to men back in the capital, men who were sent home to recover from wounds, and discussed the situation here. Certain of the strategies and tactics have shown limited usefulness and will likely be discontinued. The patrols along the railway line, however, will continue, since they do at least have the benefit of finding places where the rebels have broken the tracks. I also have several plans in mind for attempting to spot rebel encampments, perhaps even with a view to carrying the fight to them. As you gentlemen have been here all this time, long before I arrived, I suspect some of you have notions as to methods to be tried. If so, I would be very interested to hear them. I am not promising to try all of them, but I should still wish to hear them. Has anyone anything to say immediately? If so, please stand, state your name, and give your piece."

The first man to stand was tall and lean, with features that showed years of facing wind and weather. "Captain Fordibrach, Lord Carrtog. Lord, we all know that the local farmers are supporting the Northies, feeding them and supplying other needs. I would suggest that we burn out every farmer who we have reason to believe is aiding the enemy."

There was a muttering of support from the captains to the rear.

Carrtog thought for a moment, then said, "It may indeed come to that, but I have a feeling that every farm we burn out will make us that much more disliked among the rest of the population. Besides that, we will be depending on those same farmers for our own rations; we shouldn't be too hasty to burn them out. Also, I have a notion in mind to use those same farms to find and track the rebel bands. I hope to do it in such a manner that the rebels begin to suspect that this or that farmer, or someone in the farmstead, is betraying them to us, which will work to our benefit."

Captain Fordibrach frowned, then said, "Lord if you can indeed do something of that sort, I'd be willing to forgo the torches."

"Good. Anyone else?"

A small man with bright red hair and a square face stood up. "Captain Kilwatin, Lord Carrtog. The local merchants have the tendency to raise their prices by about half when selling to any of the king's men. I would like to see a heavy fine put on such merchants."

Murmured voices agreed with this, and even one or two spoke out loud. "Yes! Make the Northies pay!"

"I have a notion in mind to deal with such double-pricing, but I shall keep the notion of a fine in mind in case it might be necessary."

Other suggestions were made, mostly suggestions of draconian punishments for such things as rude behavior toward the king's men, and Carrtog was able to show sympathy toward the point of view without completely agreeing.

When he finally dismissed the men, Carrtog felt almost confident of having won over a few of them. Most of the rest, he felt, would wait to see how his first ideas worked out.

"Well," Yakor said, "At least a few of them will wait until they hear your first notion before they decide you're totally worthless."

"You think I've won over that many?"

Yakor spat. "No, not really, I was just trying not to dishearten you."

Carrtog chuckled. "Ah, Yakor, my reliable old friend! I can always depend on your honesty. Well, there are almost certainly some who I should remove, but I think I will wait a bit and see if some of them will not save me the trouble and ask to be replaced. First of all, I shall have to come up with some sort of miraculous plan to turn the morale of my command completely around."

"I wish I could reassure you that it won't really take a miracle, but I'm afraid it will require something of that sort. Do you have a ready list of available miracles?"

"Actually, I do have the beginnings of one. Would you find Captain Fordibrach, the one who wanted to put the torch to every farmer who gave a sack of grain to the rebels, and ask him to come see me? Assure him that I merely wish to get some assistance from him in carrying out a plan of my own."

Yakor gave him a look. "You plan to win that one over to you in hopes that some of the others will follow him?"

"Well, no, that had not been my main intention, just that he would likely be the man to have certain information I want. When we talk, you will see where my trail leads. And of course, you are partially right; if my plan succeeds to any degree, I might well win him over, and indeed, some of the rest."

"I'll be very interested to hear this interview."

Chapter 19

Captain Fordibrach, from the expression on his face, had not really believed any assurance Yakor might have given him about his position not being in danger. He looked around at Carrtog and Yakor as though expecting immediate remonstration for his previous words in the gathering.

"Captain, I am beginning a plan for dealing with the continual aid given by the farmsteaders to the rebels. This is a plan in the making, so it may not be ready for tomorrow, or even likely the next day, but I do hope eventually to have a project to set in motion. The beginning point will be the farmsteads who are supporting the rebels. From what you suggested, I would suspect you have certain farmsteads in mind right now that you suspect. What I need is to mark them out on a map. What I hope to do is to put a magical watch on one or more of them, and if I can manage it, I would eventually hope to track the rebels to their campsites, and attack them there."

Captain Fordibrach's eyes lit up. "Could you actually do that, Lord Carrtog? We had asked the general to have his magicians try to find the rebels by their own magic, but they could not seem to manage it. No one ever bothered to explain to us why."

"I don't know what approaches they used, but I will ask them and see. I make no promises, but I have several different methods to approach the problem, and one of them should surely work. Now, can you show me on the map where one or two of the suspect farms are?"

There was a map of the immediate area on the table, held down by weights at the various corners. The captain bent over the map, scanning it carefully.

YAKOR WAS FROWNING. "It seems you've given that man reason to hope. I'm afraid, though, that if you don't fulfill that hope, he will be seriously disappointed."

"I know. Now to work on these plans I said I had."

Yakor gave him a sharp look. "You gave him hope based on some foggy thought in the back of that mind of yours? By all the Gods, I hope you can come up with something, boy!"

Carrtog smiled. "Easy, now, Yakor. It's better than that. I do have some specific notions in mind. I'll have to see just how well I can make them work. In the very last extremity, I'll make myself a Cloak of Invisibility, and go out tracking the rebels down myself."

"Joke about it if you will, but in the last instance, it might be you turning over the command to someone else who is hoped to make something out of your failure."

"Before I do too much else, I'd best get together the magicians who served with General Hartovan and see what they have to say about tracking the rebels by magic. I'd be surprised if General Hartovan didn't ask them, and I wonder what their answer was."

THE MAGICIANS WHO HAD served with General Hartovan were an unprepossessing lot. There were only three of them and none of them were very well-dressed. One was tall with a long white beard, wearing a long gray robe with several brass badges attached to it, stars, moon-phases, comets, and lightning bolts. It was the kind of dress that a fellow might wear to make an impression. The other two were dressed in more ordinary clothing, one of them was short and stout, the other medium height and stringy.

"The three of you are all the magicians who served with General Hartovan?"

The man in the robe answered. "No, Lord, there were two others, but one was killed by a rebel magician. Some sort of magical plague, but we managed to halt it before it went further. The other left with the general; apparently he felt the general's loss reflected badly on him."

"I see. Before I go too much further, then, who was responsible for dealing with the plague you mentioned? I should hate to have the only one capable of that gone off with the general."

The man in the robe answered again. "Well, yes, he was the one who dealt with it. But he also taught the rest of us, since it was too big a risk to have only one man able to deal with an attack that had already been tried once, with some success."

"Some success? Were there other deaths besides the one magician?"

The spokesman flushed. "Yes, Lord, twenty-two soldiers and one captain. The other magician, Gwirisanth, he taught us not only how to deal with that particular plague, but several others, as well as methods to discover when practically any magically-caused plague was being attempted. Every day since then, one of us has checked to see if another plague were being launched, and in fact, twice such attempts were halted without fatalities."

"Very well done, then. Now, one of the captains mentioned having asked the general about tracking the rebels by magic. Has anything on that line been attempted?"

From the rapid glances between the three, Carrtog could tell that nothing had been. Without waiting for an answer, he asked, "Why not?"

"We were continually working at either discovering a method to counter the latest attempts to hide destruction of the railway line, or to discover when rebels were near the line. The railway line, you see, is the most important thing to be protected here."

"I see. Are there any other men you know of who have any magical talent, who might be willing to work for us?"

"Few at all, if any, Lord. The people in the town, by and large, are on the side of the rebels. The people who have come up to provide services for the king's forces are not usually the sort to wish to work too closely with the forces enforcing the king's law, if you know what I mean."

"I believe I do. Well, I would appreciate it if you would take a bit of time to think of methods to track the rebels. You can come to me if you have any ideas, indeed, if you have any notions at all as to how best to carry out our task here."

As the three went out, Yakor said, "I hope you don't rely too much on that lot."

"Actually, I've been thinking of other things. You recall, while we were coming down from Tenerack, among the annoying things we had to dodge were gliders. I've been wondering just what use we might make of them here."

"You know that the king is not at all in favor of gliders."

"Well, I'm not surprised. He did suggest that when he was able, he might have people who manned the locomotives running along the line sought out and killed. I understand he's been making good on that threat, too. Do you think he'd actually command me to stop if he heard I was working with gliders?"

"He might well do so."

"Well, then, best we don't tell him of our plans until after they've proved successful. In the meantime, there's at least one notion I'd like to work at. I'd like to set some kind of magic eye on one or several of those suspected farmsteads, and see if I can spot rebels coming and going. At the very least, we might get some sense of the direction to look for them."

"I wouldn't want to put too much hope on a direction to look; those fellows are too smart to just go in a straight line, you know."

"Yes. I'm hoping to be able to come up with a bit more in the way of tracing them. Something like making a line around the farmstead, and when they break that line on the way back home, they pick up some sort of magical trace that we can follow back to their home."

"You don't think they'll all have people back in their home camps who'll be able to see that magic and wipe away that trace?"

"Quite possibly. That's why I'm going to have to do some thinking to come up with a trace that the ordinary combat-magician won't spot. For the time being at least, if we try several farmsteads, we should be able to find one band who doesn't have a magician with them to spot the trace."

"That'll be better than nothing."

FOR TWO WEEKS, THE Kilgarhai Garrison maintained their habitual round of continuous patrolling, occasionally skirmishing with bands of rebels caught out in the open. The garrison commander was also responsible for seeing to the storage of supplies sent up from the south and the loading and sending off — under heavy guard — of wagon trains to the north. The wagons, with their guard, were sent back to Kilgarhai, where the wagons were repaired and made ready for the next shipment.

In the meantime, Carrtog set up his home in a fairly large house that had stood empty for some time. At the same time, he bought a plot of land and had work started on a building to be his own.

He had workers hired locally for the project and paid them fair wages, though he might have required them to do the work unpaid, as conquered enemies. "It won't necessarily make them like me any better," he said, "but they still have to eat, conquered enemies or not."

As much of the building material as possible was bought locally, though certain special woods had to be sent up from the south. Also, nails in the quantity necessary for a house of the size projected could not be produced locally, so those and other special items were sent up from the south as well.

In the middle of the second week, Captain Fordibrach and two other captains came to Carrtog's office. "You wished to see us, Lord?"

"Yes, Captain. I have done some study on the problem, and I have come up with a possible solution."

He set three stout leather bags on the table, each about the size of two fists, tied with a strong leather cord. "Each of these is full of a fine sand into which a magic has been set. Each of you will take one of the bags, and Captain Fordibrach, you and each of the others shall choose one of the suspect farmsteads. Each of you, or a man you choose, shall ride around each farm, pouring the sand in as near to a circle as you can manage.

"I shall give each of you a crystal, which is sensitized to the magic in the sand. When the rebels break the circle, they will carry the magic with them, and it will show up in their trail as a pale green glow. It should last long enough for you to be able to trail one or more bands back to their camps."

Captain Fordibrach smiled savagely. "A fine surprise to some Northies! You are certain this will work, Lord?"

"I'm fairly confident it will, Captain. Please report back to me afterward."

"Yes, Lord, and willingly!"

"One last thing, Captains. Even if you do track the rebels from any particular farmstead, do not return to punish that farmstead. If the rebels don't immediately suspect magic and seek traces of it, we might be fortunate and have them suspect betrayal by someone. If we leave the farm unharmed, who might they first suspect?"

Captain Fordibrach stood looking puzzled for a moment, then suddenly his face lit up again. "Of course, Lord!"

As the captains continued on their way, Yakor spoke. "You actually think to sow suspicion among the rebels this way?"

"It's possible. The rebel bands know that we offer rewards for anyone giving information about them, which means they must always be on the watch against someone who lets a desire for gold get the best of their desire to be free of the king's reign. So when something strange happens, like the king's troopers finding them just a little while after they have visited a certain farmstead for food, why, they might just make a certain sudden decision of their own."

Yakor nodded. "We suspect that the king was hoping for you to fail badly at this task. You should best be ready to deal with his reaction when you disappoint that hope."

Carrtog sighed. "I'm aware of that, though I could wish life were a little simpler. The Gods run things the way they wish, though, so I suppose I'll just have to deal with whatever comes."

WHAT WAS TO COME NEXT was, however, despite being expected, a complete surprise. Early in the morning, Addy shook Carrtog awake.

"It's happening, Carrtog! The baby's coming! Call the servants!"

"I thought it was too soon, yet?" He was struggling to wake up.

"I thought so too, but it's happening!"

Despite his state of near-sleep, Carrtog was already reaching for the cord that would ring the bell in the servant's quarters. They had arranged, some time earlier, that the servants should expect a certain series of rings to indicate that the baby was on the way.

On that signal, certain of the women servants, particularly a few who had already borne children, should come immediately, while at the same time a messenger should be sent to fetch the midwife.

Carrtog got himself dressed and waited. When the first of the servants arrived, he would still have stayed, but the looks they gave him told him that his presence was not really wanted. He left, going to the room that had become their library, and sat down to read.

After reading the first part of the first sentence of the seventh chapter for the fifth — or was it the eighth? — time, he tossed the volume aside and got to his feet.

He began pacing up and down, his mind rushing up and down, seeing all the various tragedies that could befall a woman in childbirth. There was a sudden scream from down the hallway, and before he knew it he was out the door and striding toward the bedchamber.

One of the serving-woman was standing outside, with her arms folded across her chest. "Go back, Lord. You won't want to come in here for some time. She'll be screaming and shouting, and she might well say things to you that you won't want to hear. Fact is, Lord, you'd be best to get out of the house altogether for some time. We'll send someone to fetch you when it's near."

Carrtog stood still for a short while; yes, he could well manhandle the woman out of the way, but he knew she was right. He didn't really want to be in there anyway.

A moment later Yakor was standing beside him, himself half-dressed. "She's right, Carrtog. Let's go out to the stables and look at the horses. Come on."

With Yakor's hand on his elbow, he went out to the stables where they met a manservant who carried a pair of warm cloaks and another who carried a bottle of wine and several heavy cups.

"Here, put this cloak on, and let's sit down and wait. The best one can say about these things is that they take as long as they take, so we might as well be as comfortable as we can."

Yakor poured out the wine, one cup for each, including the servants. "Since you must bear the cold with us out here, it's only fair that you should have a share of the wine." He gave them an eye. "I'll assume you won't go bragging about this to the rest of the servants. This is one special circumstance; don't fool yourself into thinking that it changes your status at all."

The two servants nodded.

They talked about various things, shying away from what was happening back in the house itself; that kind of discussion, even though it began with assurances that nothing was likely to go wrong, inevitably brought to mind the various times when something did go wrong.

One of the servants began to shiver, despite his cloak. Yakor looked at Carrtog. "Could you do something to keep us a bit warmer?"

Carrtog pulled his mind away from what might or might not be going on in the house. "A stable full of dry straw and horses is not the place to risk a fire. But yes, I believe I could do something. Probably best not to fire a pistol either. Let me see—"

He turned to one of the servants. "Go back into the house and bring me out a cup, preferably a metal one. Yakor, you go find us four small stones, about the size to fit in one's hand."

The servant was back fairly quickly with the cup, and Carrtog poured a careful measure of gunpowder into it. He took a wooden stool from the corner and put a bit of tinder on top of it, along with a bit of straw.

"Yakor, I intend to be very careful here, but I do need a bit of fire. I'd appreciate it if you'd empty your wine cup and fill it with water to stand by to douse the fire when I'm done, or if it looks like getting away. Hand me the four stones, first."

Yakor nodded, tossed back the wine, and went to fill his cup at the half-butt of water standing in the corner. Carrtog set the four stones down on the floor of the stable, and when Yakor returned with the water, he started the small fire.

Taking up one of the lit straws in his left hand, he held up his right hand, palm down, toward the four stones. Then, speaking an incantation, he dipped the burning straw into the gunpowder. Not being enclosed, it did not explode, but rather burst in a flash of light, filling the air with the scent of burned gunpowder.

"The fire, Yakor."

Yakor doused the fire, and automatically looked around to make sure no flying sparks, either from the fire or the gunpowder, had landed in the dry straw around.

"If you'll each pick up one of those stones, you'll find that it'll keep you warm. Even if you drop it into a pocket, it'll keep your whole body warm. It should last about eight to ten hours."

No one spoke for a few moments, then Yakor, heaving a small sigh, said, "Now, that is one little trick I could use now and then. Such as waiting in an ambush on a winter's day for someone to come marching down the road."

"This one's not so good for waiting in hiding anywhere. For anyone with anything more than a whiff of magical talent, it shows up like a dead crow on a snow bank. There are others that are less obvious, or which can be more easily hidden. Of course, those ones are also more difficult to do. For just sitting around in a cold stable, waiting, this one is as good as any."

"But if the fellow doing the waiting has no magical ability, it's still impossible."

"That's common misunderstanding, Yakor. Everyone has at least a small amount of magical ability. Many people don't believe they have it, so they might as well not. On the other hand, if you manage to convince yourself that you do have some ability, you could manage this particular spell easily."

Yakor thought for a bit, then shook his head. "Risking a tiny fire and a powder-flash in a stable one time is allowable; doing it twice or more to teach a lesson isn't. Perhaps another time and another place."

One of the servants spoke up. "Lord, could even someone such as I actually do magic?"

"I see no reason why not. It would be easier if you could read. You can't? No matter, we'll try something simple, something that doesn't require the burning of powder. Mind you, the burning of powder can make practically any spell easier to work. Let me see. Ah, yes, this is easy, and not likely to go awry. Yakor, do you want to try it too?"

"For certain, why not? But first, what does it do?"

"This one just lifts a small weight, something such as a coin. Mind you, continued practice will let you lift even more."

He took out a small coin, set it on the stool, pointed at it, and spoke an incantation. The coin slid across the top of the stool.

He put it in the center of stool's face and looked at the servant. "Now, you point at the coin and say what you heard me say."

The servant spoke, but the coin sat stubbornly still. "No, not quite. Listen carefully." He repeated the phrase slowly, carefully.

The servant repeated the phrase, and the coin jerked suddenly.

"You've done it! Now, you notice that it moved with a sudden jerk. That was because you weren't really sure you could do it. The next time will be easier. Try it again."

After three tries, the servant had the coin moving smoothly across the stool.

"Now, Yakor, you take a try."

Yakor made the coin move smoothly, halfway across the stool, on his first try.

"That was because I saw someone else do it first," he said, self-deprecatingly.

After each of them had taken several turns moving the coin, each eventually moving it right off the stool, Carrtog taught them another small spell, to lift the coin straight up.

Shortly after each of them had had two successful tries at this, the stable door opened and another servant entered. "Lord Carrtog, the child is born. It's a girl!"

"And my Lady?"

"She is quite well, Lord. They said for me to tell you that you could come to see her immediately."

"Thank you."

For a moment, Carrtog was disappointed that the child was not a boy, but he soon pushed that aside. Addy was well and could have more children, and a daughter deserved his love just as much. He strode toward the house.

Chapter 20

As he reached the door of the house, Carrtog realized that he had not been thinking much, if at all, about Addy for the last while, concentrating as he had on the impromptu magic lessons. Had Yakor planted that request with the servant? Well, it had saved him a lot of needless worrying.

The babe was a wee red thing, wrapped in a white flannel, lying close by her mother's breast.

The midwife looked up at Carrtog as he came in. "The babe is just fine. She looks a bit misshapen, but that's just normal, being squeezed as she was by being born. A week or two from now, she'll look much better. Your lady has had a burdensome time of it, so it would be best if you let her rest." This was all said in a tone that seemed to expect that he, being a man, would understand little or none of this and insist on forcing his wife to undergo a long discussion.

"Of course," he said, then approached Addy. "The child is well, then, and you?"

She was smiling, as though she had not gone through a long and painful process. "Well enough, considering. She seems to have been born hungry." She smiled. "The first thing she did was to start yelling, but she quieted down immediately when they put her to my breast."

He smiled in return. "This lady seems to be ready and willing to fetch me a clout with one of these basins if I stay around and tire you any further. Let me give you a quick kiss, and I'll be gone."

She smiled again. "Ah, the brave warrior Carrtog, put to flight by the wrath of a midwife! Yes, come give me a kiss and make your retreat."

Smiling himself, he followed her commands.

MUCH OF THE OPEN SPACE in the workroom was taken up by the glider, or at least, by what would become the glider. It was an open framework of lathe-work, a long body with what appeared to be a stubby pair of wings at the rear. The main wings were not yet attached, since that would require more space than the workroom allowed.

At present the wings, or at least the open lathe-work of them, were leaning along one sidewall. The body of the craft itself showed a pair of protrusions along the side, to which the wings would eventually be attached.

These projections were slightly higher at the front than at the rear, which would make the wings angle slightly upward for better lift. This was one of the things that had proven useful on small models, things that Gwaitorr had suggested in the bundle of writings on the subject which he had sent up by rail just before they had begun work on their full-size model.

Carrtog and Gryff were tightening the last connections on the body of the craft, and Addy was sitting by, watching with the baby in a basket nearby. Also sitting and mostly watching the baby was a young dark-haired woman whose task was to look after the child.

"You still plan to be the first one to fly her, do you?" Addy asked.

"I can hardly ask someone else to do it. It's a risky thing, from all accounts, even though we're generally following the plan that's been the most successful."

She glanced at the basket. "I don't like the thought of leaving little Aderyn without a father just because you don't want to ask someone to do something dangerous. After all, you don't ride out on patrol all by yourself just because it's dangerous."

"That's a different matter, Addy. My soldiers are expected to go out on patrol, and nobody expects me to do anything but send them out." He didn't mention that he was likely to accompany an occasional patrol; that wouldn't help his cause at all.

"You see a difference; I don't."

Carrtog didn't say anything immediately. This was seeming too much like one of those discussions that was going to turn into an argument, ending with him on the wrong side. He looked over at Gryff. "Gryff, I think we've done enough on this for now. I'd like to go see how work is going on the house."

"You don't need me for that, Lord. I can stay here and keep working on this."

He hesitated a moment; all he really wanted to do was to get away from the immediate presence of the glider, in hopes that he'd be able to take Addy's mind off of it.

"All right," he said, "You carry on here, I'll go up and look at the house. Addy, did you want to come along?"

"Yes, I do. But don't think this discussion is finished. Minnia," she turned to the dark-haired woman, "Please bring the baby."

So, with little Aderyn carefully wrapped against the cold winter air, they left the relatively warm workroom and went to the site where the house was under construction.

For all the fact that he represented the foreign occupying power, he hadn't had great trouble getting workmen to build his house. Winter was not usually a time for building projects in Kilgarhai, so many in the building trades were either unemployed, or taking any odd jobs they could get. An undertaking such as a house, in particular a house of this size, was something of an unexpected gift for any such, some of whom had misjudged the amount they had saved from their summer wages.

Some people might have taken advantage of the situation and pushed down the wages they paid for a job done at this time of year, but Carrtog had another purpose in mind, besides building a house of appropriate size for the station he was to fulfill.

Some might have taken the aforementioned station as requiring an imposing structure; what Carrtog had designed, with the help of people knowledgeable in the field, was a building that proclaimed the status of the resident without using its size or design to hammer home just how important that resident was.

At this point the building was little more than a fenced-off plot with several piles of lumber stacked here and there. The digging for the foundation had just been finished, requiring several fires to thaw out the winter-hard ground — this was among the reasons that a building project of this size was more often undertaken in summer — and the setting of the foundation itself had just begun.

This meant that there was not much to be seen and thus not really enough to distract Addy's attention from the previous conversation.

Even worse, he could see that she realized what he had been trying to do.

Yakor spoke up at his elbow, laughter in his voice. "I think you've just got yourself into trouble."

"What am I going to do, Yakor? I can't order one of my soldiers, or worse, one of my servants, to try that machine."

"Ask for volunteers?"

"That still amounts to me saying 'Somebody please try this thing for me because I'm afraid it'll kill me.'"

"Tell the truth. 'My wife is afraid it'll kill me, and I'm afraid of my wife.'" There was still laughter in his voice.

Addy came marching over. "It's a very nice hole in the ground, Carrtog. I'm very sure it'll be even nicer when the walls go up and they put the roof on it."

The worst part of it for Carrtog was that she had previously told him that she could just see the house when it was built and after Carrtog was happy with it. Having her now use it like a truncheon to beat him with was hard to bear.

"I'm afraid, though," she continued, "that the sight of this very nice hole in the ground does not serve to take my mind off the thought of you taking that glider up and killing yourself."

"We'll do everything we can to make it safe."

"You will, will you? What can you do when that thing falls out of the sky? Magically produce a haystack for it to land in? Don't try to jolly me along, Carrtog! We both know that thing may be dangerous, and I don't like the thought of you being the one to show just how dangerous it may be!"

"And I should tell some other man to undertake a danger that I myself shirk? What would that say about me?"

"Then forget the whole thing and don't ask anyone to do it!"

"And thus forgo what might well be a great advantage in this war?"

"If necessary, yes!"

Carrtog took a deep breath. This discussion was rushing headlong toward disaster. "I—" He stopped as Yakor elbowed him sharply in the ribs, and he clenched his teeth to prevent himself from speaking words carrying more anger than argument.

"I think," he said carefully, "We had best put this discussion aside for a while. We're beginning to shed more heat than light on the topic."

Addy was still looking at him fiercely. "I scarcely think you'll find my mind changed another time."

He was trying to find something to say that would not inflame matters further when he heard the beat of horse hooves. He turned to see Captain Fordibrach coming in at a gallop. Whatever he's coming to tell me, he thought, I think I'm going to have to give the fellow a commendation. He may have just saved me from a nasty family argument.

The captain pulled his horse to a stop, jumped down from the saddle, and saluted. Carrtog returned the salute. "What news, Captain?"

He could tell from Fordibrach's expression that the news was good. "Lord, one of the farmsteads we circled was visited! I thought it might be best to follow the track with more than a patrol's strength."

"Very good, Captain. What strength were you thinking?"

"Nothing too large, Lord. I'd say only two troops; we'd want to be moving fast."

"I suppose you'd like to take your own troop, for one?"

"Yes, Lord. We're not that worn."

"Good. Go talk to your squadron commander, have him pick another troop. Tell him that I'll accompany them."

He turned to Addy. "Addy, I'll have to go with them; this might just be the changing of ill fortunes for this command."

She said nothing. Perhaps he had been a bit early in thinking that the argument had been stopped. In fact, she might as well have read his thought, and this was only going to defer the altercation to a later time.

This was on his mind as he walked back toward the house. Yakor walked just behind his elbow. "You're going to have to put that out of your mind, boy. You can't let family arguments distract you when you're going into a fight."

"I know that. I'm just not certain how to manage it."

"You'd better find out how, and quickly."

"Very helpful advice, Yakor. Much like telling me to be careful not to be killed when I go into battle."

He grabbed a young servant boy and told him, "Go to the stables, and tell the grooms to saddle horses for myself and Yakor. We're riding with the troops, so we'll need war-horses."

"Yes, Lord."

It was something of a scramble to get into proper uniform and do it in time to meet the squadron commander before he began to get annoyed.

He took along three wheel-lock pistols, one tucked into each boot-top, and the third in the sash at his belt. This brought to mind his situation when he and Yakor had set out to find a place for himself. At that time, he was hoping that sometime soon he would be able to afford a pistol, even one of indifferent quality. Here he was now, not only the possessor of three good-quality wheel-locks, but his man, Yakor, had at least three himself, and very likely more.

Yes, he had found quite a place for himself, but it seemed like a place where he was like a swimmer, paddling desperately to keep from sinking out of sight.

SQUADRON COMMANDER Cargiodd was a stout man, but agile. He swung himself up onto his gray horse as Carrtog and Yakor approached, and the two troops with him followed suit. "Captain Fordibrach informs me that you wish to accompany us, Lord Carrtog."

"I do, Commander. In part, I wish to see how well my magic succeeded in tracking them down, and in part, I just wish to accompany my troops from time to time."

"As you wish, Lord." Carrtog could not tell from the man's expression whether he approved of his commander accompanying his troops or not. Not that his disapproval counted for much; Carrtog would come along and the squadron commander would have to make up his mind to accepting the fact.

As they rode out, Commander Cargiodd took a place beside Carrtog. "I understand you have undertaken a great study of combat magic, Lord?"

"Yes, combat magic and other magics as well. This particular magic might not be quite considered combat magic."

"I see. But you have some confidence in it?"

Carrtog smiled. "If I admit that I do, am I then a braggart? Or if I say that I have never tried this particular spell except in a workroom, am I then risking all these troops on a mere speculation?"

The commander scowled. "Neither one, Lord. I would prefer, though, that you yourself had some confidence in your ability."

"I see. My apologies, Commander. As I suggested, I have never used this spell except in the workroom, and there, it was successful. How successful it will be in the field depends on many things, such as whether or not there is a particularly skilled magician among the enemy, and whether or not the mere searching for traces causes the farmstead to send out someone to warn the rebels."

Captain Fordibrach spoke up from Carrtog's other side, "I thought of that, Lord. Instead of leading the whole troop up to look at the ground around the farmstead, I sent two men to look it over on the sly."

Carrtog nodded. "Good. If your two men were sufficiently crafty, and there was nobody in the rebels' camp who could notice anything magical about the tracks that led from the farmstead, we might well have a successful venture."

They rode along the packed-snow trail in silence for some time with the dark trees watching on all sides until, at last, Fordibrach announced, "We take the branch to the left here."

Shortly thereafter they angled off to the left and continued in that direction.

The trail led round a large grove of trees, leafless branches reaching toward the dull winter sky. "The farmstead's just beyond these trees," Fordibrach said.

As they reached the curve of the trail, they could see the edge of the fenced yard. The yard was of considerable size and housed the sizable garden that during the fall provided vegetables not only for the farmer, his family, and the hired hands, but also a considerable quantity for sale to the town (and likely to the rebels in the woods as well).

Beyond that was another fenced-off area, which had most likely been a tilled field, but now, with the crops harvested and the grain stored, held a number of long-haired, long-horned cattle, who pawed at the snow to reveal the stubble of grain beneath. A hayrack mounted on skids, still half-full of hay, sat on the outside of the fence for when the farmer would toss over forkfuls to supplement the cattle's winter grazing. As they came up on the farm, they saw other enclosures holding sheep and goats, as well as sheds for the storage of the harvested grain.

Now the dogs came out, barking ferociously, letting the inhabitants of the farmstead know that strangers were approaching.

The door of the low-slung farmhouse opened to let out a tall, heavy-built man, who held a pitchfork upright in his right hand.

He called his dogs back in and stood waiting while the troopers came closer.

They were now surrounded by all the scents of the farm; the scents of the cattle, their manure, and their feed, as well as the almost hidden scents of the other animals.

The farmer spoke. "A good day to you, Commander Cargiodd. To what do we owe the honor of this visit?"

"Good day to you also, Farmer Parllon. I'd like to introduce you to our new general, Lord Carrtog. And we have come for the usual purpose, to track down some of the rebels who are supplying themselves off your farmstead's produce."

The farmer's face took on a broad smile. "A good day to you, also, Lord Carrtog. So you've come about the same old business once more? Well, look around; I doubt you'll find any rebels under arms. More likely you'll find only some farmers ill-pleased by interruptions to their work by soldiers of the Southern king."

"Oh, we won't bother you or your family or farm-workers just now; we're looking for tracks."

The farmsteader shrugged, his expression changing not a whit. "Ah, tracks you'll probably find. We have deer coming by from time to time trying to see what they can get from our hay-supplies, and thus hunters coming to see if they can get a deer or two. Indeed, some of our men have been known to take a deer or two to make a little change to our usual winter fare."

Commander Cargiodd lifted his chin. "Good luck to them. So long as these hunters do not slip over to try to cut the railway line. We'll just be on our way, now." Commander Cargiodd urged his horse on the way, curving leftward around the farmstead's perimeter.

"We're near certain this fellow feeds the Northies, Lord Carrtog," he said, "but General Hartovan said that 'near certain' was not sufficient evidence to burn him out."

"The general was right," Carrtog replied. "In fact, I'd think careful about burning out any farmstead, no matter how good the evidence against him; we start burning them out, the ones that are left will start taking against us, besides which, the rebels will start pushing the rest harder to make up the loss. And the biggest problem with burning them out is that we ourselves need to get our own supplies from somewhere."

The commander frowned, almost as though he would prefer he and his men to starve. Carrtog decided not to push home the fact that hungry soldiers made for poor soldiers; the commander would probably not care to hear that.

Captain Fordibrach pointed. "The circle was broken over there."

"Good." Carrtog could see the crossed tracks for himself. "We don't really need the magic just now, but somewhere up the way, they'll start hiding their trail, so it's better to have the benefit of the spell from the start."

As they reached the appointed spot, he repeated the incantation, and a faint green line showed up along the track that crossed the circle. "There we are," he said, "now we just keep on following the green line."

Fordibrach called out two men from his troop. "You take the point," he said. "You know what to do; look out for ambushes, snares, all that sort of thing. If you find the camp, one of you come back to let us know, the other keep watch until the rest of us come up."

"Yes, sir." The pair turned their mounts and were off at a trot along the trail. Commander Cargiodd eyed the faintly glowing green line in the snow. "Isn't that line rather visible? I mean, if we can see it, can they not see it just as well? If they're lounging around their camp and this ghastly color shows up won't they know that something magic is on the way and be wary?"

Carrtog nodded. "Yes, if they saw it. But the magic doesn't work like that. They can't see it, since they're the objects of the spell. We, being on the other side of the spell as it were, can see it."

The commander still looked doubtful, but said, "If you say so, Lord."

They rode on, following the trail as it wound through the trees, until they met one of the two point-men coming back. His face shone with scarcely-controlled excitement.

"They're up ahead, Lord! They have guards posted all around, so we can't get close enough for more than a guess at their numbers, but I'd say we're about equal."

"All right," Carrtog responded. "I might be able to give us some advantage. Commander Cargiodd are any of your men familiar with the Grove of Battle?"

The commander gave the matter a moment's thought, then said, "Yes, some of them are. You can handle the magic itself?"

"Yes, I can." Carrtog thought of the last time he had used that incantation and about how much his ability had improved since. "I'd suggest you fall out anyone who knows the Battle Grove at all well, and then break up the rest into groups, so that one of those can give the rest a quick explanation of what to expect. During that time, I'll make my preparations. When we're both done, I'll give the signal, then set off the spell."

"Yes, Lord."

The commander quietly gathered the men in a group where they could all hear him, and said, "Lord Carrtog is going to cast the Grove of Battle spell for us. Hands up those who have any experience with it!

"Good! Those of you who put up your hands, fall out over here. Now each of you with experience with the spell, pick two to four of the others and take a bit to explain it to them. Lord Carrtog has spent some time studying magic just recently, so I think we can expect his version of the spell to be fairly powerful, but as with every bit of battle magic, much depends on how well the common soldiers take advantage of it. Now, you lot, pick your men!"

By this time Carrtog had already taken out one of his pistols, one that had not yet been loaded, and put in approximately

three-quarters of a usual charge of powder. On top of that he put a
couple of pinches of pine needles, then some wadding, then the ball.
He then opened the pan and primed the pistol, then closed the pan,
and slipped the pistol into his sash beside the one that had already
been there.

Yakor was beside his elbow.

"You recall the last time I used this spell, Yakor? Some things
have happened since then, haven't they?"

"Yes, indeed. Among them, you've increased your ability in this
sort of thing."

"Just what I had been thinking. I should then be able to do
something better this time than last, right? Unless, of course, there's
someone in that camp capable of pushing their way through my spell.
Of course, if there were, he'd have noticed my spell on the track and
we wouldn't have gotten this far so easily."

Cargiodd gave the command, and the troops moved out toward
the rebel encampment. They moved as quietly as that many men
and horses could manage, but of course the enemy eventually heard
them. The forward point man came riding back toward them.

Carrtog shouted "Now!" and swung his pistol skyward,
squeezing the trigger. He hadn't used the ball the last time, he
recalled, but he'd read various things in his studies, some claiming
that the use of the ball increased certain effects of the Grove, others
stating that those increased effects were mostly imagination. One
of the studies on the increased effect side had actually listed several
such effects, such as metal men appearing in the Grove, and Carrtog
thought that even the possibility of extra effects warranted the
expenditure of a piece of lead.

A mass of flame and sparks shot heavenward, and suddenly the
grove was there. He remembered, too late, that the forward point
man had not been warned about the Grove of Battle, and muttered,
"God of battles, protect him!"

He dropped the empty pistol back into his boot-top, then took out the other one from his sash. He heard shouting and gunfire from within the Grove and thought, it must be having some effect, even just making them waste their ammunition.

Carrtog and the first rank of troopers entered the Grove. There was a moment of sheer black darkness, then light returned. Further in amongst the trees and still out of sight they could hear more shouting and clashing of swords. Who's fighting who? Or have they been deluded into fighting each other?

He did recall that the spell, as he was casting it now, involved delusions, but the types of delusion were left unspecified.

There was a feeling about the Grove, a feeling of danger, but not danger to those on this 'side' of the spell. He worried briefly about those of his men who might just feel the danger, but not feel that the danger was not for themselves. No, look to your own feelings, don't worry about everyone else.

"The Gray Stone!" He shouted, "The Gray Stone for the King!" It was the war-cry of his own estate, Nandycargllwyd, 'The Brook of the Gray Stone.'

After a moment he heard Yakor take up the same cry, then the other troopers joined in until it ran among the evergreens.

Suddenly they were among the enemy, who seemed to be fighting against each other in little groups here and there. He raised a pistol and fired, then drew his sword since they were now at close quarters.

The delusion seemed to lift off the enemy, though here and there some were still fighting an invisible foe. From the expressions that he saw briefly on their faces, whatever they were fighting was something terrible.

No more time for looking around, then. He swung his sword, a blow that was barely parried, then another stroke that went home. Many of the enemy had not managed to get themselves mounted, and one of those, a wild-eyed fellow who swung his sword fiercely, came rushing at him from the left.

Carrtog managed to interpose his own blade, then cut the man down with a backhand blow. Sometimes rebels tried to hide behind trees, but there was always something, the tail of a cloak, a sword sheath, or just a feeling that someone was there, to give them away. The last effect seemed to be a sudden conspiracy of ravens all squawking and diving at the faces of rebels, distracting them at just the right — or wrong — moment.

The Lord of the Brook of the Gray Stone was satisfied that the Grove of Battle, this time, was far superior to the last time he had used it in battle. At last, they appeared to have dealt with most of the rebels, and Carrtog called out the words that would disperse the Grove.

Chapter 21

Carrtog looked around. The trees seemed to have changed their positions, or perhaps there were not quite so many of them as there had been. The ground was covered with bodies, most of them rebels, but no small number of the king's men as well.

What remained of the rebels were holding up their hands in surrender, but a few still fought on. Those who continued to fight very rapidly grew less, as many who saw that their comrades were yielding decided to follow suit.

"Do we take prisoners, Lord?" Asked Commander Cargiodd. "It has not been the custom under General Hartovan."

"We will take prisoners," Carrtog declared. "Otherwise, consider the fate of our own men taken by the rebels."

"The king may not be pleased, Lord."

"If the king is not pleased, I will explain my thinking to him. Carry on, Commander."

"SO THIS ENDEAVOR WAS a success, Lord."

Carrtog turned back to see Yakor at his left elbow. "So it would seem. What's your feeling about prisoners, Yakor?"

"Your point about the treatment of captives taken by the rebels is a good one, Lord. On the other hand, the king might well see all these people as traitors against his rule and therefore executable out of hand."

"So we kill the prisoners we take, and they answer by slaughtering every person of ours who falls into their hands, and in the end the whole North stinks of death, and who is left to till the fields or inhabit the cities, or give praise to the king?"

Yakor smiled slightly. "I'm not the one you have to convince; he is the one who wears the crown and gives orders to the commanders under him. Are you ready to be so persuasive to him?"

Carrtog took a deep breath. "If I must, then I will." He looked around at the battlefield of his first victory, limited as it was. "I'm afraid that is not the quarrel uppermost in my mind."

Yakor lifted his eyebrows. "Indeed?"

"Indeed." He looked to the sun beginning its descent in the western winter sky. "You haven't forgotten, have you, about the dispute back home, about who should take the risk of taking the glider up, and a risk it is, no matter how careful we might be about it. I escaped that brangle by riding out here to raid the rebels, and that is no real escape, is it? When we return, it will not have escaped Addy's attention that I rode out into danger in order to escape discussing a different danger."

"I'm not proficient in dealing with women, but the best advice I can give you is to apologize, first, and with sincerity, and go on from there."

"You feel I should give up on testing the glider myself?"

Yakor shrugged. "I don't believe I can give you useful advice on that. You may have to decide just what is most important and accept the results of that decision."

Carrtog frowned. "You're right, Yakor. It is no easy choice, and I'll have to deal with it. I just hope I can make a decision and follow through, no matter the cost."

THEY RETURNED TO KILGARHAI victorious, though none of them were deluded into thinking that this was a major triumph. It was, however, a win, one that had been achieved under the new general, with the new general taking a major part in the fight — it was certain that the battle would not have been quite so successful if it had not been for his magic.

Addy was waiting outside the front door of their quarters when Carrtog and Yakor came up.

Carrtog, fully conscious of being splashed with blood and smelling of horse and gunpowder and other uncomfortable odors, felt very unequal to the discussion he was afraid was coming.

"Addy, my dear, I'm sorry. I took advantage of a battle to escape a discussion I didn't want to have. I—"

"Carrtog, hush! You went off to a fight, which was almost necessary to make sure of your new command. When you first went, I was angry, right enough, thinking that you had only taken advantage of the fight to escape a quarrel. After a bit, though, I realized that, even in the best of circumstances, you would be riding out to battle from time to time, and no matter how much the odds might be in your favor, there was always that chance of one bullet, stray or aimed, or one man with a sword who just might be lucky that day.

"Because of who you are, there is no way I can keep you safe for certain, and I am just going to have to accept the fact that, along with the wife or lover of the lowliest trooper under your command. I have to accept the fact that you are in danger, and lift my eyes up to the Gods, praying for your safety."

She paused. "I'm still not happy with the thought of your taking that glider up, unsafe as we both know it is. But I also know that, if the glider functions as well as you hope it will, it can provide you with information that might just make a coming battle a little less dangerous, setting aside the bad luck that just might go against you or that lowliest trooper on that one day.

"So perhaps I must grit my teeth and clench my fists when you test the flying machine, and try to convince you to assign it to some other of your men when you've made it as safe as you can, just to take one risk out of your hands, leaving you to deal with all the other chances of battle. Can I ask at least that of you?"

He looked at her face, and knew that, though he had not thought much of the risks of this battle, she had been afraid every moment he had been away.

"Yes," he said, "I think I can promise at least that. I wish I could promise not to take too many or too great risks, but I never know just what might—"

She stopped him there. "Hush, my dear. We both know what your duty requires of you, and while I can't promise to be happy every time you ride out, I can at least promise to not send you off with a fearful face. And as for little Aderyn, I"m sure you will be the best father to her in every moment you have with her, and she and I will have to be satisfied with that."

"No," he said. "I will have to be the best father to her and the best husband to you that I can manage, in every moment we have. I know it's not enough, but I hope it will do."

She put her arms around him, dirt and odors and all, and said, "We will make it do, both of us."

LIFE WENT ON. CARRTOG had brought up several kegs of nails, as well as various other bits of finishing materials in order to build their house. When the building was near to being done, it was clear that there was a good deal of material left over, including at least one full keg of nails, and another partially full. All of this material

Carrtog put out on consignment to local merchants, and, in order not to seem to favor one merchant over another, he divided it among all who were interested. Further, in order not to damage local enterprise, he charged a little more than the going rates. As he told the merchants when making his offers, "I'm already losing money because I'm not charging enough to make up for the costs of shipping these things up from the south. All I want to do is cut back my losses, but if I try to charge what it cost me, no one would buy."

The rebels continued to break up sections of track, and the engineers under Carrtog's command continued to send out parties, carefully guarded, to repair those tracks.

Carrtog himself tried to work out spells to watch the tracks more carefully, sending out an alarm when anyone first attempted to tamper with them in hopes of cutting down delays in train schedules.

Finally, one morning the glider was ready for its first test flight. Carrtog had delayed as long as possible, adjusting everything that could be adjusted without taking it off the ground. The newly designed high-pressure steam engine was set up at one end of a long field; the engine's sole purpose was to rapidly wind a length of rope around a pulley. The rope was attached to the nose of the glider at the far end of the field. At a signal from Carrtog in the pilot's seat, Gryff would engage the pulley, which would rapidly haul the glider along the field and hopefully get it airborne by at least halfway to the steam engine. At that point, Carrtog would hit the lever to open the hook attached to the rope, and from there he would attempt to find a rising current of air to help him climb further toward the clouds.

So, on a cool winter morning, he climbed into the pilot's seat, having first checked that the rope was securely fastened to the hook at the nose of the craft. He looked down the field to where Gryff waited, one gloved hand on the lever that would engage the pulley. Addy was there, too, having forced herself into a state that she was able to believe that the glider would not only go up, but would come down in one piece, bringing her husband back safely. Carrtog raised his hand high, high enough to be sure Gryff could see it, and chopped it down sharply.

He could see the movement as Gryff pulled the lever, then the rope, already tight, tautened with a jerk, flinging his head back, and the glider was rolling down the field, picking up speed.

He pulled down on the controls that would make the machine go up, and felt it lift slightly, then a little more, then it suddenly leaped into the air. He slapped a hand down on the lever that released the rope and continued to pull steadily on the controls to keep it going up. Not too much, he warned himself, we don't want to stall out.

He used the controls to swing up and to the right, still using his forward momentum to climb, but trying to be careful not to climb too much.

He eased the controls slightly forward avoiding a stall, which would likely be followed by a sharp dive toward the ground. Suddenly he was climbing again!

Looking around and up, he saw several birds in the area, wings extended, and going up as well. He was caught in the same rising air current as they, and if he wished, he could probably go much higher.

He pulled himself back from that thought; the purpose of this day's flight was merely to make sure that the glider could actually fly, and then get it back down without damage, either to the craft or to himself.

He eased the controls forward, moving to the left as he did so, sending the machine into a downward spiral. After some careful maneuvering, he was still about twenty feet in the air, approximately over the spot from which he had started.

He continued to lose height, but he still had considerable speed. He pulled back on the controls, started climbing a bit, and rapidly began to lose speed. He pushed the controls forward again, carefully, so as not to come in nose first, then pulled back. The undercarriage touched the ground, and the sudden jar slammed his head forward to hit the controls, dazing him.

At this point, all he could do was hold on until the glider rolled to a stop. Blood was running down into his eyes, and he had a moment's thought for how Addy would greet the sight of him stepping out of the glider, face awash with blood. A moment later, the left-side wheel gave way, and the stump of the undercarriage dug into the ground, slapping him forward again, and swinging the glider sharply around to slide sidewards for a bit, losing its final momentum when the right-hand wheel collapsed.

The glider tipped rightwards sharply, then lost all momentum and slammed back down on the ground.

Carrtog sat still for a bit, estimating how badly he himself was injured. Aside from two blows on the forehead, he seemed to be all right, and though the head wound was bleeding badly, as head wounds will, he was mostly unhurt.

He began to haul himself out of the pilot's seat. As he did so, he was aware of rushing feet coming toward him. Gryff and Yakor were almost there, with several other servants and guards close behind.

Addy, encumbered by her skirts, was coming as quickly as she could.

"Yakor, have you got something I could wrap around my head? I'm sure I look like I'm half-dead, and I don't want to frighten Addy too badly."

Yakor found a scrap of linen and bound it round Carrtog's head with a leather thong, just as Addy came up, her face white.

"Carrtog? Are you all right? Shouldn't you lie down?"

"No, Addy, I'm fine. I just banged my head, that's all, and head-wounds always bleed badly. I may have a bruise here and there, but otherwise I'm fine."

"You certainly don't look fine, with blood all over," she answered, skeptically.

"Has nobody in your family taken a tumble and banged their head? As I said, head-wounds always bleed ferociously."

"I still think you should be lying down, or sitting at least."

"When I get off this field, I'll be glad to sit down. I'd also be grateful for something to drink, a nice cup of wine, for instance."

"Yes indeed, we did bring along some wine. All we need is to get you over to where the wine is waiting."

"All right. Gryff, would you go look over the glider, see what repairs need to be made before it can go up again?"

"Yes, Lord."

He saw the look on Addy's face, and knew that she was very close to demanding that he not try to take the glider up again. He turned to Yakor. "It won't go up again until we've done some strengthening of the undercarriage, at the very least. It's quite the experience, though."

"I'm sure it is," Yakor said, grinning. "I don't think it's an experience I wish to try, though."

CARRTOG MADE IT A POINT to go out from time to time with the patrols that patrolled the line, at the very least to make himself familiar with the situation that the ordinary troopers faced day-to-day.

He also took the opportunity to set up tentative magical 'watch-posts' along the line, usually high up in a tree. For this he used a small device attached to a crossbow quarrel which was shot up into a tree-trunk where it could 'see' a fair section of the track and the cleared right-of-way.

They also marked the perimeter of several other farmsteads which were strongly suspected of supplying the rebels. Twice more, parties went out and followed the rebels to their camps.

He hadn't accompanied either group, and the first time they didn't quite catch the rebels by surprise, ending in a hard-fought victory, the insurrectionists dying almost to the last man and the king's soldiers suffering near fifty per cent casualties. The second time, the rebels had already left the camp, going off in several directions. The magical trail eventually died out, so they had to track by normal means and were only able to track one band to a place were they had been forced to stop to rest. Since the pursuers themselves had broken up into separate parties to follow, they ended up with just a slight numerical advantage over the enemy. In addition, they too were worn out with riding. The battle, therefore, seemed to be a succession of missed sword-strokes and, more unfortunately, missed parries, ending with the surviving rebels heading off into the brush with the surviving troopers too tired and battered to pursue further.

WITH THE CONSTRUCTION of the house finished, Carrtog ordered in a number of bolts of cloth for his servants to make up into clothing for his household, including all the servants and people attached to his house. When that was done, he ended up with several bolts of cloth left over.

As he had done with the leftover construction materials for his house, he took the cloth and consigned it to local merchants for sale, again being careful not to attempt to undercut the prices of the local suppliers.

One of the merchants, after having completed the arrangements for the sale of the cloth, commented, "Not that I object to taking your goods for resale, Lord, but it seems you estimated your needs as a little larger than they ended up being."

"Yes, I suppose so, but if I'd estimated too low, then I'd be in the situation of having to order more cloth, and hoping to be able to get the exact shade and quality again. This way, though I lose a little money, I get just what I wanted. And with luck, I won't lose all that much, for someone will surely be willing to take the stuff off my hands."

As they rode back from the store, Yakor spoke up. "Tell me, these goods you ordered from the south and discovered that you had too much of, was this possibly some sort of deeper plan to get the merchants on your side?"

He twisted his head to look at Yakor. "Have I been that obvious?"

"No, not really. I just hope you aren't counting too heavily on their suddenly becoming your partisans."

Carrtog grimaced. "I'll admit that had been my hope at the start. Now, though, I'll settle for them perhaps disliking me a little less than any other royal general."

Yakor grinned broadly. "Well, perhaps you have some chance of achieving that."

AS WINTER BEGAN TO draw to a close, the rebels began to grow more active. Partly in response to this, Carrtog accompanied more patrols and forces sent out to track the rebels to their camps.

They flew the glider several more times, Carrtog at the controls for the first two, but for the third and following flights Gryff volunteered. By the time of the third flight, Carrtog had managed to develop a technique of landing safely and was able to instruct Gryff in the method. The flights were not very long, though on one of his flights Gryff managed to catch an updraft and had flown in an upward spiral until he began to worry about going too high. His concern almost undid him and at first he tried to lose altitude too fast. He was in a dive when he pulled up on the controls in order to cut down on his speed of descent. As he'd relayed to Carrtog, he'd felt and heard the wooden frame of the wings starting to crack, so he eased the controls forward again. He was still coming down fast when the undercarriage touched down, and the glider actually bounced twice. He banged his forehead on the control-bar, as Carrtog had done, but they had put up padding to prevent the kind of damage Carrtog had suffered. Furthermore, in light of Carrtog's experience, they had developed close-fitting leather caps, padded with wool, to protect the pilots' heads so he came away with only a nasty-looking bruise. When the glider bounced, the right wing had partially broken away from the fuselage, but the damage was repairable. Gryff was extremely apologetic, but Carrtog said, "In my first flight, I did even more damage to it. The most important thing is whether or not you learned anything useful from this flight."

Gryff thought a bit. "Yes, I caught an updraft and took it pretty far upward, but I started to worry about whether I'd be able to come down slow enough to land on the field I took off from. But you were wanting to take the thing up high, high enough to fly a fair distance and be able to look down from up there and possibly see where the rebels were camped. If we got a good updraft, we could go quite a way before we came down, but we might have to be ready to come out with a team and wagon and load the glider up somewhere out along the road."

"If we managed to land on the road itself and not come down in the middle of the trees. But I suppose that would be part of our problem, to make sure we stayed within range of the road so we could come down on it."

Chapter 22

Carrtog read for a second time the message he'd just received. It was a royal message, brought by courier from Waliauchel, having just arrived this afternoon. He looked up at Yakor. "The king's going back up to take command of his troops again. He plans to spend a day, perhaps two, here at Kilgarhai, to see how we've been managing. How have we been managing, Yakor?"

The older man shrugged. "You're the general here, you know better than I."

"Well, we haven't managed to put an end to rebel activity in the area, but our trains are mostly keeping their schedules, and we've fought several successful small actions against the rebels. I'd say we've done pretty well."

"Now all you need to do is to tell that to the king and convince him. You might want to be wary of seeming to be doing too well, though. We suspected he might have given you this task in hopes that it would defeat you, as it did General Hartovan, and that he could then have you retire in disgrace. You might want to ask yourself what action would the king take if he felt you were being too successful."

Carrtog dropped his hand to his side, still holding the king's message, and looked thoughtful. "Yes," he said, "what might he do in that case? Might he simply declare that I hadn't been successful enough and go on from there?"

"If he thought that through carefully, he'd likely decide it was too big a risk to him. All he has against you is suspicion of passing rumors. There are too many other powerful lords who could see themselves as more of a threat to him and might conceivably wonder what he might do about them."

"That would be more reassuring if we were certain that His Majesty always thought things through carefully."

Yakor scowled.

ALONG WITH THE KING'S message to Carrtog, the courier had also brought a letter from Princess Ellevar to Addy. After she had read it privately, Addy brought it out to Carrtog and Yakor. "Listen to this, my dear," she said, "'My father will often not concern himself at all with Lord Carrtog, but when he does, he often notes how well Lord Carrtog has done for him, but on a few occasions, he will seem to put on another face and be determined that Lord Carrtog is against him, and therefore wishes to see Lord Carrtog fail. I do what I can, but there is only so much I can do. Please tell your husband to guard himself, to see that there is no grounds for my father to call him to account. If he ever finds such grounds, I fear it will go badly for both of you.'"

Carrtog scowled an expression to match the one on Yakor's face. "Now, there's a difficulty the Gods would be hard put to unravel! I can work hard to please the king, but if I must defeat the phantoms that arise in the king's mind, then the Gods alone can give me success!"

"So what's your plan, then? Go hang yourself to save His Majesty the trouble?"

Carrtog turned a glare in Yakor's direction. "No, I believe I'll prove to the king that his efforts to turn me into a well-trained magician were not in vain."

Yakor nodded, smiling. "That sounds better than the whimpering you were aggravating us with just now. Do you have something specific in mind?"

"Not exactly, but I had been thinking of something, I just hadn't done anything with it, having been too concerned with making a glider that would fly longer distances. Perhaps I should spend some time on something a little less flashy, but perhaps with more immediate use."

He took out the communicator he had in his pocket, and spoke the words that would cause the communicator in Gryf's pocket to ring. Shortly he heard Gryff's voice saying "Yes, Lord?"

"Gryff? Find the notes I made on carrying things by means of hot air and bring them to me. I think I have a notion to make this of use to us in attempting to track the rebels."

"Yes, Lord. I'll be there directly."

"'Directly?'" Yakor smiled. "The young farmer's son is taking on the ways of speech of an upper-class servant."

"Please don't mock him, Yakor. He's trying to better himself, which is all to the good. I wouldn't care to have him think all it earned him was a sneer."

Yakor held up his hands in feigned surrender. "No, he'll hear nothing from me. I just hope he works at more than just using the right words."

"I don't think you need fear on that score, Yakor. Gryff's work is his first concern, putting the right words to it is only secondary."

Shortly Gryff was there with a small sheaf of papers in his right hand. "These are all the relevant papers, Lord, but there seems to be very little here, just a note about hot air rising and how light things, such as dry leaves or feathers, are lifted in the air over a fire, and a suggestion to yourself to look into this."

"What do you think about it, Gryff?"

The young man looked at him a little doubtfully. "To tell the truth, Lord, I had noticed the same things that you did, but had not thought beyond that. However, it does seem to me that if we were to gather enough heat, it could lift at least a little weight."

"Suppose we were to make an arrangement whereby a small weight could be lifted, and that weight given to a magic device that could seek out the rebels? What would you say to that?"

"Lord, I know practically nothing at all about magic, but I do know something about mechanics. We will first have to make some tests to see just how much weight can be lifted, then see just how heavy the magic-bearing device needs to be. I assume you were also thinking of having the whole thing pressed to go in certain directions, also by magic?"

"Yes. I'm going to have to work on several different spells, perhaps even using some magic to help in the lifting. Could you start work on the methods of using heat to lift something? Some kind of very light bag, for instance?"

"Yes, Lord. If you wish, I'll begin at once."

"Do so."

As Gryff left to carry out his instructions, Carrtog turned to Yakor once more. "We've still had no luck in discovering how the rebels manage to keep their gliders in flight for so long? None of our spies have even come close?"

"Exactly. They've managed to maintain their secrecy, in part because of their determination to release themselves from the king's rule. The people in charge of their gliders police themselves severely, never letting any one of their number even go off drinking alone where some stranger might join him in drinking and lead him to let his tongue go loose. All we've managed to discover is that magic is involved, somehow."

"Yes, we've suspected that, but..." Carrtog's voice trailed off as he went into deep thought.

Yakor looked at him sharply. "What now? You look as if you have an idea."

"Yes. It's one of those ideas that seems so simple that you wonder why it never occurred to you before. In many cases, what magic does is to increase some naturally occurring phenomenon, or cause it to occur in spite of actual conditions, such as those little devices I made to warm our hands. So the glider uses warm air to lift itself higher. Can I make some sort of device that will produce its own warm air in a large enough space to allow a glider to take advantage of it?"

Yakor smiled. "I hope I wasn't supposed to answer that question. I know a few bits of combat magic, that's all. You're the one who's been given all the magic lessons."

Carrtog chuckled. "It's not likely to be a matter where either you or I just say here's the answer, more likely it'll take a whole lot of work, trying this and that, adjusting here and adjusting there, and finally saying, 'That seems to be as close as we're going to get.' Now I think I'd better find Gryff; I set him to work on what is likely to be the first step on the way, and I should put myself there as well."

IT WAS A BRISK SPRING day and the king had rested well overnight in Carrtog's newly-built house. They had breakfasted at a fairly early hour, as befit men on a military assignment, and were now out in the field where Carrtog was about to demonstrate a new weapon in the fight against the local rebels and their constant attempts to cut the railroad line between Gwarasai and Kilgarhai. Though the glider was still expected to play a large part in Carrtog's strategy, it was presently disassembled and stacked in a locked shed across town. Carrtog had decided, after some thought, that it was best not to admit to the king that he was attempting any work with gliders. It did not seem like the path of wisdom, considering the king's antipathy to such mechanisms.

"The prime difficulty, Your Majesty, is to find them in the woods. We can and do patrol the woods as best we can, but if their bands break camp and move every two to three weeks, it's only a matter of luck that we ever come on them. Well, luck and the highly developed skill of my patrol-commanders.

"But patrols can only cover so much territory in any given time, so we need a better way of tracking the rebels through the brush. My first success was when I put a magic circle around certain farms that were strongly suspected of giving food to the rebels.

"When their foraging parties broke the circle, they carried a magical trace all the way back to their camp; even when they broke their trail by riding up a stream or any such tricks. We would follow the magical trace all the way to their camp and attack them.

"This, though, still has us waiting for them to move and only moving in response to them."

He paused and stretched out a hand, palm up, toward the small wooden table that held the objects on display.

There was a small wooden rack supporting a bag made of sheets of paper pasted together. The bag narrowed at the mouth, and fastened below that mouth was a small tray on a cradle of light straps. On top of the tray was a small package of cloth tied with string and tied to the top of that was a small flat pebble about the size of a curled index finger.

"We have all seen light things lifted into the air over a fire. If we have a bag to capture more of the heat, we can lift a little more.

"The pebble contains a spell which, when put into operation, produces a good deal of heat, though not enough to cause anything to burn. The hot air, concentrated in the bag, will lift the whole thing into the air. The wrapped package contains another spell, or rather, a set of spells. When the bag has reached a certain height, in this case, slightly above treetop level, measured by the trees just outside the town, it will move along the line of the streets. As it moves, whatever is in its view will be shown in the basin of water there on the table. It will continue to spin slowly as it moves, and when we can see the Railroad Station in the basin, it will move straight in that direction. When it reaches a certain distance from the station, another spell will come into effect, and the Railroad Station will begin to shine with a pink glow as we view it in the basin."

He paused, looking up at the king. "I will now speak the spell that will begin the operation, causing the pebble to heat and the bag to lift."

He spoke the incantation, and for a moment nothing happened, then the bag began to quiver. The bag continued to quiver, shaking more rapidly, then almost suddenly it leaped into the air.

As Carrtog had predicted, it went almost straight up, though it was blown a little to the south by the weak northern breeze. Having reached its treetop level, it began to move along the streets. A picture of the street-scene appeared in the basin of water, moving as the bag continued to move, spinning slowly.

Gradually, the Railroad Station began to appear in the basin of water, and when it was fully in the center of the basin, the bag ceased to spin, and the picture grew larger as the bag approached the Station.

Then almost suddenly it stopped. There was a long pause, and then the Railroad Station began to glow a deep pink.

The king began to applaud, followed by the rest of his party.

"The balloon was lifted only by hot air," Carrtog stated, "with no lift at all supplied by direct magic. It was indeed steered by magic, in particular when its target came in sight."

"A very pretty demonstration, Lord Carrtog. It would have been more effective had you actually used this balloon to hunt down and kill some actual rebels."

"Of course, Your Majesty. This was merely a demonstration of the balloon's capability, with proper magical direction. Our next step is to produce enough of the balloons that we can put them in place where we are fairly certain the rebels will come, then track the rebels to their camps. At the very least, we will force them to move their camps more often, leaving them less free to attack the rail lines. Guarding the rail lines is my main task, to ensure that supplies can pass from here on up to Your Majesty's forces."

"Until such time as rebel magicians begin plucking your balloons out of the sky."

"Of course, Your Majesty. But I will not be slow in adding magical protections to my balloons, and the rebels will not likely risk magicians of the necessary caliber in the woods with the wandering bands."

The king nodded. "Keep up the good work, Lord Carrtog."

THE KING BROKE HIS journey at Kilgarhai for only two days, but it was a time of considerable stress for Carrtog and his command. There always seemed a feeling that the king was looking for something with which to find fault, and Carrtog was pressed to explain all his actions in ways that showed them to be more successful than any alternative he could mention.

At last the king went marching on up the road with his regiments of reinforcements for the forces at the front.

When the last of the rear-guard had marched out of sight along the road north, Yakor turned to Carrtog. "Well, that's done at last. And none too soon, either. I could see you were having more and more difficulty refraining from saying something on the lines of 'You were the one who had me so well trained in magic, Your Majesty. Don't consider it my fault that it worked so well.'"

Carrtog smiled. "All I can do is wonder what he will come up with next. I'm afraid he won't leave me alone forever."

"Don't start thinking those despairing thoughts again, or I'll have to speak sharply to you, most Noble and Successful Lord Carrtog!"

"No, I won't let myself get into that sort of mood. But now that we've got His Majesty off our hands, shall we try to hire local people to make balloons for us?"

"You'd trust the local people for that? Most of them are not particularly on our side, if you'll remember?"

"Yes, I know. But they'd only be making the balloons, and it's difficult to damage something like that so subtly that it couldn't be discovered quickly by the briefest inspection. And we'll need a lot of the things if they're to have any success against the rebels."

THE BUILDING WAS A long, open shed whose roof was held up by wooden pillars along the center. Down the middle ran two long tables. At each of the tables sat three pairs of workmen in staggered positions along each side of the table. In the middle of each table stood a completed paper balloon to serve as a model for each group of workmen, and in front of each man was a stack of paper, a glue-pot, and a pair of scissors. Also in front of each man was a partially completed balloon.

"They're doing quite well," said Carrtog to Yakor. "I have Gryff inspecting the finished work, mostly because if I were inspecting it, it would give the balloons more importance and thus make them a more likely target for sabotage."

"That won't last, you know. The mere fact that you're having them make so many will finally bring someone to guess that they're important. All it will need then is a small spark in the storeroom."

"Give me credit for some sense, Yakor! Both they and the building they're stored in are fully covered in fire-proofing spells."

WHEN THE FIRST TWO balloons were fully prepared Carrtog sent them down along the railroad to Gwarasai, watching for anyone approaching the railroad. "They won't replace your patrols," he told his officers, "not by any means. But I'm hoping they'll be of some assistance. When our spells tell us that someone is attacking the railway lines at some point, I'm hoping to be able to steer the nearest balloon to that point and sometimes to track them as they head back to their camp. We'll also use our little communicating devices to inform the nearest patrol and give them directions as to where to go to follow the rebels."

Captain Fordibrach was frowning. "If you have a dozen or so of those balloons in the air at one time, Lord, how will you know which of them is sending a particular message?"

"That's no real problem, actually; I'll give every one of them a number, or perhaps a name, and when their controllers send a message, they'll speak their designation first of all. So we look at the map and see where that balloon is supposed to be at that time and inform the nearest patrol."

"The Northies'll probably start carrying crossbows to shoot the things out of the sky, Lord."

"They won't be that easy to hit in the first place, and in the second place, I plan to put spells on them to delude the eyes as to just where they are. Any further problems?"

Fordibrach drew a deep breath. "Nothing further, Lord. It just seemed a little too good to be true."

Carrtog smiled. "Oh, I'm quite sure that we'll find problems enough as we try to make these things work. We'll just have to solve the problems as we go."

After talking with his officers, Carrtog spoke to Yakor. "I need to find someone to watch the pictures as the balloons send them back.

For this, I'll need someone I can trust to do the job, not just anybody off the street. They'll also need to be willing to learn a little bit of magic, enough to command the balloon to hold its place, or to carry on along its previous path. Do you think you can find someone like that here in Kilgarhai?"

"I might be able to. There've been some folk moved up here from down south, hoping to get jobs with your household, or in shops that opened up to serve you and your soldiers. Trouble was, you brought most of your household with you, and you've been dealing mostly with shops that were already here so there've been a lot of people doing what work they could get, sometimes even begging in the streets just to get by. We'll have to do some sifting to find the ones who'll really work and aren't just looking for a comfortable position somewhere, but they'll be out there. How many do we need?"

"I'd say half a dozen to start, but keep some names in hand in case we need more."

Yakor nodded. "And to replace those among the first half-dozen who don't work out. Yes, Lord."

Some of the people who had moved up to Kilgarhai from the south had done so in the expectation of finding a fortune in the wake of the advancing Royal Army. The defeat of General Malgwyn's army had disillusioned many of them, some to the point where they took on illicit trades, some to the point that they found themselves begging in the streets.

When it became known that Lord Carrtog, general in charge of the garrison at Kilgarhai, was hiring men his official quarters were immediately besieged by several score seeking work. Yakor immediately set them to work turning earth for a garden behind Lord Carrtog's house.

The second day found the numbers halved, and by the fourth day, the garden was ready and the number of workers was down to eight. Two of these were put to work planting the garden, and the rest, nursing their blisters, were led away to a room inside the lord's quarters where the lord himself explained to them what he wished of them.

CARRTOG SURVEYED THE group before him. "My first question is, 'Do any of you know anything of magic?'"

He paused and looked over the group. They were all looking at each other and at him, and most seemed unsure as to how to answer the question. "Let me assure you, if you know nothing of magic, you will not be discharged; I will just know how much I have to teach you."

There was still doubt on several faces.

"I can see that some of you are feeling doubtful about magic. Tell me your difficulty, and I will try to ease your mind. I need people to learn some little bits of magic to help me in the fight against the rebels, so let me assure you I will discharge no one unless there is some serious reason why you cannot or will not deal with magic. Even in such case, I will let you go with a small fee for your time, so you need not think you have spent all this time for nothing."

He looked around, but there was still silence. No one was willing to be first to speak against a lord. He chose one man whose face looked very grim and pointed at him. "You, you look like you have serious reservations about this project. I cannot ease your concerns if I do not know what they are."

The man stood slowly. "Lord, don't lay heavy punishment on me for this, but though I need work badly, I can't see myself working at laying curses, not even on the enemies of the King, long may He reign."

"Will you accept my assurances that you will be asked to lay no curses, only to work spells that will allow my troops to track down the rebels who are out to destroy the track between here and Gwarasai?"

"Begging your pardon, Lord, but if I'm working some magic, how will I know that it is no curse?"

"I can assure you of that. Listen for a bit, and I will explain just what will be needed of you. First, I will have balloons floating up and down above the railroad line. You may have seen them being tested. These balloons will be moving along the railroad line with a small package attached below them, which has several spells on it. One of these spells will keep watch on the ground to one side, and another of these spells will keep the balloon slowly revolving so that it is continually looking all around. Another spell will send the picture of what is seen back to a device in this room.

"When any picture of rebels, or what look like rebels, appears on the device in front of you, your task is to speak the words that stop the balloon's rotation, and 'fixes its gaze' so to speak, on the rebel party. You will then pass the word to a soldier on duty here, as to where the party was spotted and when, and troopers will be sent out to deal with them. You will also set the balloons to following the rebels so that you can give directions to the troopers who will be pursuing them. Does that satisfy your concern?"

"Yes, Lord. Thank you, Lord."

"Good. Now is there anyone here who has any concern about using magic? No? Then we will commence. Magic consists of drawing power from something, in the cases you will learn from burning gunpowder, and using that to perform the task at hand. Drawing the power from the burning powder is done by means of an incantation, speaking certain words in a certain way.

"The reason we use certain words is because, having been used for the same purpose often before, they have a certain amount of power in themselves. I am told, by men whom I have reason to believe, that if one is sufficiently practiced in drawing of the power, one could use any words, so long as the intent is clear in your mind, and have the same result. I myself am nowhere near that state, and I doubt that any of you, in the amount of time we will probably be working together, will reach that state either.

"It is easiest to use a pistol to burn the powder, since a pistol-shot burns the powder rapidly and produces more power. Firing off pistols in a garrison town, however, is not a good idea, so we will simply burn a pinch of powder each time."

He paused for a moment then went on. "The procedure of watching the images from the balloons is a complex one, so we will start with something simple. You will each cast a spell to make a glass globe light up. On the small table behind me are a number of glass globes. There are also a number of powder-flasks, some small lamps, and a handful of straws for each.

"You will all need one of each. Before you go to pick them up, the powder-flasks are to be left closed until I tell you to open them, and each time you open them to pour out a measure, you are to close them immediately. If I see any man with the powder-flask open when it ought not to be, he will be dismissed immediately, without pay. Do you all understand that?"

He paused, and there was silence. He asked again, "Do you all understand?"

There was a mutter of assent.

He looked them over. "Let us try that once more. If I see any man with his powder-flask open when it ought not to be, he will be dismissed immediately, without pay. Do you understand?"

This time the answering "Yes, Lord!" was loud and clear.

"I assure you that this is not a mere matter of my not trusting you. The fact is, each of you will have enough gunpowder to cause severe damage at a loose spark, and accidentally leaving your powder-flask unstoppered when you are about to set off a small charge of powder is an invitation to setting off an explosion which might well kill the lot of us, including myself. And if you don't care whether you kill yourself, let me assure you that I do care if you kill me. I will therefore always be cautioning you to stopper your powder-flasks when you have poured out the measure for a particular spell. Now I know that you are very careful yourselves, but the man next to you might not be quite so trustworthy, so please understand if I am always harping on caution.

"So, each of you now come up and get your equipment, and we will begin."

THE SIX MEN SAT LOOKING at the glass globes before them, all shining with a green glow. "Well-done," Carrtog said. "This one took you only three tries before you all succeeded. I know of times when it took well over three tries before the whole class was successful. Best of all, no one has been discharged for failing to stopper his powder-flask. That is nothing short of admirable." He raised a hand in warning. "Don't become complacent, however. Complacency can lead to carelessness, which can lead to disaster. Now, let's try another. This time..."

Chapter 23

The first balloon was sitting on a table across the track from the Railway Station fully inflated and ready to go. The full group of balloon-controllers were standing round watching with the man in charge of this particular balloon seated at a chair by the table. Carrtog was also seated at the table; he would give the final order, after which the balloon-controller would speak the words that would send the balloon into the air following the railway track toward Gwarasai.

They had all been fully trained up to the point that each one had sent his balloon down along the track to the first bend, then had that balloon turn round and come back, all the while watching what the package beneath the balloon 'saw.' They had all practiced taking shifts at watching the balloon's progress, and checking when the spell needed to be renewed on the basin of water in which they saw what was below the balloon. This involved emptying the basin, cleansing it, and refilling it with clear water. Even still, Carrtog hadn't spent all day, every day, training these men. After he finished seeing this first balloon off, he would be going out to watch another flight of the glider.

"Go ahead, Hwydach."

The stocky, dark-haired man touched a lit splinter to a touch of gunpowder in a small bowl, at the same time speaking the incantation that increased the heat, lifting the balloon into the air. As it rose, he spoke the further incantation that set it moving down the track, slowly rotating as it went.

There were a few cheers from the gathered group; though they all had successfully sent balloons up and along the track for a short way, Hwydach was first to be sending his the full length to Gwarasai.

They all watched as it went out of sight, then Carrtog spoke. "Now, back to the balloon-shed, and set up your basin there to watch the balloon's progress. All is arranged as to who is taking the following shifts? Good. If everyone has their equipment in good order, you may have the rest of the afternoon off.

"Hwydach, you may have the equivalent time off after your shift is over, and the same for those taking shift from you. Parmavon, you will be ready to launch your balloon about eight hours from now, and Hachenbra, eight hours from then. All clear?"

"Yes, Lord."

"Then off you go."

THE GLIDER, IN ITS present form, was somewhat different from the original form, different even from the gliders that had hunted them out of the North. It was somewhat narrower, and the wings were somewhat longer, and a bit narrower as well. All this had the effect of increasing its lift, and thus increasing the distance it could go before it finally set down.

It was piloted, this time, by a volunteer from among the troopers. Carrtog — after a discussion with Yakor — had been forced to admit that it was at least a little more important that he stay alive than that he demonstrate to his men that he was not afraid to do anything he might ask them to do.

There was a large flat space of cobblestones somewhat beyond the steam engine that would provide the power to initially put the glider in the air. This section of cobblestones had a spell on it that was putting out heat, sufficient heat, it was hoped, to provide a significant updraft, which would permit the glider to climb to a fair height.

Another new thing about the glider, a thing that was not immediately visible, was that the wooden frame of its fuselage had been remade into a magically reinforced material that Carrtog had developed using inspiration from Enemantwin's near-iron conversion spell. Not only was the craft lighter than it had been when constructed of wood, but the fuselage was further strengthened magically as it was shaped to make it much more sturdy.

All this had rendered glider flight a much less dangerous occupation. Though, it was not so much less dangerous that Addy did not become tense whenever Carrtog took the glider up.

He'd only tried once to convince her how much more safe the glider had become, and decided, having escaped a quarrel by the skin of his teeth, that he wouldn't try to convince her again. He would force himself to settle for only the occasional flight.

CARRTOG GAVE A TUG at the rope where it was attached to the nose of the glider, then turned to the pilot. "All solid, Pilot Brachgwyn. Do you want to test it yourself?"

"With your permission, Lord." The pilot tugged fiercely on the rope himself. There had been a time when the pilots were leery of checking anything that the lord had checked until they had found that he encouraged them to check things for themselves.

Carrtog held out a hand, and Brachgwyn took it. "Gods be with you, Pilot."

"Thank you, Lord."

He did not bother giving the pilot any last-minute instructions; the man knew quite well what was expected of him. Brachgwyn climbed into the cockpit and fastened the belt that would prevent him from being flung around at the shock of landing.

He looked around to be sure that the lord and the other people were well out of the way, then gave a wide wave of his hand to Gryff at the control of the steam engine. Gryff, in his turn, engaged the pulley, and the glider began to roll down the field.

Carrtog, hiding his restiveness, watched until the undercarriage pulled free of the ground, only then noticing that he had been holding his breath. The glider's forward momentum allowed it to continue picking up speed, which in turn allowed it to gain a bit more altitude. It was just beginning to lose speed when it reached the edge of the area of rising warm air. Brachgwyn clearly knew what to do, for the glider began to move in a circle, nose up.

The artificially warmed air would cool soon, losing its upward motion, but he would take advantage of every inch of climbing force it provided.

Carrtog found himself muttering, "Keep it climbing! Keep it climbing!"

Yakor chuckled beside him. "That's not one of your incantations, is it?"

Carrtog turned, grinning. "Perhaps it is, it seems to be working."

"You plan to stand here watching, muttering, during the entire flight?"

"I think not. He's trying for distance."

"Which I already knew, boy."

"Of course you did. Sorry. I'm just a little on edge. Those balloons bid fair to be quite useful, but having a working glider, perhaps two, would be a serious advantage."

"You think so? They didn't do so well spotting us when we were on the run."

"No, but there were only a few of us. There're what? Thirty to fifty of the rebels, maybe two or three bands of that many? They'll have a harder time hiding themselves, I'd think."

Yakor pursed his lips and nodded. "Possibly so. I haven't had any experience trying to spot groups of men from the air, let alone trying to do that spotting while trying to keep a glider up in the air. Speaking of which, what do you plan to do while you're waiting for Brachgwyn to get back?"

"I'm going to do some shopping. Well, actually, I'm going to put some more things up for sale."

"What is it this time? I don't recall your having ordered anything from the south that you have an excess of."

"No, I haven't ordered anything from the south, this is something I've produced myself."

THE STOREKEEPER WAS a stout man, very good-humored, with a ruff of gray hair surrounding a bare crown.

"Good day to you, Lord Carrtog!" he said. "Have you come to sell me some of your surplus goods again?"

"Not this time, Storekeeper Carfwyn. This time it is something I have developed myself." Carrtog motioned for Yakor to set down the armload he'd been carrying. "You may have noticed the glider that I and my men have been building? This is a material that I created specifically for its construction."

"You mean to sell me lumber, Lord?"

Carrtog smiled. "Not mere lumber, Storekeeper. You see, one of my tutors in magic was a man who was interested in plant-magic. Not only healing herbs, but ways to make those herbs more effective and various ways of processing plants to make them serve various purposes.

"This material here is made from a slurry of certain plants, mashed in water, then poured into forms and solidified both by drying and the use of special spells. This leaves one with material that is strong and is light, but not so light as to be blown away in a high wind.

"It can be cut with a saw, fastened together with nails, and takes a coat of paint, if you want. It will probably last longer than wood, though of course I haven't had the time to actually test its duration.

"It can be produced in a wide variety of shapes and sizes, from studs for wall-framing to sheets to make the walls themselves, or even, if you wish, round poles for making fences. I suggest that I supply you with a number of what you would guess would be most desirable forms, with the suggestion that customers tell you what they would prefer. I promise that I will attempt to make whatever form they desire, with the proviso that extreme lengths or widths might be more difficult, and thus more costly.

"What do you say to that?"

The Storekeeper's face took on a doubtful expression, an expression that Carrtog recognized not as rejection, but more as the 'bargaining face.' "Well," he began slowly, "There is first the question of magic, Lord. You understand that many people will be loath to build anything that depends so heavily on magic. For many, there will be the fear that magic, a power they understand only vaguely, will suddenly fail, leaving their house fallen down around their ears."

Carrtog spread his hands, palms upward. "I'm sure you can deal with most such questions. Point out that I have used this material extensively in building the glider that you will have seen flying around, here and there. Since I am willing to trust the lives of my men and myself to this work, surely they can trust it for building."

The Shopkeeper still looked doubtful. "Still, Lord, there will be those who will be cautious, at least until they see some other using the material. I would not want to ask too high a price, for fear of adding cost to the reasons not to buy."

"I, on the other hand, would not be willing to give the stuff away; after all, I did invest a lot of time into its development."

"True enough, Lord, but I think it might be risky, for the both of us, to set a price here and now. If none of my customers are willing to pay that price, then it will sit here, taking up space, no matter how much you assure me of its quality. Would you be willing, Lord, to leave it with me, and trust me to get the best price I can get for it?"

Carrtog had dealt with Carfwyn and had heard others telling of their own dealings with the man sufficiently often to be willing to trust the Storekeeper, so he held out his hand and they clasped hands over the agreement.

When they went back out into the streets again, Yakor said, "Seems to me you're putting a good deal of trust in the man, him being one of the people who object to the king's rule, and by extension, have little regard for you, being the representative of the king in this area."

"True enough, but Carfwyn is a businessman, and I am a customer who often has a good deal of money to spend. Will he want to cheat me and lose the money I might spend in his store in future?"

"So you've taken thought of every eventuality, have you?"

"Not necessarily every eventuality, but all that I could come up with. If the fates toss something at me that I haven't thought of, that's the time when I try to think fast and act faster. Now, shall we go see whether or not our glider has returned?"

IN FACT, IT HAD NOT yet returned. The pilot's instructions had been to keep the field in sight and to try to get back to the field before he lost too much altitude. In an emergency, he was to pick any open stretch of road or field of sufficient length and come down there.

He had both a communicating device and a locating device, so they would be able to find him even if he crashed and was unable to tell them where he had come down.

It was now somewhat past the time when he was expected back and everyone was scanning the skies anxiously. Carrtog was sure he felt at least as anxious as any other, though he tried hard not to show it.

Suddenly his communicator buzzed. He had discovered somewhat earlier that the blinking light was fine if the device was on a table in a dimly-lit house, but not so fine if the device was in a pouch or saddle-bag. He had been holding the thing in his hand for the last half-hour; even so, the sound caught him by surprise.

"Lord, I'm coming down. I'm landing on the road about ten miles south of town. I'll try to call you when I'm down." The communicator went silent.

Carrtog forced himself to say no more than, "I hear you, Pilot."

The man was going to be too busy to listen to any advice he might have, let alone any scolding for not coming back sooner.

He turned to Yakor.

"Get out a couple of wagons. Load in a lot of tools and bring along a full troop. We'll have to dismantle the glider, at least partially, in order to bring it back, and I wouldn't like to have a bunch of rebels jump us in the middle of things."

"Yes, Sir! I'll take care of it." He turned and began calling out orders.

Carrtog sent a man off to see to getting his own equipment organized for the march, after which he stood or sat, working hard at pretending not to be anxiously waiting for Brachgwyn to call.

When the man still hadn't called, nor answered when Carrtog called him, and a good half-hour had passed, Carrtog got hold of

Yakor and said, "Bring along someone who can deal with wounds and broken bones."

Yakor gave him a look. "Already done, sir."

"Of course." Carrtog felt himself redden slightly.

Finally they were on the road with Gryff at the reins of a team of horses, the locater close beside him. Carrtog rode in the seat next to Gryff, his own mount being led by Yakor close behind.

The locater showed the glider as down somewhere off to the left, but since everyone knew that the road curved to the left they held to the road. If they went round the curve and the locater still pointed off to the left, they would have to make a decision.

They finished rounding the curve, and Carrtog noticed that the locater still pointed slightly left. Gryff looked at him. "What should I do now, Lord?"

"Keep going on the road, until it points directly leftward, then we stop and start looking for ways to get off the road in that direction."

"Yes, Lord."

As it happened, though, they saw the glider shortly thereafter, its right wing sheared off by a tree. Brachgwyn was leaning against it, looking a little dazed. He pushed himself upright when they approached.

"Sorry, Lord, I misjudged the length of the straight patch of the road, and ended up breaking the glider against this tree. In the collision, my communicator went overboard, and I wasn't steady enough on my feet to go look for it. I'm sorry about the glider, Lord."

"The glider can be repaired, or in the worst case, rebuilt. How are you?"

"Oh, I'm fine, Lord. Just took a bit of a jar, that's all. Give me a night's rest, and I'll be ready to fly again, if you'll allow me, Lord."

"I'll allow it, for certain, so long as this mishap hasn't put you off flying."

"Oh, not at all, Lord!" Brachgwyn was smiling. "I'll just be more careful to judge the length of my landing field and the speed I'm coming in at, that's all."

Carrtog returned the smile. "Good. While I'll always be glad to see my pilots safe, I'd prefer not to have to rebuild the craft too often."

The crew were already at work disassembling the glider and preparing to stow it on the wagons they had brought along. The fellow who knew about wounds and broken bones waited patiently for Carrtog to be through talking to Brachgwyn so he could examine the man for breaks and bruises.

"Well, Yakor, we got out of that one all right."

"Yes, we did. And that young madman is quite willing to go flying again, just determined not to come down so hard the next time."

"But as you said, he is willing to go up again."

"Is there not perhaps some magical thing you can do to keep them from breaking bones if they make some sort of misjudgment? For depend on it, they will indeed make misjudgments from time to time."

Carrtog brought his head up sharply. "Nothing that comes to mind immediately. I'd thought that my improvements to the fuselage would be sufficient. Just because these young madmen, as you call them, are willing to take all kinds of risks is no reason not to try to limit those risks. Thank you, Yakor, for the notion."

CARRTOG PUT THE EGG into the wooden chest, then closed and latched the chest. Drawing a wheel-lock pistol from his sash, he pointed in skyward and spoke an incantation, then squeezed the trigger.

He replaced the pistol, picked up the chest with both hands, then tossed it into the air. He watched it tumble, then hit the ground on one corner, and roll to one side.

He strode forward, noticing that Addy, Gryff, and Yakor were right beside him, apparently as anxious as Carrtog himself to see the results of the experiment.

He righted the chest, unfastened the latch, and opened it. The egg sat in its place, unbroken. He heard the others cheering, just as they might have if the chest had been a crashed glider, and the egg its unharmed pilot.

Addy had her arm around his waist. "It worked, my dear, it worked! You've just made flying much safer."

"I can certainly hope so, my most very dear. Before I can say that for certain, though, I will have to test the spell to see if it can protect a full-sized man. And no, that does not mean intentionally crashing the glider just to test the spell."

TWO WEEKS LATER, THEY were busy reassembling the glider when Parmavon came rushing in. "Lord! We've found them!"

Carrtog looked up. They were rebuilding altogether the wing and the fuselage where that wing connected to it, a job that required tedious exactitude.

"Who have you found, Parmavon?"

"The rebels, Lord! A Gods-lost great camp of them, Lord!"

"Well-done! Let's go have a look at the bowl, then we'll see if they're close enough to make a run at them."

He looked around at the group and called, "Gryff."

The young man looked up. "Lord?"

"One of our hunter-balloons has spotted a rebel camp. You carry on here, while I go see what's needed to deal with that. I don't expect

I'll be done before day's end, so you'll have to take care of locking up here. Can you manage?"

"Yes, Lord!"

He turned back to Parmavon. "I assume you managed to hold on to the final picture, along with the direction and distance?"

"Of course, Lord."

Parmavon led the way back to the shed where the balloon-control stations were set up. The scrying-bowl still showed a still picture of a camp in the woods, a scatter of tents, with men caught in the act of walking to and fro among them. Beside the bowl was a sheet of paper and several sticks of charcoal, while on the sheet of paper was a list of directions: So many miles this way, so many miles that way, and so on.

"Good." Carrtog announced. He wrote briefly with a charcoal stick on the sheet of paper, picked it up, and turned to one of the ubiquitous young boys who hung around the various places where Carrtog's people were working. "Take this to Commander Cargiodd. Tell him I want him to organize a raid here. He's to find me here if he has any questions."

"Yes, Lord!" Taking the paper, the boy dashed off.

Yakor spoke at Carrtog's elbow. "Are you sure he won't just lose that somewhere, or at least go tell someone who has a contact with the rebels?"

Carrtog laughed. "Watching Gods, not that one! His father is one of the balloon-controllers. That means he's pretty much on the outside in this town. And no, he won't try to use this information to put himself on the inside, because it would take too long to find someone who'd talk to him for long enough for him to explain how important this information is. And by that time I'd start wondering why I hadn't heard from Commander Cargiodd, so I'd be looking for him. And as I said, his father is one of the balloon-controllers; that gives him some status among the boys he already knows. He won't jeopardize that."

Yakor gave a brief nod.

Carrtog summoned one of his pages. "Go on back to my quarters and ask the servants to set out my field gear. The commander may wish me to come along with him on this little jaunt."

"Yes, Lord." The page set off at once.

Carrtog said, "I'll just stay here a little longer in case the commander wants to find me, then I'll go back and get dressed."

"Good. If you're deciding to come along, he won't want to be waiting long." Yakor was already in field clothing, including sword and at least one pistol visible.

After a little longer, Carrtog and Yakor set off toward his quarters, leaving instructions to the commander if he came or sent messengers to the balloon-controllers' shed.

Carrtog was dressed and going out the door when the commander drew up on his own horse with a small group of troopers as guard. "You wish to come along on this venture, Lord?"

"Unless you'd strongly prefer not to have me, and even than I would like to hear some good reasons, Commander."

The commander's mouth took on a sour expression. "I really don't want to be the man in charge of a venture in which my commanding officer gets killed, but I don't suppose you consider that a good reason, Lord."

"Not at all, Commander. I assure you I have no intention of getting myself killed in this undertaking; I don't suppose that satisfies you at all."

Commander Cargiodd said nothing, but his expression said a good deal about young commanders who had all sorts of ideas, but who could just possibly be more trouble than they were worth.

Addy also came out to see them off, carrying Aderyn wrapped against the cool spring air. "Come back safely, my dear," she told him.

"Don't fret too much, dear. We'll be back as soon as may be."

Even as he swung up onto his horse, though, he knew that she would fret all the time he was gone, and he felt himself a fool for giving her reassurances that were nothing but wasted breath. Who knew what wild shot, what chance sword-blow, might hit when he least expected it.

"You're sure these rebels will still be there when we get there, Lord? That's some distance away."

"I can guarantee nothing, Commander. If they spotted the balloon and guessed what it meant, they might well pack up and leave immediately. On the other hand, they might decide to delay leaving long enough that we get there before they disperse, or perhaps in enough time afterward to track them before they've gone too far."

They started down the south-west road at a fair pace, though a pace which allowed for supply-carts behind. The rebel encampment was some distance away and would require a day and a half to two days to reach, thus they were required to forage as they went or take supplies with them. Trying to catch highly mobile rebels required fast movement on the part of the royal troops, so foraging was not feasible.

The first part of the trip went quickly since the road was in decent shape. The next part, along a trail that crossed the main road, went a little less quickly, and when the trail degenerated to a mere track, speed was near impossible.

"I'd suggest, Lord, that the main force continue on at the best speed we can make, and let the supply carts come up behind as best they can. We can leave a small force with them in case the rebels go after them. It may be hard on the people with the supply-carts, but it will give us the best chance to catch the rebels in their camp."

Carrtog nodded. "Give the necessary orders, Commander."

As they came nearer to the rebels' position — though still more than a day away — Carrtog spoke to the commander. "It's impossible to render a force this size invisible, but I can make our scouts harder to see. I'd suggest I do that when we start tomorrow's march. It won't be a great advantage, but it will give us a bit of an edge. What do you say?"

"I was never taught this fancy 'now it is, now it isn't' stuff, but if you think it'll give us any help, go ahead. When it comes down to the battle itself, will you be able to do that Battle Grove thing?"

Carrtog looked up at the sky; the clouds were in a pattern resembling a cooked fish. "'Mackerel sky means snow nearby,'" he quoted. "The snow itself isn't a problem, but if there's any wind along with it, the Grove of Battle may be more of a hindrance than a help. We'll see. If I can't use the Grove, there may be other tricks I can use in our aid."

The next morning brought fine flakes of snow, not many, but sufficient for Yakor to warn Carrtog, "If this snow gets too heavy, we'll be slowed even more, not to mention that we may be hard put to see the trail, such as it is."

"True, but the balloon didn't exactly show a trail, it told us so far this way, then so far that way, and so on. If we try to follow those directions, we ought to get there."

Yakor scowled. "If we can; but the balloon-controllers are reckoning, best they can, and we have to reckon best we can, and hope that the snow doesn't confound all our reckoning."

Carrtog grinned. "Perhaps I ought to find a spell to make you think more positively."

Yakor's scowl lessened, slightly. "Perhaps you'd be best-advised to find a spell to make yourself think in the first place."

Chapter 24

O ne thing he could do, though, was put out a spell to detect any spells directed at his force. It could not necessarily say what the spells were, but it would definitely say that there were inimical spells out there. The sort of magic that could hide all such spells from detection was the sort that Enemantwin, or someone better, could accomplish. Such a person would scarcely be willing to live out in the wilds with a small band of rebels; his magic could be best used in other places, which meant Carrtog was reasonably confident his detection spell would find no such challenge.

The result was sobering; "There's significant hostile magic out there, Yakor."

"What does that mean?"

"Well, either there're a lot of people out there with minor spells up, or there's one person with a very large spell up, or some combination of the two. I'd be best off wagering on one or two large spells."

He took his findings to the commander, who received them with his usual contrary attitude. "So does this mean you are to be outdone, magically, Lord?"

"No, I think not. It does mean, though, that I'd be best advised to put up some powerful protective spells. This means that my active spells must be lessened to compensate."

Commander Cargiodd did not quite snort, since he was speaking to his own commander, but his air was one of smugness. "Then it must be a matter of our own men and their non-magical abilities."

Carrtog let the man have his seeming victory; spending his own magic on defense would still be using his magic to aid in fighting the battle even if it were not outwardly visible on the field.

One of the scouts returned with a report that the rebels appeared to be preparing to defend themselves, at least temporarily. "There's a fair lot of them, Sir. They haven't usually stood to fight us, it's very likely that they'll let us come up near to contact, then fire a volley and run off just ahead of us, Sir."

Cargiodd glanced at Carrtog. "It is indeed likely that they'll fire a volley and take off. With the weather the way it's looking to be, they might well get away from us if we aren't prepared for that course. We should attack now with a portion of our men, flush them out, and swing around to catch them as they retreat."

"No, rather than firing a volley and running they'll stand fast while their magicians hit us with something of their own. This is likely the magic I was sensing. Give me a moment to prepare, else we'll be caught where they want us. I'll spend a lot of power on simple defense, something to counter or quash whatever they try. The way the wind is looking, I doubt it'll be the Grove of Battle or anything related to that. There's always a chance they'll try something I'm not familiar with, and I won't be quite able to quash it completely, but I'll try to bring out something of my own they won't expect to balance things."

"That doesn't seem to bode well for our chances today, Lord. It appears that we will indeed be depending on our non-magical weapons and the courage of our men to face whatever horrors their magicians can bring on."

"Don't worry, Commander, I'm sure I can provide more than just another body on another saddle. Give your orders."

THE ROYAL TROOPS MOVED forward in their formation, the snow whirling around them, preventing them from seeing more than a few feet in front of them. The situation, of course, would be the same for the enemy, so the disadvantage was equal.

Carrtog heard a shot far off in front of them and suspected someone had fired in advance of orders.

Suddenly, there was a large dark figure in the blowing snow before them. A moment later the dark figure showed itself to be a large human figure, giving off an unearthly glow. It carried an ancient shield in one hand, an equally ancient sword in the other, and wore a metal helm on its head.

Several of the troopers in front of it fired, but the bullets seemed to have no effect. Carrtog's first thought was that this was some apparition, and its main purpose was to cause fear and consternation among the troops it approached.

Even as that thought came to him, the apparition stepped forward, almost into the royal ranks, and swung its sword. Men it touched crumpled to the ground and did not move.

Obviously, this was more than a mere apparition. Carrtog raised his pistol and fired, repeating an incantation as he aimed. The apparition disappeared in a flash of light.

"Time for my own magic," he muttered, and drew another pistol. Speaking an incantation, he fired toward the enemy.

The smoke of the pistol's discharge had a sickly greenish glow, which expanded into a large mist of the same hue. Then came the sound of a huntsman's horn, and the tone of that horn caused men to shiver. Carrtog knew that the effect of that horn, while it was felt by his own men, was directed mostly at the enemy.

As the sound of the horn died away, there came the sound of horses galloping. Then, sweeping from the rear of the royal force, came a host of galloping riders, all of them glowing, brandishing weapons and whips, and preceded by ferocious, large-eyed hounds, their baying a horrible sound out of the storm.

Yakor grabbed his arm. "The Hunt! You've summoned up the Hunt of Annwn?"

"Only an illusion, but an illusion that can have its real effects, depending on the reactions of the men against which it's directed. And if men see others suffering from those real effects, they'll be even less likely to fight."

"You suspected there was strong magic behind the enemy; might their magician, or magicians, dispel this seeming of yours?"

"Perhaps, if they themselves can hold their own minds steady enough. Even so, by that time, it may be too late for their army."

The Hunt of Annwn swept over the royal troopers, ignoring them. Several of them, already shaken by the enemy's apparition, wavered, all but two brought back into line by harsh-voiced under-officers.

The Hunt did not ignore the rebels; ghastly weapons struck, and several men fell. Weapons among the rebels fired to no effect. Others fired back behind the rear ranks and Carrtog felt the power being used, and saw the Hunt falter, then carry on again.

Many of the rebels began to flee, and there was more firing back behind their ranks. The Hunt faltered again, and began to fade, but by now the royal troops were closing with the badly-shaken rebels, whose own under-officers tried to keep them in order.

For a time they did hold, but when they broke, it was a sudden thing, first twos and threes, then half-dozens at a time.

From then it was a wild chase, galloping here and there through the wind and blowing snow, sword to sword, trying hard not to strike at your own men. Carrtog knew that twice he had parried and pulled a sword-stroke when he realized he was facing one of his own troopers. Worse still, one of those times he had to parry a second blow before his opponent, a very young man with a desperate expression on his face, realized that Carrtog was not an enemy.

Yakor and five of Carrtog's guard had managed to stay together through most of the pursuit, and finally, when there was nobody in sight, and no sound that seemed close enough to ride to, particularly in the poor visibility, Carrtog pulled his mount to a stop.

They all stopped with him.

"I'd say this is as good a place as any to stop and try to rally. I'm going to load several pistols to be ready for any general spells, and I'll also send up an illusion to tell people where to gather to. I'd suggest the rest of you load a pistol, more if you have them, but do it in shifts, with two standing guard while the others reload."

He went to work with his pistols while Yakor selected one other to keep watch. When he had loaded his three pistols, Carrtog announced, "I'm about to fire off the illusion, so don't be alarmed when my pistol goes off. Everybody understand?"

When all the others answered, Carrtog spoke his spell and fired nearly straight up in the air. The pistol flash was bright and white and extended far up into the air, where it rapidly expanded, taking on the shape of a large, pale squarish boulder with a sword lying above it.

Carrtog's magic forced the illusion to keep its shape for several heartbeats longer than any firework could normally be expected to, and while it began to fade, Carrtog explained, "That will have been visible for a good distance, and I'll do it again once or twice so people can gather here, or at least, if the commander has a better place, or a larger group of men with him, he can send a messenger here to call us in."

Yakor grinned and said, softly, "As long as a crowd of those Northies don't rally here as well."

Carrtog grinned in reply. "There's quite a few of them won't rally much south of Tenerack."

AS MATTERS WORKED OUT, however, Commander Cargiodd and about a half-score troopers joined Carrtog even before he sent up his second rallying-signal. The storm blew itself out shortly before noon, and by that time most of the troops had joined them, with the supply-carts as well, so tents were being set up and preparations made for a hot meal for the men.

"Yakor," Carrtog said, "See to having a message sent, in particular to Lady Adengler, telling her that I've survived. Best just send it along with the group that our commander sends to generally inform Headquarters of our success."

Yakor nodded, smiling. "It's good as done, sir."

They spent another night camped out there, while parties scoured the wood for surviving troopers, particularly those who might have been too badly hurt to come to the summons by themselves. Another part of their task was to gather up the dead of both sides, allied and rebel. Carrtog oversaw proceedings to ensure the rebels were given fair burial. The troops didn't seem to mind as even the most hard-hearted balked at mistreating the bodies of enemies; the Gods frowned on such behavior — it was not unknown for the spirits of such mistreated enemies to find ways to be revenged. As he looked on over the grisly task, he kept his eyes open for the body of any man who might be considered a magician, looking for traces of magic on clothes and weapons. He found little evidence to suggest they had killed the magician that had given them grief and at this revelation he sighed, knowing the man would be out there to cause them trouble again in the future.

The next day Cargiodd had a meeting with Carrtog. "Now we must decide what is our next move, Lord. In my own opinion, it is not worth the trouble to try to pursue the beaten enemy. They are badly scattered and we are not supplied for an extended effort. By the time we remedied that lack, we'd have no chance of catching them."

"I agree, Commander. What I would suggest is that we set up camp here, for those too badly wounded to travel, and for a sufficient force to guard them against any other band of rebels happening on them. The rest of us should set out back for town and when we get there send back sufficient food and transportation to bring in the rest."

Then followed a discussion of just which troops should be left to guard the camp, which should be sent back to town immediately, and all the myriad details that distinguished an organized army from a mere mob.

Two days later, Carrtog rode back into Kilgarhai at the head of a significant portion of his force. They came with an air of triumph, for all that they were lacking somewhere over a third of the number that had ridden out. He was well aware of the fact that the rumor would have them beaten by the rebels, but when the troopers began to get leave to visit the wine-shops and ale-houses, that rumor would begin to correct itself.

The people, of course, barely paused to watch them march in, and while nobody had the nerve to mock them, the glances they gave the troops told where their sympathies lay.

However, once the troops had been dismissed to their barracks, Yakor and Carrtog had arrived at last to their quarters, and their horses had been taken care of, the greetings more than made up for the grim mentality of the townsmen.

"Here I am in the dirt of three days' travel and a filthy fight and you hold on to me as if I might disappear if you slackened your grip in the slightest! Let go of me for a moment, only long enough to sluice the greater part of the grime off me, and we can be much more comfortable."

She leaned back a bit to look up at him. "It does seem that whenever I let go of you, you go rushing off to do something so dangerous I do seriously fear that you might not come back. Allow me to hold on to you when I can, please."

But she did release him then. "Yes, please get rid of your dirt, and let us spend more time holding each other, so I can try to have less fear when I next see you go off."

So Carrtog went off for a meeting with warm water, and came back to greet his wife and his daughter, who then went off with her nursemaid (the daughter, not the wife) leaving the pair of them alone.

IN TERMS OF THE ENTIRE war, Carrtog's victory over the rebels was only a minor affair, but in local terms, it was a large success. As such, it required a report be sent to the king.

When a message came from the king, several weeks later, Yakor said, "Well, how delighted will His Majesty be with your success?"

"I suppose the real question is, 'Does he think I ought to have done better?'"

"So will you stand there all day wondering, or actually open it and find out?"

"Don't rush me, now. Anticipation is so enjoyable."

His statement to the contrary, Carrtog broke the seal on the message and opened it.

"'To Lord Carrtog, Commander of the Garrison at Kilgarhai. Greetings. I read with gratification the news of your recent victory over the rebels. Such news is in scant supply these days.'

"Now, is that a dig at me, Yakor, or merely a reflection on how badly my predecessor had done?"

He went on reading. "'I hope that I may continue to expect such news from your command. It is very difficult to bring the rebels to a fight, save in petty skirmishes, or in situations where it is almost obvious that there is a trap laid. With the situation being thus, it is even more important that the supply-lines be maintained, and therefore that any interruptions to the railway traffic be curtailed, preferably prevented completely.'

"Now, does that mean that if one of the trains is an hour late due to rebel activity, I'm in trouble? Or is that a foolish question?"

"My Lord, I don't think anything like an hour's delay is likely to be serious, but to have an interruption of rail service that lasts more than one night and a day is going to require grave explanations."

Carrtog nodded. "I'm sure you're right. So I suppose my response is to continue on as I've begun, 'curtailing rebel activity' as completely as possible."

"Does His Majesty have anything further to say in that document?"

Carrtog looked back at the letter for a moment, then said, "Well, he does say, 'I repeat, it is extremely necessary that the supply-line be maintained safe, in order to bring this war to a successful conclusion as soon as possible.'"

He frowned. "I'm afraid I keep seeing hidden threats wherever I look, and perhaps all he's doing is urging me to continue doing the same good job I've been doing."

"And perhaps this is not the same king who had taken to calling me 'Lord Yakor' because he was unsatisfied with the way you were leading us out of enemy territory."

Carrtog pursed his lips in annoyance. "Sometimes I have a great desire to give up being a Lord and just go to being an ordinary man, building machines."

Yakor gave him a stern look. "If I seriously thought you felt that way, I'd give you a severe scold. Now get out there and curtail some more rebels."

Carrtog grinned.

AFTER THEIR SUCCESSFUL excursion, there was a period of about six weeks when no rebels were seen. Then slowly, as if in time with the turning spring, they began to take action again.

"They took a shot at the balloon, Lord," Hwydach reported. "They used a crossbow, but near as I could tell, they missed by a mile. They went and hid under the trees for a long time, afterward. I would have stayed around to trail them, but the warming-spell needed renewing."

"It's harder than one might think to hit something flying. Still, you might think of flying a bit higher; pass the word to the rest."

"Yes, Lord."

ADDY WAS DRESSED IN a blouse of white over a tartan skirt, with a sleeveless gold jacket. She was accompanied by a nursemaid, carrying baby Aderyn.

"So you're not going out this time?"

"No. Unless the full garrison is going out, it's best if the commander doesn't go out every time. The sub-commanders need to know that he trusts them. And this time it's only two troops, and there's a couple of them that know some battle-magic, if necessary."

"Then you don't foresee any difficulty?"

He grimaced. "Actually, the man in my position foresees all kinds of difficulties, but he hopes that he's also foreseen solutions to them and that, whatever he might have missed, his commanders in the field will react adequately."

He smiled, ruefully. "And all the time they're gone, he wishes he'd gone out with them, because he knows the fault is his, whether he goes or stays."

At that moment Aderyn stirred in her nursemaid's arms, muttering fretfully. Both parents turned to look at her; for the last while she had been 'making strange' with people, save for those she was commonly with, her parents, her nursemaid, and gruff old 'Uncle' Yakor, who had fallen in love with her practically from birth.

"Is anything wrong?" asked Addy.

"No, Lady, she's just stirring. She'll be back to sleep in a moment," answered the nursemaid, looking at the baby gently.

"Give her here for a moment, then, Minnia."

Minnia passed the baby over, who stirred and muttered again and, opening her eyes, saw mother, and closed her eyes, snuggling in comfortably. "She is a dear, isn't she, Carrtog?"

"She is indeed. And Gods willing, she will grow up to be as dear as her mother."

Addy laughed quietly. "Don't say that sort of thing as she grows up; first she'll be flattered out of all good sense, and later on, as her mother grows old and gray, she'll be insulted."

"Don't be foolish, my love. As we grow old together, you'll just continue to grow more dear to me."

She laughed again. "You're the foolish one! Just you make sure that we do grow old together."

She stopped suddenly. "Oh! I'm sorry, that's just the kind of thing I shouldn't say. Neither one of us needs to be reminded."

They stood in sober silence for a bit, then, until Carrtog put an arm around his wife and daughter. "No, don't fret over it; however long the Gods give us to live together, let us enjoy that time and everything else the Gods give us."

It was just then that one of the ubiquitous little boys who hung around the works and occasionally ran errands came dashing up, a fearful expression on his face. "Lord, it's Hwydach! Something dreadful's happened!"

Carrtog drew away from the warm embrace of his wife and daughter with more than a little reluctance.

"Let's go have a look, then. Addy, forgive me this sudden departure, I'm sure it won't be long."

Addy shook her head, concern clear on her face, "Do as you need. We will be here for you when you're done."

Carrtog kissed them both and left for the balloon-controllers' shed.

"What happened, boy?"

Trotting along at Carrtog's side, the boy answered, "He was working his balloon, as usual, looking over a Northie camp, when there was a flash in his bowl, and he went dead white, collapsing off his stool, holding on to his throat."

"I see."

The boy looked up at him. "You know what happened, then, Lord?"

He shook his head. "I know several things that might have happened, I'll have to look at him to be sure."

Shortly after, they were at the door of the shed. Carrtog opened it and went in. There, gathered around Hwydach's area, were all the men who weren't presently working, and some who ought to be.

"All right, then, everyone back to your places! Parmavon, what happened?"

Parmavon's response was mostly a repetition of the boy's story, with the addition of an odd smell and a dark blue color in the water in the scrying-bowl, which had faded gradually.

"I see," Carrtog said. "Well, I believe I can help. Bring me a bowl of clear water, and I'll get to work."

Parmavon was back shortly with the bowl and a pitcher of water, which he poured into the bowl.

Meantime, Carrtog had laid Hwydach out straight and checked his breathing, which was shallow. He frowned, then, realizing that everyone was watching him, calmed his features. The onlookers were already worried, and there was no sense in adding to that worry by his own expression.

He looked around at them, and announced, "I'm about to cast a spell, and I'll be firing a pistol so no one be alarmed."

He took out a pistol, making sure that this was the one that held only a powder-charge, but no ball, the one that he held ready for immediate use if a spell were necessary. He pointed it toward the floor, next to the unconscious balloon-controller, and fired it, repeating an incantation.

For a moment, nothing happened, then the water in the newly-filled scrying-bowl turned green, and there was the scent of new-cut grass. He took a deep breath; good, so far.

He watched, forcing himself to show no impatience, and then, long moments later, Hwydach began to breathe more deeply. Carrtog himself took a deep breath, and smiled. "I believe he'll be well, now. Parmavon, send someone for a healer, just to be sure."

Parmavon called the boy who had fetched Carrtog and told him, "Off with you, bring the healer. Tell him Lord Carrtog has done what he can for Hwydach, but wants a healer to look at him to make sure."

"Yes, sir!" The boy was off at a run almost before Parmavon had finished speaking.

Parmavon turned back to Carrtog. "Lord, what happened to Hwydach?"

"Someone among the rebels used a spell to strike at him through the link of the scrying-bowl. My carelessness, I'm afraid. I never thought they'd convince anyone with that level of ability to go out, even for a visit, to one of the camps in the wild." As he said it, Carrtog realized that in fact the chances were good that this was the same magician as had escaped their last raid. Careless indeed ... he should have known something like this was coming.

"Can you strike back, Lord?"

"Strike back? I'm not sure, I'll have to look into that. First thing I want to do is to protect the rest of the balloon-controllers. That I can do. If you'll excuse me, I will begin work on it immediately."

"Of course, Lord." Parmavon was a little flustered, and Carrtog, though he did not show it by his expression, was at least equally flustered. Best get hold of yourself, Carrtog, or you'll have them all thinking you've gone mad. Asking a balloon-controller to excuse you, indeed.

It took only a few moments looking at the traces left by the attack on Hwydach before he was able to formulate a protective charm for the rest of the balloon-controllers. All that was needed then was to summon them so that he could place the spell on all of them at once rather than waste the time by spelling each one as they came on duty.

"SO ALL THE TO-DO'S done, then, sir?"

"For the time being, Yakor, for the time being. Until that magician, or another one, finds another spell that he can send over the link from the balloon, a spell that can slip past my protective charm, then I'll need to make another."

He thought for a moment. "Of course, I should get myself busy thinking up attack-spells so I can devise defenses for them. Try to keep ahead of them."

Yakor chuckled. "And all the time they're trying to get ahead of you so that you both wear yourselves out without actually doing anything."

Carrtog grinned. "You know, sometimes you can be a very unhelpful old man."

Chapter 25

"So, the rebels are out in greater numbers now?" Carrtog looked around at his officers.

"Definitely, sir," answered Cargiodd. "Tracks torn up in two places yesterday, three the day before, Gods know how many today. Either they have more men out there, or the men they've got out there are working themselves to death." He glared around as though daring any of the others to gainsay him.

One of the other officers, Ffyldarch by name, asked, "Have none of those balloon-things been able to track any of these new troops?"

Ffyldarch was not much in favor of anything new, or indeed in favor of much beyond swords and, just possibly, firearms. Carrtog occasionally considered getting rid of the man, but held off for fear of having him replaced by someone worse.

"The balloons have not so far found a trace of them," Carrtog said, and refrained from speculating that the enemy had some new spell of concealment. That would seem like making excuses, and he didn't feel he needed to make excuses.

What he did need to do was spend more time and trouble trying to find out what he could. This involved taking charge of one of the balloons himself and checking the wilderness for what traces of new magic he could find. After that he would see what any such new traces suggested about concealment spells.

"There is no blame to be attached to the balloon-controllers, they are doing the job they were trained for, and doing it well. I, as the most highly-trained magician here, will have to look into refinements of their training, if such are necessary, to deal with whatever new methods the rebels might be using.

"If there is nothing else, gentlemen, you are dismissed."

He watched them as they got up and left. It might be a good idea to train the balloon-controllers for more, but it was a long step from training men to utilize the spells necessary for handling the balloons to giving those same men sufficient grounding in magic that they could not only notice traces of magic, but go from there to speculating on what those traces meant.

It would be much better for him to do what he had already decided; take a balloon and fly it out along the track, particularly in the area of the latest track damage, and see what he could see.

There was no difficulty acquiring a balloon; they had produced a number of spares, just in case. The difficulty came when he got it up in the air and sat down at a table in the balloon-controllers' shed to send it out along the track. He'd gotten his balloon traveling down along the track at a good speed, when he suddenly noticed that the controllers' shed had gone quiet. Instead of the usual light chatter between controllers, they were all quiet, looking at him and quickly back to their own scrying-bowls.

He stopped his balloon and stood. "Gentlemen, I apologize. I should have told you what I intend before I started. I am not checking on your work at all. I am working at a whole different chore altogether. I am trying to find out if the rebels have any sort of new concealment spell in use, and this requires me to travel up and down the line to see if I can find any traces of magic, after which I will try to see what kind of spell was used. When I discover the remains of some new concealment spell, I will then go to work on a spell to defeat it, after which I will pass this on to you."

He paused, looking around at them. "For now, just carry on with your work as you normally do." He stopped and sat down.

As he went back to work, he heard the other balloon-controllers begin to chatter, but nowhere near so much as usual.

"They don't quite believe you're not here keeping an eye on them, no matter what you say."

He looked up at Yakor. "I suppose I ought to have taken up a room in the house, but I didn't think this would happen."

"If you have people under you and you hang around where they're working, they're almost always going to think you're spying on them. Reassuring them that you're not just makes them more certain you are."

"Gods help us! I suppose it's too late to pack up and go over to the house."

"That'd be worse. They'd just think you were going to hide your spying."

"I just hope they don't get so worried about me spying on them that they stop doing their work properly."

"The best thing you could do is stop worrying about it yourself. When you actually start training them to spot new spells and to defeat those spells, most of them will stop worrying about your spying. The rest, well, they'd be the ones who always thought you must be spying on them, even before you started to work here."

"Thank you, I think."

Yakor just grinned.

IT WAS A LONG AND ARDUOUS task; this being a wilderness area, traces of magic were few and far between. Many of those that were present were baffling for one reason or another. What was a trace of a very minor love-charm doing out in the wilderness? Others were baffling because the remnant did not give enough evidence to do more than guess what it might have been.

By the end of the day, Carrtog had found nothing at all hopeful.

"Don't be so down," Yakor said. "You said yourself that it's a wilderness; how could you expect to find your answer on the first day?"

Carrtog forced a smile. "Of course I expect success on the first day! Am I not the young hero who saved the king's daughter and was rewarded by special training in magic? And did I not go on to make serious inroads into the rebels attempting to cut the rail lines? Success on the first day is therefore nigh to mandatory."

"Being the greatest fool on the Gods' green earth is also mandatory, it seems. Now you'd best be getting back to your quarters and stop your fretting. You'll end up yourself being scant comfort to Lady Adengler."

THE LADY ADENGLER, it seemed, had just received another letter from princess Ellevar. "She urges you to use caution, Carrtog, though she can't be more specific than that. She says that her last two letters from her father mentioned you unfavorably. The most recent said, 'Be careful of Lord Carrtog. Though he has done well in keeping the railway line clear, I do not altogether trust the man.'"

Carrtog looked down at the third finger of his right hand. No, the ring was not prickling, but neither was it infallible. It was possible that some danger was coming and the ring was not warning him, or perhaps not warning him yet.

"Gods' mercies! The rebels appear to have found a way to hide themselves from our searchers and it's now that the king is looking for something to accuse me of! Well, I suppose the only thing to do is to take whatever measures we can for our safety, given that we know so little. Addy, my dearest, would you like to pack up Aderyn and go stay with your parents for the time being?"

Addy straightened and gave him a severe look. "Carrtog, is that all you think of me, that I should go running home to my father at the first hint of danger? If you want to send me home, you'll have to tie me up and take me there, and then persuade my father to lock me up in a room somewhere! Otherwise, I'll just slip away and come back to wait with you for whatever danger might be coming. Are you ready to do that?"

He held up his hands as though to ward off her anger. "No, no, I'm not ready for that yet! I'd prefer to see you out of danger, but neither am I ready to do all sorts of useless things to try to accomplish that. All right, we stay and face what comes together."

DAY FOLLOWED DAY, AND Carrtog continued to seek for spell-remnants in the wilderness. Most often what he found were spell-scraps, too brief to prove anything, or else he found bits of hunting spells, or other equally useless remnants.

He also worked from the other end, dealing with all sorts of spells of reversal and other spells which would banish all magic in a certain area. He also tried spells to reverse various invisibility spells with indifferent success.

The other balloon-controllers, having by and large gotten over the notion of Carrtog spying on them, were still having occasional good luck finding other rebel bands, bands to whom the new magician had not come to with his new spells of invisibility. Such successes helped to make up, at least partially, for the bands which were invisible.

"This will only help for a while," Carrtog said to Yakor after they had seen the latest force go after another band of rebels that had been tracked down. "Once we've finished off all the rebels who we can still see, we'll be left with the ones we can't see."

"I assume you've looked over all the places these hidden gowks have attacked the railway?"

"Yes. Whatever spell-traces they might have left seem to fade out fast." He smiled, crookedly. "I'd say that's very inconsiderate of whoever that magician is."

"Very inconsiderate." Yakor smiled back.

VERY LATE THAT SAME afternoon, just as Carrtog was about to stop his searches for the day, Hachenbra called out, "Lord Carrtog!"

Carrtog looked up from his bowl. "What is it?"

"Something's pulling the rails apart, Lord!"

"Whereabouts?"

The other consulted a list of landmarks beside his bowl, then said, "About twenty-five miles south from here, Lord."

Carrtog consulted his balloon's own whereabouts, and a thrill went through him. "I'm a bare five miles south of that! Thanks, Hachenbra, I'll turn my balloon and come up there immediately!"

He sent his balloon northward as quickly as he could manage, but by the time he arrived, the rebels had done their work and were gone.

Hachenbra spoke up again. "They've got a spell covering their tracks, Lord, but it doesn't seem to work immediately. I see a bit of horse-track go down, then it disappears. They're heading roughly north-eastward."

"Thank you once more, Hachenbra."

This time, he did find several spell-remnants. A couple of them were extra-strength spells, just the kind of thing one might want if one were looking to tear up railway tracks quickly.

"This one's for improved sight, Yakor. What in the name of the Gods was that for?"

Yakor grinned. "Perhaps someone was trying for another improved strength and mistook his wording."

Carrtog merely snorted and continued making notes; several of the spell-remnants faded even as he made note of them. These ones he did not attempt to identify immediately, but just made what notes he could and went on to the next.

"It seems almost certain that one of the features of the spell they used was that any remnants of it disappeared quickly. Very inconsiderate of them, Yakor."

"Yes. You've said that before."

"They may be even more inconsiderate by using spells that are difficult to identify from bits and pieces."

"Surely they can't be that foul!"

Apparently, they were at least that foul. Two evenings later, Carrtog was penning a letter to Enemantwin, explaining the new situation and asking if the older magician had any further suggestions for him.

THEN, JUST TO ADD TO the problems of the Royal Garrison of Kilgarhai, Yakor came in to set down a broadsheet before him.

Broadsheets aimed at lowering the morale of royal troops were a common sight on the streets of Kilgarhai, tacked up on walls and fences. A whole squad was tasked, every day, with going through the streets and removing these broadsheets as they found them. Often as not the topic of these broadsheets was sufficiently futile that they might well be ignored, save that the king would surely not approve of their dismissal.

This one, though, could scarcely be ignored.

Soldiers of the king of Cragmor!

Have you considered how much your king cares for your welfare? When the rising first began in Tenerack, certain of your fellow-soldiers were wounded too badly to be able to ride. Do you know what your brave king did then? He abandoned them in the middle of the night, and fled with the few who could still ride, leaving those wounded to the mercy of the people of the land they were occupying.

If this brave king of yours finds himself in any sort of military difficulty, how much thought do you think he will give to your welfare? Surely not much more than to those he abandoned in Tenerack.

Think of your own welfare, Soldiers of Cragmor!

Carrtog looked up at Yakor. "You notice they don't deny that their own people massacred wounded men?"

"I scarcely think our king will be inclined to notice a fault in their propaganda. More likely he will think of you as their source of information, no matter how unlikely that seems."

Carrtog sighed. "Unfortunately, you're quite likely right. We still have come no closer to finding the source of these broadsheets. They appear to have a very well-qualified magician hiding their source. Even assessing the paper and the ink has not allowed us to track the people who handled them."

"A very well-qualified magician you say? Perhaps even the same magician as the originator of the invisibility spells?"

"If so, then he has been a thorn in our side longer than I realized."

"You sent a letter to Enemantwin about those spell-fragments you're working on. I think it may be time to send him a letter about this."

Carrtog scowled at the broadsheet. "I'm afraid you're right; up to now these things have been a mere nuisance, but this is serious."

He pulled over a blank sheet of paper and began to write.

ON THE AFTERNOON OF the next day, a train of five horse-drawn wagons came into Kilgarhai from the south. The man at their head was a tall and well-built fellow. He was well-dressed, as were all the top men among them. His face was square, his hair a dark red, and his nose was flat.

He presented to Carrtog a letter with the king's seal introducing him as Llodcar, a merchant, head of a band of merchants with the permission of the king to look into setting up businesses in Kilgarhai. The king's note asked Carrtog to extend all hospitality and assistance to them.

Carrtog returned Llodcar's letter to him. "Go see my chief servant, and he will see to rooms for yourself and your men. Take your wagons to the stables; I am quite sure we will be able to put up your horses there."

After the wagons had gone on their rattling, creaking way, Yakor said, "I don't trust them."

Carrtog held up his right hand, showing the polished bone ring. "My ring is prickling. It could mean something so simple as them making the local merchants upset at their possible competition, but I'll take precautions. Among other things, I'll put a spell on all the house guard, and certain other people, protecting them against certain magics. That'll mean you and me as well."

"Good start. I'll keep an eye on these traders and assign some of the guard to them as well."

"Good. I hope they don't expect me to personally escort them around and introduce them to the local merchants; I've been spending a lot of time and money making connections with the local merchants, and I wouldn't want to ruin that by having to go round and introduce some possible competitors. Worse still, these competitors appear to have the backing of the king himself.

"Well, enough of this fussing over what might be; I've got to go back to work at those spell-remnants. Something just occurred to me regarding some of them, and I've got to see if it's actually a good idea, or just my mind trying to convince me that it's actually good for something."

Yakor grinned. "Oh, I'm sure it's good for something. What that might be, I don't know, but it must be good for something."

"Thank you very much. Now I've got to get to work."

His first notion as to how to deal with the spell-remnants did not work out, but it did suggest another possibility. Unfortunately, that possibility, when investigated, showed that while it might indeed belong to an invisibility spell, it was an invisibility spell with certain unusual features. It would thus require special handling to reverse it.

Later that evening, he was still hunched over a table full of scribblings by the light of a flickering oil lamp when Addy came in. She was dressed in a soft nightgown with a warm housecoat over it, belted at the middle. She was unaccompanied, but carried a single long candle in a holder.

"My dear, an hour and more ago, you told me you were coming to bed shortly. Surely you'd be able to work better if you put these things aside and gave yourself several hours' rest."

He looked up at her blankly, then rubbed his eyes. "It's not been that long, surely?" He shook his head. "Of course it has." He looked down at his papers and took up his quill again. Then he carefully set aside the pen, capped the ink-horn, and stacked the papers with little heed for order.

"You're right, of course. It's just that every hour those rebels can ride around unseen allows them that much time to wreak havoc with the railway line. And every hour the rail line is cut is another mark the king can set against me if he wishes."

"And every hour you take away from your rest is another hour you are working at somewhere less than your best ability and therefore that much less likely to find the solution you seek."

He grimaced. "You're right, of course. I'll go back at it in the morning."

Chapter 26

The next morning however, the spell on the railway itself warned of tampering along the line. The nearest balloon to the spot got there in time to see nothing but a stretch of broken track. The repair-crew, along with a troop to guard them, went out almost immediately after the first alarm was received.

Carrtog, a new spur to his efforts, went back to work. He had already discovered that the spell was a complex one and was beginning to discover that some of the complexities seemed to have been added intentionally.

"Enemantwin would be scandalized," he muttered to himself. The old magician had considered elegance in spell-craft to be an absolute, that the grace of simplicity was the mark of an experienced spell-crafter. This spell, with all its unnecessary flourishes and embellishments, seemed to indicate the caster was a novice intent on demonstrating his mastery of the art and in doing so demonstrating just the opposite. Once one had discovered just how unnecessary the flourishes were, one could ignore most of them in deriving a counter-spell. The trick was to be certain which ones could be ignored.

Carrtog was beginning to suspect that not all of them were frivolous.

Carrtog wanted very much to go out as soon as possible to track down this hidden band and their thorny magician, but he was also quite aware of the danger of going out not fully prepared. He forced himself, therefore, to be meticulous in his work, not scrimping in his efforts to be certain of his goal. While doing this work he was also aware of the fact that the magician who had produced this spell, with all its unnecessary flourishes, might well also be a formidable foe when it came to combat-magic. Just because he was not as elegant as Enemantwin would desire did not mean that he would not be effective. It was almost certain that he would be able to counter the Grove of Battle, so Carrtog must be ready with an alternative. That, and be certain that he could overcome the spell of invisibility in the first place.

He leaned closer, examining his work.

At last he leaned back, giving a long sigh of relief. It was done. As it turned out, the spell was almost a common one, save that one of the embellishments had to be taken into account when producing a counter-spell. Now, was it a tricky use of what looked like amateurish spell-craft in order to produce something hard to deal with or was it just the good luck that sometimes favored amateurs? Best he should treat it as someone being tricky, rather than convince himself it was an amateur getting lucky. Thinking the alternative would be the fastest way to be caught unawares in actual battle.

"Yakor! Send someone to tell Commander Cargiodd to prepare a force for a raid. Probably four troops."

"Yes, Sir!"

Shortly after, Yakor returned. "You've worked it out, have you?"

"I believe I have. No, let's be definite about it. Yes, I have. It was overly complex but not uncommon. Maybe a lucky amateur or a sneaky master of the trade. I'm going with the sneaky master, just to avoid being caught by surprise."

Yakor nodded approvingly. "Good! Always best to be ready for the worst."

"Yakor?"

"Sir?" Yakor's expression demonstrated that he expected something unusual.

"I want you to stay behind. My ring is still predicting trouble, and I want you to keep an eye on the family and all. I'll renew the protective spell on you and the others,for whatever help that might be."

Yakor didn't argue. "I'll do my best, sir."

"Yes, I know you will. Thank you."

IT WAS LATE AFTERNOON, and they were marching along the road beside the railroad. Commander Cargiodd turned to Carrtog and said, "So you are accompanying us this time to cast the spell to reveal the Northies' tracks, Lord?"

"No, not their tracks, but the rebels themselves. Unless their commanders are total fools, they will have their men hiding their tracks, not totally depending on the spell to hide them. But the fact that someone among them has a new spell of invisibility suggests that a magician is one of their number. Very likely the same man as before who knows a good deal more magic than your average soldier. My main purpose in coming is to be present and ready for whatever he might throw at us."

"You foresee magic you might not be able to deal with, Lord?"

"Such as the invisibility spell that I had to work so long at? Possibly. But in combat-magic, it is not always necessary to be able to reverse an enemy spell, only to cast a more powerful spell. Preferably to cast that powerful spell first. Also, shield-spells in combat magic are usually proof against a number of attack-spells. I shall be carrying several loaded pistols for the purpose of casting several spells in succession. This should be sufficient for the number of spells I will be facing."

"Very good, Lord." The commander's expression said that he feared the situation to be somewhat less than very good.

When they arrived at the point where the repair-crew was finishing the repairing of the line that had been broken, the time was late afternoon. "What now, Lord?" asked Commander Cargiodd. "If you won't be able to reveal their tracks, how do we proceed?"

Carrtog smiled. "Perhaps I misled you a little, Commander. The spell they used will only take effect where there is a track to be hidden. I have added a touch to my counter-spell, something that not only counters the spell but also adds a slight touch of dark blue to every place where the spell had taken effect. No, you needn't worry about the rebels suddenly noticing that they all have a touch of dark blue; the color will only be visible to those wearing the uniform of Cragmor."

He paused. "On the other hand, the magician out there, if he has any sort of competence at all, will know when his magic has been dispelled. I doubt very much whether we will be able to come on them unawares. On the other hand, I doubt that they will be able to conceal a proper ambush. Just as their magician will know that I've dispelled his invisibility spell, I will know if he has been able to deal with my little color-effect. If he does, I have a spell or two in mind to deal with ambushes."

Carrtog chose a spot which seemed the most likely place for the rebels to have entered the wood, assuming that their camp was somewhere to the northeast of the railway line. He fired a pistol without a ball into the air, speaking the appropriate incantation, and looked around.

For a time he saw nothing, then just a little off in the wood, he saw a dark blue spot. Hiding the traces of about thirty men on horseback was a difficult matter. A lot could be done in that direction, but there were always traces that escaped.

He pointed it out to the commander. "There we are. Start our men on the track, Commander. I'll clean and load this pistol, just in case I need it for another spell."

Shortly thereafter, the first elements of the force, a pair of scouts, were advancing along the marked track. Commander Cargiodd allowed them to get a bit of a lead on the main body, then led the rest of the force up behind them.

Marching through the wood in late springtime was a different proposition from their previous marches; it was warmer for one thing, and the smells of springtime were far more pleasant than those of winter.

It was still springtime, though, which meant that their day's march would have to be curtailed by the early approach of night. Their scouts had orders to seek for a good camping-spot, preferably before dark made it impossible to ensure that the enemy had not left any nasty little surprises there.

Suddenly, in the middle of the night, Carrtog felt a feeling as if a band around his chest had been released. He turned to talk to Yakor, only to recall that his armsman was not with him. If the older man had been present, he would have said, "The rebels' magician has just countered my spell. Of course, that only means the blue marks on the trail are gone, not that the rebels are invisible again."

In the morning, Commander Cargiodd was annoyed to be informed that the blue traces of the enemies' passage had disappeared.

"I was expecting as much," Carrtog said. "I had a feeling that the rebel magician was reasonably competent. However, I have another plan in mind. Having tracked their magician by use of bits of his spell-craft, I will now cast a spell directing me to the one who cast the spells himself."

Commander Cargiodd frowned. "Why did you not begin with that spell instead of using those bits of blue color, Lord?"

"Because this spell is somewhat more difficult and may not work at all."

"Have you a plan in mind, then, in case this spell does not work?"

"Of course." He smiled more confidently than he felt.

Shortly thereafter he set his spell, using a flash of burned powder rather than a pistol shot. "There's no telling how near they are, and there's no sense in firing a shot to warn them of our presence." He told the commander.

Almost immediately a broad green line showed on the forest. "They won't be able to see this, either, will they, Lord?" The commander was clearly a little worried.

"No, not until the magician discovers what I've done, which he may very well do sometime before the day is out. In that case, I shall have to take other measures."

How magnificently confident you sound, he told himself.

The commander, mirroring Carrtog's feigned self-confidence, gave abrupt and concise orders, getting the troops on the way with little wasted time.

The scouts, having been given some time to take up their positions, slipped up along the marked trail with a commendable lack of noise. The main body followed along as quietly as possible, but being a large number of men and horses with all their accouterments complete silence was near impossible.

Near midmorning, the green trail disappeared with no warning.

The scouts, however, had followed the practice of marking their own trail with bent branches or tied tufts of grass at intervals so the force continued along the trail with hardly a pause.

Carrtog, whose ring was continuing to warn him of danger, wondered how matters were going back in the town. He considered using his communicator to get in touch with Yakor, but put the thought aside for two reasons. Firstly, they were attempting to do a

silent march, and secondly, what if he called Yakor just as his man
were in a dangerous situation where he was trying to remain hidden?

A few moments later one of the scouts, all his horse's harness
muffled with rags and his own metal equipment similarly silenced,
appeared before them.

"The trail's gone, Lords, but we got close enough before that to
be able to hear sounds from their camp. They started to quiet down
right quick, though, most like because someone figured we might be
getting close. Besides that, they'd started to get a bit careless about
leaving traces by then, being almost home as they were. If they don't
send someone out to find my partner, we ought to be able to come
on them nearly by surprise. If they do send someone out to find him,
he figures to fire a pistol-shot to let you know."

"Thank you," Carrtog said. "Commander, let us carry on."

So they carried on.

They finally reached the second scout, with no pistol-shots
having been fired, and he gave a quick outline of how the enemy
camp was laid out; he had been able to creep up close enough to look
at them without having been seen himself.

Carrtog and Commander Cargiodd set up a quick plan of
attack; Carrtog would use no spells immediately, waiting to see what
the enemy magician could come up with first. His response would
depend on what the enemy did.

He knew that responding to the enemy was not good tactics,
but he wanted some further idea of what the enemy magician was
capable of before he did any serious magic.

It was difficult to spread out in the woods, but the king's forces
did so. Then they descended on the rebels. The sound of their
coming gave the enemy full warning, so they were well prepared.
On the other hand, the rebels were outnumbered by a considerable
amount, a fact they soon discovered and immediately took them to
flight.

Their magician sought to gain them some time to flee by a spell calling up something that was mostly an illusion, but capable of physical effects as well. It was a large black wolf which shrugged off sword-blows or pistol-shots, but could savagely rend a man with its massive jaws.

Fortunately, Carrtog recognized it for what it was. He drew a pistol, said a spell-disbursement charm, and fired. The illusion was at long range for a pistol, but the charm, in effect, extended the range to reach the illusion it was directed at. Without any flashy effects, the wolf disappeared.

Carrtog drew a second pistol, spoke another charm, and fired it in the direction he believed the rebel magician to be. The discharge of the pistol came out in a cloud of tiny sparks, each of which grew as it flew to become a tiny person about the size of a man's thumb carrying a sword that seemed to be about shoulder height on the person carrying it, though each tiny warrior brandished it with ease. The little glowing warriors flew on wings as colorful as those of a butterfly and each wore a tiny back-and-breastplate as well as a helmet. They dived and struck at the rebels, at their exposed hands, faces, and necks, and each stroke seemed to pain like the sting of a wasp, if the wasp were as quick as any real wasp and about the size of a man's thumb.

Carrtog's next move was to cast a spell to counteract any spell the rebel magician might cast. Being such a general spell, it might not work against certain specific spells, but it should give him a bit of breathing room.

Unfortunately, while he was taking that moment to decide which spell to cast next, the enemy magician fired a pistol of his own, and a moment later a frigid wind came blowing from the north carrying a cold rain that froze on the faces, hands, and clothing of the royal troops. It also blew away the lightly-built tiny winged swordsmen, freezing them in the air and dropping them to the ground.

Weather spells were not much used in battle because of the possible deleterious effects on the weather in the longer term. Carrtog was ready, however, not with a counteracting weather spell, but with a spell to counter the spell itself, making the cold wind fade away as if it had never been.

Carrtog then loaded a pistol as rapidly as possible and waited for the rebel magician to make his next move.

The magician's next move was to draw back himself. The rebel troops continued to scatter and pull back with the royal troops in pursuit, but not allowing themselves to scatter too much for fear that the rebels might make a sudden rally and outnumber the royal troops at some specific spot. This left the rebel magician exposed, except for five men guarding him from mundane weapons.

The rebel troops were too scattered for any magic to be fully effective; using a spell against one to five men was a waste. However, using a spell against a magician could not be considered a waste, so Carrtog, after loading another pistol, cast a spell called Confusion to the Enemy. Its intent was to cause the enemy to see things that weren't there, misjudge distances, stumble over things, run into things, and anything that might slow him or cause him to not act in his own best interest.

Carrtog was not surprised to see that only the magician's guards suffered any confusion and only slightly at that. Carrtog himself had put strong defensive spells on himself and his own personal guards, so it was no surprise that the enemy had done the same.

He loaded two more pistols, at the same time trying to close some of the distance between himself and the enemy magician.

Suddenly a thick, white mist appeared around the rebel magician and his men, spreading rapidly toward Carrtog himself. He fired a pistol and called out the charm Clear Sight, a simple but strong spell.

The mist stopped about twenty yards from him, maintaining that twenty-yard clear space from him even as it carried on spreading past and around him.

He cast another spell, a very strong one named See the Man, one which might well put him on the edge of exhaustion. The result was a clear corridor some three yards wide, cutting straight through the mist. Its pace slowed as it neared the enemy magician's position then stopped suddenly.

For the space of about ten heartbeats it stayed still, then in a sudden rush, it moved to reveal its quarry.

"Come on!" he shouted, urging his horse forward along the corridor, which rolled back and forth over the rebel sorcerer.

The magician fired a pistol in his direction; beyond range for a pistol-shot, so it must be a spell of some kind. Well, he would just have to hope that his own spell-protection charm was still in effect.

He felt something like a heavy blow across his whole body, and almost fell out of his saddle. His mind told him that his spell-protection charm was indeed in effect, otherwise he would have been driven to the ground, likely with a number of broken bones. As it was, he and his horse continued in their charge, though the horse was a little slowed.

The question now was how many loaded pistols did that fellow have left? That last spell might well have taken the last of Carrtog's own spell-protection, leaving him — and his men — vulnerable to whatever the man threw next.

But no, the magician was fumbling with pistol and powder-flask. Gods be blessed, he's out!

His foe fumbled and dropped his pistol, then hastily turned his horse to run. Carrtog was bearing down on him. The other man's horse didn't have enough time to build up the speed to escape.

At the last moment, a trooper in the uniform of Carrtog's force came rushing out of the mist in front of the magician, looked around wildly, and swung his sword, cutting the man out of the saddle.

He came rushing on toward Carrtog, lifting his sword for another blow. Carrtog brought up his own blade to counter, only to have one of his own guards rush forward, slamming his horse's body into the body of the other man's mount, sending the horse staggering, and the man struggling to stay in the saddle.

As the trooper regained control of himself, he suddenly realized who he had been attempting to attack. He dropped his sword-hand to his side. "Lord Carrtog! Forgive me, Lord, I didn't mean—"

"No, you just came to a space in a magic mist, saw armed men, and started to swing. You killed the enemy magician, for which you have my thanks, and you have my guard to thank that he just knocked you off balance and didn't chop you down to save me. I suppose it's a futile question to ask if you know where your troop-commander is?"

"I'm sorry, Lord. Before that Gods-cursed fog came down, I sort of had an idea where he was, but not anymore, Sir."

"Well, I and my men will be riding this way; perhaps you might wish to come with us."

A suggestion from a lord was as good as a command, so the young man said, "Yes, Sir," and fell in behind them.

They rode on for quite a while, never finding any sign of the battle save for dead or wounded men. For their own wounded, one of the people in his party stopped with them to do what they could, then catch them up again. For the enemy wounded, they only made an effort to mark the place, then went on again. If possible, someone would come back to try to find the rebels.

After an hour and a half or so, Carrtog stopped his party, which by now had grown by ten men all from various troops.

"We'll stop here to make a temporary camp, at least. I'll send up a signal to let the rest know our general position, and I hope they'll be able to find us."

He loaded a pistol and fired off a charge. The incantation he spoke with it caused the pistol-flash to spread out into the now familiar form of a large grayish rock with an unsheathed sword above it.

As the illusion began to fade, he said to those around him, "There. Now anyone who sees that will know where to find us. Now, the head of my guards will be the commander of this group, and he will be responsible for setting up whatever camp and sentries seems best to him. For my part, I will see to a ring of wards around us to warn us if any enemies approach. However, I would not like to hear that the sentries took the wards as an excuse to slack. Magic is useful, but depending on it to the exclusion of all other methods is not only foolish but dangerous."

IT WAS NOT UNTIL LATE that afternoon that Carrtog and Commander Cargiodd decided that all the troops that were going to rally to that point had arrived. By that time Carrtog had repeated his gray rock illusion twice more. After the second time, he said, "I'd say that should be it. If they don't come now, they're either dead or deserters."

Chapter 27

Two days later, shortly after noon, they were marching back into Kilgarhai. They had barely come past the edge of the town when Yakor came riding up. Even before he spoke, Carrtog knew something was wrong.

Carrtog turned to Commander Cargiodd. "Commander, see to getting the men to barracks."

"Yes, Lord."

He pushed his mount out of the line of troops.

"What's happened Yakor?"

"Last night that Gods-cursed Llodcar and his so-called traders attacked; they've taken Lady Adengler, killed several servants and guards. I barely kept them from getting the babe."

Carrtog felt his heart slide to the pit of his stomach, but close behind the panic came anger. "Why did you not contact me immediately?"

"Change one disaster into two? Call you and have that magic thing squawking when you're about to ambush the rebels?"

"Of course." Carrtog recalled his own decision not to call on Yakor for the same reasons. "You say you kept them from taking Aderyn?"

"Their intent had been even worse, Lord. From what I heard them say, they were to take the Lady but slay the child."

Carrtog felt his teeth clench. "Tell me how it came about."

Yakor nodded. "Last night, I was just taking a last turn around the quarters to see that all was well. When I came to the stables, I found all the stable boys sound asleep. When I couldn't get them to stay awake, I realized that it was magic of some sort, so I ran out and shouted the alarm. That protection-spell of yours kept me and the guards awake, and we ran first for the Lady's chamber. I could hear fighting round the corner next to the baby's room, so we hurried round there. One of the two guards was dead and the second wounded but still fighting against three out of an original four. We managed to weigh in and turn the tide, but, by the time the three attackers were dead, there was nothing we could to for Lady Adengler; the two guards set to her door were already dead and she was gone. It was during the fight when I heard one say to another, something like 'We're not going to be able to kill the brat; let's get out of here.'"

He paused, looking at Carrtog. "It's a good thing you decided to make the nurse maid one of the ones under the protective spell; she was awake and soothing the little one already, a water-jug in her hand to fight off murderers if necessary." His expression was grim at the memory. "It took a bit to convince her that we were not Gods-cursed baby-murderers, but when that was done, she was quick to get the girl ready to carry away; I decided not to leave them in the room; I didn't have enough men to keep them safe and also try to go after the ones who'd taken your Lady.

"I'm sorry, Lord. They had it well planned; before they started much else, they'd already used some Gods-cursed magic to sicken all our horses. That let them get well away before we could wake anyone in town to sequester horses for our own use."

"You did follow them?"

Yakor spat on the ground. "Your commanders, being extremely careful of the improper use of His Majesty's troops, refused to allow me to take more than the particular troops assigned to your guard.

Despite my position as your sworn man, they do not consider me to speak for you in any matter regarding disposition of troops. A commendable attitude, so far as it keeps me from taking troops off for some purpose of my own which has nothing to do with the purposes of the garrison of the town, but when it comes to preventing me from pursuit of the kidnappers of your family, I find it a little less laudable. I sent three to pursue the false traders as far as possible and send back word when they reached some final destination.

"Lord, they did not go north, as one might expect, but back into Cragmor."

Carrtog could feel the rage building in the back of his mind, but he knew very well that acting only on that rage would likely lead to disaster. Instead, he began to funnel the rage toward careful steps to take.

It did not matter much who had taken Addy, what mattered was to get her back. The fact that they had taken her back into Cragmor was confusing. Or was it? Was this perhaps a plan by the king to inhibit his effectiveness, thus giving His Majesty a reason to retire Carrtog in disgrace?

It seemed sort of roundabout and fraught with danger for the king, but Carrtog recalled the day on the trip back from Tenerack when the king had suddenly refused to listen to Carrtog, and began addressing Yakor as 'Lord.'

He pulled his mind away from that. He could look into who precisely was behind it later. The first thing to do was to see if he could track Addy. If he could track her, the next thing to do would be to track her and free her, and— No! Thinking of particular punishments for culprits was much too previous.

How many, if any, of his troops could he reasonably take? Taking the whole garrison was out of the question. Aside from leaving the railway line unprotected, there was the fact that his leading of his entire force back into Cragmor, without any orders for the movement, could be construed as rebellion and might just accomplish the king's desires — if it was indeed the king behind it.

Of course, leaving his command without the king's permission might achieve the same end but Carrtog would not leave Addy a prisoner for any longer than he could help.

They had arrived at the house now, and he turned to Yakor. "Summon all my guards, at once. After that, send a boy to ask Commander Cargiodd to call on me at his earliest convenience. Issue orders to the servants to pack for a journey of at least two weeks. No, cancel that. Gather the nursemaid with Aderyn and enough servants to look after us. We'll be living rough, with enough allowances made for the baby. Have them load enough wagons with sufficient supplies for us."

"We're going after them?"

"Was there any doubt?"

"His Majesty might be unhappy."

"Had it occurred to you that His Majesty might be behind the whole thing? That the reason why those 'merchants' had such well-forged letters was that they were not forgeries at all?"

Yakor scowled. "Surely even the king would not put out papers like that, under his own hand?"

"Might he not, if there were no copies made for any official record and the 'merchants' understood that the papers would be denied if matters went wrong?"

Yakor spat on the ground. "All right, then, I'll start with carrying out your orders. Where will we find you?"

"Either in the machine-shed or my office. I have a good many preparations to make before we go."

THE COMMANDER'S FACE was grim when he approached Carrtog in his office an hour later. "It reflects badly on my troops, Lord, that these scoundrels should so brazenly carry out such an outrage in their midst. My troops are at your disposal, Lord, however you need them."

Carrtog frowned. "I appreciate the offer, Commander, but I must not lose sight of the fact that the railway line needs to be kept open. I will take only the troops assigned to me as guard. I will ask, though, that you allow me to draw supplies for this excursion, as well as necessary transport."

"Of course, Lord."

"You might not wish to be so obliging to me, Commander, if the king should send people to ask questions as to my deserting my station and the amount of assistance you rendered to me in the matter."

"Lord, I believe that I and my troops owe you a good deal, considering the losses you have prevented through your magic. For that reason alone, I am willing to suffer the king's displeasure."

"Thank you for your gratitude, Commander, but I am unwilling to pull down another in my troubles. I will take only my guard, and supplies and transport for two weeks, and that is all. You may demonstrate your gratitude by continuing to protect the railway line in my absence."

"Yes, Lord."

AFFAIRS IN THE HOUSE in order, Carrtog moved next to the machine-shed where he would find all the special supplies he would need for the excursion. Gryff was in the machine-shed tinkering with a large machine that took up most of the workspace. The machine was something Carrtog had never seen before, though he was not entirely surprised as he had known Gryff had been working on something in secret for many weeks. The young engineer looked up as Carrtog came in. "Lord, I'm sorry, I wasn't able to do anything to prevent what happened." His face showed extreme anguish, a knowledge that he had not done enough.

"Gryff, you were hired as a mechanic, not a warrior, and I had no desire to see you getting yourself killed fighting men who've spent all their lives learning how to fight. I'm going out after those murdering scoundrels, you need have no doubt as to that, however, I could use your services as a mechanic. It will very certainly be dangerous, but I will have men guarding you while you do your part. What do you say?"

Gryff's expression blazed. "Need you ask, Lord? In fact, I wished to speak with you. I have been working on something that may be of use. I had hoped it would make the glider more effective in the fight against the rebels, but my hope is that it can serve us now instead." Gryff turned to the wagon-like contraption in the center of the workroom. "I call it the Stew-pot."

"The Stew-pot?"

"Er yes, as that's what it sounds like while it works, Lord."

"You've successfully built a steam driven wagon, Gryff?" Carrtog hazarded a guess based on the steam engine that was secured the center of bed between the four wheels. He circled the machine, suddenly immeasurably pleased with his protégé despite the grim nature of the current circumstances. The wheels were much wider than a wagon's, two large in the back and two small in the front, and there was room in the front for at least three passengers to sit facing forward.

Gryff pointed to the center of the machine. "The wagon-bed has been extended a bit," he explained, "in order to allow for the steam engine itself, as well as passengers or cargo, or both. Just like a steam locomotive, it has the capacity to pull heavy loads for greater distance than a horse drawn wagon though it is not constrained by following any track."

"I see you have the power going to the rear wheels."

"Yes. Powering the front wheels and steering from the rear would have required the driver to sit with the engine in front of him, blocking his view, and it seemed to me that steering with the rear wheels would have required a bit more care to be able to turn the vehicle at the corner and not just a bit too late. Of course, one of my concerns was to give some leverage to the mechanism turning the wheels. I made the front wheels smaller to make them that much easier to turn."

"It is an ingenious design Gryff. And you said it runs?"

"Yes. Even over dirt roads, as you might have guessed by the width of the wheels themselves. But I have added purpose to it beyond the carting of equipment, Lord."

"The hauling of heavy loads sounds useful in its own right, are you sure you haven't outdone yourself by added further functionality?"

"I would hope not, Lord." Gryff reached for a lever on the side of the stew-pot and four large clamps closed around the spokes of the wheels to lock the machine in place. Another lever dropped four heavy metal arms to the floor from the undercarriage. The metal plates on the ends were equipped with spikes that could be set in place to dig into the ground. The final lever unlocked an extendable arm on the top of the engine that split into three branches at full extension. The arm was more of a wide tray in the shape of a shallow V with a groove down the center. The two offshoots locked into place at the end to form what looked to be the branching arms of a crossbow.

Gryff cranked another handle until the platform contraption was pointed at an angle towards the ceiling. At Gryff's request, Carrtog stepped forward to wind a knob on his side and a broad hook moved in the groove from the highest point to the lowest end. The motion of the winding made a ratcheting sound as hidden gears moved and tension seemed to be wound into the mechanism. And indeed the perpendicular arms curved by a fraction with the winding.

"There. Now it's in the set position. The engine will do the remainder of the winding and the arms will store the tension until it reaches maximum and the release is tripped."

Suddenly the aim of this contraption became infinitely clear.

"You mean to launch the glider into the air from a standing position as a crossbow looses a bolt."

"Yes, Lord."

Ingenious indeed!

"Has it been tested?"

"Well, I had hoped to do so in the coming days but..."

"Then we'll do so on the road."

THERE WERE FIVE TROOPERS at the head of the column, two of them out of sight, scouting the trail. The stew-pot, with a train of three wagons, came next. Gryff was at the controls with Carrtog and Yakor in seats, their mounts hitched to the back, trotting along.

Behind that group were another thirty troops, including some newly assigned to Carrtog's guard to replace the ones lost in the attack by the false merchants. Behind those were another ten wagons, drawn by horses, hauling the supplies for the expedition.

Carrtog looked down at the brass-bound wooden chest next to his feet that carried his supplies for magic casting. Yakor followed his glance. "You know the water won't hold still enough in a scrying bowl on this thing for you to take a reading on her direction. Besides, they're probably still following the road themselves. You can take another reading this evening, and one again tomorrow morning, just to make sure. Other than that, just be patient."

Carrtog gave a half-smile but said nothing. Loading up and setting off had taken longer than he'd anticipated and he was afraid that anything he said might just be anger, anger at anyone and everyone, which would be futile.

The road, of course, was familiar from having ridden along it in patrols, though traveling it in the hissing, clinking stew-pot was very different. There were still the trees and bushes giving off their various scents, though these were competing with the smoke from the boiler and the oil, heated by the friction of the moving parts. Riding up here on the wagon one got only the occasional whiff of horse, which Carrtog found himself missing.

From time to time Yakor would toss fresh fuel into the stove that heated the boiler, and Carrtog would wield the oilcan. Parts of the pistons and their shafts could be oiled while the device was moving, but they had found it necessary to stop once in a while to oil the wheels. Still the promise of using the glider to scout far ahead of their path made the effort worthwhile.

By the first evening, Carrtog had gotten sufficient control of himself that he did not feel quite so near to breaking out in anger if he spoke. He still begrudged the time spent resting overnight, but realized that it was necessary.

As they walked around the campsite, Yakor stuck out his jaw at the wagons that had been pulled along behind the stew-pot. "You really feel it was necessary to bring all the contents of the machine-shed?"

"As Gryff pointed out, better that than to suddenly find ourselves lacking some particular thing."

"He may be right, at that."

AS THEY MOVED FURTHER southward, the countryside was less forested, the trees transitioning to more and more farmers' fields, until towns, villages, and hamlets replaced the forests as the main feature spotted along the length of the road.

They stopped occasionally for provisions at this town or that, but when they stopped overnight they set up camp just off the road, somewhere a fair distance from any town. Only the younger troopers grumbled about not having the chance to rest in a town where beer and fresh food might be available, but these were quickly hushed by the older and more serious among them. They were bound to rescue the lord's wife from whoever had kidnapped her and were therefore on campaign, so any diversions must be whatever they could devise in camp. In the meantime, each evening they saw to the condition of their weapons, removing each scrap of rust, making the edges of their blades keen, but not so keen as to risk splintering, making sure barrels of their firearms were free of the least remnant of burned powder, the flint not too worn, and so on. After that, most of them, particularly the older veterans, took any opportunity to sleep.

Carrtog spent some part of each night reading over the notes he had taken while studying under Enemantwin and Gwaitorr, as well as notes he had made from his own researches. Then he devised spells to improve the effective properties of the oil so that it would not clump in the dust and so that it would resist evaporation or burning at high temperatures. After that was done, he turned his attention to altering the wood that they used as fuel for the stew-pot so that it would burn more efficiently. Eventually Yakor would shoo him off to sleep and he would lay awake for a time, thinking about Addy.

BY THE FOURTH DAY, Carrtog was growing tired of blindly following the faint trail left by the kidnappers and decided to take the glider up to gain a better view of the path ahead.

He told Yakor, "I want to have a good look at that road, specially any turn-offs they might have taken further on."

"So you're using the glider? Wouldn't it be safer to use the balloon?"

"True, but the balloon gives poor visibility over long distances and that's what I'm looking to gain."

Yakor shrugged and spat. "Your choice. I wouldn't want to be in your shoes if you rescue Lady Adengler and die in the process. She'll kill you."

"Doesn't that sound a bit contradictory to you? It does to me. Are you sure you're not afraid she'll kill you?"

It didn't take long to set up the stew-pot, in fact it took longer to assemble the glider which had to be transported without its wings attached. Once assembled, it took five men to lift the glider onto the launching platform, but thankfully, the shallow trough did a passable job of holding the undercarriage of the glider in place once seated.

Carrtog settled hat and goggles on his head, preparing to climb into the mounted glider.

"Perhaps I should go instead, Lord," Gryff said nervously from his position near the controls. "I haven't had a chance to test the launch. What if...?"

"I have faith that you've done your job as I've taught you. There's no cause for concern."

"But the forces on launch, the sudden burst of speed. What if it's too much for the glider to handle, or the pilot?"

"The spells we devised to protect the pilot on landing should work the same for takeoff. And the glider itself has been reinforced three times over. As I said, there's no cause for concern."

Yakor snorted and crossed his arms, "And I suppose that's what I'm to tell Addy when I rescue her without you?"

Carrtog glared at his armsman and climbed into the glider. Seated and secured in the harnesses, he gave Gryff the signal to engage the engine.

The stew-pot chugged into action and the tension arms began to flex. Carrtog took a deep breath and hoped his words of confidence didn't prove unfounded.

Carrtog was forced back against the seat as the mechanism tripped the release and the glider leaped forward. His stomach did an uncomfortable flop as he was launched into the air. He felt the flex of the spells all around him as they did their work to buffer the shock. Without them things would have been very different. As it was, the glider shot into sky like a lead ball from the barrel of a pistol. Five times the height of the tallest tree the momentum was spent and Carrtog had a chance to gasp a breath before remembering he needed to engage the controls to point the nose level so as not to stall. From there the flight became normal and Carrtog circled back to the stew-pot once to ensure everyone knew he was still in one piece before angling back to the road and playing out a ways. Below him the road stretched onwards through the trees towards Waliauchel. Unfortunately there was no caravan of wagons on the horizon that could be labeled as his target, though Carrtog hadn't expected there to be. The kidnappers had a head start and were likely travelling much lighter; that was if they'd chosen to keep the ruse of travelling merchant and hadn't ditched the wagons completely.

The glider started to settle. "God of the Winds!" He muttered. He was going to have to turn the glider round and fly back to the stew-pot. There must be some way to cause the air to lift up on the wings and keep him in the air longer! The craft continued to settle; no, there was no time to fool with spells right now. Time to get back as close to the stew-pot as possible. He would have to put some work into that, though.

THE TRAIL LED RIGHT through and past Waliauchel. As they approached the city, Carrtog spoke to Yakor. "I think we'd best stop and talk to the princess. Someone is sure to report our passage to her, and I'd prefer for her not to think that we were sneaking by."

Yakor gave him a look.

"Think about it, Yakor. She hasn't got much power on her own, but she could certainly interfere if she thought something was suspicious. And on the other hand, she might just have some notion what, if anything, her father might have been up to."

Yakor nodded. "Even if she knows, do you think she'll tell you?"

"Gods help me, Yakor, I'm not going to go in and say, 'princess, do you happen to know if your father has given orders to have your best friend kidnapped and her daughter murdered?'"

"Just so long as you actually give some thought to just what you will be saying."

It took a while longer to get an audience with the princess than Carrtog wanted. In fact, he found himself barely hanging on to the rags of his temper by the time they were finally ushered into her presence. When she saw them, concern immediately flooded her face. "Where is the Lady Adengler?"

"She has been kidnapped, Your Highness. A group of merchants came to Kilgarhai, bearing letters of introduction purporting to be from your father, the king. While I was out with a force attacking the rebels, they attacked my house, killing several people, and taking away the Lady Adengler. They also attempted to murder our daughter, but were foiled by our guards and by Yakor. I have brought my guards and a few other people and am on her trail."

"And the trail leads down here? I would have thought it would have been a rebel maneuver."

"So would I. It may still be rebels, but rebels who have found a hiding place down here. I am fairly certain, though, that this is no false trail being laid for me; I have checked several times to be sure that the trail we follow is real and no false stratagem."

"Tell me the truth, Lord Carrtog. Do you suspect my father?"

There was no use hesitating, or trying to give her some kind of pacifying response; she knew as well as he of her father's changeable moods.

"Your Highness, I cannot deny that there is a strong possibility your father is involved. I hope you will not attempt to turn me aside."

She shook her head. "No, Lord Carrtog. Lady Adengler is a good friend of mine, and I would not see her harmed. All I would ask is that before you turn yourself irrevocably against my father, you should be quite sure that it is he who is behind this."

He bowed. "Yes, Your Highness, I will certainly promise you that."

The princess sat still for a moment, then spoke again. "My father still writes to me often, and he is constantly troubled by the rebel broadsheets alluding to his behavior, calling him a coward." Her expression showed her own concern. "The Gods do not give it to every man," she continued, "to show bravery in each and every circumstance, and yet most men, perhaps even all men, find it a fault that any man cannot always press forward in spite of his own fears. I worry over what he might do, just to prove himself."

Carrtog nodded. "I understand, Your Highness."

He left unsaid his own concern, that the king's care for his own reputation might cause him to take actions which could only lead to more trouble.

The princess thought for a moment longer, then asked, "I am limited in the things I can do, but can I give you any help? After all, Adengler was my lady-in-waiting and a friend for many years."

Carrtog thought, then shook his head. "Thank you, Your Highness, but I am well-supplied and have sufficient funds of my own. I will only ask for your good wishes."

"That goes without saying, Lord Carrtog."

"Thank you, then, Your Highness. With your leave, then, I will continue on my hunt."

"Go, then, and may the Gods go with you."

"SO, THEN, DID WE GAIN anything from that stop?"

Carrtog glanced at Yakor. "Not much, I confess, save for a bit of a closer look into the king's mind. I can't say I'm certain just yet, but it seems more likely now that he might just have set this plan into motion in order to pull me down. I suspect that perhaps even now a message has come to me at Kilgarhai suggesting that my wife is being held against my being less efficient in the protection of the railway. Supposedly, I will be held in a bind; if I agree to such a demand and become less rigorous about pursuing the rebels, then the king will relieve me, with regret. If I refuse, on the other hand...." He stopped there, unwilling to force his mind to face the consequences.

"But you will be doing neither. They will have to wait a certain time for the message to reach you before they act, and in that time we will track them down and pull their hiding place down around their ears."

"With relish."

Chapter 28

Two days west of Waliauchel, travel became more difficult. What had been roads degenerated to mediocre roads, then to rough trails, then something just better than game trails.

Still, the scrying bowl said that Lady Adengler was further along the road.

The green forest closed in round them once again. Every day the scouts went out ahead of them, every evening they set sentries around their camp, but nothing came of it.

CARRTOG MOVED THE GLIDER controls slightly, adjusting his course; he noted the slight drag on his muscles caused by the spell that prevented his body from bouncing around and breaking his bones against the frame.

He was checking the road on which the kidnappers had traveled. This was his second consecutive day at this endeavor.

They had learned they could launch the glider and travel ahead a ways before Carrtog would find them to land nearby — though the landings had grown more and more difficult in the rough wilderness. Scouting in the glider took much less effort than riding ahead and with the stew-pot's ability to transition quickly back into a wagon they didn't lose any forward progress waiting for the glider to return.

On the fourth morning, Carrtog spotted a rough log-built house off to the right of the main road a ways in the distance. The spell guiding him to Addy lined up with the house. He still had some altitude left so he turned in that direction. As he approached, the spell remained steady, still pointing to the house. Just to be certain, he circled, and at every turn the magical trail stopped at the house.

He took the glider back to the stew-pot, landed, and slid out onto the ground. Yakor came over at a brisk pace.

"I've found her! There's a rough wood cottage up a ways and to our right." Carrtog reported. "Now to get there and bring her out before they know we're nearby."

"So we stop here and make some plans," Yakor said.

"The first thing I want to know is whether or not they've got anything up to protect themselves against magic. I'll get started at that right now."

"Be careful, for the Gods' sakes. You don't want to go poking them with a magical stick and letting them know we're here."

Carrtog gave him a look. "Give me credit for a bit of sense, will you? His Majesty's tutors taught me how to do more than poke people with sticks."

Yakor gave a slight smile. "Sorry. I'm sure they did; carry on."

In fact, being cautious about it required the better part of a half-hour, but at the end of that time Carrtog took a deep breath and said, "They do have some protection spells up, but nothing really powerful. I'm guessing their magician doesn't want to extend himself too soon, so as to save his strength for when he has to deal with me. And they didn't really expect to deal with me at all, I suspect. As far as they're concerned, I'm still sitting up at Kilgarhai, either waiting for their message, or trying to decide how to respond."

"At least, you hope so."

"Actually, I'm going to plan on the basis that they suspect we're out here somewhere and planning to come on in. I hope that makes you feel better. And before you ask, I believe there are no more than about a dozen men in there."

Yakor turned aside and spat on the ground. "My first suggestion, maybe my only one, is that you go in fast and furious, to give them less time to think."

Carrtog nodded. "Exactly."

Gryff spoke up, a bit diffidently. "I've been working on some devices to help us out, including something to bring down the front door."

Two grim faces turned to him in unison, and he jerked, almost as if struck.

"Uh— it may not be all that good an idea," he muttered.

"Nonsense!" declared Carrtog. "I've been fiddling with notions along the way but putting the finishing touches on your work would probably be quicker than my working things out from the start."

"It will probably require the destruction of one or more of the balloons."

"Out with it, boy!" growled Yakor.

Gryff was still cowed by having the full attention of both Carrtog and Yakor, but he continued. "If we hang a container, preferably metal, full of gunpowder under a balloon and float it over to the door, then set off the powder. Uh... could you do that by magic Lord?"

"By magic or by some other means. Perhaps best if we put in a handful of pistol balls as well. Before we do this, I would like to make certain that Lady Adengler is not being held anywhere near that door."

"Of course, Lord."

"We have something to make this canister out of?" asked Yakor.

'SOMETHING' ENDED UP being one of several short lengths of fallen tree that they had brought along, already hollowed out, metalized, and turned into short lengths of pipe. They blocked one end with another short round piece of wood and patched all the cracks with short chips. They spread pistol balls across the bottom and placed a bag of gunpowder on top. They made a small slit in the bag and stuck a fuse into it, then spread more pistol balls on top. They made another round lid, put it in with the fuse protruding, then fastened it with more chips.

"You think this will do?" asked Yakor, doubtfully.

"It might," answered Carrtog, "but I'm going to take it a step further, working on Enemantwin's lessons. I'm going to change the wooden parts of this thing into metal, specifically iron."

"Won't that make it too heavy for the ballon?"

"I've been working on a spell to increase the lift produced by hot air. So far the effect is limited in both effect and time, though I hope to increase those limitations in times to come. Now's as good a time as any to test those spells."

He set the wooden container carefully on the ground, then walked a short distance away and poured a small charge of gunpowder onto a wooden chip. He used a taper to set off the charge of powder, at the same time repeating an invocation.

He then took his belt-knife and tapped the blade against the container. It gave off the familiar near-metallic 'ting.'

"It worked."

Yakor's eyebrows rose. "Had you doubted it?"

"No, not really; I've practiced it several times since Enemantwin first taught it to me. It's just that this attempt has a lot more riding on it."

"I see. Before we go breaking down doors, you don't suppose they might have someone inside there watching for balloons to come floating up the front road carrying big packages of gunpowder?"

"Actually, I was planning to put a charm on it to make it less easy to notice."

"Invisibility?"

"No, invisibility is hard to get right on something that's moving. Nor is it a spell that I've practiced. I plan to use something more like 'Don't Really Notice This,' but with a fair bit of power behind it."

"'Don't Really Notice This?'" Yakor repeated. "You'll convince someone not to notice a great big round thing drifting up to their door?"

"I will admit that it would work better on someone or something drifting up between the trees, but I think we can get away with this."

"You think so seriously enough to take the risk?"

"Yes, I do. But just to make sure, I'll be ready to rush the door before the noise of the explosion starts to die down."

"You? Who's going to control the balloon?"

"I am. But I plan to get right up close before I set up the table and the scrying-bowl to control it by."

"You do, do you? And do you plan to use this 'Don't Really Notice Us?' spell to hide us as we get up close?"

"'Us?' I hadn't really intended there to be an 'Us,' just me and the equipment."

"How many people did you expect to waste getting me tied up so you could leave me behind?"

"I was hoping you'd have sense enough to let me do this by myself."

"You were, were you, boy? My job is not to let you go taking boneheaded risks by yourself. If I can't talk you out of it, my job is to go along and lessen the risk as much as I can."

"What if I tell you that the chance of failure of the 'Don't Really Notice Me?' spell is increased for every extra person included?"

"Then we won't let anybody else come along. They'll just have to start running from further back as soon as the charge explodes."

CARRTOG MANEUVERED the balloon and its cargo toward the door. It was nearly impossible to believe that nobody in the house could see the balloon; it was so clearly visible out here, with neither trees nor brush to hide it. But no one opened a door or a window, nor fired a shot at it.

He and Yakor were out behind a bush, possibly the only bush within a stone's throw of the house, with the scrying-bowl set carefully level on a clump of grass.

A moment more and the balloon would touch the door. Carrtog picked up the stick that had been magically connected to the fuse. When he broke the stick, the fuse would immediately catch fire. The fuse itself would burn quickly; within two to three heartbeats it would set off the powder charge. After that, they would go in through the door, and after that...

He snapped the stick.

For a moment, he thought the thing had failed, then there was a roaring explosion and the whole front of the building was obscured by a cloud of smoke. Several things, either pistol balls or bits of the container, whipped through the bush above them, clipping off bits of twigs and leaves, and Carrtog was glad that he and Yakor had lain down on the grass behind the bush that hid them.

But Yakor was already on his feet, and Carrtog was only a little slower.

Yakor and Carrtog leaped up the three steps into the acrid powder-smoke to face the door. Several pistol balls and bits of the canister had gone right through, but it had not been blown down in its entirety. Carrtog brought up his right foot and stamped forward against the door; the lower half of it flew inward to land somewhere beyond, and the upper half hung there for a moment, then clattered to the floor.

Carrtog went through the doorway at a run, pistol raised. A man came out of a hallway across the room, pistol in hand. Carrtog fired, then tucked his pistol into his sash, switching his sword to his right hand. Through the smoke, he saw the man stagger back against the wall and slide down.

More men came pouring into the room. Yakor's pistol fired, adding to the smoke; a man in front of Carrtog lunged forward, sword thrusting. Carrtog's blade was up and parrying in a moment, the two blades clanging and screeching together.

The man was no poor swordsman, either; he and Carrtog matched thrust for thrust, parry for parry, until Carrtog managed to hit home with a thrust to the throat.

The fight then became a melee in the dim confines of the main room of the house; Carrtog vaguely had time to be grateful that Yakor had insisted on not having the full force of his guard take part in the attack.

Suddenly, there were no more men to be fought in the front room, and Carrtog was racing down the hallway where they had estimated that Addy's room was located. He flung open the first door and, seeing it was empty, turned aside to the next one. This one was locked, so he stamped his heel into it, and the latch pulled free with the sound of splintering wood. The windows were blocked by shutters, but some light came in by means of the cracks between them. He could see a figure standing beside a bed. "Addy?"

She rushed over "Carrtog! You're here!"

"Of course I am. Did you just think I'd sit by while some group of bandits stole you? Come, let's get out of here."

"Oh Carrtog!" There was anguish in her voice. "They've killed Aderyn!"

"Is that what they told you? They lied. Yakor got to her room before they could get in. We've brought her along with us just to be sure she stayed safe."

She turned to Yakor. "Yakor? I could kiss you!"

"Not right this moment, if you please, Lady. We might still have some fighting before we get away clean."

That statement was accentuated by further clashing of swords back in the front room, along with shouts of fighting men, as well as more than one scream as men fell, wounded or dying, as the main body of Carrtog's guard entered the house. The battle was done a moment after that.

It was Yakor who gave the orders to their men. "Let's go! We don't leave anyone behind, wounded or dead. Make sure of it."

"Yes sir!"

GRYFF HAD BROUGHT THE stew-pot up to the door towing the wagon set up for carrying passengers in relative comfort. Carrtog saw Addy on board where Aderyn was waiting in the arms of her nursemaid.

"None of us want to stay around here in the company of all the dead, so we're going to pack up and be gone immediately."

Holding her daughter tight in her arms as if she were never going to let her go again, Addy merely nodded quickly.

'Immediately' turned out to require a bit more time than the word inferred. It was Yakor who suggested, "We should search the place, see if there's any sign who hired them. I know we suspect the king, but it might have been the rebels. After all, you were being fairly effective in keeping the railway line open."

Carrtog stood still for a moment, then nodded. "You're right, of course. Would you go give the orders?"

Yakor glanced at Addy, smiling, then said, "Yes, of course, sir."

Carrtog sat quietly in the doorway of the passenger-wagon along with his wife and daughter. The child was holding on to her mother, afraid she would go away again, and Addy was trying to comfort her as best she could. As for Carrtog, all he could do was to sit quietly with them, giving silent assurance that all was well.

Yakor finally came out of the house. "We searched everywhere and everyone. I don't suppose we actually expected a written letter from the king requesting that they kidnap your wife and kill your daughter. There was, of course, nothing like that, only a suspiciously large amount of money amongst the lot of them. We found most of it on that Llodcar; there's no saying which of our bunch killed him, but if we could find out, we should give him some kind of reward. That Llodcar's the kind of gowk I always think's better dead."

"Well, take about half the money and share it out among our men. You take one in ten of the rest, and I'll use what's left to help defray the costs of the rescue."

"One in ten? Isn't that overly generous?"

Carrtog smiled. "Argue, and I'll make it two in ten."

Yakor nodded, smiling. "All right, if you insist, sir."

THE RETURN TRIP WAS less hurried and they took greater care for the comfort of their passengers. They also stopped overnight more often in towns, having a good deal more money then they previously had.

Thus it was on the night before they reached the capital, that they discovered the drapery of mourning black adorning the small inn where they stopped. The window sashes were black, the staff were all dressed in black, and at the peak of the roof of the porch there was a black streamer.

Carrtog called the innkeeper over. "We've been off in the back country. Who's passed away?"

"Why, King Bornival, may the Gods be good to him, Sir. He fought a great battle, and beat the Northies right well, but in the very end, some Gods-cursed Northie fired a shot and hit him accidentally.

Accident or no, it took him in the heart, and he died there, victorious. The leader of the Northies that Rhadfel Llorsan, was killed as well, so it looks as if the war is over, at least until some other Northie takes it into his head to rise up against the queen."

"The queen?"

The innkeeper looked at Carrtog sharply. "You have been off in the back-country indeed! Why, Queen Ellevar, of course. Everyone knows that the king, Gods keep him, had no male heir, and his wife had passed away some time ago. There's this lord and that lord think only a man should rule over a country, but Queen Ellevar has shown herself to have a good head on her shoulders, and she's had a good few lords behind her from the start. So, long may she reign, I say!"

He was looking at Carrtog gravely, so Carrtog answered, "Long may she reign indeed! I was taken by surprise because, as it happens, my wife, the Lady Adengler, was, until our marriage, a lady-in-waiting to the then princess Ellevar."

It seemed clear that the innkeeper did not really believe this tale, but was polite enough not to say so out loud, in particular to a lord who had a large following of armed men.

IN PRIVATE, CARRTOG, Addy, and Yakor talked this over.

"If it wasn't so late in the day, I'd suggest we carry on to Waliauchel today," Carrtog said. "I wonder just how much of our landlord's story is fact, and how much is elaboration as the tale's passed on."

"I think we can depend on the fact that the king is dead. Just how he died might not be exactly as the landlord's version has it," Yakor answered. "This could be a dangerous turn of events. You'll recall, you have no few enemies because you had the king's favor. Cause could be made for the accusation that you abandoned your post, no matter what the circumstance. There might be any number of them willing to try to force the queen to have you disgraced over it."

"She wouldn't agree to something like that," Addy said.

Yakor shrugged. "Being a ruler doesn't necessarily mean that she can do anything she likes. She will need the support of her lords. If a large enough group of them demand something, she may have to fall in with it simply in order to be able to do anything that requires the support of those lords in the future."

"On the other hand, even if I wait until I get back to Kilgarhai to send her a message, I'll still be in the same situation. I think I'll be better off altogether to stop by, if only to let her prepare for whatever trouble comes."

Addy nodded, "Though she had nothing to say about matters of government, she was more aware of how the kingdom was run than you might think. I'd say that you'd be best to stop in and talk to her. At the very least, you can give her your condolences on the death of her father, even though you may be nearly certain he paid those brigands to kidnap me."

Carrtog nodded. "Then its decided, we'll stop by to give our condolences and to let her know that we were successful in dealing with those outlaws."

NEXT MORNING, THEREFORE, they set out for the capital, in a mood of uncertainty. Conversation was sparse for most of the day, and even little Aderyn caught the mood and was fretful, requiring her mother's attention to the point that her nursemaid could barely conceal her relief when Addy took charge of her in the afternoon.

As they rolled into the outskirts of Waliauchel later that day, it became clear that their landlord the previous night had the story essentially correct. The whole town seemed to be in mourning, and broadsheets posted on town walls extolled the bravery of King

Bornival, who had died boldly leading his men in the charge that led to victory.

"You can't call down a king who dies in battle, especially if the battle's won," Yakor observed. "So that's the official version, no matter what the facts might be."

It was too late, of course, to call on the queen that day, but they left word that they would be calling the next day and found lodgings for themselves for the night.

Getting in to see Princess Ellevar had been one matter, getting in to see Queen Ellevar was quite another. The ruler of Cragmor had numerous demands on her time, and visits from old friends, no matter how dear, had to take second place to the requirements of the nation.

However, late in the morning, a servant came into the antechamber where they were waiting with numerous others, to announce, "Lord Carrtog of Nandycargllwyd and Lady Adengler, Her Majesty will see you now."

They rose and followed the servant.

The princess had always dressed in clothing that showed her youth; as queen, however, she dressed in a manner to demonstrate maturity. Her expression was grave as they entered and bowed, but then she smiled.

"A good day to you both, Lord Carrtog and Lady Adengler. I hope the day finds you well."

"Very well, thank you, Your Majesty. As you can see, I have brought Lady Adengler with me and there is a nest of bandits that is no more."

"I'm glad to hear of that, Lord Carrtog. Good news is in somewhat short supply, these days."

"My condolences for your loss, Your Majesty. Of course, the war is now ended, though the cost was severe."

The queen's expression saddened, then she regained her composure.

"When you last passed through here, I spoke about my father's concerns. With the news of his death, I also received a last letter he had written the night before the battle. In it, he declared his intention of proving himself to all on the next day."

She paused. "Everyone says he died leading the charge that won the battle. I had already found that being daughter to the king means that every bit of news coming to me is shaded to prevent giving offense; you can imagine how much more so that is now that I am queen. However, I had already made acquaintances who were willing to tell me something closer to the truth.

"The fact is that the battle was already won when he led his charge. The rebel leader had already fallen to a random shot across the field, and the rebels were beginning to break. But someone among the rebels apparently fired one last shot before fleeing, and given the range, it was probably only bad fortune that put my father in its path.

"So, most of the soldiers saw only the king leading the final charge against the rebels and demonstrating his courage for all to see. For my part, I would prefer to have my father alive, with all his faults.

"But I am allowed only a short time to speak with mere friends, no matter how valued; my time must be spent on meetings that will hold the realm together, often enough only smoothing the ruffled feathers of this lord or that. Before you go, what can I do for you?"

"Nothing, Your Majesty; we had only stopped to offer our condolences."

The queen's face grew grave. "I must tell you that someone has already seen it necessary to inform me that you have left your post to go rushing back into the interior of the kingdom. I have let it be known that you have gone with my approval, to rescue the Lady Adengler, an old and dear friend of mine. Of course, someone may indeed find the nerve to point out that my approval appeared to have come after the fact.

"On the other hand, your record in Kilgarhai speaks for itself. No accusation of slighting your task will stand. You may have to defend yourself against personal attacks, but you need not fear Royal disapproval."

She smiled.

"Thank you, Your Majesty."

SOME SIX WEEKS LATER, they were once again in Waliauchel, by the Queen's invitation.

"Well," said Yakor, "They don't seem to be in mourning any longer."

Addy looked around. "No. But then the queen has invited us, and most likely everyone of any importance, to tonight's victory celebration. They could hardly stay in mourning for something like that."

"No," agreed Yakor.

"It does seem that they've gone out of mourning a bit soon, for having lost a king," Carrtog mused, his arm firmly around his wife's waist.

"Not really," Addy said, "Six weeks is reasonable. Especially given that the queen is taking over and has to show that she's in charge. There will be a good many lords giving out not-so-subtle hints that the realm would be better run by a man and offering themselves as possible husbands. And she isn't going to want to accept any such offers, since she knows that would mean relegating herself to the position of wife of the ruler, possibly even eventually dying of some 'fever' or other.

"No, don't look at me like that, Yakor, you know very well that I'm right! She's going to have to show that she's in charge and doesn't need some man to stand behind her, or eventually in front of her, to legitimate her orders."

"No, Lady, I agree with you. She's probably spent much of the last six weeks sounding out various lords to see where they stand, if they'll support her or not. I'm a little surprised she hasn't sent some message or other to Lord Carrtog."

"She probably hasn't, since she most likely sees him as one of her supporters already."

Yakor smiled. "We can certainly hope so."

FOUR DAYS LATER A MOUNTED messenger from the palace, wearing a tabard in the royal colors, appeared at their door. "A message from Her Majesty to Lord Carrtog of Nandycargllwyd."

"I am Lord Carrtog."

The messenger presented the scroll, and stepped back.

"Thank you. You may tell her Majesty that the message has been delivered."

"Actually, sir, my instructions are to bring back any message you might wish to send in return."

"I see." Carrtog broke the seal on the scroll, and unrolled it.

He read it quickly, then read it again, then looked up.

"Her Majesty wishes to speak to us this afternoon, just before the celebration commences, on matters of great importance to the nation."

He looked around at them, then at the messenger, and said, "Please tell Her Majesty that we will wait upon her this afternoon at five o'clock, according to her desire."

"On behalf of Her Majesty, I thank you, Lord Carrtog."

When the Messenger had gone, Carrtog looked at Yakor and said, "Well, I believe this will be the occasion for Her Majesty to ask for my support for her reign."

A LITTLE BEFORE FIVE, Carrtog, Adengler, and Yakor were waiting in an antechamber of the palace for the queen's summons.

They had already discussed the possibilities of the meeting in private among the three of them. Here, with servants nearby and quite possibly willing to supplement their income by selling private conversations to anyone willing to buy, they kept their talk to such things as possible uses for the sort of balloons they had used to track the rebels.

"To make them large enough to carry any amount of cargo, they would have to be enormous, and the production of the hot air to allow them to rise, with that cargo, would require some kind of fire. Those small heat-producing stones we make would have to be so much increased in size as to add an extreme weight to the thing."

"So it's impossible, is it?" inquired Yakor.

"No, not impossible, just a matter of great difficulty. There's also the matter of making it go where we want it to go, not merely depending on the winds. That difficulty is increased by the size the thing would have to be, which would mean that the wind would always be pushing on it."

"For someone protesting that it is not impossible, just a matter of great difficulty, you are doing a very good job of lining up more and more difficulties," said Yakor with a large grin.

"If one begins with a list of difficulties to be overcome, one encounters less surprises on the way to success," replied Carrtog with an only slightly smaller grin. "Actually, the notion of moving air around has led me to think that gliders might be more useful for the task of carrying cargo. I've already worked out some—"

The door opened and a servant stepped in to announce, "Lord Carrtog, Her Majesty will see you and your party now." They rose and went past the servant, who announced them.

They all knelt, but the queen almost immediately said, "Please rise. I hope the day finds you well."

"Quite well, Your Majesty."

"Good. I have been told that gossip says that this evening's celebratory ball will involve various awards to people who have served well in the recent war. As is often the case, gossip has a good deal of truth at the foundation.

"In your particular case, Lord Carrtog, the award is not only for your service in the war, but also for your prior service to me, personally. I know that my father rewarded you for that when he was alive, but now that the power is in my hands, I can and will give you a further reward.

"Since I am led to understand that you have an interest in various things mechanical, I shall be awarding you the position of Artificer to the Crown. The position will come with an annual purse to fund your researches, with the proviso that at least some of your researches shall always go to the betterment of the realm.

"I shall also grant you an increase in your lands, for any researches you care to undertake which cannot be clearly shown to benefit the realm."

She smiled. "I've been told that many a research project is undertaken merely to satisfy curiosity, and actual benefits may only show up later, if at all.

"I hope this will be pleasing to you."

"Very much so, Your Majesty!"

THE WIND WHINED THROUGH the wire struts supporting the glider's wings, large wings to support the large body capable of hauling significant cargo.

Carrtog had already cast the spell to produce the continuous wind against the lifting edges of the wings, and now that he was airborne, he could cast the spell that would continually nudge the craft forward in the direction the nose was pointed.

For a whim, he tilted the craft so he could see the small figures lining the hillside. The queen and a number of her advisors, all in the fanciest dress they could manage, were watching the test flight of the glider named Queen Ellevar's Enterprise.

A very well-kept secret was the fact that Queen Ellevar's Enterprise had already been thoroughly tested. Carrtog had no desire at all to suddenly discover, in the midst of showing off his new invention to the queen, that there were faults in the design, which would change the initial flight to a disaster.

Two pylons had been set up miles apart. His goal was to do five rounds for this first test. There was another group of advisors up at the far pylon to testify that the glider had indeed traveled the whole distance on each round.

It was a well-known fact that certain of the queen's advisors were antipathetic to Carrtog and would find against him for the slightest reasons, perhaps even no reason at all.

On the other hand, it was also well-known that Lord Carrtog stood high in the queen's favor, so an advisor would have to be very determined to go against that fact.

He completed his fifth round, at which point he dipped his wings as a salute to the queen, then carried on to do a sixth, unnecessary, round, just to make sure.

He landed and rolled to a stop near to the queen and her party, which included Addy, Aderyn, Yakor, and Gryff. As the glider settled into silence, he could hear the shouting. Most of it would be cheering of course.

He slid out of the glider, and walked over to the queen, saluting as he came, but as always his eyes were mostly for Addy.

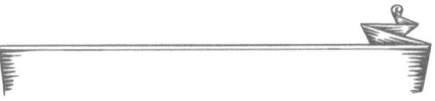

About the Author:

J. P. Wagner was both a sci-fi/fantasy writer and a journalist. While his editorials and informative articles could be found in publications such as the Western Producer and the Saskatoon Star Phoenix, Railroad Rising: The Black Powder Rebellion is his first published novel.

A self-proclaimed curmudgeon, but known to his family as a merry jokester, his words have brightened many lives. Sadly, J. P. Wagner passed away in 2015 before the publication of Railroad Rising: The Black Powder Rebellion.

While this may be the last book he finished before he died, it doesn't mean that this was his only book. In addition to his career in journalism, he wrote many novels throughout his lifetime. All of these works have been passed down to me, his daughter and now I will share them with you.

Other titles by JP Wagner:

C heck out his other fantasy novel, The Search for the Unicorns available now in ebook and paperback where all fine books can be found!

If you want to get the latest updates and quirky news, head over to the JP Wagner Website[1] and sign up for the Curmudgeon Newsletter!

Don't miss out!

Visit the website below and you can sign up to receive emails whenever J P Wagner publishes a new book. There's no charge and no obligation.

https://books2read.com/r/B-A-EKQG-LIIEB

BOOKS 2 READ

Connecting independent readers to independent writers.

www.ingramcontent.com/pod-product-compliance
Lightning Source LLC
Chambersburg PA
CBHW060421030726
47495CB00003B/676